Uprooting

Roots Series
Book 2

Jenna Rogers

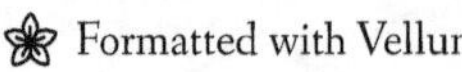 Formatted with Vellum

*For all those trying to be everything to everyone all the time.
For the ones who are constantly going, going, going and
putting on a face even when you're exhausted.*

*May you find your power and strength in saying no, resting,
and making yourself a priority.*

Uprooting Playlist

I created this playlist to help me write *Uprooting,* and I hope you can use it to enhance your reading experience. I have noted any songs that are paired well with specific chapters.

different us 2.15.23 - Erin Kinsey (Prologue)
paint the town blue - Ella Langley (Ch. 1)
I'll Be A Bartender - Dylan Scott (Ch. 1)
Dance Away My Broken Heart - Abby Anderson (Ch. 6)
That Dog - Caylee Hammack (Ch. 6)
Whose Bed Have Your Boots Been Under - Shania Twain (Ch. 6 & 55)
Brave Girl - Callista Clark
I Know She Ain't Ready - Luke Combs
Indifferent - Megan Moroney (Ch. 9)
monsters - Ella Langley (Ch. 11)
Two Steppin' On the Moon - Josh Turner (Ch. 12)
Sold (The Grundy County Auction Incident) - John Michael Montgomery (Ch. 15)

I Can Love You Like That - John Michael Montgomery (Ch. 15)
Annabel - 49 Winchester (Ch. 16)
Russell County Line - 49 Winchester (Ch. 16)
She Won't Be Lonely Long - Clay Walker (Ch. 18)
All I Want for Christmas is a Cowboy - Megan Moroney (Ch. 22)
What Could Go Right - Thomas Rhett (Ch. 22)
Still Believe in Crazy Love - Ryan Kinder (Ch. 23)
Wondering Why - The Red Clay Strays (Ch. 27)
Drowning - The Red Clay Strays (Ch. 28)
Carry Me - Anne Wilson (Ch. 28)
Settlin' - Sugarland (Ch. 28)
Country Classic - Kane Brown
Hard to Leave - Riley Green
She Don't Know - Walker Montgomery
Ain't Missin' You - Dylan Schneider
I Love the Way You Love Me - John Michael Montgomery (Ch. 42 & 53)
Don't Tell Me You're Not in Love - George Strait (Ch. 42)
Am I Okay? - Megan Moroney
The Girl I Was - Jenna Paulette
Gorgeous - Kane Brown
10-90 - Muscadine Bloodline (Ch. 53)
Hope That I'm Enough - Parker McCollum
Heartbroken - Jessie Version - Diplo, Jessie Murph
Painted Sky - Mikayla Lane
What Not To - Tucker Wetmore (Ch. 54)
Rope the Moon - John Michael Montgomery (Ch. 55)
Dirty Looks - Lainey Wilson (Ch. 55)

hold my beer - Alana Springsteen (Ch. 55)
Wildflowers - Sophia Scott

Content Warning

Uprooting is a brother's best friend small town cowboy romance that explores self-acceptance, allowing yourself to rest and ask for help, and the strength of family ties. In order to tell this story, I made the choice to include topics that may be sensitive to some readers, including alcohol consumption, an off-page heart attack, discussions of domestic abuse, and discussions of a parent who deals with gambling addiction and alcohol abuse. Reader discretion is advised.

Prologue

December, 9 Years Ago

Jax

With ten seconds left on the game clock, I take a deep breath and search the crowd for the one person I need to see most right now. If I can just find those stunning hazel eyes and let their calming effect ground me, I know I'll be okay.

I catch a glimpse of Lauren's golden hair, drawn back into her signature braid, and in the bright lights overhead, I swear I can see every one of her freckles on display. Her eyes are closed and her hands are clasped as if she's praying for our victory, and it's the cutest thing I've ever seen.

Charlie, our quarterback and my best friend, hollers to indicate the start of the play, and I surge down the field. Even in the chaos, I swear Lauren's voice rises above the others, and I use it to push me farther and faster, like my life depends on it. With our team down by five, it kind of feels like it does.

A streak of green darts into my field of vision, and I deftly dodge the opposing player in time to catch the ball.

The second I step into the end zone, the whole stadium erupts into a wall of sound. Back in Roots, Texas, everyone takes football seriously, but our stadium is nothing compared to this one, home of the Cowboys and, for tonight, our state championship game.

A group of students hop the railing that's been holding them back the last four quarters, surging onto the field. My teammates surround me, wild grins on their faces. This is the first season in twenty years the Spurs have made it to state, and it's been nearly forty since we've clinched a win.

Through the mass of people bombarding me with congratulations and pats on the back, my attention once again splits. I can't help it. From the moment I met her, I've searched for Lauren in every crowd.

Finally, I catch sight of blonde hair braided down the back of a Roots Spurs jersey with Charlie's name on the back. I'd be insanely jealous if that jersey didn't belong to her brother. Lauren wraps Charlie up in a hug, and then the two make their way over to me. As her gaze catches on mine, the noise in the stadium quiets. All I see is her.

I've never felt this way about anyone before, and I hate myself a little bit for feeling it now. After everything I've been through, I know I could never have a woman as smart, kind, and beautiful as Lauren. She deserves someone brave and strong and who can give her the world, but I'm not that person. I'm good at school and football, but I'm not good at protecting the people I love. It's a miracle my mom and I made it out of Oklahoma this summer, and that miracle had nothing to do with me.

I try to remind myself why I'm unworthy as she and Charlie continue my way, but the second Lauren flashes me a grin, the only thought I'm capable of is *she might be my favorite person in the world.*

"Nice catch out there." Charlie claps me on the shoulder.

"Nice throw." I nudge his side.

"Just like we practiced, right?"

I don't get a chance to answer before a group of guys dogpiles on Charlie. I may have made the game-winning catch, but he had a heck of a game tonight. We wouldn't have won without him.

Lauren tucks a strand of hair behind her ear before saying, "Good game, Jax."

Hearing my name on her lips cartwheels my stomach a dozen times. I love the way she says it, like I'm someone special, not just another man in my family destined to hurt those he loves.

"Thanks. I heard you cheering out there."

"No way!" She tosses her hand dismissively. "Not in an arena this big, not with all these people."

"I swear I heard you. You were my good luck charm."

She grabs on to my wrist, lifting my cheesy cereal-box bracelet and giving me a pointed look. The touch sends warmth throughout my entire body. "I thought this was your good luck charm."

It used to be. I've worn it to every game since I found it. My teammates thought it was ridiculous until I went on to make three touchdown catches.

I shake my head, pulling it off. "Not after tonight. I need *you* at all my games instead." I slip the bracelet over her wrist as color fills her cheeks.

"Come on. I didn't do anything more than the rest of the fans."

Except she did. When I came to town, Charlie was the first to make me feel welcome, but Lauren was the one whose presence silenced my mind enough to forget the pain that forced my mom and me to stay with my aunt. Two nights ago, when I was too nervous to sleep because of our upcoming game, Lauren was the one who sat up in the dim light of the Rhodes' kitchen, hyping me up. When the nerves of the game made me nauseous during warmups, Lauren's smiling face in the stands is what calmed me down. There's a spark between us that I've felt from the moment I first laid eyes on her, and as much as I try to ignore it, I can't.

Charlie rushes back up to the two of us. He's drenched, and when he lays his hand on me, it's sticky.

I jerk back. "Dude, what the hell's that?"

"Gatorade." He beams. "There's going to be a huge party tonight. We have to go."

"I don't know. I'm not really into—"

"Come on! It'll be fun. The place will be crawling with girls, and they'll all want a piece of the guy who made that catch."

I scoff and glance at Lauren, who practically splits my heart in two when she drops her eyes to the ground. "You should go."

"Lauren, you're coming too. I need a D.D.," Charlie announces.

She opens her mouth to protest, but Charlie is already bouncing off to the next group of people.

————

A giant bonfire flickers in the center of an empty field just outside of town as at least fifty teenagers sit around the flame, drinking and laughing. There's another group of people playing games of pong and rage cage behind us, and I can't help but feel out of place. I've never understood the appeal of alcohol. It heightens every emotion. Sometimes, that's joy, but more often it's something twisted, like sadness or anger.

I get up from my spot on a tree stump, not feeling like being the life of the party tonight.

At the movement, Lauren glances up at me. "Where are you going?"

"I don't know. I just need to get away from all this."

"Can I come? I don't want to be here alone." She nods to where Charlie's enthusiastically recounting his adventures on the field earlier for probably the millionth time.

I bite back a smile, trying not to get too excited she chose to be with me. "Sure."

We put distance between the fire, and by the time we reach the river, the music and laughter from the party is drowned out by the trickle of the water. The darkness nearly swallows us whole out here, but I still feel Lauren's presence on every inch of my skin. I take a seat on a boulder along the bank, and she sits on the opposite side, heat radiating off her.

We're quiet for a few seconds until finally Lauren asks, "Now what?"

A giggle slips from her lips, a sound I've come to adore so much. It's one of the things that immediately drew me to her—her boundless joy for life. She can be reserved and cautious, but when she lets herself break free of it all, she's impossible to look away from.

"I don't know. My whole plan was just to sit here and listen to the water," I admit.

Again, her laughter tumbles out, and it sounds like music I never want to turn off.

"I have a feeling we're going to be here for a while." She glances over her shoulder. "Charlie is living it up out there."

"As he should. This is his night of glory."

"It's yours too."

I shrug.

"Come on." She leans her shoulder into mine, filling my nose with her sweet scent. "We wouldn't have won without you."

"It was just luck."

"I've seen you and Charlie practicing over the last few months. That wasn't luck."

Silence falls over us again, and I dig the toe of my boot into the dirt below us, beating myself up. Give me any other girl and I could flirt my pants off, but Lauren makes me tongue-tied.

She turns to me. "Are you going to miss being in season?"

"Yeah, I love the game and the camaraderie that comes from the team."

"What do you do during your off-season? Obviously going to parties isn't on the list."

"No, it isn't." I chuckle. "Hopefully I'll spend more time with my mom and aunt. I didn't get much time with Mom before we moved here, but I think that'll change."

"That sounds nice." She picks up a rock from the bank, skipping it perfectly. "What do you like to do with her?"

"Cook or watch movies."

"What's your favorite movie?"

"*Top Gun*."

She skips another rock before asking, "Are you Maverick or Goose?"

"I don't know." I pick up a rock of my own to skip. "Maybe Goose? Your brother would be Maverick. He's a little more bold."

"And more stupid," she mutters.

I burst into laughter, but I cut short when I catch her watching me closely. "What?"

"I don't think I've ever seen you laugh like that."

I return to digging my boot into the dirt, not knowing what to say back.

"It's nice." She nudges me with a smile.

I have to bite my lower lip to keep from grinning like a little kid.

Her phone lights up between us, and she lifts it before locking it and putting it back down. I nearly ask her if she's going to answer, but decide on "What's your favorite movie?" instead.

"*The Proposal.*"

I crinkle my nose. "What's that?"

"You don't know it?"

I shake my head.

"Ryan Reynolds and Sandra Bullock?"

"Nope."

She blushes. "It's a rom-com."

"Are those your favorite?"

"Yeah, I guess so." She gives a sheepish grin, shrugging a shoulder. "I love romance. It's full of hope, and the idea of finding someone who adores you, quirks and all, is pretty cool."

I'm so close to blurting out that I'm that person, but I know better than to cross the line. This is my best friend's little sister. He's fiercely protective of her, and even if he weren't, I'd still feel an inclination to protect Lauren from myself.

"Do you have a favorite movie-watching snack?" she asks.

"Oreos and peanut butter."

She sticks her tongue out. "That sounds nasty."

"Don't knock it till you try it. There's no greater combination than chocolate and peanut butter. Add a little cream and a little crisp from the Oreos and—" I bring my fingers to my lips and blow them up in a chef's kiss.

"I guess I'll have to take your word for it." She raises her brows, looking doubtful.

"I'd have to say the same about *The Proposal*."

Her jaw drops as her phone lights up again, but she flips it over, focusing back on me. "What do you—"

A twig snaps behind us, and we both whip around to find a lanky kid stumbling our way. It's Austin Moore. He's a year behind me, in Lauren's grade, and he's the other starting wide receiver on our team. I kind of hate the cocky freshman.

"There you are! I've been looking everywhere for you, Lauren. I've been texting you." His glossy eyes are filled with hope.

"Oh, yeah, sorry. I just didn't want to be out in that chaos."

He crouches down into her space, holding out his hand and flashing a grin. "We don't have to go back. I just wanted to spend time with you. Is that okay?"

Lauren's gaze flicks to me, and I give her a nod. "Go on. I'll be fine."

She gets up, leaving with Austin, and I remind myself this is a good thing. Austin has had his eye on Lauren all school year. It's been so obvious. As much as I want to be upset about him being with her, I recognize a guy like Austin comes with a lot less baggage than I do. He's better for her than I could ever be. I should be relieved he came to take her because this needs to end, or it's going to be impossible not to fall for my best friend's sister.

Chapter One

Lauren

Never drink hard liquor. That's a rule I've always followed. I prefer beer and wine over the burn of spirits, and I watched my brother, Charlie, do too many stupid things when he drank whiskey, back in high school.

Tonight though, I came into the bar just wanting to feel...nothing. Too many emotions have been swirling around inside of me over the last few months. So here I am, sitting at the Long Neck Bottle drinking my second glass of Jim Beam on the rocks, and I can't help but think this isn't working. Because despite my desire to feel numb, I'm feeling a whole host of things when I register the tall, broad figure of Jax Greer.

I watch his biceps flex as he mixes what looks to be a whiskey sour for one of the locals at the other end of the bar. When his blue-eyed gaze latches on to mine, heat rises in my chest. My curiosity is piqued, and I'm almost giddy, a sensation I haven't felt in too many years to count. It all feels borderline too much, but at least I'm no longer thinking about the weight I came here to escape.

When Jax realizes I'm sitting at the bar alone, a surprised smile spreads on his face and he approaches me.

"What're you doing here by yourself, Freckles? Are Callie and Olivia meeting you?"

"Why do you insist on calling me that?" I huff. "Just call me Lauren like everyone else."

"I've been doing it for years. There's no sense in stopping now. Where are your friends?"

"It's just me." If the girls knew I was here alone, they'd throw a fit.

He narrows his eyes further. *Gosh, they really are beautiful eyes.* "What's going on?"

"Nothing."

"People don't sit in bars and drink alone over nothing."

I spin my glass, watching the ice clunk around inside. "Maybe I do."

"No, you don't." He leans against the bar, inspecting me. The motion pulls his plain white T-shirt taut against his chest in a way that makes my head spin more than the alcohol. "Tell me what's going on."

I tap my fingers on my glass. "I came here so I wouldn't have to talk to anyone about what's going on."

He clenches his teeth, highlighting his strong, stubbled jawline. I'm pretty sure that thing could cut glass.

Still tapping my fingers, I ask, "Can you just get me another Jim Beam on the rocks?"

He doesn't tear his gaze from me. Between being in my orbit over the last nine years and working at this bar, he knows my drinking habits. "You sure you don't want a beer?"

"Nope."

He hesitantly moves from the bar, sweeping across the room to grab a bottle of bourbon off the shelf. When he sets the glass down in front of me, his eyebrows rise in concern. "You're sure you don't want to talk? I can be a good listener. It's one of the requirements of being a bartender."

I shake my head. "Right now, I just want to sit and sip on this toxic sludge."

His lips slip into a half-hearted smile, but I don't miss the concern in his eyes when he gives me a curt nod and draws away from the counter to help another customer. Even as he mixes up their pink cocktail and nods along good-naturedly, he watches me carefully.

The feel of his eyes on me sparks a flicker of a flame, and I sip my drink in an attempt to put it out. I'm not sure why alcohol is my solution for everything tonight. It's never been known to put out a fire.

When my phone buzzes in my pocket, I know who it is before I even pull it out. I decline the call and send a text.

ME

Please leave me alone.

AUSTIN

I just want to talk. Come on baby

When Austin and I first started going out, I was so excited the most popular boy in our grade wanted to be with me that I somehow ended up letting him call me *baby* for the next eight and a half years. Now, five months post-breakup, I should be able to tell him the truth. I wish it were that easy for me.

I type out a message, thinking of Callie's words two weeks ago, when Austin last texted me. He doesn't get to keep popping back into my life and refusing to let me move on when *he's* the one who cheated on *me*. It feels good to type the message, but as soon as I read through it, I erase it all. They're not my words, so I rewrite the text and hit send.

ME

> I don't want to talk. I'm trying to move on. Please stop calling.

Naturally, that makes him call again. *What is wrong with this man?*

I decline the call and then block his number. I don't know why it took me this long to finally do it. Maybe I needed some liquid courage. Either way, I feel lighter now.

Eager to ride this wave, I take a big gulp of my drink. And another. *And another.* Fifteen minutes later, my third drink of the night is gone, and it's working. I'm floating on a cloud.

Things with Austin felt off for a long time before we finally broke up. I couldn't express my feelings to him, and I pushed my own needs to the backburner to keep him happy. Even so, it hurts to end a long-term relationship. It aches to know that after everything I sacrificed, I wasn't enough. He still cheated on me.

I thought I'd been doing a good job of moving on, but when you're constantly running into your ex at the grocery store or the local diner, it becomes notably harder. It doesn't help that every few weeks he likes to call to try to make amends, as if he senses when I'm starting to move on.

I'd like to think I could deal with Austin today if I weren't already having a nightmare of a week. Three days ago, I reviewed the books for my family's ranch and realized Copper Hill is at the end of its rope. Then, my dad wound up in the hospital. He spent two nights there and when we finally got him home this morning, my ex reappears after almost two weeks of silence.

As the alcohol courses through my veins, the pain lessens. I feel more empowered. *I don't need him.* It may have been comforting to have Austin's support with the ranch, but I can handle it on my own. I can do it *all* alone. I'll do it better. I'll fix the ranch and fix my dad, and everything is going to be great. I just need to buckle down.

When Jax comes back to check on me, I ask him to refill my drink.

"How about I drive you home instead?"

"I'm good. I just want one more. There's nothing wrong with that."

He crosses his arms. "I can't in good conscience serve you another."

"Then please just leave me alone."

He stands there for a moment like he's going to argue with me, but finally releases a breath and storms off.

I'm watching him whisper to the other bartenders, probably telling them not to serve me, when a firm hand lands on my shoulder.

As I spin around to greet my new friend, the room tilts.

"Baby, you have to hear me out. I've given you your space, but it's time we get this sorted out. You *need* me."

Austin's words turn my earlier joy into pure rage, but instead of standing up to him, I sputter. "I...what? What do you mean?"

"Look at you." He thrusts his hands out, as if my mere existence is explanation enough. "You're pathetic without me, going to the bar by yourself. You and I both know the ranch isn't going to hold itself up. You need me."

People watch us as Austin raises his voice, and I scoot out of my barstool to face him. "Go home, Austin."

He grabs hold of me, and I try to pull back, but his grip is tight. The stench of alcohol wafts off him.

"Austin, let go." My voice waivers.

"No. I came here to talk with you." He shoves me back into my seat, but our combined alcohol consumption quickly turns everything into a complete mess. My butt clips the edge of the barstool, and I fall to the floor.

When he reaches down to help drag me up, I pull away. "Ow! No, Austin. That hurts."

Shuffling footsteps drag Austin's attention up just as someone growls, "Get your hands off her."

Jax is suddenly there, pulling him away from me, but Austin resists, flailing his arms and making a bigger idiot of himself.

Instead of entertaining Austin's aggression, Jax cocks his arm back and slugs Austin in the face.

Holy crap! I've never seen Jax hit someone, and I hate that watching him stand up for me is officially the hottest thing I've ever seen in my entire life.

The fury in his eyes softens to concern as he crouches down next to me, placing his hands on both my shoulders. "Are you okay?" He inspects me, as if the damage Austin caused can be seen with the naked eye, but no one can see my shattered heart.

"I'm fine. Will you take me home?"

Jax nods. As he scoops me off the floor, he turns to Earl, the bouncer. "Get him out of here."

When Jax steps through the back door into the cool night air, I nuzzle into his touch. It's been a long time since I've seen him in this way. When he first came to town, over nine years ago now, he was one of the only people who made me feel free to be myself. I didn't have to be perfect to win his affection. But time drew us apart, and Jax became my brother's best friend who gave me an annoying nick-name solely to get on my nerves. Now, I'm seeing traces of the Jax I used to know, the soft one who once swiped away my tears when he caught me crying in the barn, the thoughtful one who bought me a pint of ice cream on my birthday freshman year.

His lips curl into a gentle smile as he runs his thumb up and down my arm. I notice the perfect bow shape of his upper lip. His lips almost look stained red. With the alcohol coursing through my veins, I know I'm not thinking clearly, but I also can't bring myself to care enough to stop the question from forming in my mind. *What would it be like to kiss Jax Greer?*

Between his full lips and the way he's gently caressing me, I bet he'd be an amazing kisser. I imagine he's passionate and experienced. He probably knows exactly what to do to make a woman feel like the only person on earth.

We sit in silence the entire drive back to my house, but when he stops his truck and puts it in park, he gently says, "I know you're not okay."

I pick at a stray thread on my flannel, trying to fight the surge of tears his words have brought on. "I'm *fine*. I don't want to think about what just happened."

I've done a great job of holding it together in front of everyone. Jax isn't about to be the one who undoes that.

I can still feel his gaze on me when I speak again. "Do you want to come inside?" He bites his lip like I asked him to break some sort of rule. Pinning him with a look, I add, "I *want* you to come inside, Jax."

He gets out of the truck, rounding the bumper to help me step down, even though I'm five eight and his truck isn't that lifted.

Once I unlock my front door and swing it open, Jax pulls me toward the couch, brushing my hair to the side. The warmth of his touch feels so good, soft but firm like I expected. He makes a tsking sound and gets up from the couch.

"Where are you going?"

"To find some ointment and Band-Aids. You're bleeding. You must've hit the barstool when Austin knocked you over."

I reach up to my head and sure enough, a small trace of blood appears on my fingertips.

I'm ready to protest, telling him I don't need a stupid bandage, but when he comes back and sweeps my hair away from my face again, I melt. I put aside my ego for a second, basking in his intimate touch until he presses an antiseptic pad to my forehead.

I wince and pull away. I guess the effects of the alcohol are wearing off now. He wraps an arm around my waist and tugs me closer, holding my gaze and making my heart pound in my chest like a stampede of wild horses.

"Did he ever hurt you?" There's pain in Jax's eyes, and I can't help but wonder what put it there. Like everyone else in town, I heard about what brought Jax and his mom to Roots his sophomore year, but people here tend to spread gossip just to keep themselves entertained, so I've always treated it as such. If he ever told Charlie the truth, my brother kept it to himself.

"He never laid a hand on me."

Jax peels open a Band-Aid. "He's still a complete asshole."

"I know."

"Then why'd you put up with him? Why'd you get *engaged*?"

"I don't know." I draw my knees up into my arms. "I did love him, at one point."

"Have you ever heard the phrase 'you'll pick a familiar hell over an unfamiliar heaven'?"

I shake my head.

"Well, Austin is your familiar hell. Yes, he's an asshole, but he's all you've known. It would make sense for you to get back with him when he came crawling back to you tonight." He's silent for a beat, intent on pressing the bandage to my wound before he finally meets my eyes, whispering, "Please don't take him back."

"I'm not going to."

"Good."

With him this close to me, I can smell the scent of his cologne, clean and masculine.

"I'm tired of him making me feel worthless," I whisper. "He called me pathetic tonight."

"He's wrong."

The alcohol must be getting to me because for the first time in so long, I don't hold back. "I'm tired of everything falling apart. It feels like him cheating on me was just the start of this downward spiral. I want to feel good again."

"You deserve that," he says with a soft smile.

I take his words of reassurance as my sign to lean in and close my eyes, but he immediately scurries off the couch. "What the hell, Lauren?"

Chapter Two

Jax

She's like a drunken deer in the headlights when she looks back at me. Both her hands are braced on the couch from when she caught herself after my swift retreat.

As she straightens and finds her balance again, a blush paints her cheeks and horror fills her eyes, making me feel bad for how I reacted. Not only did I reject the woman I've been in love with since I was fifteen, but I rejected her right after she had to hear awful things said to her by the man who was supposed to marry her in six months.

I plop myself back down on the couch. "What was that?"

She presses her face into the palms of her hands, groaning. "I don't know. I'm sorry. I just wanted to feel good again, to feel wanted. Obviously that backfired." She laughs, but the sound is coated in embarrassment.

"What are you talking about?"

"When I first broke up with Austin, I felt relieved because it was an end to the pain I'd been feeling while our relationship fell apart. It was nice to stop pretending I was happy, and seeing new possibilities for my life was exciting for a little bit, but now that the excitement has worn off, reality has set in."

Noting the flush still in her cheeks, I rise from the couch and head into the kitchen to grab her a glass of water. When I hand it to her, she gives me an appreciative smile before taking a sip.

A lock of her golden hair falls over her face as she stares at the glass in her hands, not meeting my gaze. "I miss being in a relationship. Plus, now, I have to go through life not only knowing that it's possible for someone to say 'I love you' and not mean it, but also knowing *I'm* the type of girl that someone would say those three words to without meaning them."

I reach out my hand, placing it on her thigh in a lame attempt at comfort. Her smile doesn't reach her eyes as she continues. "Toward the end, Austin made me feel like something was wrong with me, and that only got worse when I found out he was cheating on me. Because of him, I don't know who I am anymore. I don't know what I enjoy doing in my free time, and I'm starting to wonder if I'm unlovable." She pauses, releasing a sigh. "For as long as I can remember, my life has revolved around me holding everyone I love together, but now *my* life is blowing up, and I don't know if I'm good enough to fix all this. I certainly wasn't enough to fix my relationship with Austin."

I hate seeing Lauren torn down. She used to be bold. She used to know who she was and what she loved. She wasn't afraid to take what she wanted out of life.

Twisting the glass in her hands, she glances up at me. "I know it was stupid to think it would fix anything, but I thought kissing you would relieve some of the pain I've been feeling and make me feel wanted again, at least for a little bit." She drops her gaze to her lap.

I sling my arm over her shoulder, leaning my head against hers. "It's not silly to have all these emotions after everything you've gone through, but kissing me isn't going to make any of it better."

"I don't know what will." She bites her lower lip, looking defeated.

I open and close my mouth as I take her hand and let silence wash over us. I want to make this better, but I don't know how.

Finally, I say, "I don't know what it's like to have your heart broken, but I've seen people fall in and out love in my lifetime. So many lose themselves when they love someone who isn't right for them, but now you're free." As I say the words, I think of my mom when she came to Roots. She blossomed into the best version of herself once we escaped my dad. "You should learn what you like and what you want in life. You're strong—you can handle anything life throws at you. I promise you're better off without that asshole. You just need to learn how to believe it again."

She throws her hands up in exasperation. "I don't even know where to start."

"Make a list of things you've always wanted to do but didn't. Then, we'll make sure you do everything on it."

She crinkles her brows. "I don't know about that."

"Why not?"

"Honestly, it sounds scary. I don't want to do *everything* alone. I like people."

"Which is why *I* will help you."

Her eyes go round. "You will?"

"Of course. Now get some sleep. We can revisit the list another day."

"No." She grabs my wrist as I get up from the couch. "I want to do it now. This is probably the boldest I'll ever be, and there's no way I'm falling asleep anytime soon."

"Are you sure? It's late."

"Yeah, I already have a few ideas." She gets up from the couch to grab a pencil and a pad of paper, her hazel eyes sparking. I love that she's biting back a smile instead of fighting off tears.

When she jots down her first idea, I immediately glance over her shoulder to read it.

1. Take swing dance lessons at the Long Neck

"I always wanted to take lessons, but I've been so busy, and the few times I could've gone, Austin shot the idea down. He said he wasn't good at dancing, but I didn't care. I just wanted someone to dance with me because I enjoy it."

I have to fight back the urge to remark on how much I hate that man or how I would've done anything she asked just to see a smile on her face because *that's* what you do when you care for someone. Instead, I opt for, "That's a good start. What else have you been holding back from?"

She writes down two more.

2. Cut my hair
3. Go to a ranching conference

She twirls the pencil in her hands. "I've wanted to cut my hair for two years, but I always chickened out."

"What about the ranching conference?"

"Austin went to plenty, but always alone. He argued that someone needed to stay back at Copper Hill and that he was better at talking to strangers. I kind of wonder if he just didn't want me to realize I could manage without him."

I wince. This was supposed to be empowering for Lauren, but it feels like it's just empowering me to beat the crap out of Austin. Thankfully she still looks upbeat, so we keep going.

"Can I add something?"

She hands me the pencil and paper, watching over my shoulder while I write.

> 4. Eat out alone
> 5. Do something that's only for me and no one else

"I like mine better," she says as she snags the pencil from me, flipping it around to erase what I just wrote.

"You can't do that!" I slip the pencil from her grasp, but she grabs it back.

"It's *my* list."

I chuckle. "But you're not going to grow if you only do things you come up with on your own."

"Fine. But I have more to add."

"Be my guest." I gesture to the notepad.

She writes down two more items.

> 6. Go to a concert
> 7. Regenerative Agriculture

"What's that?" I point to number seven.

She assesses me for a minute, as if she's trying to decide whether she can trust me. Finally, she sighs, admitting, "The ranch isn't doing well. Our profits have been down, and the cost of maintaining the ranch continues to creep up. We need to do something different, or we aren't going to make it."

There's fear in her eyes, and it spurs me to wrap my arms around her without hesitation. She allows me to do so, even leaning into me in a way that makes my heart melt.

Talking into my chest now, she continues. "Regenerative agriculture, or 'regenerative ag,' is supposed to not only be better for soil health and the environment, but it's been proven to cut costs and improve yields. I think it could work for Copper Hill, but I've been afraid to suggest it."

"It sounds like a great idea. I think it could work for your family's ranch, especially with someone passionate like you leading the charge."

"I think so too," she says softly.

She turns back to the notepad, jotting down another idea, and curiosity has me peeking over her shoulder.

8. Kiss someone new (when I'm ready)

I can't help the grin that curves on my lips as I watch her add the little note in parentheses. I look over the list once more.

"What about hobbies? Are there any you want to pick up again?"

"Well sure, but I don't have time. Now that Austin's gone, I'm the one in charge, and I'm managing the ranch with one less cowboy. If I'm being honest, I already don't know how I'll manage to get away for a weekend to attend a conference or find time to research regenerative ag."

"What if I helped you?"

"When would *you* have the time? I thought you just took an ownership stake in the bar. You're probably just as busy as me."

"It's only a ten percent stake. If anything, it's given me more time because I'm starting to supervise and cutting back my late shifts. I can help you in the morning with whatever you need, whether it's an extra set of hands or help with admin work."

She worries her lower lip. "When are you going to sleep?"

"I'll take naps." I smirk.

"This sounds like a terrible idea. You need to take care of yourself."

"So do you," I counter, pinning her with a look. "Let me help."

"Are you sure?"

"I'm sure. Add some hobbies on there." I tap the notepad. "You need to let yourself enjoy life again."

She stares me down for a while, and I feel her gaze on every inch of my skin, but I hold it, determined to show her I'm not going to change my mind. I've watched Lauren lose herself over the last several years of her relationship, and I've had to bite my tongue because she said she was happy. Now that I know she isn't, I'm going to make sure that changes.

She lifts the pencil.

9. Start reading again
10. Ride Lucky for fun

I point to number ten. "When was the last time you took Lucky out for a trail ride?"

"I honestly couldn't tell you. The poor guy needs a break just as much as I do. He's always working."

"That's going to change soon." I give her an encouraging smile. "I like this list. You can always add more to it later if you come up with something, but for now, you should get some sleep, and I should go."

She pouts. "I'm too tired to go all the way to my room."

Sighing, I scoop her up and carry her down the hall, setting her on her bed. "There."

She's still pouting.

"What's wrong now?"

"I'm too tired to get ready for bed." A small smile spreads on her face, like she's testing me more than anything.

"All you have to do is brush your teeth."

"Nuh-uh. I have to get the bar smell off me, and then I have to do my full face routine. I don't get clear, youthful skin like this by neglecting crucial steps."

"Then do it." I turn to leave, knowing I've already over-stayed my welcome. I'm not used to spending extended periods of time with her alone. It's been years, and even when she didn't have a boyfriend, I knew better than to let myself get attached. I don't protect the people I love, as evidenced by my fantastic failure at doing that for my mom nine years ago. Being with Lauren isn't going to change that.

She glances down at her floral bedspread. "Will you stay here tonight? Please."

When she looks back up at me with her hazel eyes, I can tell she needs this, and if I'm being honest, it's impossible to say no to Lauren.

"I'll stay."

Chapter Three

Lauren

I BOUNCE UP FROM MY SPOT ON THE BED AND JAX GIVES me a look. He doesn't say anything, but I can tell he's suspicious of me springing up after claiming to be too tired.

The truth is I don't want to be left alone yet. I know sleep won't come easily, and I don't want to lie there by myself, stewing in my thoughts.

I quickly run through a shower and change into my pajamas. I brush my hair and then lean against my bathtub, groaning.

"What's wrong?" Jax creeps into the doorway of the bathroom, gaze averted like he's afraid of invading my privacy.

"I have to braid my hair or it's going to be all tangled in the morning. I spent all day lifting bales of hay, and I don't think I can hold my arms up long enough to do it."

He chuckles. "I'll braid it for you if you want."

"You know how to braid?"

"No, but it can't be that hard."

I raise my eyebrows. "Do you even know what one looks like?"

"I was raised by two women. Of course I do. Now sit still and let me braid your hair."

This should be interesting.

He sits next to me on the edge of the tub, gently brushing his fingers across my hairline as he gathers the locks back, then breaks it into three sections. I'm impressed.

"Now what?"

"I'll do it." I giggle, reaching back for the strands of hair he separated and ignoring the ache in my shoulders. "I'm sure I can do a better job than you, even if I can only lift my shoulders halfway."

When our fingers tangle, a spark jolts up my arm. I pause what I'm doing, meeting his gaze, which only makes everything worse. My heart races in my chest. *This is new.*

It's been so long since I've allowed myself to acknowledge his good looks and charm, not to mention the occasional soft side that makes me want to snuggle up in his arms.

I break eye contact and focus on crisscrossing the chunks of hair over one another. He carefully studies my technique, making it nearly impossible to focus, but I get through the braid with only one minor mistake.

I twist a band around the bottom and inspect my work in the mirror. Turning to Jax with a smirk, I note, "It's still better than you would've done."

"Ouch."

I give him a mischievous grin, and he returns it with his own smile that stops my heart from beating. For the second time tonight, I see glimpses of sixteen-year-old Jax. I picture him holding his hand out to me as he tries to convince me to get on the rope swing he and Charlie built over the river out back. I remember the pride he wore on his face when he slipped his good luck bracelet onto my wrist at the state game. I pushed aside all these happy memories when I built my life with Austin, but in this moment, they're front and center, and I can't shake them.

"Time for my skincare routine!" I clamor off the tub, humming as I crouch by my cabinets and collect what I need, decidedly ignoring what just happened between us. "You should do it with me. Your skin could use a little extra care," I say as I pop back up.

"What does that mean?"

"I just think it'd help bring out the natural shine of your skin if you used toner and moisturizer like I do." I press my hand below my chin, putting my face on display for him.

As I place my bottles of product on the counter, he picks them up, reading the labels. "No way am I letting you put this on me." He folds his arms and leans against the doorjamb. "I'll just watch you do it."

I grab my cleanser, doing my best not to stare at his biceps. "Don't make me say it, Jax."

"Say what?"

"I could use the distraction."

He groans, tilting his head back. "I'll do a lot for you, Freckles, but I have to draw the line somewhere. It's not happening."

Not willing to accept his answer, I place a dollop of cleanser in my hands, swiping it across my skin as I explain what I'm doing. "This is an oil cleanser, so I rub it on for about one to two minutes. It's important to rub down my neck and around my lymph nodes to help with lymphatic drainage and circulation. Then I'll wipe it off with a warm washcloth."

"That was a lot of words I don't understand. You don't

need to explain it to me. I already told you I'm not—" Before he can reject me again, I apply some of the cleanser to his cheeks, rubbing it around. "Lauren!"

I draw back from him with a wild grin on my face. "Now that it's already on there, you might as well rub it around for a couple minutes."

He gives me a scowl but, to my satisfaction, does it anyway. After about thirty seconds, I reach over, grabbing his hand and guiding him along.

I hand him a warm washcloth, but instead of setting it aside when he's done, he turns it over, grabbing my waist. He tugs me toward him and lifts my chin with his other hand. At his touch, chills echo down my spine.

"What are you doing?" My words are barely above a whisper.

"I'm helping you remove your cleanser. Please let me do this. You asked me to stay so you wouldn't be alone, but it feels more like you wanted me here to take away my masculinity and force me into doing your skincare routine."

"I'm not taking away your masculinity by giving you nice skin."

He gives me a stern look that reminds me I'm supposed to be holding still for him, so I stop what I'm doing and stay quiet as he takes over.

His motions are gentle and methodic, and they lull me into noticing how blue his eyes are. Deep, like the ocean.

When he draws back, I don't move, still looking into his eyes. It's only when he speaks again that I realize I'm staring.

"Okay, what's next?"

"Toner, followed by my magic serum, and then moisturizer to finish."

He tsks. "No wonder you don't have time to read a book or ride Lucky. This must take up two hours of your day."

"It's only ten to fifteen minutes tops. Here." I drip some toner onto his fingertips and show him the motions to rub it in, then guide him through the last two steps.

When we're done, he turns to me. "Is my skin shining yet?"

"No, you have to do it daily."

"I don't think I can."

I shrug. "I guess you're just not dedicated enough."

"I'd need your help to stick with it."

My heart speeds up inside my chest. I can't believe how much I like spending time with Jax. I appreciate that he willingly sat here with me through this elaborate process. I like how gentle he is with me, the way he teases me, and the softness in his gaze. He makes me think maybe, with the right person, moving on won't be as complicated as I'd thought.

"Is it bedtime now?" he asks, breaking me from my thoughts.

"Yeah, I'm tired."

He heads toward my bedroom door, saying good night over his shoulder, but watching him walk away only unsettles me further.

"Wait!"

He turns, a look of concern laced in his brows. "What's wrong?"

I search for an excuse. "The guest bedroom gets pretty cold at night. You should probably just stay in here."

He assesses me for a moment before nodding and heading toward my linen closet, gathering a pillow and some blankets. When he's made a bed on the floor, guilt floods me. I should be able to be on my own, and Jax shouldn't have to sleep on the floor. He's already done enough for me tonight. I'm asking too much of him.

What has gotten into me? I shake my head and blame the alcohol I ingested earlier.

"Are you sure you'll be okay down there?"

"Yup." He pulls the sheet up below his chin.

"It doesn't look very comfortable."

"At least this way I can make sure you don't try to kiss me again," he teases.

I throw my pillow at him. "I changed my mind. You *should* sleep on the floor."

He chuckles. "Good night."

"Good night."

Even though Jax is on the floor, I can hear every time he rolls over and every time he takes a deep breath. Still, I sleep like a baby knowing he's there.

———

When I peek my eyes open in the morning, I'm surprised to see the sun shining through the seam where my curtains meet. I'm usually awake before the sunrise, even after a late night.

Jax is gone, and I start to think last night was a figment of my imagination until I roll over and find a glass of water and Advil sitting on my nightstand. The list Jax and I created is taped to my wall just above it.

I take a sip of water, leaving the Advil. Surprisingly, I feel okay. I grab a sweatshirt and as soon as I swing my door open, my nose is greeted by the scent of bacon and—*is that pancakes?*

I pad down the hallway and into the open area that includes the kitchen and living room.

Leaning my forearms against the kitchen island, I take in Jax, shirtless and flipping pancakes on the griddle. He still has a lingering tan from the summer, and his abs look like they're sculpted by God himself. His Spidey senses must be tingling because he pauses, mid-whistle, and spins around to face me.

"Hey! How are you feeling?" He grins.

"Actually, pretty good."

"That's great because I was hoping we could check an item off your list today."

"Already?" I draw back from the island, my nerves building. I no longer feel as brave as I did last night.

"Sure. Why not?"

Chapter Four

Jax

Hesitation floods Lauren's face. It's sad to see the bold and excited version from last night gone so soon. I hate Austin for doing this to her, and I hate myself for not stepping in to help her sooner.

"I just made the list. I should probably—"

"It doesn't have to be anything big." I pull the bacon out of the pan and split it between the two plates on the counter. "We could just buy you a book at the bookstore so you can start reading."

"That's all I have to do?"

"Yes." I flip a golden-brown pancake. "In case I didn't make it clear last night, you don't have to do all of this alone."

"Okay, well maybe we can do it later?" She bites her lip as she pulls her phone from her pocket. "I have a couple things I need to do this morning, and I'm already getting a late start to the day."

"Let's eat some breakfast and then I can help you before we go to the bookstore."

I add three blueberry pancakes to her plate.

"Thank you."

Grabbing my own loaded plate, I join her at the kitchen island. I drizzle syrup across my pancakes, slice into one, and am half a second away from chomping down on my bite when she asks, "So is this the Jax Greer treatment?" When I furrow my brow at her, she cheerily adds, "You know, after you sleep with a woman? Is this what you do?"

I set my fork down, my stomach churning. "No, it's not. When you're trying to keep things casual, making a woman breakfast the next day doesn't make any sense."

My words have a bite to them, but Lauren doesn't seem to notice. I hate that she sees me as someone who sleeps around. I guess I did it to myself: I've been too afraid of hurting anyone and too caught up in my feelings for the same, unavailable girl. But I want to be more.

"Too bad, because these pancakes are amazing!" She assesses the ingredients on the counter. "Is this store-bought mix? I didn't think I had any in the pantry."

"They're homemade. Aunt Carol used to make them for me in high school."

"Wow. Make sure to tell her thank-you for me."

She shamelessly shovels pancakes into her mouth, doing a giddy little dance as she does so. Wisps of hair fall out of the braid she slept on last night, framing her freckled face. Her skin is still glowing, which makes me somewhat reconsider my judgments on her time-consuming regimen.

She glances up at me, her smile gone. "Why do you always keep things casual with women? Why not have a real girlfriend?"

"I don't want one."

"Why not?"

I kill some time and take her empty plate, unwilling to dive into the fact that I haven't believed myself worthy of caring for someone like that after I failed to stand up for my mom every time my dad drank too much. And how would I even explain that I haven't met anyone who's held a candle to Lauren since we met *nine years* ago. "Are you ready to go?"

"Sure, just let me change." She pauses, eyeing me and pointing her finger from my head to my toes and back again. "I hope you have a shirt lying around somewhere because that outfit is very impractical for ranch work."

She slips past me with a smirk.

"You were looking, huh?"

"You wish! Don't flatter yourself." Her bedroom door slams closed.

She's right. I've been wishing Lauren Rhodes would notice me from the day I first laid eyes on her.

———

It took Lauren a while to get out of work-mode in the bookstore. She made a beeline for the Ranching and Agriculture section, and I had to peel her away, but once she started exploring other sections, her eyes filled with wonder.

When we walk out of Molly's five minutes before closing, I'm still riding the high of seeing the smile on Lauren's face when I bought her both the romance books she was torn between.

"Thank you again for these." Lauren lifts the bag in her hand. "I'm excited to start. I'll have to figure out how to work it into my routine a couple times a week."

"That's the whole point of this list, to bring some joy into your life."

"I think it'll help." She scuffs her boot on the sidewalk. "Do you have some in your life?"

Her question catches me off guard, and I tense up. It's not like she asked me to tell her about my past, which I've hid from most people in town, both out of shame and a desire not to revisit it. Yet it still feels like she's asking me to give her a piece of my heart, something I don't normally do with women, but especially not with Lauren. I'll never get that piece back from her.

I lift my hat, raking my hands through my waves before putting it back on my head. "What do you mean?"

"I was just wondering. If you're the one who's supposed to be helping me check things off this list, I should probably vet you and make sure you have some in your own life."

"I do," I say, automatically.

"Like what?"

We're still just standing outside Molly's place, so I take her hand, leading her to our parking spot while I figure out how to answer this question without saying *you*.

Once we're in my truck, she buckles up and swivels toward me expectantly. I guess I should've anticipated that.

"You still haven't answered my question."

"Okay, fine." I turn my key in the ignition. "I like my mom's cooking, and I like seeing her happy. She and Aunt Carol are both very important to me."

"That's nice, but you should have things you can do for yourself that make you happy too, right?"

Right. I glance over my shoulder as I back out onto the road. "I like hunting. There's no better feeling than being in a deer stand, disconnected from nature. I like the concentration it takes to keep my hands from shaking when I draw my bow back, the satisfaction of getting a whitetail."

"When was the last time you went hunting?"

"I guess it's been a while." I used to be better about that when Charlie was around, but I've spent the last couple years focused more on making something out of myself than enjoying hobbies.

"Good thing it's hunting season now."

I glance her way as I flick my blinker on and turn off Roots Road. The corners of her lips are curving into a smile.

"I guess I could try to find some time for it."

"There you go."

I wonder if she's doing this because she thinks she owes me after I helped her make the list. I open my mouth to tell her this isn't supposed to be a transactional arrangement, but she speaks first. "What about work? Do you enjoy your work?"

I punch in the code at the gate to Copper Hill and marvel in the beauty of this place. Even in November, there are still some wildflowers growing along the fence line. The cattle graze peacefully to our right. There isn't a cowboy in sight. I'm sure they'll all gathered in the bunkhouse for supper. It's such a different lifestyle from mine—getting up with the sun instead of going to sleep just before it rises. I loved working on this ranch with Charlie back in the day.

"Jax?" Lauren leans forward to inspect my face.

"I don't mind bartending."

"Is there something else you'd like to do someday?"

I stopped wanting things for myself a long time ago. "Maybe." I shrug.

I brace myself for her to ask me more questions as I pull into her driveway, but instead, she leans in to give me a quick hug. "Thank you again for the books. It was a delightful surprise." She puts her hand on the door. "I guess I'll be seeing you around?"

That's it? I'm not ready to say goodbye. If I'm not careful, I'll close in on a full twenty-four hours spent with Lauren, but I can't help it. She's like a drug.

I shuffle out of the truck, walking to her doorstep. Before she can reach for the doorhandle, I blurt, "Do you want me to cook you dinner?"

She hikes her thumb toward the house. "I have leftovers in the fridge that need to get eaten and a couple hours of research to do tonight. Besides, you've done enough for me already."

"I don't mind."

"That's okay." She swings her door open. "I really need to get started on regenerative ag research if I'm going to implement it in the spring."

"Of course." I glance down at the ground. "I'll, uh, see you soon then. I plan on following through with my promise to help out around here."

"Thank you."

I take the cue and head out, bounding down the steps of her front porch and trying to block out the shame of her rejecting my offer.

As I open my truck door, she calls out, "Do you make dinner that's as good as your pancakes?"

I glance up, unable to stop my grin. "Better."

"Can you make pasta?"

"The best pasta."

"Then sign me up for dinner soon." A smile paints her lips.

I spend the entire car ride home plotting how to get more one-on-one time with Lauren as soon as possible.

Chapter Five

Lauren

I untack Lucky and put him in his stall for the night, releasing a sigh as I take in the gorgeous sunset. When I pull out my phone, I have yet another text from Jax. They've been coming all week, but this one still sets butterflies loose in my stomach, and I don't know what to do with the feeling.

Little does he realize how unmotivating that is. I *want* Jax to come over again. He's been around the ranch for the past week, like he promised, but he's mostly been working with the other cowboys. I miss the smile in his eyes when I talk with him and the feeling of his gentle touch. It's both torturous and confusing.

My list has been staring at me for a week. Jax has been

texting me to check in on my progress, but all I've been able to tick off is reading for fun, which I only did because he dragged me to the dang bookstore.

I've told him I've been busy. It's true. Even at this time of year, there's still a lot to be done on the ranch, and I've been spending any free moment I have on research. I'm now hoping to implement adaptive multi-paddock—or AMP—grazing at the ranch. It involves dividing our fields into smaller pastures where we plant different crops and continuously moving our livestock through each paddock. This should help return the cattle to their natural inclination to graze and cut down on the cost of feed.

Except implementing this strategy means I have to get a move on studying what the soil needs in each section of the ranch. Everything I've read tells me I need to consider what the cattle need and how they're going to best move through the various paddocks so we can begin zoning and planting in late winter to early spring. I'm trying not to let myself spiral thinking about all the work that will be involved in making this happen.

My phone vibrates in my hand again, and I'm grateful for a distraction from the chaos in my head.

JAX

Don't ghost me Freckles. I know where you live.

ME

I need to look at the list again. Let me check when I get home in 5 mins. I'll do something tonight

Promise?

Promise

I'm going to check in on you so don't lie

I bite back the stupid smile on my face and slide the barn door closed behind me, getting into my truck and driving to my corner of the property.

As soon as I get to the house, I walk into my room and scan the list. My eyes snag on number two. It seems simple enough. If I don't put too much thought into it, I can do it.

I quickly send two texts. One to Jax—

ME

2) Cut my Hair

And one to the person I know will be supportive when I want to make a rash decision.

ME

I'm feeling impulsive. Can you hang out tonight?

CALLIE

Hell yeah! What kind of trouble are we getting into??

———

"This isn't exactly what I had in mind when you sent your text," Callie says as she plays with my hair, carefully assessing it. "What inspired the sudden impulse?"

I swing my legs off the chair I'm sitting in, assessing the decorative pattern in the tile of Callie's bathroom floor. "Jax helped me make this stupid list of things I could do now that I'm single again. This was number two."

"Jax?"

"Yeah." I try to keep things brief, but she stares me down with this look that cracks me open. I leave out the parts about all the crap I've been dealing with, but I wind up spilling the story of Austin harassing me at the bar, Jax punching him, me trying to kiss him, and everything that followed.

"Oh my god! You and Jax!"

I leap from my seat as if I'm afraid someone will hear us, even though we're in the privacy of Callie's house. Even if someone were trying to eaves drop, the sheer volume of plants on her bathroom windowsill would surely do something to muffle our conversation.

"No way. Jax is a player, and he's my brother's best friend. Plus, I *just* got out of a relationship. Nothing is going on." My words are as much for me as they are for her.

She nods and presses her lips together tightly as she digs through the top drawer for scissors. "I'm not saying you're ready for anything yet, but maybe someday when you are...I don't think Jax would do all that for just anyone."

"Probably not, but he's doing it for Charlie. He's always just seen me as his friend's little sister."

Callie shrugs then claps her hands. When she shifts the direction of the conversation, I'm incredibly grateful. "Okay, what length are you thinking? I have some ideas, but I want your input first."

"I'm thinking just past my shoulders." I hold my hand up to show her where I want my hair to sit. It'll be a substantial change from my hair now, which sits at the middle of my back. "I still want to be able to put it up in a bun or a braid."

She continues to assess my hair, then grabs a chunk. "I have a vision. Be patient and let me work my magic."

Before I have a chance to say anything back, she snips

off the first piece. A whole bunch of curse words I won't say out loud cross my mind. This is actually happening.

"No going back now." Callie smirks.

She goes to work, and I play a game of counting the number of colors in Callie's bathroom to distract myself from the nerves. I'm at ten, but it's not working, so I close my eyes. Maybe I shouldn't have been so impulsive. I've never been the kind of person who acts on a whim. I like to plan. And plan. And plan.

Callie catches me pinching my eyes shut. "Lauren, you look amazing! Stop worrying."

"I think I should've thought this through."

"You had it on your freaking list. That means you've been thinking about it for years. Jax was right. It's time you finally did something for yourself." She fluffs my hair. "You look incredible."

"Are you almost done?" I peek an eye open.

"Yeah, I just need to do one final check." She circles around me, her eyes laser focused on my hair. She snips two more pieces around the back and then shouts, "Bellissimo!"

She opens her middle drawer and pulls out a tiny hand mirror, decorated with yellow suns on the rim. Tugging me from the chair she hands it to me and spins me around.

When I take in my reflection in the large mirror, I feel a whole swirl of emotions. Without even trying, I'm smiling, and I can't stop. I feel beautiful and lighter, and not just because I have less hair on my head.

Putting her hands on her hips, Callie says, "How does it feel to have finally done something for yourself?"

"Really good." I press my hands to my cheeks, which are growing red from all the excitement.

"We have to show you off. Let's go to the Long Neck!" Callie is already scrambling out of the bathroom and grabbing her purse from the hook by her front door. "This will be perfect. You can show Jax your new look too. We *have* to go."

"Are you serious?"

"Of course." She looks down at her sweatpants, grimacing. "But we both definitely need to change first." She wraps her hand around mine and bolts down the hallway.

———

When I walk into the bar, I'm incredibly nervous. Nothing about my look tonight resembles the old Lauren. My hair is five inches shorter. I'm wearing a black leather top Callie gave me and a pair of her bootcut jeans which she said made my "peach look extra juicy." Whatever that means. All that's mine are my boots and the necklace my mom gave me on my sixteenth birthday. Even the eyeshadow and lip gloss on my face belong to Callie, but between her knack for knowing how to accent a person's best features and her constant compliments, I've managed to keep my head held high and even start to feel kind of pretty. Scratch that. I feel *really* pretty.

As we make our way to the bar, I can't help but notice the way people are looking at me. My mind takes off running with all the bad things they must be thinking. My new look probably seems like a cry for help. I'm sure they think I'm having some sort of breakup crisis. I start to shrink back, my shoulders caving in as I keep my head down.

"Hey, gorgeous, you better keep your head up or people won't be able to see your beautiful face." Callie tilts my chin.

"People are staring. I already know what they're thinking."

"They're only staring because you're *glowing*. You are crushing the single life right now, and it shows." She links her arm in mine. "Come on. Let's go find Jax."

As we approach the bar, my eyes immediately fall on Jax. He's already looking at me, despite the chaos of the other bartenders scrambling to serve their demanding customers.

He meets us at the bar with a wide smile on his face. "You did it. You look..."

"Doesn't she look stunning?" Callie clings on to me, beaming with pride.

Jax just nods, swallowing thickly. I tuck my hair behind my ear and draw my eyes down to the ground as heat rises to my cheeks. When my eyes bounce back up to him, he's still looking.

"Earth to Jax." Callie waves her hand in front of his face. "Can we get some drinks?"

Jax nods his head. "Ranch water for Miss Callie. What about you, Freckles. Not whiskey this time, I hope?"

"Definitely not whiskey. How about a Lonestar?"

He barrels off, and I watch him go. Callie spins to me, her eyes wide. "Oh my god! Did you see his face? He couldn't stop staring! I *told* you you're glowing."

I wave her off. "That doesn't mean a thing. You know Jax is a flirt."

"Has he ever flirted with you before?"

I pause. "I don't think so. That'd be kind of wrong considering Charlie's his best friend."

"Ooh, forbidden romance. I like it." Callie wiggles her brows.

I roll my eyes and shoot her a glare as if to say *zip it* at the same time Jax returns with our drinks.

Chapter Six

Lauren

I THINK EVERY MAN IN THE BAR HAS ASKED ME TO dance tonight, and I've said yes because I can. Callie has been incredibly supportive, dancing with the guy's friend or happily standing off to the side, giving me a cheesy two-thumbs-up whenever I glance over at her.

Jax has not been so supportive. He's been watching me closely, his brows pinched and arms crossed.

"Maybe we misjudged Jax earlier," I say to Callie as we walk back toward the bar to close out our tab after last call. "He's been glaring at me all night like a protective older brother. He probably saw what I was wearing and had an internal crisis, thinking he was going to have to watch me all night. He's already punched a guy for me once."

"A protective older brother wouldn't look at you like he was. Trust me."

Jax sees us coming and grabs my card, printing the receipt. When we meet him at the bar, he slides them over to me, gritting out, "Did you ladies have a nice time?"

"The best. I like single Lauren. She's fun." Callie beams.

"Where's Olivia tonight?"

I sign the bottom of the receipt, sliding it back to Jax. "She's out of town with Rhett."

"Who's going to keep you two out of trouble?"

"Nobody." Callie bites back a devilish smile. "You ready to go, Lo?"

I glance between Callie and Jax, who still looks angry. I give him my best innocent shrug and follow behind her, but Jax grabs hold of me.

"How long is Rhett gone? Does that mean you're short a cowboy?"

"Yeah, but it's only for a couple days."

"I'll come over tomorrow to help out."

"You don't need to do that. You've helped a lot lately."

"I *want* to. I'll see you tomorrow." I'm fighting between being thankful to have someone there for me and upset he's going out of his way to help me when Jax swivels on his foot and calls over his shoulder, "And for the love of god, please stay out of trouble."

I laugh. "I'm a perfect angel! Are you kidding me?"

"But you're hanging out with the devil tonight." He shifts his gaze to Callie.

"I heard that!" Callie scrunches her nose at him.

"I'm kidding...mostly."

Callie sticks her tongue out at him before linking her arm in mine and spinning us toward the exit.

When we step out into the cool November air, a memory of Austin and me sneaking out to see each other pops into my mind. I physically shake my head, as if that will get rid of it.

Callie furrows her brow, holding back laughter as she watches me. "What the hell are you doing?"

"I was just thinking about when Austin and I used to sneak out to meet each other in high school. It was starting to get colder in the evenings, but I always pretended it didn't bother me because I wanted to be with him. It took him a while to catch on that I was faking it." I tip my head. "Well, he didn't exactly figure it out on his own. I had to ask for his sweatshirt."

"Did he give it to you?"

"Of course. Why would you ask that?"

"I don't know. He just didn't strike me as the most attentive boyfriend in the world." Silence washes over us for a moment as we step onto the sidewalk. It's only a ten-minute trek to Callie's, and, in a town like Roots, it's plenty safe for two young women to walk alone in the dark.

She glances up at me again. "Can I ask you something?"

"Sure."

"Were you two actually happy?"

On instinct, I answer, "Yeah! Of course. We wouldn't have been together so long if we weren't."

A breeze whips Callie's auburn locks into her face, but I don't miss the knowing look she's giving me.

Sighing, I relent. "I think we were both really happy for a while, at the start. Things slowed down after about a year and a half, but I figured that was normal for a couple. You know, you get used to being around each other and the excitement of every little touch feels a little more normal. You fall into a routine." I glance both ways before we cross the street. "When we finally moved in together after college, things were exciting again for a couple weeks, but then the stress started to eat away at us. We didn't have as much time to spend on our relationship, and I tried to latch on while he pulled away. That's probably when I really lost myself."

"Or maybe you were just starting to find yourself." Callie leans into me, looking me in the eyes. "I always thought you deserved better than Austin. You have no idea what you're worth."

How I ever got so lucky to have a friend like Callie is beyond me.

She squeezes my arm as we trudge down Roots Road. "No more being sad. Tonight was about making you feel empowered and excited about your new life! Tell me something you didn't like about Austin." When I give her a surprised look, she adds, "Don't hold back."

"I guess it sort of bothered me that he never put his laundry away." I shrug. "It'd just sit in the laundry room all week until I finally did it to make space for the next load. He never once said thank-you either. It made me feel a little used."

"I would too. Give me another one," she instructs as we enter the residential side of town.

"I didn't like how obsessive he was about work. I understand work is important. I love the ranch, and we obviously need it to do well in order to afford our lifestyle, but it became everything to him. We didn't go to bed or wake up together. He went on trips alone and used it as an excuse to miss out on family dinners or birthdays. It scared me a little that I was going to start my forever with someone who cared more about work than family or the rest of the people who cared about him."

"That's a really good one. Give me another."

Suddenly fired up, every little thing that's bothered me about Austin boils to the surface as we pass Mrs. Liens's perfect home with its freshly painted white picket fence.

"He was a bad dog owner." I glance toward her. "Did you ever meet Poker?"

She shakes her head.

Callie and I didn't become close until right before Austin and I broke up. Before Olivia came to town, I swear she was making an effort to avoid me altogether.

"He got Poker our senior year of high school. When we moved in together after college, I was the one who fed him and bathed him. I *loved* that dog. Meanwhile, Austin basically forgot he even existed. It killed me."

She lets go of my arm to do a little hop off the curb and lead the way across the street. "Why didn't you keep Poker when you two broke up?"

"He was Austin's dog. I cared for him, but Austin picked him out and gave him a home for his first five years of life. It seemed like the right decision, but I really miss him." I hop off the curb like she did. It makes me feel free, just like my hair, my outfit, and the night we had. "I might even miss him more than Austin."

"Hell yeah! Say that again but leave out the *might*."

"I miss Poker more than I miss Austin."

We keep walking, but then it hits me where we are. I turn to Callie, excitement filling me. "You know, Austin's parents live on the next street up. Maybe we could swing by, just to check on Poker. I worry about him sometimes."

"I don't know..." She makes a sour face. "Maybe it's not the best idea to get so close to the enemy."

"But Poker isn't the enemy."

"Okay, we'll just swing by."

Callie hooks a left, and I trail behind. We pick up the pace until we're jogging in the direction of Austin's parents' house, a soft yellow rancher.

When we approach the driveway, all the lights in the

house are off. "I don't know what I was thinking. Of course we won't be able to see him. It's almost two in the morning. They're all asleep."

"Looks like Austin's parents aren't home either." Callie points to the empty driveway. "Any chance they took Poker with them?"

"I guess."

I hang my head and start to spin away when I hear a gentle whimper.

"Poker?" The whimpering grows louder. "Oh my gosh! He left him outside. See!" I point toward the crack in the fence where a shiny blackberry nose is peeking through. "Austin's the worst. He doesn't deserve to have a dog."

Callie peers through the slots in the fence and immediately starts cooing at the dog. "You're right. Let's take him home."

"What?"

"Let's take him. Then you can have your dog back, and Poker can have an owner who lets him sleep inside. Win-win."

"We can't do that."

Callie is already reaching over the fence, her tongue out as she focuses on unlatching the gate.

"Callie!"

She doesn't pause what she's doing. "Don't just stand there. You gotta help me. I can't get this open."

"It's a sign we should just go."

"No, wait. I have an idea." She gets down on one knee, patting the other. "Come on. I'll help you get over the fence."

"Then what?"

"You grab Poker and open up the fence from the inside."

Normally I would say no, but I have three beers coursing through my veins, and when Poker whimpers again, something about it all makes me think maybe even he needs someone to look out for him because life is overwhelming and can be torn from us expectedly. In those puppy-dog eyes, I see another lost soul, so I rush over to Callie, stepping on her knee as she hoists me over the fence.

"Stand back, Poker," I whisper just before I hitch my leg over the fence and fall onto the other side.

"Are you okay?" Callie whisper-shouts.

"Yeah, I'm fine."

As I unlatch the fence, a light in the backyard flickers on. Austin swings open the back door, wearing nothing but his boxers and a scowl.

When I look to Callie for guidance, she's focused on her phone, blasting "Whose Bed Have Your Boots Been Under" by Shania Twain at full volume. She holds it high above her head before shouting, "Run!"

So I do what any sane person would do: I grab on to Poker, and I bolt.

Chapter Seven

Jax

WHEN I GET HOME AFTER MY SHIFT AND SET MY KEYS on the counter, I'm still thinking about Lauren. Her haircut framed her face perfectly, highlighting every little freckle the sun has dusted across her nose and cheeks and illuminating the dimple that appears whenever she gifts the world a genuine smile. The top she was wearing was bolder than the simple blouses she normally wears, but she looked absolutely stunning, and her jeans accentuated every one of her curves.

Watching her dance with guy after guy was maddening. Even now, hours later, the thought sparks jealousy inside me. I wanted to be the one who held her waist, the one who made her tilt her head back in laughter. I want to be the one who gets to call her *mine*.

As torturous as it was to watch her with other men, it was great to see her looking happier than she did last week. Maybe the list is starting to serve its purpose.

My phone lights up, and my heart soars when I see

Lauren's name on the screen. But then I realize it's two thirty in the morning. *Why is she calling so late?* The last time she called me at this hour, she wanted me to drive her to Amarillo so she could find out if Austin was cheating on her.

I swipe my thumb across the screen to answer. "Hey, Freckles. What's up?"

"Oh thank god you answered." My stomach sinks. "Jax, I need you to pick me up."

"Is everything okay?"

"Yeah, I'm fine."

"Where are you?" I'm already walking out my door, keys in hand.

"I'm at Austin's parents' house."

Shit. "What'd you do? Never mind. Just stay there. I'll be there in five."

"Okay." There's a weighted pause before she adds, "Thank you."

I barrel out of my driveway and flip through radio stations, searching for something to calm me, but nothing does the trick. I end up giving up and turning the radio off, but the silence and anticipation swallow me whole, so I turn it back on.

When I pull onto the street, Sheriff Baker's car is in the driveway. Lauren and Callie sit on the porch steps while he stands in front of them with his hands on his hips. Behind him, Austin paces back and forth, fuming.

I slam my truck door closed behind me, rounding the hood. "What's going on?"

Sheriff Baker spins around and opens his mouth to explain, but Austin catches sight of me, throwing a hand in my direction. "What is *he* doing here? He's the one you called? Seriously, Lauren? First you try to steal my dog, and then you call *him* to come to my house and pick you up? What the hell is wrong with you?"

I don't like the look in his eye or the tone of his voice. It reminds me too much of a past I've tried to bury, and it sets a fire inside of me immediately. I step up to him, pushing a hand hard against his chest. "Don't talk to her like that."

Sheriff Baker inserts himself between the two of us, turning toward me. "They were trying to take the dog." He looks as if he's biting back a smile.

"I'm sure there's some other explanation." I turn to the girls for help.

Callie shrugs, and Lauren says, "He was left outside overnight. He was whimpering!"

It takes everything in me not to throw my palm to my face. "You're kidding. You actually tried to take the dog?"

Lauren grimaces, raising her brows in a way that's supposed to look innocent. I hate how cute it is because it makes it so much harder to be mad at how irresponsible they were tonight.

Sheriff Baker steps forward. "Austin isn't pressing charges for breaking in and theft, but I figured someone should drive them home and make sure they stay out of trouble."

"I can do that." Glancing at Austin, I ask, "Why'd you call Baker? You of all people should know Lauren wouldn't hurt a fly."

"I would've driven them home myself, but Lauren refused, and Callie was causing a scene."

"Austin didn't call me," Sheriff Baker explains. "It was a noise complaint from the neighbors. I guess there was a lot of shouting."

I can't help but feel a small amount of pride for the women, but there's also concern rising inside me. If the neighbors called the cops, there's a good chance Austin was a complete asshole to Lauren again.

"Let's get you two home. Thanks, Baker. Sorry about all of this."

He shrugs. "This is the most exciting thing to happen to me all year. I can't wait to tell my wife in the morning."

Lauren and Callie get up from the steps and follow me to my truck. They're both quiet until we turn off Austin's street.

"You can't tell me that jerk didn't deserve it," Callie mutters from the back seat.

"To have his dog stolen? What were you going to do with him? Did you think no one would notice you suddenly had Austin's dog?"

"I guess we hadn't really thought that far ahead." Lauren crosses her arms.

"This doesn't help anything. This isn't how you move on."

"It wasn't about moving on. I was just worried about Poker. Austin clearly isn't fit to look after him."

I pull into Callie's driveway, and they both unbuckle.

I reach out to Lauren. "I don't think you should stay here tonight. We should talk about this."

"But—"

"I'm worried, Lauren. This isn't like you." Not to mention I'm concerned Austin said some nasty things to her again. I don't mention that part though. I don't know if Callie knows about the night at the bar, and it's not my place to tell her.

"But my truck is here."

"We'll get it tomorrow."

Callie glances between the two of us before wisely deciding to extricate herself from the situation. "Sorry, Lo.

I'll call you tomorrow." Callie leans in for a hug before rushing out of the truck.

Lauren looks at me with hurt eyes as I back out of the driveway. "I don't need you to act like my big brother right now. I need a friend."

"That's what I'm being. I want to make sure you're okay."

"I'm *fine*."

"Baker said he was there because of a noise complaint. What happened?"

"Austin was obviously not happy about being woken up or having his dog stolen. He shouted a bit."

"What did he say?" I pull onto Roots Road, heading toward Copper Hill. "Did he try anything?"

Lauren slowly uncrosses her arms. "Like I've already told you, Austin never hurt me, not physically anyway."

Relief washes over me for a brief moment, but it's quickly replaced by concern. "I don't want him to hurt you in *any* way. You deserve better."

"Thanks. I'm okay though. Nothing happened." She stares out the window, even though it's pitch-black on this gravel road. "We had some words, but it's fine."

I pull into Lauren's driveway on the east side of the ranch. When I park and help her down, she's stiff, like she's restraining the emotions inside her, and it breaks my heart in two. I stroke my hand over her head in a soothing motion, clutching her close to me.

When she murmurs against my chest, I have to strain to hear her. "I was being stupid. I don't know what got into me. Alcohol, I guess? I clearly need to stop drinking, and that'll solve all my problems." She glances up at me, laughing lightly.

"Did he say something awful to you again?"

She nods.

"Do you want to talk about it?"

"Will you just come inside and sit with me while I get ready for bed? I'm not ready to be alone yet."

"Of course." I follow her toward the door, determined not to ruin the little seed of trust she gave me by admitting that. "You know, I've been missing your skincare routine. My skin hasn't had the same shine since you helped me."

When she looks up at me, I feel like I said the right thing because she says, "I can do it for you again."

"I'd like that. I've been watching some YouTube videos on how to braid hair too. I think I'm ready to give it another go."

She laughs. "I don't believe you."

"I'm not kidding. I'll prove it right here, right now."

We shuffle quietly through the front door, and I can tell her thoughts are still swirling. I want to make her laugh and smile again. I try to think of something clever to say, but once she locks the front door, she spins toward me. "I want to check another thing off my list tomorrow. I need to do something for myself again. I'm tired of being the old Lauren, lost and hurting."

"Is this because of tonight?"

"No." She drags her lower lip through her teeth. "Maybe? I don't know. I think it's been an accumulation of things, but tonight opened my eyes to everything I was missing out on when I was with Austin. It made me realize he didn't treat me half as well as I deserved, and I'm ready to let go of it all and be better. I need your support though. I need you to bust down my door and drag me kicking and screaming if I'm being shady."

I laugh as I drape my arm over her shoulders. "I can do that. Where do you want to start?"

Chapter Eight

Lauren

Jax met me at five o'clock this morning to help me around the ranch, but we haven't spoken much. I'm sort of relieved. I've needed the time outside with my horse, working with my hands, to process everything. Plus, I really don't want to talk with him about the nasty things Austin said to me last night. I don't even want to *think* about any of it.

The silver lining is those belittling and shaming words opened up my mind to the possibility that maybe our relationship ending wasn't because I wasn't good enough to keep us together. Maybe that's at least one place in my life I didn't fail, because no human should ever talk to someone the way Austin did to me last night. I'm thankful Callie was there with me to help me see that, but I kind of wish she were around today to keep me from beating myself up for not seeing it sooner.

"Will you help me with this last bale of hay?" I ask as I lift one end.

Jax lifts the other end, drawing my attention to his taut forearms, just as my phone starts ringing.

"Shoot! I need to check this." I drop the bale. "I've been trying to get ahold of someone from Herford about a bull for our July calving season."

Jax sets down his end of the bale, swiping his forehead. "Go ahead. I can wait."

When I pluck my phone out of my pocket, my brother's name is staring at me on the screen. *Huh, not who I was expecting.*

I swipe the answer button, lifting the phone up to my ear.

"Hey, Char. What's up?"

I briefly register the wince on Jax's face before Charlie explodes. "What the hell happened last night? Why did Jax have to pick you up from the sheriff at Austin's parents' place?"

"Well, hello to you too. Things are going well. Thanks for asking."

As a strained silence hangs on the other end of the phone, I scrunch my face in annoyance at Jax. Charlie starts yelling at me again as I spin around and step out of the barn.

Unable to stand the chastising anymore, I cut in. "I know I was being stupid. It's not going to happen again, but honestly, I kind of needed last night."

"What do you mean? You needed to break into your ex-boyfriend's backyard and steal his dog?"

"Technically it was his parents' backyard, but no. I needed the clarity. Stop being so harsh about all of this. You're my brother, not my dad."

"But Mom and Dad don't know, right?"

I dig my boot into the dirt. "I don't know. Up until thirty seconds ago, I didn't think *you* knew either."

"I couldn't believe it when I heard. What happened to goody-two-shoes Lauren?"

"I had a couple drinks and was influenced by Callie."

Charlie clears his throat. "Callie Fletcher? How long have you two been hanging out?"

"I don't know. Since June or July?"

"How come I didn't know about this?"

I shrug, leaning against the wooden fence behind me. "Because you're never here."

"You know it's hard for me to come home. It's complicated, but that doesn't mean I don't want to hear about your life."

"But you get weird when I mention Callie's name."

"I do *not*," he says, his voice coming out two octaves too high.

"Yes, you *do*." I mimic his tone, fighting back laughter.

"Okay, this isn't about me. This is about you. Are you okay? Do I need to tell Mom and Dad? You're worrying me."

"Char, I love you, but if you tell them, I will come to California and murder you with my bare hands. You know they don't need the extra stress in their lives." I glance past the fence, grounding myself by counting the cattle spread across the pasture. "Besides, last night was nothing to make a big fuss about. Like I said, it was exactly what I needed to finally feel like I can move on."

"Would you tell me if you weren't okay?"

"Yeah," I say automatically, shoving my free hand into my back pocket. "And I promise I am. The best I've been since I broke up with Austin." Swiveling back in the direction of the barn, I catch Jax checking on me through one of the windows. My heart flutters, and I realize I might actually be telling the truth.

"I know I'm not there, but I'll always pick up the phone when you need me. I love you."

"I love you too." I peel myself away from the fence. "Promise you won't tell Mom and Dad?"

"As long as you don't get into any more trouble, which I will hear about. You know Jax is always keeping an eye on you for me."

I steal a glance back at the barn, doing my best to deflect from what these nonstop flutters might mean. "Yeah, I do. That little snitch."

Charlie snickers.

"Talk to you later."

"Wait." There's a long pause, and I can tell he's working up the courage to say whatever it is he has left to say. "Have you and Callie ever talked about me?"

Charlie and Callie dated for a couple years in high school and into college, but they broke things off when Charlie decided he wouldn't be returning to Roots. I know it was his decision, but I still think he broke his own heart in the process. I can't help but think there's more to the story. They seemed so happy together.

"No, she hasn't said anything," I say softly.

"That's okay. That's what I figured. It's been years."

"It doesn't mean she doesn't still care for you."

"I mean, why would she? I changed my mind on her. I was the one who left."

I'm quiet. I can't argue with him, and I don't know how to make it any better.

"Anyway, I'm glad to hear you're doing better, Lo. Can you give me a call every now and then, so I don't have to hear all about your life from Jax?"

"Yeah, I can do that. Talk later."

I hang up, brushing aside the little bit of sadness that

has come over me and putting on my game face as I storm into the barn.

"You tattled to my brother?"

Jax straightens up, sticking his hands out in defense as I barrel toward him. "I didn't tattle. I just thought someone close to you needed to know what was going on. I figured he was better than your parents."

I press my finger into his chest and step so close that the toes of our boots touch. My pulse is pounding faster and faster, and I can't decipher whether I'm angrier than I thought or if it's just being this close to Jax that's causing it.

"You don't have any business going to Charlie about things. I'm almost twenty-four years old. I run the largest ranch in the county. I can handle myself."

"I'm sorry. I was only looking out for you."

I soften a bit at his words, dropping my finger from his chest and taking a step back. "I know. I guess I've forgotten over the last couple weeks that you're *Charlie's* friend. You've almost felt like—" I shake my head. "Never mind. It's stupid."

"What?"

"You've been there for me lately, but this was a wake-up call. Your loyalty obviously lies with Charlie."

"That doesn't mean I don't care about you too." He reaches out to me, pulling me into a hug, and I allow it. He's covered in dirt and smells like a mixture of hay and manure, but I still don't think there's a better feeling than being in Jax's arms.

"Can we talk about last night yet?" he whispers.

"What about it?" I glance up at him as nerves bundle in my stomach.

"Well, for starters, you clearly need a dog."

I laugh to cover the flash of pain his words bring. "I'd

love a dog, but that's not in the cards for me right now. Life is too hectic. I do miss Poker though, more than Austin apparently."

His chest vibrates against me, and the rich laughter that pours from his lungs sends shivers down my spine. *What is happening to me? This is my brother's best friend. I shouldn't be looking at him like this.* But I can't help the way his presence simultaneously calms me and ignites me.

"That's my girl. I like hearing you laugh and seeing you look less...beaten down."

His blue eyes shimmer as he gazes down at me. I stiffen, but inside I'm melting. *That's my girl.* I love the sound of that.

He must sense my hesitation because he clears his throat and releases me, backing away. "You said you were ready to check another item off your list. Are you still going to dinner alone tonight?"

The nerves are back, swirling in my stomach. Now that the excitement of last night has worn off, I'm not feeling so brave anymore. I shake my head. "No, I changed my mind."

He bends down, wrapping his arms around the lower half of my knees and throwing me over his shoulder like a sack of potatoes.

I gasp. "What are you doing?"

"I'm just doing what you asked: dragging you kicking and screaming. If you could *not* kick and scream though I'd really appreciate it.

Chapter Nine

Jax

I'm in the middle of typing out the third reason when
another text from Lauren comes through.

ME

What's wrong?

Austin is here.

With Shelby Miller. You remember her? She
was the most beautiful girl in high school

I start to type out "No, she wasn't," but I stop myself.

ME

Stay calm

LAUREN

How can I stay calm?! I'm eating alone and
my ex is here on a date with another
woman!

You don't know it's a date

I can tell. I just watched him pull his first
move on her

I don't think they've seen me yet. Maybe
they won't

Jk he saw me

He must be doing this to get back at me
for last night

Oh no. They're walking this way

HELP!!!!

I get up from my seat, grabbing my keys off the hook by
the door on my way out. It's only a five-minute drive to the
Pork Screw, and as I pull into the parking lot, I realize I have
no plan. I'm just on autopilot, ready to do whatever is necessary so that Lauren feels safe again.

I step out of my truck and through the windows of the
barbecue joint, I can see Austin and Shelby hovering over

Lauren's table. Lauren's face is ghost-white. She's got a smile plastered on when I walk into the restaurant, but I can tell even from here that it's designed to hide her sheer panic.

I'm about to shove past Austin with some sort of lame excuse about Lauren meeting the rest of our friends at the wrong restaurant when she glances over Austin's shoulder and says, "Oh no. Someone's truck is getting towed in the parking lot." Turning back to Austin with a look of concern, she adds, "Did you drive your Ridgeline here?"

Austin swivels toward the front door in disbelief. "They're towing my truck? What the hell?" He barges out of the restaurant, and Shelby follows, looking concerned.

Lauren pulls money from her purse and grabs my hand. "We have about two seconds before he realizes they're not towing his truck."

I follow her from the table. Lauren hands the money to the waitress, breathlessly rushing out an excuse, and we slip out the side entrance.

Once we know the coast is clear, I lead her to my truck and drive us half a mile down the road before pulling up to Sweet Mae's.

It's only when I park in the diner's lot that we both release a breath and burst into laughter.

"Did you see the look on his face? That was priceless!" Lauren beams. "I kind of wish his truck actually was being towed."

"Me too. That was brilliant."

"I don't know what made me think of it. I just couldn't stand sitting there with the two of them looking down on me anymore."

"Well, it worked like a charm." Meeting her gaze, I tell her, "I'm proud of you."

Her brows pull together. "Why?"

"You could've sat there and taken his shit, but instead, you came up with a way out."

"I think you're forgetting I ran away from him."

"But I've seen you cower and freeze in front of him before, and you didn't do that."

"Well, thank you." She glances out her window as the smile on her face slowly fades. "Hey, Jax?"

"Yeah?"

She turns back to me. "I'm still really hungry."

I chuckle. "I knew you would be. How about we grab some dinner? It'll be my treat. I know it's not the barbecue you picked for the evening, but I'll buy you a sundae to make up for it."

"No, not the diner! I hate the diner." She tries to fight the smile that's growing on her face. "You owe me two sundaes now."

"You're such a liar. I know you love Sweet Mae's burgers and fries."

She nods and we head inside, where my palm gravitates to her lower back. A couple of prying eyes laser in on us as we walk past a row of tables, but I don't let it bother me because being this way with Lauren feels so natural.

When the waitress comes to greet us at our corner booth, Lauren looks ravenous, so I let her order and tell the waitress I'll take the same.

"Thank you," Lauren says. "If this food doesn't come soon, I'm liable to eat *you*."

"I better tell the waitress to speed that order up then." I pretend to get up from the booth, and she quickly grabs my arm, her eyes going round as she laughs in surprise.

Thankfully the diner is dead, so our food comes quickly. A natural silence falls over us while Lauren puts all her attention on the big burger in front of her, and I try to keep from putting all my attention on Lauren.

When she finishes her food, I figure it's okay to speak again. Swiping a french fry through a puddle of ketchup, I ask, "Are you okay?"

"Yeah." She plucks a fry from my plate. Hers are already gone. "It's kind of weird. I should maybe be bothered by all of this, but seeing him with another woman didn't even hurt. If anything, I felt bad for Shelby."

"What changed?"

"I guess I've started to reckon with all the pain he put me through before we even broke up, and all the ways he didn't treat me right. I used to think maybe our relationship going down in flames like that was because of something I did wrong, but last night helped me see that wasn't the case. The realization gave me a lot of peace."

I lower my burger, narrowing my eyes. "Why would you blame yourself when he cheated on you?"

"I don't know. That's where my mind always goes when something is wrong."

"It shouldn't. Austin is just an asshole. You deserve better." I take a sip of water.

Her cheeks flush. Turning her gaze down to her empty plate, she says, "Enough talking about me and my problems. Tell me something about you."

I lean back. When I first moved here, there was an instant connection between Lauren and me. I felt like I could tell her anything, and she wouldn't judge me. But it's been over nine years since I came to town. We haven't had a conversation without both of our walls being up in a long time. We haven't taken the time to ask each other how we are or what's going on in each other's lives, which was necessary because I had to protect my heart. I'd fallen for a woman who wasn't available. But since I wasn't having these conversations with Lauren, I wasn't having them with anyone. I don't know how to do this, especially after intentionally sticking to the type of relationships that never involve connecting on more than a physical level. It feels like talking to her would be going against everything I've built, but then again, Lauren feels so safe.

"What do you want to know?"

"Anything. I've known you for so long, but I don't *know* you."

"I think you know me better than you think. I know *you* pretty well."

She arches an eyebrow, leaning back in her seat. "Oh, do you?"

"Yeah, your favorite movie is *The Proposal.* Your favorite color is yellow because of the sunflowers you and your mom grow in the little garden behind the big house every year. You're always cold, but—and you'll deny this—your favorite food in the world is ice cream." She bites her lip to stifle her smile, and it stirs up something in my chest. "You constantly put pressure on yourself to be the perfect daughter, the perfect rancher, the perfect everything to everyone, but you're tired. And while you do a great job of hiding it, *I* still see it."

The smile she was hiding no longer needs to be hidden because it's long gone. She picks at her crumpled napkin on the table, and silence falls over us. *Crap.* I definitely crossed a line.

Setting her napkin down, she leans toward me. "Your favorite color is green, and your favorite movie is the original *Top Gun.* You're obsessed with any song by John Michael Montgomery. You have a scar from when you and Charlie built a rope swing along the creek, right here—" She reaches out, setting my body on fire when she traces a finger along my collarbone. "You'd never admit it, but you have a deadly fear of snakes. You've always stayed away from committed relationships, which I think stems from some sort of messed-up fear that you're not good enough to commit, but *I* see you, and I can tell you you're wrong."

Whoa, she might know me better than I know myself.

I lean back against the booth, crossing my arms. "I'm not afraid of snakes."

"You totally are! I've seen you scream and run like a little girl."

"Yeah, probably when I was ten."

"Jax, I didn't meet you until you were a sophomore in high school." She giggles.

"You're a liar."

"I never lie."

The waitress brings us the two sundaes we ordered, and Lauren gleefully digs in. I can't resist sneaking glances at her as she daintily spoons her fudgy chocolate ice cream, closing her eyes as she savors it and lets it melt in her mouth.

Between bites, she says, "You never answered me. Tell me something I don't know about you."

My instinct is to deflect. Any time a woman tried to get too personal, that's what I would do. I've never wanted to be close with someone, but this is Lauren. She's felt familiar since the day I met her, so I do something I've never done before. I break the one rule I've always had. Only, it doesn't feel like breaking the rules with Lauren. It feels like I'm finally finding my way.

Chapter Ten

Lauren

I'M CERTAIN JAX IS ABOUT TO CLOSE DOWN. HE HAS this look like he wants to run away, but slowly, that look fades. His eyes soften, and he leans toward me.

"Promise not to judge me?"

I nod, too eager to hear what he has to say.

"Not a soul knows this, so you should feel privileged."

"What is it? Just tell me."

He holds up a finger. "You can't laugh."

"I won't." I'm hanging off the edge of the booth now, my elbows resting on the table.

He spoons some ice cream, taking his time with it before he finally admits, "When I'm having a bad day, I like to watch *Bachelor in Paradise*."

I bite my lip but epically fail at holding in my chuckle.

"You promised you wouldn't laugh!"

"Actually, I didn't *promise* anything."

He shifts uncomfortably in his seat, holding up his

spoon. "At least let me explain myself before you judge me too much."

"I'm not judging at all. I just didn't expect it from you. Please go ahead and explain. I'd love to hear about why you love the show."

"Love is a strong word." He winces. "When we first came to Roots, my mom and Aunt Carol used to watch it together. I'd sit there with them, complaining the whole time, but they'd laugh and laugh at all the drama. It was a breath of fresh air after coming out of some dark days back in Oklahoma. Watching it reminds me that the bad days eventually end, and there will be good ones ahead."

I sit there, in awe. This is the first time Jax has spoken about what happened back in Oklahoma. I'm terrified I'll say the wrong thing and scare him off. I want him to feel comfortable sharing more with me.

"That seems like a fair reason." I nod, keeping my tone light.

My words don't seem to be the right ones because he's sitting rigid in the booth, looking completely freaked out from his moment of vulnerability. Doing my best to steer the conversation in a lighter direction, I point my spoon at him accusingly. "I'm a little suspicious of you only watching it on a bad day though. There's no way you could watch a few episodes, see all the drama, and casually set it aside."

A half smile creeps onto his face. "I swear. I'll spend hours binging it, but then go months without watching it."

"You're a special kind of psychopath," I say before taking another bite of my ice cream.

His lips quirk again, and this time, laughter breaks free, making me wonder when I last saw him display genuine joy like this. In high school, his smile in every picture was closed-lipped, and in those early days, it felt like he was trying to keep himself from being happy.

When did that change? Was his smile always this radiant? Maybe I was just too focused on the ranch, on Austin and keeping us together, that I didn't pay Jax enough attention.

"Your turn." He leans back in the booth, crossing his arms and watching me intently.

"I think you already summed me up earlier."

"Come on. I know you're so much more than that. There has to be something I don't know about you."

I dig into my dessert, searching for any remaining bites of cookie as my mind races with what to tell him. Finally, a thought hits me, and the words spill out before I think too hard about it.

"When I first took over the ranch, I didn't want it."

"Really?" He sets his spoon down. "But you seemed so excited, and you've done such a good job with it."

"I know. I didn't want to disappoint Austin or my parents. I guess you were right earlier about putting pressure on myself to be perfect."

I chew on my lip, feeling vulnerable. I don't want him to feel bad for me. This is just my nature, so I rush to explain. "Charlie was the troublemaker. He was the one who'd sneak out in high school and do all these stupid things that could've gotten him killed. Then he chose a different life for himself and rejected the family, so I naturally felt like my role was to clean up after him and to try to make our family whole again. To be the peacemaker." I scrape a bit of fudge off the side of the sundae glass. "When he left, I had to take the ranch. If I didn't, I'd be killing a family legacy that's lasted for generations."

"Why don't you tell your parents? I know you want to

keep the ranch in the family, but I'm sure there's someone else who could step in."

I realize then that Jax and I aren't that different. He likes to fix things too. Except, in this case, there's nothing to fix. "I came around to it. I've never had big career aspirations. I did well in school, but I didn't feel like any of it fit. When I think about working a corporate job and climbing the ladder, it makes me queasy. I was scared of the responsibility that comes with running Copper Hill, but once I stepped in on the ranch, I found ways to improve our systems, and I still have more ideas. It gives me a sense of purpose, and now that Austin is gone, I truly have free rein to make this mine. It's all slowly starting to click, and I'm realizing that this *is* what I want."

"I can't believe I didn't notice before."

"How would you have? I never told anyone, not even Austin." His lips quirk the slightest bit at that, like he feels validated for getting an upper hand on Austin. "Like I said, I'm happy with how things are now."

"What other things did you hide for the sake of your parents or Austin? Did you ever hide something from me?"

"What do you think? I've had no problem telling you how much I hate your stupid nickname for me." I smirk, ignoring the way my gut is twisting at the thought of the big thing I'm hiding not just from Jax but from everyone.

"No need to emphasize it more."

"I don't think it hurts." I give him a soft smile, and when he returns it, I feel just a little more at ease.

"Would it make you hate the nickname less if I told you why I call you Freckles?"

I shrug, but my curiosity is piqued.

"I know you think your freckles are these splotches on your face, but I love the way they fleck your nose and dust your cheekbones. They're part of what makes you *you*. You're gorgeous, Lauren. I love your freckles."

My cheeks heat, and I quickly take a heaping bite of ice cream to avoid looking into Jax's eyes. I know if I do, I'll wind up a melted puddle in this booth, and I'd prefer to finish the night with at least a shred of dignity. Not to mention, I'm kind of curious where the rest of this conversation is going to go.

"All this time, I thought you called me Freckles because you knew how much I hated them. I thought you did it to bug me."

"I hoped it'd help you appreciate them like I do, but I guess it didn't quite work that way."

"Maybe not before, but it might now that I know." He gifts me a lopsided grin, and my stomach somersaults. So much for not turning into a puddle. "What else have you been holding back from me?"

He licks a dribble of ice cream off his upper lip, making my chest squeeze. I don't like the way I'm reacting to Jax right now. I don't want to have feelings for someone for a long time after what I went through with Austin. I may have matured enough to recognize Austin was not the guy for me, but it doesn't mean I'm ready to love someone else. It doesn't mean I'm secure enough in myself to put my heart out there again, especially not with a guy like Jax who is known for being a flirtatious commitment-phobe. This needs to stop.

"Nothing else that I can think of." His cheeks turn pink, but my eyes must be deceiving me because there's no way Jax Greer is the blushing type.

The conversation lulls, and I take it as an opportunity to pull us away from this more intimate territory we're heading into.

"I think I need a do-over of my solo meal."

"Really? You want to do it again?"

"Yeah, I don't feel right about checking it off my list when I didn't actually manage to."

"I think this meal should count. You endured everything you needed to get out of the experience and then some in a very short amount of time." He chuckles. "What else is still on your list?"

I pull out my phone, then swipe open to the picture I took of it. "Go to a concert, attend a conference, implement regenerative agriculture on the ranch, do something for me and no one else, and attend swing dance lessons at the bar."

"What do you want to do next?"

"Swing dance lessons are bi-weekly." I pop open my calendar app. "I can't make it this Tuesday or Thursday, but I can go the Thursday after that. I'll plan on attending then." My eyes settle on another event on my calendar. "Also, I did some research, and there's a cattle conference being held early next month in Tulsa."

"Look at you, doing your research. This is great. Are you going to take your dad with you?"

My heart stops. I definitely can't take Dad right now. It'd be too much for him, but I don't want to get into all of that with Jax, so instead I give him a little half-truth. "Everyone in the ranching community knows him, so I'd end up completely ignored in the corner while he inadvertently steals the show. I have to go alone."

He glances up from his sundae. "Are you planning on driving?"

"Of course. It's only a five-hour drive. I don't need to fly there."

"Please don't go alone. I know the drive isn't that far, but the roads can be rough this time of year."

"I'll be fine. Like I said, if my dad comes, it'll defeat the whole purpose of having that on the list."

"Then I'll go with you."

I scrunch my nose. "Are you sure?"

"Of course. It's good for you to do some things alone now, but you don't *need* to be alone. I'll come with you. It'll be fun."

A smile curves on my lips. I can't help but look forward to this.

Chapter Eleven

Jax

IT'S BEEN OVER A WEEK SINCE I TOOK LAUREN OUT TO dinner and agreed to go with her to the conference in December. I admittedly crossed a line I didn't mean to, but I'm just trying to be a good friend and look out for her like I promised Charlie I'd do when he left. Except, this feels like more than that.

I busy myself with putting all the high-end liquor back on the shelves while we prepare to open, but my mind keeps wandering. I picture Lauren brushing her hair behind her ear and daintily eating ice cream. I imagine how soft her touch was when she did my skincare routine for me. I think of the texts we've sent each other recently despite me telling myself I'd give her some space. To be fair, only texting her instead of spending time with her after I help at the ranch or after my shifts at the bar *is* giving her space. That's me showing self-restraint.

My phone vibrates in my pocket, and I pull it out to find a text from Charlie. He's been texting me a lot more lately since Lauren tried to steal Poker, and only a quarter of it has been about Lauren. It's nice to feel like I have my friend back in some capacity. He's been so distant these last few years. I guess I should've expected it after the way he left for LA.

"I'm going to miss you." I shrug, trying not to act too mushy.

"Nothing will be different." Charlie swats his hand dismissively. "I've been away for school for the last four years."

I nod, even though we both know he's saying that to soften the blow. It will be different. Charlie always came home for breaks, and we've worked on the ranch together every summer since high school. Now, he's going off to live his own life. He may come back for the holidays, but we'll no longer get busted for playing Cowboy Poke instead of actually working.

Charlie grabs on to his truck door. "Will you look out for Lauren while I'm gone? She tends to close herself off when she's going through hard times. I blame myself a little bit. I'm the one who had to break the mold, and I think she feels like she has to make up for it. I know she has Austin, but you know how I feel about him."

Yeah, I do. I feel the same and probably more. "You already know I will."

"Thanks. There's no one else I'd trust more to look out for her."

"You sure about that? She might fall in love with me." I wiggle my eyebrows.

Charlie punches me in the arm, and thankfully it's half-assed. "If you pull any of your player shenanigans on my little sister, we will not be friends anymore. You hear me? I will kill you."

"Hey, we could actually fall in love someday." My tone is lighthearted, but inside there's still that tiny fiber of hope. I haven't been able to shake the feeling I get when I'm around her, even all these years later.

"Yeah, right. You let me know when that happens because I want to see the pigs flying." Charlie grins, slapping me on the back.

Hearing those words are like a dagger to the heart. Charlie is the only person in my friendship circle who knows about my dad's gambling addiction or the drinking and abuse that followed when bets didn't go his way. Charlie is also the only one who knows I blame myself for not standing up for my mom in those dark times. He's always insisted I'm too hard on myself, that it shouldn't have been my responsibility to protect my mom from my dad when I was only fifteen.

His words used to provide me with at least some comfort. Now, hearing him imply I'm not enough for his sister to love only goes to show that his words have been nothing more than empty platitudes. Even my best friend knows I'd never be good enough for Lauren, or anyone else for that matter.

"Jax!" Callie's cheery voice brings me out of my head. Lauren and Olivia trail behind her, each of them clad in jeans and cowgirl boots.

I plaster on a smile. "Can I get you ladies anything to drink before your lesson?"

"Am I chopped liver?" Rhett murmurs as he joins the women.

"Ignore him. He just doesn't like dancing much, but I needed a partner." Olivia presses her hands on his arm and leans into him, a goofy grin on her face.

"We don't need drinks. We're sober tonight," Callie says, exchanging a meaningful look with Lauren.

"All right, then I guess I'm useless to you. I'm going to go help Jorge get the rest of the bar prepped."

Before I can swivel around, Lauren's hazel eyes snag my gaze. I give her a gentle grin before barreling off, the memory of Charlie basically telling me even *he* wouldn't trust me with his sister enough to keep me away.

People continue gathering on the dance floor, making the bar feel more vibrant. The overhead lights dim, but all the neon signs come to life. Betsy Hogan, a Roots local in her mid-sixties who's been teaching these dance lessons since she was in her mid-twenties, mics up and takes her spot at the front of the dance floor.

"Okay, everyone. The first step to swing dancing is finding a good partner. The best dancers use a partner they're familiar with. In fact, some of the best I know are siblings."

Despite trying to focus on my duties, my eyes keep drawing up to Lauren. She's looking at Callie, scrunching her nose in disgust at Betsy's last comment.

"If you don't have a partner you're familiar with, don't worry. We will find you one. Anyone who isn't partnered up, raise your hand."

Lauren and Callie grab on to each other, but two other unfamiliar men raise their hands. They're in Wranglers, boots, and hats, but they don't have the kind of build that suggests they're familiar with ranch work. Their clothes are too clean, and their boots aren't even the slightest bit scuffed. I dislike them immediately.

Callie wiggles her brows at Lauren suggestively, and my stomach lurches. I don't like them even *more* now.

Betsy moves quickly, pulling Lauren and Callie apart and pairing them off with the men. "You two can't be together."

"Come on, Mrs. Hogan. You know I can lead and follow for just about any dance you have to teach," Callie says.

"I know, honey, but these gentlemen need someone to dance with."

One of the fake cowboys approaches Lauren with a lopsided grin, and it takes all of my restraint not to step in and take his place.

I'm working. It's not my place to interfere. I don't need to get further tangled up with Lauren. I start my mantra, repeating it over and over again while I grind my teeth together.

I don't move from my spot at the bar while Betsy rattles off detailed instructions. From here I have a clear view of Lauren as Fake Cowboy #1 leans in, whispering something in her ear. She pulls back, blushing and grinning at him. When she turns to Olivia next to her, Olivia gives her a big thumbs-up in between her attempts at following the steps with Rhett.

This is torture. I should've requested the night off. I don't want to watch Lauren dance with someone else. That should be me holding her close and making her smile.

One of our regulars comes in, and I take the opportunity to distract myself as Betsy demonstrates the next move. While I mix up Benny's Manhattan, my eyes are drawn back to the dance floor. Everyone is following the steps Betsy demonstrated except for Fake Cowboy #1, who decides to improvise a little as he finishes the sequence with Lauren. This time, she doesn't just smile when she pulls away. She tilts her head back and laughs. *No. No. No.*

I clench my jaw, white-knuckling the stir stick in my hand.

"I think that drink has been stirred enough," Benny says.

"Right." I swivel to the bar, slamming the Manhattan down as the damn fake cowboy flashes Lauren a grin. At the contact, the glass shatters into a million tiny pieces, sending whiskey all over the counter and the floor.

"Shit!"

Chapter Twelve

Lauren

We're in the middle of the most complicated part of the dance sequence when the sound of shattering glass grabs my attention. I'm supposed to lift my arm up and over my partner's head and then slide apart from him, but I can't focus when I look over to find Jax and Jorge scrambling to wipe down the mess at the bar. Across the room, Jax meets my gaze for a second. The look on his face can only be described as desperation. For what, I can't be sure, but having his eyes on me makes me understand what people mean in romance books when they say their heart skipped a beat because I swear mine stopped for half a second.

That fleeting moment of peace is gone quickly when I accidentally stiff-arm my partner in the face. He keels over, groaning loudly.

"Oh my gosh! I'm so sorry." I reach toward him in an effort to console him, but he shoves me back, holding his nose.

When he finally straightens, blood drips down his face

and onto his clean shirt. "Look what you did! You have to watch what you're doing."

His words feel familiar, like something Austin would say to me.

"I'll get you some ice," I offer, trying to keep myself calm.

"That's the least you could do," he grumbles.

I know it was my fault for being distracted, but I'm not okay with someone talking to me like that anymore. It was an accident.

I stop on my way to the bar, crossing my arms. "On second thought, you can get it yourself. Maybe ask them if they have some manners to give you while you're at it." I storm off, weaving through the groups of dancers and sitting down at one of the picnic tables on the other end of the dance floor.

I take several deep breaths, processing what just happened. I didn't mean to be so rude, but everything that's happened over the last few weeks has only showed me the ways I've been weak, and I'm tired of it. I'm ready to find my strength, and I'm certainly not going to let some man in a clean pair of Tecovas make me feel like garbage.

Betsy comes to my side, flicking her mic off as she places her hand gently on my knee. "Is everything okay?"

"I gave my partner a bloody nose."

"I saw." She laughs.

"He might need some ice. I was going to help, but he was being a jerk, and I lost my temper." I sag, feeling guilty already.

"No one likes a fake cowboy anyway." Betsy makes a sour face. "I'll be sure to get him some ice. In the meantime, do you need a new partner so you can finish your lesson?"

I pause. I should probably stop being a child and fix

things, but I also don't want to keep dancing with that man, and I'm not about to let another item on my list get derailed. "Please."

Betsy swivels, turning her mic back on. "It appears we are down a dancer. Do one of the bartenders over there want to lend a hand?"

Jax calls out before Betsy's even finished speaking. "I'll do it."

As he hops over the bar, she turns to me with a mischievous smile. "Someone is awfully eager to dance with you."

A few women watch with curiosity and murmur amongst themselves.

My cheeks heat, and I loudly tell Betsy, "Mr. Overprotective over there. He's always keeping an eye on me for Charlie."

"Right." Betsy purses her lips, giving me a sideways look. "He's hopping a counter for Charlie."

As Jax joins me, the adrenaline seems to catch up to him. He glances around, looking almost shy before turning back to me and saying, "I figured after watching these lessons the last three years, I should see if I've actually learned something. Besides, chicks love a man who can dance."

I try not to let the words eat at me as I take his outstretched hand.

He pulls me closer to him, his warmth and masculine cologne curling around me. My gaze snags on his eyes, noting the juxtaposition of light and dark blue in them as my heart pounds in my chest.

I push down my tingling excitement. "Show me what you've got."

He steps away, still holding on to one of my hands. He does some fancy move where we pass each other in opposite directions. There's a brief moment where our hands break apart as he switches which hand is holding mine. Anyone watching wouldn't be able to tell, but I noticed. It's impossible not to notice a moment where I lose Jax's touch, no matter how brief.

When our hands reconnect, he spins me around with a wide grin on his face. Then we're back to where we started, chest to chest.

The whole move lasts less than five seconds, but when we stop, we're both breathing heavily. Our gazes lock, and the smile on his face brings one to mine as well. Our fingers remain laced together, and I don't want to pull them apart. This feels so natural.

I want to spend the rest of the day and all of forever with his hand in mine. I don't care if they get clammy. I wouldn't even care if someone told me right now that I had to choose between holding hands with Jax or eating an ice cream sundae. My hand is meant to fit in Jax's.

Something in his soft eyes makes it clear that the flicker of excitement I'm feeling isn't just in my head. He's feeling it too. I open my mouth, but Betsy's mic squeals in the speakers as she makes her way back to the front of the dance floor and begins instructing again.

She demonstrates the next move in the sequence with the help of a volunteer. As Jax and I reset, my fingertips vibrate.

Throughout the rest of the lesson, the seconds pass in slow motion so that I can feel Jax's presence on every inch of my skin, but the minutes fly by.

We finish the last of the sequence just as Betsy claps her hands together, announcing, "That's it for today. Great work everyone! Don't forget to practice. It truly does make perfect. I hope to see y'all again soon."

We clear the dance floor, and I follow Jax back to the bar where I figure I'll reconvene with my friends.

Jorge greets us at the bar, a look of defeat on his face. "I should've been the one out there. I need to up my game so I can have a chance with the ladies for once." He crouches below the bar then quickly pops back up. "Do we have more paper towels, or do I need to make a trip to the store tomorrow?"

Jax rolls his eyes, plowing past him to conduct his own search.

Heather, one of the other bartenders, steps in. "Your lack of dance skills isn't the reason you don't get the ladies, Jorge. Besides, from what I hear, Jax has been out of the game for a few months." She shifts her gaze to me, a smirk on her lips. "Now I see why. I heard y'all were at the diner together the other night too."

"Oh, that was nothing." I swat the rumor away.

Heather mixes a drink with her lips pressed together. "Sure." Lowering her voice, she says, "I've seen the way he looks at you. It's not like the other women he's picked up."

"Jax and I are just bonded because of Charlie," I explain as Jax comes back, tossing a roll of paper towels to Jorge.

Callie, Olivia, and Rhett come up behind me, Callie slapping a hand on my shoulder. "What'd you think of your first swing dance lesson? Was it everything you hoped it'd be?"

"And more," I tease.

"I bet," she mutters under her breath.

I narrow my eyes at her and turn away, not willing to have this conversation, especially not with so many nosey people around.

"Should we head out?" Rhett asks, pulling his keys from his pocket.

"Yeah, I just need to pee real quick." I spin on my heel toward the bathrooms.

"Do you want company?" Olivia asks.

"Don't be ridiculous. I'll be fine."

I cross the bar, use the restroom, and am barreling out of the women's room when I bump into Jax's chest.

"Oh, sorry." Out of habit, I throw my hands up to Jax's firm chest. When I look up at him, my breath catches, and I find myself rooted to the ground. "I guess I'm a bit of a klutz today."

His chest vibrates against my hands as he chuckles. His smile fades, and he grabs my arm, pulling me to the side of the hallway and even closer to him as Ms. Sanchez comes down the hall behind me.

Once she's in the restroom, Jax turns to me. "I saw what happened with your other partner. The lesson wasn't the right time to talk about it, but I'm proud of you for sticking up for yourself."

"Thank you." My voice is small. *He's proud of me? I lost my temper! It doesn't matter if he's a jerk or if he reminded me of my ex. He's still a human being. I should've shoved my feelings aside and helped get him some ice.*

"Hopefully today showed you that you don't need to fix everyone else all the time. Not everything is on you. You can let things be imperfect."

I nod, and we both stand there, letting a heavy silence settle over us as Ms. Sanchez exits the bathroom and eyes us suspiciously.

In the quiet, my thoughts move at a million miles an hour. He's right. I've been feeling guilty about how I handled the situation. Some part of me always feels the need to fix things. It's eaten away at me that I didn't perfectly handle the situation, but maybe I shouldn't look at today as a loss of control but me taking control back. Today could actually be a step in the right direction, whether I realized it or not.

I glance up at Jax to find his eyes are trained on me. There's a spark there that makes me think the chemistry I've felt tonight is mutual, and the revelations of this evening make me want to do something about it. I want to stop holding back.

Stepping closer to him, I ask, "Did you really just dance with me to test your dance moves after all these years, or was there another reason?" It *definitely* felt like something else.

He winces, remaining silent, which gives me all the space I need to analyze my actions from every angle. *Maybe I shouldn't have asked.* It feels like things between us have shifted so quickly, and I don't know what it would mean if we admitted we had feelings for one another. *We can't be a couple, can we? He's my brother's best friend.* That feels like a line I shouldn't cross. Not to mention I'm still healing. It's been almost six months since ending things with Austin, but I'm still trying to figure out how to trust again. Jax has never once in the entire time I've known him been in a real relationship. It's always been hookups and flings. I don't want that for myself.

There are a million reasons I shouldn't be with Jax, but I can't bring myself to care enough about them. All I can focus on is the way he looks at me and how it feels when he touches me. He makes me believe I'm stronger, braver, and more worthy than I truly am, like maybe I actually can be as good as he sees me.

"Your question is kind of silly, don't you think?" he murmurs.

"What do you mean?"

"Isn't it obvious?"

I shrug. "Not to me."

"Of course I didn't just come out there to try out my dance moves. I couldn't care less about that, but I knew this lesson was important for you and your list. Your brother would've stepped in too."

Disappointment floods me, even though I should probably be relieved right now. He's looking out for me because of Charlie. This keeps things simpler, but there's a large part of me screaming inside, saying maybe I don't want simple.

Chapter Thirteen

Jax

"Thank goodness for the holidays to finally get you to spend some time with us, huh?" Mom gives me a teasing smile as she sets down the hand mixer and wraps an arm around me.

"I'm trying to take on more responsibility at the bar. I told you it might take up a little more of my time."

She arches a brow. "Don't lie to your mother. I know you've been spending more time at Copper Hill than the bar."

"Yeah, I like the work, and Lauren could really use the help." I busy myself with grabbing plates and silverware to set the table. "With Austin gone now, the weight of running things has fallen on her. I know her parents help out as much as they can, but they were already helping before, so she's still down a person."

"That's awfully nice of you." Aunt Carol comes into the room, sitting at the kitchen island with a glass of water.

Mom joins her sister on the other barstool, and I eye

them suspiciously. "Why do I feel like you're about to have an intervention?"

They exchange a glance and tilt their heads back in laughter.

"Yup, this definitely doesn't feel right." I glide to the dining room table, which is in the open area next to the kitchen.

"Oh, stop it!" Mom rolls her eyes. "We're just trying to take advantage of our time together to see what's going on in your life. I fed you, bathed you, and clothed you, and now I get nothing."

"I did a lot of that too," Aunt Carol chimes in.

"I hate it when you two gang up on me, which in case you haven't noticed, is *all the time*." I set a fork down. "And you wonder why I'm not here more often."

"Just tell us what's going on. It's Thanksgiving. I want something to be thankful for." Aunt Carol presses her hands together in a way that can only be described as diabolical.

"How about the turkey in the oven or the sides Mom spent all day prepping?"

"Come on!" Mom pleads. "We just want to know what you've been up to. Is something happening with you and Lauren?"

"You wish!" I scoff, but something on my face must be a giveaway because they devolve into giggles.

I roll my eyes, setting the last of the silverware on the table and disappearing into the living room to watch the end of the Cowboys game. There's a part of me that wants to talk to them and get their advice, but the even bigger part knows better than to open that can of worms. Since I intervened at dance lessons the other night, things have been tense between Lauren and me. We've been tiptoeing around one another, unsure how to act and desperately trying to get a read on one another.

I wanted to tell her how I feel. I think she might be ready for that, but I'm terrified I'm not. My one-night stands haven't exactly turned me into a relationship guy, which only reminds me that there's a reason I've never been in one before. Everyone around me knows the truth. My mom and Aunt Carol have drilled into me how terrible the Carter men are. When we came to Roots, I had hoped changing my last name to match my mom's would be enough to distance me from the terrible legacy the Carters have left, but even my closest friend has told me I'm not enough. I can't even imagine what Charlie would think if he found out—

Beep! Beep! Beep! The sound of the smoke detector screeching throughout the house pulls me from my thoughts. I leap from the couch, searching for the cause, but it doesn't take long to spot the big black cloud billowing from the oven. Aunt Carol pulls a charred turkey out of it, and Mom grabs the burnt stuffing out after her, fanning the smoke.

"Well, I guess we're going out for dinner tonight." There's defeat in Aunt Carol's voice. I can't blame her. Mom has always cooked the turkey because she's been so busy with Resilient Paws, the dog rescue she runs right in her backyard. This year, she had time to help prepare dinner because of all the work Olivia has been stepping in to help with, but her attempt clearly failed.

Unable to refrain, I snap a picture of the crusty turkey and send it to Lauren.

ME

Do you know where all the failed turkey chefs go to eat on Thanksgiving?

I instantly regret sending the text. I'm not sure this is the way to break our recent bout of tension, but to my surprise, she immediately responds. Maybe we needed something light-hearted to get our relationship back on track.

LAUREN

Oh no! Maybe there's a Bucc-ee's open?

ME

We aren't getting Thanksgiving dinner from a gas station

Hey! You could do much worse than Bucc-ee's!

I can't hold in my laughter. She's not wrong. Texas's most infamous gas station has everything from refrigerator magnets to swimsuits as well as a vast selection of food, which isn't half bad. I used to beg my mom to take me to Bucc-ee's for a brisket sandwich and an Icee, but the nearest one is easily an hour away, so I was often unsuccessful.

"What're you smiling about? Dinner's ruined," Aunt Carol sasses as Mom tries to look over my shoulder.

I pull my phone tightly toward my chest, but another text vibrates.

"Oh, I bet he's texting Lauren!" Her smile is radiant, and it surprises me. I wouldn't expect the same woman who told me all Carter men are scum to be the one who supports me having a relationship with someone she likes as much as Lauren.

LAUREN

Dad just pulled the brisket off the smoker. It still needs another 30 mins to rest and as usual he made way too much. Y'all should come over

"How do you two feel about Thanksgiving brisket at the Rhodes'?"

"I don't care where or what we eat. I'll take anything besides this burnt turkey." Aunt Carol throws down her oven mitt on the counter, grabbing her coat and heading toward the front door without further discussion.

———

"How about we play a few games of poker to round out the night?" Mr. Rhodes offers as we finish cleaning up after our spectacular dinner. I don't understand how he could spend so long making that delicious brisket and not even eat it for dinner tonight.

"I don't know, Dad. You get a little excited when you play." Lauren pins him with a look.

"Come on. It's Thanksgiving! I want to play poker with my family, like we always do. I'm not ready to give up everything I love in life."

I look between him and his daughter, noting the sudden shift, but Mr. Rhodes simply claps his hands together and presses on a smile. "Are you three in for a game?"

I glance at Mom, weary. Growing up, poker wasn't something I learned how to play. In our house, it wasn't just a game. It was a trigger for a cascade of darkness.

Mom gives me a gentle nod before she says, "Sure. It's been a while since I've played a hand, so you'll have to remind me of the rules."

At her words, Mr. Rhodes's face fills with joy. Grabbing a deck of cards, he takes his spot back at the dinner table, explaining as he shuffles.

My stomach churns as the cards feather together in his hands. Sweat beads on my palms, and as I brush them off on my jeans, I try to remind myself I'm safe. My dad isn't here to hurt us, and I'm not my father. I don't need to ruin their tradition just because of things that happened years ago. A few games of poker can't hurt, especially the way the Rhodes family plays it. It's the most innocent version out there. They use chips to place bets, but they never actually put any money on the line. For them, the only reward in the game is the pride of winning.

We make it a full time around the table before anyone folds, but once it starts, everything unravels quickly.

"I fold." Mrs. Rhodes groans, setting her cards down.

Lauren nudges her mom in the side, whispering something to her that makes the two of them laugh.

Nana Rhodes assesses her cards with pursed lips before sighing. "I suppose I'm out too."

We make it around the table once more, upping the bets by what would be the equivalent of fifty dollars in chips before Mom folds.

Nana Rhodes picks up her cards to peek. "Oh, Aimee, you should've folded when I did with a hand like that."

Mom tugs the cards back with a frown. "It's called bluffing, and you're not supposed to look at my cards without my permission!"

Aunt Carol snickers as she snatches the cards up next.

"What are you laughing at?" Mom frowns at her sister. "You folded before the rest of us. At least *pretend* you have a good hand once in a while."

Lauren rolls her lips, like she's trying to hide a smirk, and I can't tell if it's because of the hand she has or the banter at the table. It's been like this all night. It feels good to be surrounded by such a loving group of people.

Raising a brow in my direction, Lauren tosses in two chips. "You ready to give up yet?"

"Nope." I actually have a decent hand.

Mr. Rhodes assesses Lauren, narrowing his eyes at her as she does the same. Finally, he tosses two poker chips on the table to match her bet. "I'm calling you, darlin'. Show me what you've got."

She leaps out of her chair, cheering, without even showing us her cards.

"Hold on a second! You can't celebrate if you haven't shown us your cards." He bolts up from the table, reaching out for her hand.

Lauren snatches them up before he does but then holds them out for everyone to see. "Read 'em and weep. A royal flush, which means I definitely won."

"Well, shit. I thought I had this one in the bag. You just robbed me of everything I had. I can't believe it!" Mr. Rhodes's bewilderment quickly turns to pride as he kisses his daughter on the head, but the shift in his mood comes too late. His words are like picking at a scab I didn't even realize I still had.

I'm not in the safety of the Rhodes's family dining room anymore. I'm back in Oklahoma in that rickety house I spent the first fifteen years of my life in. Dad is barging through the front door, a glassy look in his eyes that only ever indicated terrible things to come. *"Shit! I thought I had that one in the bag. I was completely robbed! They took everything I had."* He slams down the open bottle of booze in *his hand, and I try to dart to the safety of my bedroom before he notices I'm here, before he has the chance to take out his rage on me.*

Lauren's hand on my arm brings me back. "Are you okay? You look a little pale."

Chapter Fourteen

Jax

"I NEED A MINUTE." I SLIDE OUT FROM MY CHAIR, darting for the front door. I need air. I need to get far away from this place and the memory I thought I'd buried.

Swinging the door open, I fling myself onto the front porch, basking in the cool air. It reminds me I'm safe. I remember the trick Mom taught me all those years ago to help ground me whenever things got bad at home and the fear settled in to paralyze me.

I inhale a deep breath, catching the hint of manure mixed with dirt being kicked up in the wind. The breeze bites at my skin and the peace of being on this ranch nowhere near a major road calms me. That peace is shortly interrupted by the sound of footsteps on the porch behind me.

I swivel around and find Lauren approaching me, concern knitting her brows together.

"Hey." She gives me a soft smile.

"I'm sorry. I didn't mean to barge out. I promise I'm not a sore loser."

She laughs. "Jax, that's the last thing I'm worried about. Do you want to talk through what happened?"

I shake my head. I've always kept my past hidden out of shame and a desire to protect my mother. She was terrified people in this town would look at us differently if they knew the truth. But it hits me that I don't feel the need to keep this from Lauren. I trust her. I just don't feel like unraveling the story further tonight.

"Honestly..." I blow out a breath. "I want to forget about what just happened."

"I know what that feels like." Shadows fill her eyes for a moment, but they're gone before she asks, "Do you want to get out of here?"

"We can't leave. Your dad wanted to play poker. I don't want to ruin the tradition."

"You're not ruining it. We got to play a game. Besides, he gets competitive sometimes. It might not be the worst thing to stop now."

"Where do you want to go?"

She grabs my hand. "I have an idea."

———

I told everyone I was tired and going home early, which was only a half lie. I didn't mean to lie at all, but Mom and Aunt Carol were already on my case earlier, and I didn't want them talking about Lauren and me being an item again. It's painful enough to remind myself I can't be with her.

When Lauren drags me into her house several minutes later, a bright smile on her face, it's almost enough to make me forget about the earlier memories. *How does she do that?*

She presses me down onto the couch and dashes into the kitchen.

"Where are you going?"

"I'll be right back."

I try to settle in, but the anticipation is killing me. I glance over my shoulder, watching her rummage around in her drawers. She disappears into the pantry and then reappears at my side with a package of Oreos, a jar of peanut butter, paper towels, and a butter knife.

She sets her items down on the table in front of us and wastes no time, turning on the TV and opening up her streaming app to none other than *Bachelor in Paradise*. She keeps her back turned to me as she spins the top off the peanut butter. It looks like it's never even been opened.

She hands me a paper towel then pulls two Oreos from the package, popping them open and scooping a heaping pile of the spread into the middle before resealing the container.

"Is that the right peanut butter ratio?" She winces.

I want to kiss her right then and there. *She remembers.* And she didn't just remember that I like to watch *Bachelor in Paradise* after a hard day. She remembered this is my comfort snack. I must've mentioned that years ago.

I already had a million reasons to love Lauren before, but this adds to it, and it's both incredible and torturous all at once because there's no better feeling than being in love with someone, but there's also no worse feeling than being in love with someone you can't have.

"The ratio is perfect," I manage.

"Which season do you want to watch?" She picks up the remote, studying the screen.

"Whichever one you want."

"Come on! It's not about me tonight. We're trying to

help you feel better. Tell me your favorite season or the one you watched last."

I take the remote from her, navigating to the episode I left off on a couple months ago. She gives me a satisfied nod before snagging an Oreo of her own and scooping a tiny amount of peanut butter onto it.

I grab her hand before she puts the top back on, trying to pretend like I'm not completely distracted by her round hazel gaze or the crackle of electricity that bolts through me at the feeling of her warm skin under mine.

"You have to add more than that."

She pulls the cookie closer. "Let me try it like this first. I might not like it."

"You're definitely not going to like it if you can't even taste the peanut butter." I grab the knife out of the jar and reach for her cookie. "Let me do it."

She relents, and I slather on a respectable amount of creamy goodness before returning the cookie to her.

She takes it gingerly, eyeballing it before closing her eyes and biting down.

It barely touches her tongue before she's moaning in delight. "This is amazing!"

"I told you."

"How have I lived my whole life without this?"

I shrug. "Beats me. The good news is now that you know about it, you don't have to go another day without it."

She polishes off her treat and hits play, curling into the couch. She doesn't even make it halfway through the first episode before she dozes off, her head bobbing until she finally gives into the exhaustion and falls asleep on my shoulder.

It hits me that this is all I want in life, quiet evenings with Lauren. Just like Lauren now knows how incredible the taste of peanut butter and Oreos are, I now know what it's like to have Lauren by my side, celebrating holidays, comforting me when times get rough, and basking in the perfection of a cozy night in. Now that I've had a taste of what our life could be like, I can't forget the sensation. I'm going to fight like hell to be the man who is good enough for Lauren because I know without a shadow of a doubt that she's everything I need and more.

Chapter Fifteen

Lauren

As "Sold (The Grundy County Auction Incident)" plays for the third time on our five-hour drive, I groan. "Do we have to listen to John Michael Montgomery the whole way?"

"What do you have against John Michael Montgomery?" Jax frowns from the driver's seat.

"Nothing. It's just that I don't feel the need to listen to him for hours on end, and I definitely don't need to listen to the same song *three* times."

"But we already established I get to be the—"

"I know. I know. It's your truck, you're driving, and if I want us to get there in one piece then you should get a say in what we're playing." I roll my eyes. "That's a really stupid rule by the way. I'm driving myself next time."

"Here, I'll skip the song if it bothers you that much." He presses a button on the dash, and "I Can Love You Like That" drifts from the stereo.

He turns to me with a goofy grin on his face. "This is a

good one. Let's listen and then we can play whatever you want."

When we pull up to a red light, the song escalates, and Jax meets my gaze, singing along as John Michael Montgomery croons about how he can love his woman exactly like they did in all the romantic movies and fairytales she grew up loving.

I shake my head at him, laughing while he belts out the chorus, but my stomach is doing a thousand cartwheels right now. It feels like Jax is singing this song directly to me, and it makes me feel giddy but sweaty.

The song winds down, and I quickly try to brush the feeling away. "Can I play Christmas music now?"

Jax throws his head back. "Do we have to?"

"I'm sorry. I didn't realize I agreed to road trip with the Grinch."

"I'm not the Grinch."

"Then why can't we listen to Christmas music?"

"Because I don't feel like it."

"Oh, I see. You don't feel like it because you're a Grinch." I cross my arms, trying to hide the smile that's creeping onto my face.

"Why are you so insistent on playing Christmas music?"

"Because I love Christmas. Thanksgiving is over. I waited the appropriate amount of time to listen to it around other people."

He turns to me as we pull up to yet another red light. "What do you mean around other people? Do you listen to Christmas music before Thanksgiving?"

"Only when I watch Christmas movies."

"I'm guessing that means you watch Christmas movies before Thanksgiving?"

"Of course." I shrug, shifting in my seat. "I watch them all year around. There's no sense in restricting the times I get to watch a good movie."

"A little heads-up next time would be nice. I wouldn't have agreed to come if I knew I was going on a road trip with a *crazy* person."

"I'm not crazy." We pull into the parking lot, and I swivel toward him in disbelief. "Did you stall on purpose?"

"I swear I didn't." He parks. "Go ahead and queue up a song. We can sit here and listen to it before we go inside if it makes you happy."

"It does."

As the cheery song slips through the speakers, I press myself up against the window to watch the swarm of trucks and cowboys. These are my kind of people. As much as I love Roots, not everyone there is a rancher. Not everyone gets the hard work that goes into the day to day. Only about one percent of the population, including both farmers and ranchers, is responsible for providing food for the rest of the United States. That percentage has drastically decreased over the last couple of generations, and the business gets a little lonely. It's exciting to finally be amongst people who share common values, goals, and life experiences.

"You've got a little drool on your chin." Jax smirks as he reaches over and jokingly swipes it off.

It sets flutters loose in my stomach, but I swat him away. "Stop! I'm just so excited. I can't believe I'm here. It kind of ticks me off that I pretended to be okay with not coming to one of these sooner."

"Well, you're here now, so let's make the most of it."

We get out of the truck, grabbing our luggage from the back seat.

"I like the vibes I'm getting already," I say with a sigh.

"This is going to be a good conference. We're going to have a good time."

"I'm getting ditched on this trip, aren't I?"

"You might."

He gives me an annoyed look, but I can tell from how quickly it wears off that he knows I'm joking.

I open the door to the hotel, telling Jax, "In all honesty, you're probably going to be the one to ditch me. Look at all these beautiful cowgirls. At least put a sock on the door or something if you're going to bring one back."

He stops in his tracks. "I'm not going to do that."

"Okay, fine. We don't have to do the sock thing, but you have to give me some sort of warning."

I glance up at him to find a frown on his face and pain in his eyes. "I'm not going to bring some girl back to my room. I'm here for you."

My heart sings, but I work to shut it down. Jax is here for me but only like a brother is there for his little sister. That's all I am to him—someone he needs to protect. He said as much at the bar the other night. No matter what he makes me feel, I can't forget the things he's made abundantly clear.

"You don't need to babysit me, Jax."

Giving him a curt nod, I march up toward the desk, but he pulls me back by the elbow. "I want to be here." He drops his hand. "Do you really think I'd come here with you just to pick up girls?"

"No, but I'm still figuring you out."

He nods then wordlessly dashes off to check-in. When the woman asks about our reservation, I give her my last name, and she types a few things on her keyboard before pulling out an envelope with two keycards in it.

"Here you go. One king bed. You'll be in room 518."

"I'm sorry. I think there's some sort of mistake. We asked for two full beds."

She furrows her brow and returns to her computer, clacking away again. After a few moments, she shakes her head. "I have one king bed on the reservation. I can put you on a waiting list in case anyone else was switched, but the whole hotel is booked out for the conference. Sorry."

"Is there at least a pull-out couch or something in the room?"

She shakes her head.

Jax takes the keys from her. "That's okay. Thank you."

I follow him in a haze, trying to figure out a way to avoid sharing a bed with my brother's extremely hot best friend who I should *not* have a crush on. Just the faintest touch from him is enough to cover me in goosebumps. I can't imagine being that close to him all night long.

As we get into the elevator, I turn to him. "I'm building a pillow fort between us."

"Are you kidding me?"

"Nope."

He shakes his head as he presses the button for the fifth floor. "Don't be ridiculous. We're both adults. We can share a bed." He smirks. "I remember you begging me to share a room with you not that long ago."

"Exactly. A room, not a bed. Plus, I was—"

"Drunk? That's the only way you'll sleep with me, huh?"

I release a puff of air as the doors open. "You're twisting my words."

"It's fine. I get it. I'll sleep on the floor."

He dramatically thrusts his hand to his forehead, giving me his best woe-is-me look before getting off the elevator and hanging a right toward our room.

"Fine, we'll share." I swipe my keycard, opening the door and immediately setting my bag against the wall.

Jax's lips quirk as he flounces onto the bed. "So, what do you want to do the rest of the night?"

"We definitely need to get some food. I'm starving."

"Okay, and then what?"

I shrug. "I guess we see where the night takes us."

Chapter Sixteen

Jax

"THAT WAS INCREDIBLE!" LAUREN DOES A HAPPY dance as we exit the restaurant.

"I didn't realize you're such a big fan of tacos. I thought your favorite food was fettuccine alfredo."

"What girl doesn't love a good taco?" Lauren leads her way down the sidewalk toward my truck. "But you're right. That is my favorite food. Give me some pasta and a glass of wine, and I'll be yours forever."

Noted. "Now what? It's still kind of early." I glance at my phone. It's only six fifteen.

"Should we explore a little? That seems like something the new Lauren should be doing."

"Is it something the new Lauren wants to do? That's important too."

"Yeah, it is."

I nod, taking her hand and leading her down the street.

"Where are we going?"

"There's a concert venue, Cain's Ballroom, around here. I thought we could pop by and see who's playing. There should be someone good since it's Friday night, and I just happen to know someone who has 'attending a concert' on her list."

She drops my hand. "How do you know about this place?"

"It's pretty well-known if you're into live music."

"I didn't know you were into live music."

"I'm sure there's a lot of things you still don't know about me."

Lauren stops dead in her tracks. "Wait, is John Michael Montgomery playing here? You probably looked it up before we came!"

I roll my eyes. "Why would you think that?"

"Because you're obsessed with him. You played his music for the entire car ride here."

"Well, he announced his Farewell Tour a while back and has been essentially MIA since then, so we definitely aren't seeing him tonight."

"You're just proving my point further."

I wrap an arm around her, leaning into her side. "Just come with me."

We head down Main Street as a gentle breeze blows through. When Lauren shivers, I stop, pulling off my Carhartt jacket and handing it to her.

"What are you doing?"

"It's cold out, and you're shivering."

"I'm not going to take your coat from you. It's not even supposed to hit freezing tonight. I'll be okay."

"Just take it." I hold it out for her and help her hesitantly slip it on.

"Thank you. I'm sorry. I would've brought a better jacket if I knew we were going to walk a few blocks."

"It's okay. I don't mind."

"Are you sure?" Concern laces her brows. I should've known she'd be resistant to my help, however small.

"I promise. Besides, I kind of like seeing you in my jacket."

Her cheeks flush, and she's saved from having to answer when we arrive at our destination. It's hard to miss considering the giant red sign on the roof that reads *Cain's* and the matching sign hanging off the front of the building.

I open the door and gesture for Lauren to go first so she can get out of the cold. As I follow, I take in the incredible building with various posters covering the brick walls. A bar sits at the back end of the venue, and the opening act must've already started because music drifts through the rafters of the high ceilings. The acoustics alone make me want to stay.

A woman approaches us, asking for our tickets.

"We don't have any." I grimace. "Is it too late to buy some?"

"You're in luck. We still have a few left."

"Who's playing tonight?"

"It's a country band called 49 Winchester."

Turning to Lauren, I ask, "What do you think?"

"Have you heard of them?"

"I know a few of their songs. They're pretty good if you're into a raspy voice and that grass roots sound."

She smiles. "Let's do it. I have to check it off my list anyway."

I hand the woman my credit card.

Lauren swivels on me, a look of frustration on her face.

"No, you're not buying our tickets! You're only here because of me."

"I may be in Tulsa because of you, but we are *here* because of me."

"Oh, is going to a concert on your list too?" She arches a brow and places a hand on her hip as if to say *checkmate*.

I sigh. "No, but I was the one who suggested we come here."

The woman looks between the two of us, tapping her foot as she waits to swipe my card.

Sensing her impatience, Lauren drops her arm. "Fine, you can pay."

We head inside and Lauren leads the way up to the bar. The opening band has already exited the stage. "Can I at least buy you a drink?"

"No, I'm fine."

She clings on to my arm. "Please."

I hesitate for a beat longer but finally relent because I don't see any way to avoid the truth. "I don't drink."

"How did I not know that?" She looks hurt, not at all frustrated or upset. There's no look of misunderstanding in her eyes, just disappointment in herself.

"I don't broadcast it. Some people think it makes me boring."

"I don't think you're boring. I'm actually really glad you're here," she admits.

"Oof."

"What? That was a compliment!"

"I know, but you seem surprised to be enjoying your time with me." I nudge her side.

"Well, our relationship has been kind of hot and cold over the years. I wasn't sure what to expect on this trip. You used to drive me crazy."

I step in closer to her. "I wouldn't mind driving you crazy now, but I hope it's a different kind of crazy."

Her eyes go round, and my stomach turns. The words sort of just slipped out. I'm not used to having to hold back with a woman I'm interested in, but this is Lauren. I don't know what the rules are now, but I'm pretty sure I just broke one.

"Jax Greer, are you flirting with me?"

I've only been trying to for the last nine years. Thanks for noticing, Freckles. "Do you want me to be?"

She opens her mouth to answer as the lights dim.

The lead singer walks to the front of the stage, grabbing the mic. "This song is called 'Annabel.'"

The crowd goes crazy, and I'm left to wonder what's running through Lauren's head right now.

———

To my delight, I've recognized more songs tonight than I expected, and Lauren has been getting into the music too. It's hard not to become consumed by it all in a venue like this. The pulse of the drums vibrates in my chest. The ground quakes with every strum of the guitar. Friends drape their arms over one another, belting out the lyrics like they speak to their soul. The energy is electric.

When "Russell County Line" comes on, I offer my hand to Lauren. She takes it gingerly, and I pull her close. Her full lips curve into a smile. I desperately want to know what it'd be like to kiss her. With her pouty lips and gentle personality that's also full of bold and pleasant surprises, I imagine one kiss from Lauren will set my world on fire.

As we slowly step from side to side, she warms up to me

and rests her head on my chest. I hope that means she feels safe with me. After everything she's been through over the last few years, she deserves to have people who make her feel safe, who she knows will take care of her and let her be free to be herself.

I press my lips softly to the top of her head, getting swept up in the moment. She glances up at me with her big hazel eyes, her mouth slightly agape as if to ask *Did you just do what I think you did?*

I give her a smirk and spin her as the music picks up. She tosses her head back, a radiant smile blooming on her face. She's glowing. I love seeing her so happy, and I love even more that I had something to do with that happiness.

"Do you still remember the dance from our lessons?" I ask her.

She nods eagerly, and I lead her through the steps as the song finishes up.

I'm so swept up in her that I don't even notice the song has ended until the lights flicker on and a mob of people swarms from the venue.

"I guess it's time for us to head back," she says, looking disappointed.

I don't want to go back. I don't want this night to end, but it's already ten thirty, and our day starts unreasonably early tomorrow. Lauren scheduled breakfast with another rancher at seven so she could talk to him about implementing regenerative agriculture before the conference starts at eight.

I grab Lauren's hand and lead her through the masses toward the door. When we step out into the cold winter air, we turn to one another, and I can see the same sense of hesitation on her face, like she's also scared the moment we shared is going to be erased as soon as we head back to the hotel room and focus on the reason we're here.

So instead of being responsible and leading us to the hotel, I say, "I did a little research on Tulsa before we came here. There's a speakeasy not too far from here. Want to check it out?"

Chapter Seventeen

Lauren

I SHOULD PROBABLY SAY NO. I'M LOOKING FORWARD TO the conference tomorrow and want to be fresh for it, but I'm also far from ready for our night to be over.

"Lead the way."

The grin he gives me makes my heart float. I'm so glad I agreed... until he starts to lead me down a dark alley.

"Jax, where are you taking me?"

"The place is down here. See the little metal bull above those green doors?" He points ahead of us. "That's it. I promise I'm not going to take you down some side street and get us killed."

I bite my lip but follow him anyway. He swings the far door open to reveal a large, dimly lit room. There are spikey looking chandeliers hanging from the ceiling that I'm sure cost a fortune and a bar crammed into the center stocked with an absurd amount of liquor bottles.

As I observe the tables covered in linen cloths and let

the piano music drift past me, I can't help but feel like I don't belong. This place looks fancy.

We make our way toward an empty table, but my phone vibrates in my pocket, stopping me in my tracks. When I see Charlie's name across the screen, I turn to Jax. "It's my brother. I should take this."

Jax nods, but his brow is laced with concern. I ignore him as I slide the button to answer the call and jog toward the door. Charlie is probably calling to ask about Dad, and apparently I'm not good at hiding my dread. I texted him yesterday about the appointment, but I'm sure he has more questions.

I step outside to get some quiet, and realize Charlie isn't calling me. He's FaceTiming.

When I answer, his whole face fills the screen. "Hey! There's my favorite sister."

"I'm your only sister."

"But you're still my favorite."

"What do you want?"

He frowns. "Can I not give you a compliment just because?"

"You're more than welcome to, but I don't know the last time you did." I lean against the brick wall behind me, thankful I still have Jax's jacket when a breeze blows up the quiet alley.

"I'm sorry." Charlie ruffles his hair. "I miss you."

His words capture my attention. He's always been stubborn about his decision to leave Roots. I know it was hard for him to tell my parents he didn't want to take over the ranch when it's been what was expected of him since the moment he was born. I'd assumed he's been happy in California, but his words now, and the look on his face, have me wondering if he's just too afraid to admit he doesn't want the life he left everything for.

"I miss you too. I'm excited to see you in a few weeks. You're still coming for Christmas, right? You're not calling to tell me you're canceling?"

"I'll be home for Christmas. I'm actually thinking of staying all the way until New Year's Day."

"Really?" I don't know the last time he stayed in Roots for longer than two or three days.

"Really. I'm able to get the time off work, so I figured I might as well."

I nod, the unspoken truth of why he probably wants to stay longer lingering between us. "Are you calling to see how he's doing?"

"You texted that he was doing great. Is there a reason I need to worry?"

"No," I rush out. Everything has been okay over the last few weeks since Dad has stepped back. Although he's been a little grumpier because of it. He misses working on the ranch.

"Okay, well, I just wanted to call and wish you luck with your conference. I'm really excited for you and proud of you for doing this on your own."

"I'm not *completely* on my own."

"What do you mean?"

"Jax is here with me."

"Jax?" He moves the phone even closer to his face. "Jax Greer? Like my best friend Jax? The one who used to drive you bonkers because he called you some nickname you hated? That Jax?"

I roll my eyes. "Why are you being weird about this?"

"Because I would think between my best friend and my

favorite sister, one of you would remember to mention that you two were going on a trip together."

I laugh. "I'm still your only sister."

"And you're still my favorite." He sits down on his couch, propping his phone against something. "Is there something going on between you two?"

I hope. "Don't be ridiculous, Char."

"I don't want you to get hurt. You just got out of a long-term relationship. I know things are tough with Dad and the ranch right now, but don't let yourself fall for someone who isn't going to give you all the things you want. You know Jax has never been with anyone for longer than a night."

My stomach turns sour. He's right. I need to squash the inklings of feelings I have for him before it's too late. Just because he's charming and kind and makes me feel like the most beautiful girl in the world, doesn't mean he's going to change his ways for me.

"Is he there? Put him on the phone."

"He's inside, but there's nothing you need to worry about."

I glance over my shoulder and find Jax standing just outside the door to the speakeasy, watching me closely. Of course he wanted to make sure I'm okay because that's what he does. But he also keeps his relationships without strings. I don't know what to think right now.

"What are you doing out here?" I call to him.

"You think I was going to let you stand in some shady back street all alone? Hell no."

"Put him on," Charlie demands.

I motion for Jax, giving him a look of exhaustion. "Charlie wants to talk with you."

He nods and closes the distance between us. As soon as his face is in the screen, Charlie goes off. "What the hell, man? Why didn't you tell me you were going to the conference with my sister? Have you been making passes at her?" Charlie presses his thumb and forefinger to the bridge of his nose. "Oh, god! Are you two *sleeping* together?" Charlie looks like he's about to barf up his dinner.

Jax looks at me with a hint of betrayal on his face, and I quickly shake my head. "He's being overprotective over *nothing*." I shove my face into the view of the camera and glower at Charlie.

Memories of the way Jax held me tonight while we danced, how he made sure I had enough space in the crowds, and even the gentle way he grabbed my hand flash through my mind. None of those actions match his reputation for being a no-strings kind of guy, and now that I'm starting to really get to know him, I'm confident Jax deeply cares for me.

Shoving his free hand in his pocket, Jax quickly recovers. "Why would you think that? Don't you have any faith in me?"

"I don't know. It's not like I've ever seen you pass up a beautiful woman before. I love you, man, but you can't commit, and I don't want someone like that making moves on my sister."

I can't believe how harsh Charlie's words are, but as I watch his face on the screen, I wonder if there's a reason for his unkind nature, like maybe there's some underlying motivation. Even so, Jax looks crushed. He brushes it off, as if he's unaffected, but I can see through it when he narrows his eyes, keeping his tone light as he asks, "Are you at home right now? Shouldn't you be out? It's almost nine o'clock on a Friday."

"Work sucked. I didn't feel like going out, and I wanted to tell my sister how proud I am of her for doing this."

"I am too."

My heart pounds in my chest like a stampede of horses. *Jax is proud of me.*

"I guess I'll let you two go. I know you have a big day tomorrow."

I take the phone back from Jax. "Good night, Char. Love and miss you."

"Ditto! And Jax, you better treat my sister with respect, or I'll whoop your ass."

"Screw you," Jax says back, but his tone is not as playful as Charlie's. There's an edge, and the pink on Jax's face that brings him to life is evaporating by the second.

I hang up, turning back to Jax. "Should we head back inside?"

"Actually, I think we should go back to the hotel. Charlie's right. This weekend is important to you, and I don't want to be a bad influence."

My heart softens for him just a little bit more, but when we take the whole trip back to our hotel room in silence, the butterflies in my gut start to feel more like termites eating away at me.

I don't understand what shifted so quickly. I can't help but wonder where things would've gone tonight if I hadn't picked up the phone. It felt like we were on the cusp of something, and I really want to see where that could lead. I don't just want to kiss Jax, although I'm sure it would be amazing. I want to *be* with Jax because he makes me feel unlike anyone ever has, and I think he feels the same way about me.

When we're back in the room, I set my purse down on the desk in the corner and rifle through my suitcase for my toiletry bag. "Do you want me to do my skincare routine for you tonight?"

Jax doesn't even look up from his suitcase. "No, that's okay. It'd take too long. Let's just go to bed."

I try to hide my disappointment as I head to the bathroom. He's completely shut down.

By the time I head back into the bedroom, Jax is already changed into a plain white T-shirt and plaid pajama pants. He wordlessly passes me into the bathroom, closing the door behind him.

He takes what feels like an eternity. It's probably only a few minutes, but it's long enough for me to convince myself whatever vibes I felt tonight were in my own head. I've been stupid to think we could become something. I've been down this path before. When we first met, I thought there was a spark between us, but he watched Austin swoop into my life, and he practically swooped right out of it.

When he draws the covers back on his side of the bed and slips underneath them, I go rigid. I'm too aware of his warmth and the muscles I know are barely hidden by that shirt he's wearing. I can't stop thinking of every tender and beautiful moment we shared tonight and how they've suddenly melted away.

He flicks the light off on his side of the bed, and the room goes dark. "Good night, Freckles."

He's so close. His words are so soft. Chills spread across my arms even though his presence makes me feel hot enough to start a fire.

"Night."

"Sleep tight."

I lie there thinking about the way he flirted, the cheeky smirks he gave me, and the feeling of his toned muscles under my hands as we danced. My heart sticks on the way he looked out for me when I stepped out to take my call and how he gave me his jacket and checked on me throughout the concert to make sure I was having a good time. *That can't mean nothing.*

His breathing quickly deepens as he drifts off to sleep. How on earth do men do that? It takes me ages to fall asleep *on a good day.*

I continue trying to piece tonight together, desperate to make sense of everything that happened from the good to the bad moments. Then Jax rolls over, tossing an arm out and draping it over me, making my heart stop beating in my chest.

His breathing is slow and even, telling me he has no clue what he's doing right now. I should move, but being wrapped up in Jax's arms feels too perfect, like it's exactly where I should be right now. I barely let myself breathe, out of fear that he'll wake up.

As I relax into his touch, my mind quiets. I'm not thinking about my dad, Charlie's warnings, Jax's reputation, or all the things I have to do for the conference tomorrow and the ranch when I get home. I just have one thought resting in my mind as I drift into a deep sleep: *I'm falling for Jax Greer.*

Chapter Eighteen

Jax

I FEEL BETTER RESTED THAN I EVER HAVE. I'M WARM, comfortable, at peace, and—*wait, is that Lauren's honey shampoo I smell?*

I register smooth skin under my fingertips and the soft warmth pressed against my entire body before I open my eyes to find a mop of golden hair below my nose. I've somehow slipped my arm around Lauren and pulled her in to be little spoon. If I wasn't terrified of her waking up and finding us like this, I'd be over the moon. Holding Lauren feels right. I remain frozen in place, listening to her rhythmic breathing, which grounds me, even after my spiral last night.

I can't be upset with Charlie for saying I don't commit. It's true. I've never committed to a woman, and for good reason, but hearing him say the words brings out the side of me that wants to prove him wrong. I'll show him. I can commit. I *want* to commit. Hell, I even think I'm *ready* to commit, especially to Lauren, the girl I've been in love with for so long, and who I've only fallen harder for over the last few weeks.

As Lauren gently blows puffs of air out her nose, I fill with a greater resolve to prove myself. I'll show her I'm capable of committing, that I'm worthy. I'm not exactly sure how I'm going to do that, but she needs to know I'm a good man who's willing to give her the world.

When she stirs, I quickly draw my arm back. I'd like to think I'm successful in doing it without her noticing because she doesn't say anything to indicate she's displeased. She just turns to me with half-shut eyes and a dopey smile that puts one on my face too. "Good morning." Her voice is gravelly. "What time is it?"

I glance at the clock. "Almost six thirty."

"No!" She shoots up. "My alarm didn't go off. I'm supposed to be getting ready. I have to meet with that rancher for breakfast soon."

I grab a hold of her shoulders and pull her back toward me, wrapping her up in my arms. I could get in my head about how this might be crossing a line, but I'm much more concerned with the look of panic on Lauren's face.

"Take a few deep breaths. You're going to make it on time to that breakfast, and you're going to knock his socks off to the point that he shares every single secret about regenerative ranching with you. I know it."

Her shoulders slowly lower, and she turns back to me, gifting me a smile. It's half-hearted, but it's something. "You think so?"

"I know so. Can I do anything to help you get ready on time?"

"Stay out of my way?"

"I can do that. That's what I'm here for this weekend."

She drags herself from my arms, turning back toward

me with her nose scrunched up. "You're here to stay out of my way? It seems like you could've done that from Roots."

A sly smirk touches her lips.

"You know what I meant. I'm here to support you."

She slides off the bed, grabbing clothes from her suitcase and scrambling to the bathroom, but she pauses briefly in the doorway. "Jax?"

"Yeah?"

"Thank you. I wouldn't want to tackle this weekend without you."

———

Lauren reaches out to grab my hand, drawing my attention away from the clock on the wall that I may or may not have been checking every thirty seconds. "What's going on with you? You seem antsy."

I have the perfect plan to show Lauren what things could be like between us, but it's going to blow up in my face if we don't get out the door in ten minutes.

"Nothing. It's nothing. Take your time finishing your food."

Pushing her plate away, she says, "I'm done."

"No, you're not." I push it toward her. "I know you. You wouldn't let a burger go to waste."

"Well, I'm too nervous to eat now." She crosses her arms and leans back.

"I'm sorry. I just have a surprise I think you'll like. I didn't expect the cocktail hour to go until seven thirty."

"I'm not trying to ruin your plans. You should've told me. We could've left early."

"And draw you away from all the wonderful connections you were making? No way! You were a rockstar in there. Everyone wanted to talk with you."

She rolls her eyes. "I talked with like three people."

"It was way more than that," I insist. "Your breakfast seemed to go well too. He kept lingering and coming back up to you tonight. He couldn't stay away." *And I hated it.*

It was incredible to see Lauren's excitement and hope after breakfast this morning, but it was less than pleasing to find out at the cocktail hour that the man she had breakfast with was a good-looking, twenty-something instead of some harmless grandpa she'd want nothing to do with.

She pulls her plate back and takes another bite of her burger as the waiter comes to check on us. I request the check, and as soon as we've paid, I grab Lauren's hand and lead her out the door.

"Okay, you have to tell me where we are going in such a rush."

I tug her into the doorway of the building right next door. We step into the threshold of an independent bookstore that looks even more vibrant than in the photos I saw online. Garland is strung along the top of the bookshelves, and a Christmas tree sits in the corner near a café with signs that say it sells both coffee and wine.

"Ta da!" I throw my arms out, feeling a little proud of myself when I catch the look of wonder in her eyes.

"Jax, this is amazing."

"I figured between the books, the little café, and all the Christmas decor, you'd like it. They close in twenty-five minutes though."

She wraps me up in a bear hug, and I press a kiss to the top of her head, just like I did last night.

Pulling back, she meets my eyes. "Thank you for

bringing me here. I love it. I don't care if we only have five minutes. I'll make every second count."

"You better pick out a book because I know you've finished the two I bought you."

"Okay, okay! I'm going." She snaps a picture of the Christmas decor in the corner before dashing off toward the romance aisle.

It's nice to see her growth in only a few weeks. I didn't have to drag her away from books that are related to work. Instead, she's fully embracing what she enjoys and letting herself be happy. It's beautiful to see, and it makes me think maybe I can get there someday too, allowing myself to be happy instead of consumed with regret. Lauren might be exactly what I need to change that.

By the time the intercom announces the shop is closing, Lauren's arms are stacked. Watching her struggle to carry the pile already in her hands but reaching out to add another on top makes me love her even more. I rush over to pull the books from her grasp.

"No, I've got it." She pulls away. "I'm fine."

"Nice try, Freckles." I shuffle through the books I've wrestled from her, a smirk growing on my face. "These look interesting. Brother's best friend. Brother's best friend. Brother's best friend... I'm sensing a pattern here."

"Clearly you haven't found the Christmas novella yet." She reaches to grab them back, but I angle away.

"I might just need to buy you all of these."

"Really?"

"Now that I know how obsessed with Christmas you are, I wouldn't dream of depriving you of the Christmas one. And I'm fully supportive of this new interest in your brother's best friend."

Her laughter breaks free. "Books are kind of expensive."

"It's fine. I want to. Think of it as your early Christmas gift from me."

"You're not buying me seven books for Christmas."

"You're right." I stride up to the counter, handing the clerk my credit card. "I'm buying you six books and a novella. There's a difference."

She buries her head in her hands, but I don't miss the excitement blooming on her face. It makes the $130 hit to my credit card more than worth it. I'd buy her a million books if it meant seeing that beautiful look of delight.

As I hand her the bag, she uses a menacing tone to tell me, "There's going to be payback for this. I'm going to get you the most outrageous Christmas gift. I hope you're ready."

"Oh no, you're going to get me a big present? I'm so disappointed," I tease.

She presses her lips together in what I think is her best attempt at looking threatening. "I mean it! It's going to be way better than your gift."

"I'll make sure to mentally prepare, but I should let you know I'm not done with my surprise."

"Oh no."

"Come with me." I grab her free hand, pulling her out the door.

"As if I have a choice," she grumbles.

Chapter Nineteen

Jax

WHEN WE'RE BACK IN THE COMFORT OF OUR HOTEL room, Lauren looks thoroughly confused. "I don't mean to sound ungrateful, but I thought you said there was more to the surprise?"

"Buying you all those wasn't enough?" I tease.

"It was more than enough. I'm actually a little relieved there's nothing else. I already have no idea how I'm going to make this up to you." She points to the stack of books next to her suitcase.

A smile slips onto my lips, and I pull her in close. "You don't have to make it up to me. I'm doing this because I want to." I tuck her hair behind her ear. "I do have one more part of the surprise. Get into something comfy, and I'll take care of the rest."

She groans defiantly, but there's a spark in her eyes, and a smile tugs at her lips as she hesitantly moves toward her suitcase to pull out a change of clothes.

While she's in the bathroom, I make a quick call to room

service, and by the time I'm done, she's coming out wearing a pair of black sweatpants that cinch at the waist and one of Charlie's football T-shirts from high school. She's taken off her makeup, and there's something about her naked hazel eyes that makes it impossible to look away.

"Will you do my skincare while we wait?" I ask.

"Only if you tell me what we're waiting for."

"No way! That defeats the purpose of a surprise."

"I don't like surprises."

"You'll like this one."

"Fine." She tosses her head back as if she's already exhausted from all this waiting. She heads to the bathroom, grabbing her bag of toiletries. "Come on then."

She puts a little dollop of oil onto her palm and looks at me with those big beautiful eyes, waiting for permission to touch me. If only she knew how badly I crave her gentle, comforting caress.

I prop myself on the counter and give her a nod, so she places her fingertips to my cheeks, smoothing the oil across my face. I have to fight to keep myself from closing my eyes as I relish our closeness. The warmth of her contact liquifies my body. I love that I can smell the scent of her honey shampoo and count the freckles on her cheeks. Flecks of gold and green kaleidoscope in her stunning eyes, mesmerizing me.

Once the oil has been evenly distributed, she wets a washcloth with warm water and wipes it across my face, explaining each methodical step again and making sure to show me the dirt that just came off my face.

I pick up one of the bottles on the counter, inspecting it. "Did you have fun today?"

"I did. Did you?"

"A lot more than I expected to have at a ranching

conference." I've found the lectures to be interesting. I almost wish Lauren would accept more help because I have a few ideas I've picked up on that might make the cowboys' work more efficient.

She pulls a bottle of toner from the bag, replacing it with the cleansing oil we just used. Music from the hotel room next door fills the comfortable silence between us as I watch her apply her own.

She hums along until she finishes up, turning to me and asking, "Is there a reason you like John Michael Montgomery so much? He has some great songs, but I don't know anyone else who'd happily listen to the same artist on repeat."

She rubs the cool liquid across my clean skin, and the sensation scrambles my brain. I drag my lip in with my teeth, trying to refocus. I could keep things light, but there's something about the curious look in Lauren's eyes that compels me to go deeper with her. Besides, the man who deserves her would be willing to open up.

She busies herself with switching out the toner for moisturizer as she waits for my answer. I can't believe I know words like toner and moisturizer, and I definitely can't believe I'm about to share this with her.

Lauren has me in a chokehold, and she doesn't even realize it.

She brushes the smooth cream onto my face and turns to wash her hands off. I use her to calm me as I blurt out the words before I can think any more about this. "His music makes me feel safe."

She gives me a questioning look as she wipes her hands off on the towel.

"I'm sure by now you've heard the stories about my dad."

She nods. The whole town wouldn't stop talking when my mom and I first showed up at Aunt Carol's doorstep covered in bruises with not a penny to our name.

"He was an addict. Gambling was his drug of choice. He just couldn't say no to a bet." I stare at the floor. "He was always convinced he'd strike it big on the next one, but it'd only lead to more debt, and when he was down, he got angry. He never took responsibility for his own actions. He found ways to blame it on my mom and me. He'd yell…" I wince, realizing I haven't told this story to anyone except for Charlie, and that was years ago. It's been easier to bury all of this down deep.

"When the yelling wasn't enough, he used his fists. We slipped out in the middle of the night, when Mom was certain he'd drunk enough alcohol to knock him out cold." I grind my teeth together, not wanting to say the next part. "I know I was supposed to be the strong one, the one who helped her, but I was terrified. I was certain he'd find us in Roots. I mean, it wouldn't have taken a genius to figure out we'd gone to stay with Mom's sister. But I don't think Dad even missed us. He was probably glad we were gone because he didn't have to hide his addiction anymore, and he didn't have to hide the fact that he was selling drugs to try to pay for all his gambling debts."

Lauren's eyes go round. She shuffles closer to me, sandwiching herself between my thighs and rubbing my back gently.

"About three weeks after we left, we found out my dad was arrested for dealing. Aunt Carol took us out to dinner at Sweet Mae's to celebrate, and John Michael Montgomery's music was playing in the diner. Something was wrong with the stereo, so it played on loop. Now, whenever I hear his voice, I have that feeling of being safe and happy again."

Lauren places her hands on my thighs. "We don't have to talk about this anymore if you don't want to. I just wanted to understand you a little better. I should've asked you if your favorite color is green or something like that."

"It's not green."

"See, I was wrong. Tell me what it is then."

"It's hazel." I grab her waist and turn her toward the mirror. "More specifically, it's the color of your eyes."

Chapter Twenty

Lauren

His favorite color is the color of my eyes. Never has someone said something so sweet to me. I feel like I could walk on water after hearing those words.

Jax watches me, as if he's waiting for me to say something, but I don't know what to say in this moment. He not only shared some deeply personal elements of his life, but I think he just confessed to having feelings for me. In a matter of minutes, he completely uprooted every belief I had about him and us.

He breaks eye contact with me, pulling my hands back to his face. "I don't think you finished rubbing the moisturizer in. I can feel it here." He points along his jaw.

I follow his guidance and note the unsteady nature of his hands. It hits me that his world might've just been shaken as much as mine. I doubt many people know the truth about Jax's dad. Hearing about his rough past makes me want to share something personal with him too. I want to show him he can trust me.

When I pull my hands away, Jax slides off the counter. "Can I do some of the steps for you?" He grabs the bottle on the counter as I nod.

When he squeezes the dropper, an absurd amount of gold syrup comes streaming out. Nervous laughter slips out as I quickly take it from him, sucking some of it back up.

As I will myself to be vulnerable with him, he swipes the serum on my face, using slow strokes and light pressure. I close my eyes and revel in the feeling of being taken care of. I don't know the last time someone pampered me like this. Heck, I don't know the last time I let someone take care of me at all, but I like it, especially with Jax. Despite his size, his touch is tender, warm, and caring. His blue eyes are soft as he watches me, almost with a look of awe that makes me feel like the only woman in the world.

When he pulls his hands away, I rush my words out, closing my eyes as if that will keep the words from being true. "My dad is having heart problems."

I can't bring myself to look Jax in the eyes or to wait for his response. I just keep word-vomiting. "That's why I came to the bar alone a few weeks ago. My dad fainted, so we took him to the emergency room. According to the doctors, it's just high blood pressure, but they've been running all kinds of tests to be sure. He already has a decent diet and gets plenty of exercise, but the ranch puts a lot of weight on him. He needs to reduce his stress and make some changes, or he can have a serious heart attack." I glance down at the floor. I feel emotions rising inside of me, and I can see pity in Jax's eyes. I'm not telling him this so he'll comfort me; I'm supposed to be showing him I value his trust.

I quickly add, "I know it could be worse. We caught things in time to make changes and do some digging." *But it's still terrifying.*

Reducing Dad's stress means almost no work on the ranch, and he's having a heck of time letting go. In the occasional times he does, I swear he's losing the essence of who he is. It makes me think about what it'd be like to lose him, and I *can't*. I love my whole family, but I've always connected more with Dad and Charlie. Charlie already left. I can't take losing my dad too.

Then there's the pressure I'm putting on myself to care for the ranch and make all of Dad's sacrifices worthwhile. It'd be selfish to complain about having to take care of things on my own when Dad needs rest to prioritize his health, but it's still so heavy.

I prop myself on the counter, trying to clear my head. If I let myself marinate for too long, I might accidentally cry in front of Jax, which is the last thing I want.

"Thank you for sharing with me." Jax grabs my hand, giving it a squeeze. "You didn't have to do that."

"I wanted to."

"For what it's worth, your dad is the strongest mother trucker I've ever seen. Nothing can take that man down or steal his essence."

His avoidance of using the actual word puts a half-hearted smile on my face. "You're right about that. He is a *very* strong mother trucker."

"I know you two are close, and I can only imagine how scary it must be to learn the person you've always looked up to has an Achilles heel. Knowing you, you're probably turning your responsibility for the ranch into a burden you have to carry alone now."

Curse him for knowing me so well. I thought I was doing a better job of hiding it.

Jax makes a point of meeting my gaze as he adds, "I'm

here for you, and when you need someone to hold you or make you smile, I'll be there."

My mind swirls as Jax squeezes my hand tightly, and I try to grasp everything that just happened, all the comfort and kindness he just provided me with. It's astounding how much peace he can bring me after I felt so defeated moments ago. *How on earth is Jax Greer still single?*

He must see my wheels turning because he narrows his eyes. "What's going through your mind right now, Freckles?"

"Why have you never been in a real relationship?" Shadows cross over his face until I continue. "You're sweet, handsome, and funny. Why not share that with someone? Why just have strings of uncommitted relationships?"

He lets go of my hand, stepping back. "I've never seen the point."

"I don't believe you."

Leaning against the counter, he sighs. "Do you really want to know?"

I nod, anticipation filling me.

"I've never felt good enough. My whole life, I've been told the Carter men are nothing but trouble. My grandpa was an addict, and he cheated on his wife. My dad's vice was gambling, but it destroyed our family just the same."

He pauses, but I remain silent, giving him the room to keep going.

"When I was younger, I was afraid of being like the two of them. I was terrified of being an addict and destroying my family if I was lucky enough to have one. I was so scared of the monsters that came before me I didn't realize I was turning into one myself every time I cowered in fear instead of standing up for my mom. People in town look at me with pity because of my past, but the people who know me best know the truth. They know I only hurt those I love. Everyone is better off without me."

The pain in his eyes and brokenness in his voice splits my heart in two.

"Jax, you seriously think that's how people look at you? Even the people you love?"

"I *know* they do." He turns around, collecting my scattered bottles from the counter and neatly placing them in my bag. "I can brush off the things some outsider in town says, but I'll never forget the things the people I love have said."

"There has to be some sort of misunderstanding. You're a good man. You always have been. Even when we were younger and you annoyed me, I still recognized you were a great friend to Charlie and a supportive son and nephew. Now, you're helping me with the ranch and pushing me to do all these wonderful things I wouldn't have done on my own. I wouldn't be here right now if it weren't for you and your refusal to kiss me that terrible night a few weeks ago."

He turns back to me. "That was the hardest thing I'd ever done."

"What?" My voice is shaky as I slip off the counter. I think I know what he means, but I have to be certain.

He steps closer, his warmth swarming my body. His presence scrambles my brain, and out of instinct, I reach out to him, grabbing fistfuls of his T-shirt.

"Choosing not to kiss you was one of the hardest things I've ever done." His words are barely above a whisper, but they echo down my spine.

Tilting his head down slightly, his blue-eyed gaze latches on to mine as he wraps an arm around my waist. The stampede of horses in my chest greets me once again.

I take another half step closer to him so that we're toe-to-toe. "Then why didn't you kiss me?"

"You weren't ready."

"I'm ready now," I whisper.

He searches my face. "Lauren—"

"I'm not trying to bury my feelings or get back at Austin. This isn't even about checking off another item on my list. I just really want to kiss you." So badly. I want to know how his lips taste, how his hands will feel in my hair. I want to bask in the glorious feeling Jax gives me whenever we're together. "Is that okay?"

"That's more than okay," he says, sounding almost pained, like he's physically restraining himself.

We're both breathing heavily as we stare at each other in anticipation. He brushes a stray strand of hair behind my ear. "You're sure?"

"More than ever."

He drops his hand to just below my chin, tilting it up ever so slightly, and then brings his lips to mine.

Chapter Twenty-One

Jax

In all the times I wondered what it would be like to kiss Lauren, I'd never considered it'd be like this. It feels like a firework display is going off in my chest as my heart beats rampantly. All my senses are simultaneously shot and supercharged. I can't feel my feet on the ground, but I'm aware of her hands brushing the hair at the base of my neck and the way she gently nips at my bottom lip.

"I've wanted to do that for so long," I say.

"Me too."

My heart soars knowing we're on the same page.

She leans against the counter. "I'm thankful you stopped me that night after the bar, but I've been wondering ever since."

I guess we aren't *exactly* on the same page. This isn't just a kiss for me. I've been waiting for this moment for *years*.

I'm not about to blow this by not communicating with

her. I open my mouth to set things straight, but a knock on the door interrupts us.

I rush to answer it, opening it to reveal room service with our giant ice cream sundae on a platter.

Lauren rushes to my side, but I shift my body to hide the tray before she can ruin the surprise.

"What is it?"

"Trust me, you'll like it. Cover your eyes."

"Jax—"

"Cover your eyes, Freckles."

She presses her lips into a firm line as she sits on the bed and follows my instructions.

"Don't even think about peeking. I'll know if you do."

"Just hurry up. You're killing me."

I glide across the room and set the tray down in front of her then gently pull her hands from her face. "You can look now."

When her eyes land on the sundae, her face fills with a smile bigger than Texas. The glass is at least the size of her head and filled to the brim with brownies, chocolate ice cream, and chocolate fudge.

"Don't get too excited because we do have to share," I tease.

"Yeah right! You'll have to get your own." She snatches the sundae with both hands and leaps off the bed.

I gasp and bound after her, just barely catching her before she can lock herself in the bathroom. "I can't believe you just did that!"

She shrugs. "I had to at least try. This looks heavenly."

"New rule: the sundae has to stay on the bed at all times."

"Second rule: I get three bites for every one bite you get." The satisfied smirk on her face makes me laugh.

"That's fine. Three of your bites are probably equal to one of mine anyway. You're the daintiest eater I've ever seen."

"What do you mean?" She picks up a spoon and curls a bite of ice cream from the sundae, savoring every second of it as her eyelids flutter in satisfaction.

"That!" I thrust my arms out at her. "You just proved my point."

She looks embarrassed, so I quickly lean in to plant a kiss on her forehead. "It's ridiculously cute."

She hides the joy on her face by taking another bite. "You better jump in before I finish this without you."

"You haven't had your third bite yet. I'm waiting."

She swats at me, laughing. "Just eat."

We sit in silence for a few minutes as we savor the decadent chocolate brownie paired with the rich chocolate ice cream and fudge. It's too much chocolate for me, but she looks so happy that it's worth the stomachache.

The lull in the conversation sets loose a swirl of questions in my mind. *What's next for us? Did the kiss mean something to Lauren or was it just about physical attraction?*

I spoon a bite out, leaving a chunk of brownie behind for Lauren. "We need to talk about this weekend."

Lauren glances up at me cautiously. "What about this weekend?"

"We kissed, for one, and I don't know what headspace you're in, but I want to let that moment stay magical without things becoming weird between us. Tell me what you're feeling."

She lowers her spoon. "A little confused."

"Confused how?"

"The last few days have been a lot to process." She finds the chunk of brownie I left and scoops it up. "It's not like I didn't notice our chemistry before, but everything changed so fast, and I don't know what to make of it. I'm scared."

"Scared of what?"

"A lot of things. I've been hurt before by the one person who was never supposed to break my heart. That makes it hard to trust *anyone*." She folds the napkin in her lap in half before glancing up at me. "You've shared some personal things with me tonight, but I can't figure out why. Why me? And I know it doesn't mean anything because you're not a relationship guy, but I still don't get it."

Her words cut me deep, even if they're true. I haven't been known as a relationship guy, but if there's anyone in the world I'm willing to try for, it's Lauren.

"It *does* mean something." I move the empty glass to the floor and scoot closer to her. "We've built a friendship over the years, and we've only grown closer over the last few weeks. That kiss, it was *amazing,* and to me—" I inhale, trying to gain the courage to say this next part. "To me, it was *everything*. I don't want only one night with you. You're not just another woman to me." She's *the* woman for me.

Her eyes go round, and she draws back a little. They set me into panic mode. *Have I said too much and ruined this before it even started?*

Finally settling her hand on my leg, she says, "That kiss was unlike anything I've ever experienced, and I've loved spending time with you. I'm scared of opening myself up to someone again, but I'm more scared of not seeing where this could go."

Hope sparks in my chest. I'm on the cusp of what I've wanted for so long.

"Where do we go from here? I love spending time with you, holding your hand"—I squeeze her hand—"and kissing you, but what happens when we get back to Roots?"

"I want to keep exploring this." She looks more certain of herself now.

"Me too."

"But why am I the one you want more than a night with? What makes me different?"

"If you don't understand that, then we have some work to do. You're the most beautiful woman I've ever met, and I'm not just talking about your gorgeous eyes or your incredibly distracting curves." I trace a finger along her waist and wonder if she feels the same tingling sensation I do. "You're kind. You're smart. You're a hard worker, and you'd do anything for the people you love. You're humble. You're brave. Do you need me to go on?"

"I don't know if I could take it if you did." She covers her blushing cheeks. "What about Charlie? Do you think he'd be weirded out by us being together? If we decide to see where things go, would that ruin your friendship?"

"I don't know. Charlie is my best friend. I love the guy, and I know he loves me, but I'm worried it'll be a different story if I'm dating his little sister."

She presses her lips together. "You're right. Maybe it is a little weird."

After a beat, she sits up straighter. "What if we don't need to tell him? Or anyone else for that matter."

"What?"

"We're *just* figuring things out. I'm worried our relationship will become more complicated if everyone in town knows. It puts pressure and expectations on us. Charlie might be weirded out at first, but you and I both know he would be so excited to see his best friend and his sister together." She pats my leg, beaming.

Did she not hear him on the phone yesterday?

She continues. "My parents would be over the moon

too. Everyone would be planning our wedding before we've even had a chance to figure out what this is. Isn't it easier to keep this between us while we figure out where this can go?"

I scratch the back of my head. "Yeah, I guess so."

That turns her smile brighter, like she's already made up her mind, but this doesn't quite sit right with me. I search for something to do with my hands, but there's nothing, no napkins close by, no loose threads on my sweatpants or the bedding, so I sit there stiff like a board. "Are you sure? You don't even want to tell Callie and Olivia?"

"Oh, there's no way I can keep this from them, but I'll swear them to secrecy."

"Not even your parents?"

She shrugs a shoulder. "I'd like them to know eventually, but for now, I don't think it's necessary."

My mind races as two conflicting thoughts battle for dominance. I guess this could be a good thing. It keeps the pressure off us, and a secret relationship *does* seem exciting. Plus, this gives me the opportunity to explore things with Lauren without the risk of hearing the one thing I'm most terrified of: I'm not enough for her. Still, I wonder if Lauren wants to keep us a secret for the same reason I would if I were her: to hide from the truth just a little bit longer.

"We can keep it quiet if that's what you want," I finally say.

She springs into my arms, pressing a kiss to my lips. Just like that, I'm putty in her hands.

Drawing back only the slightest bit, she says, "I need you to know keeping this a secret has nothing to do with you and everything to do with me. When Austin and I got together, it felt like our fate was decided for us, and I guess I'm afraid it'd be the same with you because, like you said, we *do* have a foundation. Our families are intertwined in a wonderful way, but it means there'd be pressure. I want to fall in love with you because that's what *we* want, not what anyone else wants."

I hear her words, but all my brain registers is that she doesn't want to tell people about us. She cares for me but not enough to share our relationship with others.

I could let this consume me, convince me I'm not enough and never will be, just like I did every time I didn't fight for my mom, but I'd rather fight for the person I love this time.

The opportunity to be with Lauren is something I've wanted for so long. I'm not going to throw that away, so I shove my feelings aside. "I'll do whatever it is you need to be happy. I just want to be with you."

"Me too."

I kiss her forehead. "Then let's do this."

We'll figure it out. I'll prove myself to Lauren and, maybe along the way, I can get her to change her mind about hiding us.

Chapter Twenty-Two

Lauren

WHEN MY ALARM GOES OFF IN THE MORNING, I'M TORN between knowing what I'm here for and wanting to stay in bed with Jax for all of eternity. We still have four hours of conference events today, and while I'm looking forward to the speakers on the agenda—there are talks on innovation and ranch management—all I want to do is lie here wrapped up in Jax's arms.

I peer over my shoulder and find his soft eyes already focused on me. "Have you been up for a while?"

"Couldn't have been too long." He pulls me closer. "Granted, time goes by too fast when I'm with you."

I turn to face him, wrapping my arms around his neck. "I have a hard time believing you're known as one of the biggest flirts in all of Texas. You're just full of corny things to say."

"Ouch."

I giggle and press a smacking kiss to his cheek. "I like it."

"Good, because you're making me this way. I promise I'm normally a lot cooler."

I swing my legs over the edge of the bed, glancing back at him with a smirk. "If you say so."

I gather my clothes from my suitcase then pause, groaning.

"What's wrong?"

"You've ruined the conference for me. I want to stay here with you."

He smiles, slipping from bed. "I'm touched, but you need to get up. You'll be glad you did. I promise."

He shoos me toward the bathroom, and as I head that way, he follows close behind.

"What are you doing?" Suspicious, I place a hand on my hip.

He doesn't answer. He simply grabs my hand, tugging me toward the bathroom and flicking on the light.

Shredded up pieces of paper with the hotel logo are taped all over the mirror. They're covered with notes in Jax's handwriting.

You're Kind. You're Funny. You scrunch your nose when you laugh. You're one of the best bluffers in poker I've ever seen. Every once in a while, you'll catch me off guard with something witty, and it makes me laugh. Even when you get knocked down, you get up. You love your people fiercely.

I turn to him, my hands hanging limp at my sides as my jaw falls to the floor. "You did this?"

"You asked me last night what I see in you, and I need you to know that it's everything. But saying it doesn't feel like enough. I wanted you to look in the mirror and see what I see."

My heart swells. I feel like I could cry. No one has ever made me feel so loved.

I shake my head in disbelief. "I don't even know what to say."

I wrap him in a hug. I want to tell him he didn't have to do this, that I'm learning to love myself on my own and it isn't his job to take care of me, but when I look up at him, he's fighting back a smile. I know what Jax needs to hear. "Thank you."

I keep scanning the sticky notes, and one in the bottom right corner catches my eye.

You've become my best friend.

I pull it from the mirror. I just want to hold it for a moment and soak it in. He watches me silently until I finally set it down and pull him to me, sinking my fingers into his hair and crashing my lips into his.

I don't know any other way to convey the things I'm feeling right now, but I can only hope this kiss lets him know whatever is happening between us means the world to me. This isn't some rebound from Austin. This isn't some misguided decision or a quest for wild adventures post-breakup. Jax makes me feel safe and adored. I only hope I can do the same for him because this is something that can very easily bloom into the greatest love I've ever felt.

———

"Okay, this is so not fair." Jax tosses his head back. "If I can't play a John Michael Montgomery song three times on the car ride, then you definitely can't play 'All I Want for Christmas is a Cowboy' three times in a *row*."

"Grinch."

"I'm *not* a Grinch." He huffs, making me burst into laughter.

I pull my phone from my pocket *again* and check how much time we have left of the drive. When I work out that there's only forty-eight minutes until we reach Roots, my stomach sinks.

"What's going through that beautiful mind of yours?" Jax reaches his hand out to rest on my thigh. "You seem nervous."

"Are you sure you're okay with hiding this when we get back?"

"I want you to feel comfortable." He doesn't pull his eyes from the road. "If this is what it takes to allow us to explore a relationship without any external pressure, then I'm on board."

There's a hint of something on his face that makes me think there's more to it. The tiny, irritating voice that developed during my relationship with Austin and always told me I wasn't good enough chimes in, but I do my best to fight it off. After seeing all the incredible things he wrote about me on the bathroom mirror this morning, I know he's not ashamed of me. Still, we will have a lot to figure out.

And what if our attempt at a relationship fails? It was easy to get swept away in Tulsa, but as we hurtle back toward reality, I'm terrified I'm setting myself up for heartbreak again.

"Are you worried about giving this a shot?" I turn the music down. "I've seen how difficult it is to avoid someone in a small town when things don't work out, and Austin wasn't Charlie's best friend. Are we being dumb?"

"Maybe we are, but there's only one way to find out. And I'd much rather try and have it not work out than live the rest of my life wondering what we could've been."

I bite back a smile. "You're a smooth talker, Jax Greer."

"Does it make you want to kiss me?" He smirks.

"I always want to kiss you."

He pulls off the highway and turns into the parking lot of a large building decorated with wooden slats and a neon image of a man on a bucking bronco.

"What are you doing?"

Jax wordlessly pulls me toward him on the bench seat of his truck and tangles his fingers in my hair as our lips meet. When he pulls away, he says, "I wanted to give you the opportunity to kiss me."

"And you needed to exit the highway for that?"

"Well, technically, it wouldn't be safe to kiss you while driving, but I also needed to pull off the highway so we can have one last adventure where we don't have to hide. Give me one more hour of just us."

"But I already told my parents when we left." I chew on my lips. "They'll be expecting me back soon. They're going to ask questions."

"If anyone asks, we had a flat tire, okay?"

"Okay."

"That's my girl." He leans in to give me one more kiss.

Those words paired with the kiss remind me how excited I am to explore a relationship with Jax. Despite all the reasons I have not to trust him with my heart, I do. And as if by magic, the fear I had a moment ago is erased.

Jax swings the truck door open, and I follow behind, ready for one last adventure.

Chapter Twenty-Three

Jax

As we walk into the dingy bar, I'm starting to think we aren't going to spend much more than five minutes here, let alone an hour.

I grab Lauren's hand as an old man with glassy eyes sitting on a barstool gives Lauren the elevator look. I stare him down, shielding her from him as we approach the bar.

"Excuse me?" I call to a woman who is scrolling on her phone and chewing gum. She looks bored out of her mind, and I can't blame her. This place is nearly empty.

Her gaze flits up to Lauren and me, curiosity sparking in her eyes. "What can I help y'all with?"

"Can you tell us if there's anything fun to do around here?" I wince. "Besides drink at a bar, of course."

Unfazed by my accidental insult, she points a finger behind her, saying, "There are a few restaurants about a minute that way." She thrusts her hand in our direction. "And there's a Christmas tree farm with some local vendors in the empty lot over there."

I look at Lauren and find her zipping with energy. She's clinging to my arm, her beautiful hazel eyes blown wide.

A smile slips onto my face. "Yes, we can go."

She spins on her heel and marches us out, bouncing with energy.

"I've never met anyone who loves Christmas as much as you," I remark.

"That's because you came down from Mount Crumpit. Here in Whoville, people like Christmas."

I toss my head back. "I'm never going to live this down. I don't hate Christmas, but I don't get *this* excited to go to a Christmas tree lot." I wave my hand up and down at her.

"Well, let me tell you, this time of year is a lot more fun when you get excited about Christmas."

Before walking down the paved road that's strung with lights and tinsel overhead, Lauren pauses, taking it all in with awe. I can't blame her, the bright colors, the shining lights, the positive energy that smacks you in the face the second you see it, all adds up to a sight that can take your breath away, but it still pales in comparison to the sight of Lauren now and always.

God, I can't believe I'm here with her right now. I wrap an arm around her waist, and she sidles up into my side with a shy smile that sets my cheeks ablaze. *What the hell?* I've never blushed with a woman before. I've always known exactly what to say and what to do, but with Lauren, I can't calculate every move, nor do I want to. I like getting to just be me when I'm with her.

"So, Little Miss Whoville, where do we start?"

She takes in the dozen or so booths surrounding us before grabbing my hand and darting toward a stand with hot chocolate. I buy us each a drink, Lauren a peppermint hot chocolate, and me an original.

With her paper cup in one hand and my palm in the other, she drags me from booth to booth. Vendors sell Christmas ornaments, fresh-baked cookies, homemade fir-scented soaps and candles, and even hand-carved wooden Santas. Lauren buys something from nearly every one.

"How are you going to explain all your souvenirs to your parents? Are you going to tell them you bought them from the AAA guy?" I tease.

"Of course not. If it comes up, I'll say I bought them in Tulsa. I had to support all the local businesses. I'm a business owner too. I get how difficult it is."

We reach the end of the aisle, and Lauren tugs me into the fenced-in tree lot.

"You understand what it's like to be passionate about your business and to try to make a name for yourself," Lauren says. "You've taken ownership in the bar. It's not that different."

Lauren releases my hand to inspect one of the Christmas trees to our right.

I take advantage of the distraction, muttering, "Yeah, I guess so."

Lauren turns back to me, scrunching her nose. "You guess so?"

"I don't know. The bar isn't exactly what I'd call a passion. It's more an opportunity I was presented with that I'm trying to take advantage of."

"What do you mean?" She slowly moves to the next tree.

I scratch the back of my head, wincing. "I care about proving to myself that I'm responsible, and I'd love to run a business I had a role in building, but the bar means little to me."

"Then why on earth would you try to take ownership of it?"

"I just told you."

"But you could do that with anything else." She leads the way to the next aisle.

"I got the job at the bar out of college because Aunt Carol was friends with the owner. Not too many people wanted to give me a job in Roots. It didn't matter I was a varsity football player, college educated, and stayed out of any trouble that didn't also involve Charlie. People still saw me as the troubled boy who came from a broken home."

"People don't see you like that." Lauren shakes her head, grabbing on to my arm. "Everyone loves you. Yes, there were rumors at the start, but as far as I know, no one knows the truth. Even if they did, they wouldn't hold it against you. People aren't like that in our little town."

She stands in the middle of the row of trees, taking them all in, but I can see her mulling something over. "You could've worked for the ranch. My dad would've given you a job in a heartbeat."

"Only because of Charlie." I toss a hand, brushing her off.

Still, I like imagining a life where that was my path. This weekend made me realize how much I love the work I do with Lauren on the ranch. It's given me more of a purpose than bartending ever has, and not just because I get to see Lauren. But the bar is my path. I've taken an ownership stake; I can't give all of that up.

"Where else did you look for a job?" Lauren pauses in front of one of the larger trees in the row, admiring it.

"I spoke with Mrs. Harving and Mr. Colt. Neither of them would give me a job."

"There's your problem!" She throws up her arms. "Did

you ever consider the fact that you asked two of the most stubborn people on planet earth? Not just in Roots, all of the planet. Neither of them likes sharing responsibility of their businesses. That has nothing to do with you. Chin up. You have no idea what people really think of you."

"This coming from the girl who didn't understand why I'd like her."

"That's because the only person who has ever supposedly loved me broke all his promises."

We reach the end of the row of trees, and instead of turning into the next aisle, I pause us under the colorful lights strung overhead, taking both her hands. "Don't let that asshole ruin things for you. You have great friends who adore you as you are. Your family loves you, and I care for you so much."

I press my lips gently to hers, stunned by the way such a simple touch can make my knees lock. *I'm in trouble.*

When we pull away, I lace my fingers in hers again and let her lead us down the next row of spruces. The music drifting softly from a speaker in the corner of the fencing grows louder as we round the corner.

Lauren scrunches her nose. "They did such a good job of creating the perfect Christmas vibe, and then they ruin it by playing non–Christmas music. Such a shame."

"Wait, this is a good song." I grin. "Dance with me."

"Is it John Michael Montgomery? I can't believe I didn't recognize him after you made me listen to him for a million hours this trip." She stamps her foot in mock indignation.

"It's Ryan Kinder." She flicks a curious gaze at me as I place my hand on her waist. "The song is called 'Still Believe in Crazy Love.' It's about how he's had his heart broken, but he still believes he'll find beautiful love someday."

"Cute."

As we sway to the music, she leans her cheek against my chest. "Do you still believe in crazy love?" I ask her.

She releases a deep sigh that makes my heart nearly fall out of my chest. *She doesn't. Whatever this is will never go anywhere. I should've known.*

"I don't know that I did a few months ago, but I'm starting to see it's possible to find friendship and love in the same place, and when you do, it creates something amazing." She blushes, turning away from me to watch two children, a boy and a girl, blaze by.

"I've realized it's possible to find someone who wants to lift you up, even when there's nothing in it for them other than to see you smile." She looks up at me, cautious hope in her eyes. "I think maybe that's crazy love, a safe love, a kind and giving love, the kind that doesn't turn you into someone you're not but instead helps you find the most authentic version of yourself. So, yeah, I think I still believe in crazy love, and I have you to thank for that."

My heart doesn't know what to do anymore. It went from feeling trampled to feeling like it's flying.

"What about you?" She peers up at me. "Do you believe in crazy love?"

"I think I might."

"What does it look like for you?"

We sway back and forth for a few more moments as I consider it. "I think it's someone who makes all the little moments feel spectacular. I want to share big, messy, tradition-filled holidays with someone, to cook and dance and laugh with someone who's mine."

Our eyes connect, and a smile blooms on her face. An unspoken promise lingers between us, but the song ends, and "Rockin' Around the Christmas Tree" blares through the speakers.

Lauren pulls away. "Now *this* is Christmas!"

I chuckle. I like this version of us, the one that gets to be together and show affection out in the open. I don't want to hide us, but I also want to give Lauren what she wants. I don't see any way to win.

I wrap an arm around her shoulder and press a kiss to the top of her head, trying not to think about that as I ask, "Should we head home now?"

"Do we have to?"

"A tire can only be flat for so long, Freckles." The sorrow in her eyes melts me, but I see this as my chance. When we get back to Roots, I'm going to show Lauren I can be someone she's proud to show off to everyone.

Exiting the Christmas tree lot with my arm still draped over her shoulder, I lean into her ear. "If you promise to go back with me, I'll promise to give you a date next weekend that will make you forget all about cutting this one short."

"Promise?"

"Promise."

Chapter Twenty-Four

Lauren

THE GIRLS

CALLIE

> Can we assume your silence over the last few days means you had a good time at the conference? Or do we have to kill Jax?

CALLIE

> Or someone else? I can kill someone else for you

Guilt swirls in my stomach. I have been MIA from the group chat over the last few days. I'd like to say it's because I've been so invested in the conference, but it has a lot more to do with recent romantic developments. I haven't wanted to be on my phone because I've been so absorbed in soaking up my time with him while I have it. I've been sucked into Jax's orbit, and it's time I return to real life. The last thing I want is for a man to become my whole world and then have it come crashing down again.

The Girls

ME

No killing necessary. I had a good time. I'll catch you up soon

CALLIE

Ohhhh our girl is growing up and she got some!

OLIVIA

Callie don't be embarrassing

OLIVIA

Wait did you Lo?

There was no "getting some"

OLIVIA

Omg Callie you were right!

CALLIE

I'm always right

OLIVIA

You can fill us in tomorrow at the puppy yoga event I'm hosting for the rescue

OLIVIA

You're coming right? You signed up last month

Of course I'm coming

CALLIE

I can't wait to hear all the details!!!

———

The second I walk through the door of the yoga studio, I'm met with squealing. Callie beelines toward me with a silly grin on her face and wraps me up in a hug.

Olivia's not far behind, though she approaches at a normal pace.

"Did I call it or did I call it?" Callie turns from me to Olivia and back again. "Are you two officially dating now?"

Perhaps overreacting, I clamp my hand over Callie's mouth, my eyes wide. "Keep it down. I don't need anyone to hear, especially not Little Miss Nosey in the corner." I tilt my head in the direction of Mrs. Liens. She retired a couple of years ago and has made it her full-time job to be in everyone's business.

"Do you not want people to know?" Olivia furrows her brow.

"Sort of. We're going to keep it a secret for a little while. I don't need everyone's opinions on us while I'm figuring this out. I know some people will think Jax is a rebound after I was with Austin for so long, but that's not what this is, and I don't need that idea getting into Jax's head." I smile shyly at my friends. "Everything felt so right this past weekend. I'm not ready for that to change."

Olivia nods along in understanding as Callie eagerly bounces up and down. "Oh, a secret relationship! This is going to be so fun for you. It's kind of hot, sneaking around."

"Yeah? Have you done a lot of sneaking around?" I nudge her side. "Got a secret love affair you haven't told us about?"

She rolls her eyes. "Nope, it's just me and Boots."

"Maybe we need to change that." I grab a rolled-up yoga mat from the bin in the corner. "You spend an awful lot of time with your cat."

She grabs her own mat, following me toward the back of

the studio. "I spend a lot of time with you two too, but I don't hear you complaining about that."

"Touché."

Ms. Easton unfolds her mat up front and clears her throat loudly, waiting for everyone to quiet down. "Thank you all for coming. I'm so happy I can support this wonderful cause. I'll let Olivia take over."

Olivia glides to the front of the room, turning to face her audience with a confidence and light she didn't have when she first came to Roots. It's wonderful to see what a new job, a support system, and some time to relax have done for her.

"Good evening, y'all! I'm Olivia Parker. I started working with Resilient Paws Rescue as a volunteer back in May, and now I'm heading up the marketing with the goal of helping keep the dogs fed, getting them the medical care they need, and, ultimately, finding the right home for all these amazing animals. This is the first time we've ever held puppy yoga for the rescue, but after today's turnout I hope to do it more regularly."

A few ladies in the front row nod along in agreement.

"The setup will be simple. Ms. Easton will lead us through an hour of yoga, and we'll allow the puppies to roam around freely in the room. Feel free to pause at any time to sit and hold the puppies. They love being loved on." She grins with affection. "The puppies that will be in here today are from Lubbock. We found them last month huddled underneath a water tank for warmth when an early snow blew through the city. They're about four months old, and they're now fully vaccinated and microchipped. The adoption process will be a foster-to-adopt, where you'll be considered a foster until the dog has been spayed or neutered. These puppies are the product of irresponsible breeding, and we don't want to perpetuate the problem."

She glances down at her phone, undoubtedly reviewing notes she took for the event. "We are having a DNA test done on them to confirm their breed, but we suspect they're Australian Shepherd, Border Collie mixes."

Olivia shares a smirking glance with Callie, and when I turn to her, she raises her eyebrows at me. They're hoping I'm going to fall in love today. They know I want a dog, and a working breed like this would be the right fit for the ranch, but puppies are a lot of responsibility, and I'm already entering a new relationship with Jax. It's the last thing I need.

Olivia wraps up her speech. "Thank you to Ms. Easton for agreeing to be our instructor today, and thank you to my friend, Callie, for getting us connected. Let me know if you have any questions, and have fun!"

Ms. Easton leads us through a gentle warmup, having us roll our heads in circles as we stand with our palms outstretched. Meanwhile, Olivia helps Carol unleash five little furballs into the room. One instantly comes up to me, her tongue hanging out as she jumps up on my legs. When I glance down at her sweet blue eyes, I melt.

"Yup, you're doomed." Callie chuckles.

Olivia finally rejoins us as we're led into downward dog. The same chocolate-colored mutt scrambles underneath me as I hold the pose. She licks my face until I have to collapse onto my knees to shield myself from the puppy's love.

"Someone has taken a liking to you." Olivia beams, then lowers her voice. "Speaking of, you have to explain how things happened between you and you know who."

"He Who Shall Not Be Named," Callie chimes in. "Ohhh, we can call him Voldemort!"

"We are not calling him Voldemort." I groan as we pop back up into Warrior I.

"I kind of like it." Olivia purses her lips, trying to hide her smile.

"Two against one. He will now be called Voldemort from here on out." Callie does a fist pump.

"You two are ridiculous."

"Hey, if you don't like it, then I guess you need to stop hiding your relationship."

"Oof." Olivia lets out a breath. "There's no recovering from that."

I glare at her, and she instantly holds her palms up before shifting into Warrior II. "Hey, I'm not the one who dished it out. I'm just acknowledging it was good."

Two furballs bustle our way as they try to bite the back of each other's necks. They pause for a brief moment when one of them knocks into Callie's leg, and she immediately drops to the ground with them.

"I don't know how I can possibly tell you two anything with the way this conversation has gone so far. It's like herding cats."

"I promise I'm still listening." Callie says from her spot on the floor, legs spread out so the two puppies can rough-house between them.

Ms. Easton leads us through a sequence of cobra pose to downward dog, and the chocolate-brown furball from earlier returns to me, nibbling on my ear. I try to shrug her off, but end up cross-legged on the floor with her in my lap after about thirty seconds.

I take the opportunity to move a little closer to Callie and Olivia, lowering my voice once again as I fill them in on my weekend. Every once in a while, my story is punctuated with an "Aww" or "Oh my god."

"I know you two are trying to keep things a secret, but are you officially dating now?"

I wince. "I don't know. I'm kind of torn between really liking... Voldemort"—I glance to the girls for their approval before continuing—"versus being absolutely terrified to trust someone with my heart again. And in a way, it being him makes it that much harder because he's never done a real relationship before. What makes me special?"

"I felt the same way with Rhett when he finally opened up to me," Olivia says. "He hadn't shown so much as an inkling of interest in a woman since he came to Roots, and that was years before I stepped foot in this town. I didn't get what made me special. But ultimately, I pushed away my fears and decided to trust him, and now I'm dating my best friend. Rhett has never given me a reason to doubt him." Olivia shifts back into cobra pose. "Sometimes you just have to take a chance and trust that someone's past doesn't dictate their future."

Callie nods emphatically. "She's right. When my parents left Roots, I kept my guard up for a little while. I was afraid to let anyone love me because it seemed like everyone who did just leaves, but that will lead you to a pretty lonely place. If you shut everyone out because of a few bad apples, you'll have no one." She scoops up the puppy at her feet. "Has Voldemort given you any reason not to trust him since you two expressed your feelings for one another?"

I shake my head.

"Then you have to give him a chance. They call it falling in love for a reason. It means you give up control. When I stopped guarding my heart, I found wonderful people like Ms. Easton, Rhett, and you two. You have to open your heart fully, or you won't stand a chance. You'll end up with the exact thing you're trying to avoid."

"Thank you." I continue stroking the puppy in my lap,

who has now fallen asleep. I'm thankful for her calming presence.

Callie watches me with a smile while Olivia leans over to pet the top of her head. "I hope you know you're taking this sweet girl home soon."

"I don't think so."

Olivia presses her lips together. "Whatever you say."

Chapter Twenty-Five

Jax

My phone rings as I haul groceries for my date with Lauren into the house. I had to buy the wine separately, on the other end of town, because I didn't want anyone asking questions. I didn't realize how complicated keeping up the ruse would be, and it's only been about five days.

I fish my phone from my pocket and answer the FaceTime call. "Hey, man. What's up?"

"You look busy," Charlie notes. "Am I calling at a bad time?"

"No, I have about an hour," I say, setting the bag down on the counter.

"Where are you going?" He tilts the phone as if that will help him see a different angle on his screen.

"Nowhere."

"Is that a bottle of wine?"

"Oh, yeah." I fold the bag over so that he can't see the

rest of the contents. "My mom and Aunt Carol asked me to pick one up. I'm having dinner with them."

"I thought you said you weren't going anywhere." He furrows his brow. "Also, none of you drink. If you did, we would've gotten into way more trouble in high school." His smile is big, but only until he remembers what's going on. "Wait, are you going to see a girl?"

"No, it's nothing."

"It's totally a girl. I can see it on your face. This isn't just any girl either. You *like* her." His face morphs into pure glee. "Holy crap! Is it Shelby Miller? I heard she's back in town."

"You think I'd be going to all this trouble for the girl Austin was seen out with a couple months after he broke Lauren's heart? No way."

"Then who is it?"

I sigh. "She wants to keep things low-profile. I'm just trying to respect her wishes."

"I hope not for long. You're not someone's dirty little secret."

I roll my eyes and flop into a chair at my dining room table. "It might not be such a bad thing she wants to keep it a secret. I'm not exactly the kind of guy you go parading around town with, as you made clear the other night."

He shifts his gaze down, a look of shame on his face. I think that's what I wanted, to know he regrets what he said.

"I'm sorry, man. I didn't mean to be so harsh." He scratches the back of his head, wincing. Charlie has never been the greatest at talking about his feelings with me. "I think the world of you. You're my best friend. I just want my sister to find someone who's willing to commit. It doesn't mean I don't think you're capable. I may or may not have had a crappy night when I called her. I shouldn't have taken it out on you. Plus, I thought calling you out would push you."

I can't help but sit a little straighter. *He sees my potential.*

Charlie waggles his brows. "I guess I didn't need to push you since you're over there pulling out all the stops for a lady."

Yep, I'm avoiding that landmine. "Do you want to talk about your crappy night?"

"Nah, that's in the past now." He shakes his head. "I just want you to know I'm not a shitty friend. I believe in you, and I love you, man."

I want to tell him my "lady" is his sister, and that I have full intention of committing, but it'd be unfair to Lauren if I burst out with this information without talking with her first, so instead, I say, "This is getting weird."

He laughs. "Okay, okay. In all seriousness, is she hot?"

I wince. This just got weirder.

When he starts to sense my hesitation, I blurt out, "She's more than hot. She's stunning, like walk-into-a-room-and-make-everyone-stop-what-they're-doing stunning. She's smart, kind, funny, and driven. She's incredible."

"Well, sheesh. This sounds like love. That was fast."

"I'm not in love," I rush to say, knowing it's not the full truth.

After a beat, Charlie adds, "I'm happy for you. I know it's scary to put your heart on the line, but there's no better feeling than opening up to someone."

"Do *you* have a girl I don't know about?" I tease, but I'm actually a little curious.

"No, I don't have time for girls with work, but I know what it's like to fall in love." His tone is soft and withdrawn, and I suddenly know exactly what he's talking about, or more accurately, who he's talking about. The only woman he's ever loved, and the woman he lost: Callie.

"You know she hasn't dated anyone since you left."

"Who?" He narrows his brows as if he's confused.

"Don't play dumb with me. You know who I'm talking about."

"I made my choice. I don't have the right to care about her love life."

"It doesn't mean you couldn't change your mind." I shift my phone in my hands, swallowing my pride. "We miss you here."

"I miss you too. I'm even starting to miss Roots a little. It's freaking me out." He chuckles, clearly trying to hide the lump forming in his throat.

"You're coming to town for the holidays, right?"

"Yeah, I'll be there in a week."

Glancing at the calendar, an idea pops into my head. If I'm going to be the kind of man Lauren would want to tell the world about, then I need to start practicing what I preach. "Will you come hunting with me while you're here?"

"Oh, hell yeah. It's been too long since we've headed up to the cabin."

"Agreed." A text from Lauren appears on my screen. "I better get going. I have a few things I gotta get organized here."

"Good luck on your date, love bug."

I scoff. "See you later."

When I hang up, I sit there for a moment, wondering what Charlie would think if he knew. After our conversation today, I'd like to think maybe he'd be okay with it. I guess time will tell.

Callie drops me off in Lauren's driveway to help us stay incognito. She talks the whole drive, but I can't focus on anything she has to say because my stomach is in free fall. I shouldn't be nervous. We've already been on a few sort-of dates, but I'm terrified that being back in town after some space will make her change her mind.

Despite the fear, there's also been more light in my days since I kissed Lauren. I care a little less about how I'm being perceived, and I have hope. I'm not ready to let that go so easily.

As I gather my bags, Charlie's words ring through my mind. He actually sounded proud of me, like maybe the problem has been the way I've portrayed myself. Maybe the secret to not turning into my father has always been to shift my perspective. I might be the only one who saw me as a monster. I'm confident this thing between Lauren and me is a positive thing, not only because I love being with her, but also because it gives me the chance to prove I'm not the man I'm scared of turning into.

Once Callie's truck is parked in the drive, Lauren rushes out of her house, thanking Callie for her help before turning to greet me.

With her excited and innocent gaze on me, I melt. "Hi, Freckles."

"Hi. Can I help you with your bag of goodies?"

She reaches out, but I know she just wants to look inside. Tugging the groceries to my other side, I brush past her. "No way. This is a surprise."

"Come on. Please." She draws out the *e* and gives me her best puppy-dog eyes. "I hate surprises anyway."

"You just don't like giving up control. It's good for you to do every once in a while."

"I think I got my fair share in Tulsa." She reaches out again.

I thrust an arm out to stop her. "If you want to see what's in this bag then let me inside. You can see it all there."

"Fine."

She opens her front door, revealing the upbeat tune of "All I Want for Christmas is a Cowboy."

"You know, I wouldn't exactly call blasting music going incognito. Are you trying to get the attention of all the cowboys who pass by?"

She and I both know not many people come to this corner of the ranch. She's tucked away from everything and everyone. I think that's part of why she chose to live out here instead of closer to the bunkhouse or the big house. With everything Lauren does in the day-to-day, she could use the peace and quiet... to blast her music, I guess.

Rolling her eyes, Lauren closes the door behind her. "I do this all the time."

"Would you like to dance?"

Her eyes light up. "Really?"

I nod, extending a hand and spinning her around. The song is nearly over, but I love the spark in her eyes as we sway for a few seconds.

When it ends, she turns the music down. "Speaking of dancing. Would you be willing to go to swing lessons again? I had a really good time last time, and I'd like to know more than one dance. I could go without you, but I don't want another partner." She twists her hands in front of her, speaking faster now. "I know we're trying to keep this a secret, so we'll have to figure out a way not to make it too obvious, but—"

I pull her into my arms to stop her rambling. "Of course I'll go with you. You can go with the girls, and then I'll offer to cut in like last time. Maybe we'll get lucky and there'll be an odd number."

"I could probably ask Callie or Olivia to sit out if there's an even number, but I don't want to ask them to do that."

"You know they'd do it for you in a heartbeat."

"I do, but I don't know that I should ask them to." She leans on the counter, trying to peer into my bag.

I pin her with a glare. "I see what you're doing, Freckles." Folding the top half of the bag over, I add, "I don't think Olivia would mind stepping out for dance lessons. She kind of sucks."

"Hey, she tries!"

"She does." I laugh. "Well, it's settled. I'll do lessons with you again. You just have to promise not to make out with me in the middle of the dance floor."

She rolls her eyes. "Oh, please. If anyone has to hide anything it's you. *You're* the one who's going to want to kiss *me*."

"We'll see about that."

Chapter Twenty-Six

Lauren

I SWING MY LEGS FROM THE BARSTOOL AT THE KITCHEN island, taking in a deep breath and trying to focus on the handsome man in front of me right now. It's been hard to relax this evening. My goal for the day was to map out at least four of the paddocks for AMP grazing, but I only got two done because I got a call about one of our cattle getting caught in the fence. It took four of us to get it out, and when we did, her leg was scratched up enough that we had to call the vet. I barely finished in time to see Jax, and now I'm both behind and exhausted.

But here he is, cooking me dinner and looking incredible in that tight white tee and those gray sweatpants. Knowing how much I love the taste of red wine with my pasta, he brought me a pretty expensive bottle, which he won't even have a sip of.

I'm trying to enjoy it all, but it's nearly impossible to let go of everything I should be doing instead of sitting around having dinner cooked for me. Plus, putting on a face is really difficult with Jax. It's like he sees my soul, which is marvelous but frustrating when I'm trying not to ruin our evening.

In an attempt to at least shift my thoughts, I focus on how to be the best girlfriend for Jax. Spinning my wineglass around in my hand nervously, I ask, "Are you sure you're okay with me drinking if *you're* not going to drink?"

Jax pulls a fettuccini noodle from the pot, blowing on it and holding it out for me to test. "I'm a bartender. People drink in front of me all the time. I'm fine."

"Why did you decide to bartend given all the bad memories you have involving alcohol?" I take the noodle off the spoon, sampling it. "Those are perfect. Pull 'em."

He turns the burner off and shifts his attention to the alfredo sauce, stirring it carefully.

"I mean, part of it was just taking the opportunity that was given to me."

"But there's something else you haven't told me."

"I like being there to look out for people." He doesn't lift his gaze from the pot. "I know alcohol can make people do dumb stuff, and this has given me the chance to step in and advocate for those who find themselves in vulnerable positions."

"Like when Austin harassed me that night."

"Yeah, I guess it triggered me to see him grab you like that."

I don't know how I never connected the dots.

He moves the sauce off the burner. "Are you ready to eat?"

I don't press the issue as I slip off my barstool and walk into his outstretched arms. When my chest meets his, he wraps his arms around me and places his chin on top of my head. I love the way his six-foot-four frame engulfs me. It makes me feel safe.

"Not to sound clingy already, but I kind of missed you this week," I murmur against his chest.

He presses a kiss to the crown of my head. "I missed you too. I'm sorry I couldn't be at the ranch more. The bar nearly fell apart without me last weekend. I've spent almost every day since cleaning up messes that shouldn't have happened in the first place."

"It's okay. I managed."

"Tell me about your week. What have I missed?" He dishes up two plates of pasta, bringing them to the kitchen table and lighting a single candle in the center.

I sit down next to him and immediately pull my phone from my pocket to show him pictures of the puppy from yoga. "I guess the big highlight is that you have some competition. I fell in love this week."

I thrust my phone in his direction, showing him a photo of the tiny girl with her paws crossed over each other. "Look at her! She's just the cutest thing I've ever seen. We joked that she is such a lady for crossing her paws like that." I swipe over. "Olivia took this video of us as we were leaving. She wouldn't stop following me. It was so cute."

"She has freckles just like you do." He points to light brown flecks that cover her snout, the whites of her paws, and the spot between her eyes.

"Oh my gosh! She does. That just makes me love her more."

"And to think you used to not like freckles." He twirls pasta on his fork, looking smug.

"I didn't like *my* freckles. There's a difference."

"Well, either way, it sounds like it's meant to be." He shrugs. "Does this mean you're going to get a dog?"

"I don't know." I set my phone down on the table, grabbing my fork. "Sometimes I feel like I can hardly take care of *myself.*"

"An animal is a huge responsibility. I'm glad you don't take that lightly. I think that means you'll be an intentional dog owner."

He hums. "Sometimes it takes caring for someone else to help us learn how to prioritize ourselves. She might be what you need to finally let yourself enjoy a walk here and there and to finally go to bed at a reasonable hour. You should consider getting her, especially if it means helping a dog in need. I like seeing the way you light up, and looking at these pictures, it looks like she's rather fond of you too."

I glance down at the picture on my phone again. "Just like that." Jax points to the involuntary smile that's grown on my face. "Do you know what you'd call her?"

"Bella." I hold up the picture. "Doesn't she look like a Bella?"

"She does."

"When I'm ready, I'll adopt, and it won't just be one dog. I want a couple, but I need to work on a few things for myself first."

"That's very honorable."

I plaster on a smile, hoping I didn't say too much. I don't want to ruin our evening by telling him how exhausted I've been lately. Between Austin invalidating my feelings when we were together and me taking over for Charlie when he left, I've learned to keep things pushed down. But Jax is so wonderful. Maybe I *should* tell him. Maybe he'd *want* to know. He'd probably even be supportive.

"You look distracted, Freckles. What's going through that beautiful head of yours?" Jax's rough voice pulls me from my thoughts, and I'm honestly a little relieved.

"I was just thinking about how incredible this pasta is. Where'd you learn to make it?" I shove a mountainous bite into my mouth.

He assesses me with a look of doubt for a little too long, but finally he decides not to press me any further. "My mom got it from a neighbor when we lived in Oklahoma. I think she knew what was going on in our house. Mom refused to accept help, but she'd occasionally accept dishes the neighbor would bring over." He shakes his head. "A couple years later, after she mastered the recipe, Mom taught me how to make it."

"That was nice of your neighbor to share her recipe. *I'm* certainly grateful." I twirl another large bite to prove my point.

As we finish our meal, Jax's gaze on me doesn't waver, like he knows I'm hiding something and staring me down is going to help him get to the bottom of it. Still, he doesn't try to pull it out of me.

I polish off my glass of wine, and by the time I swipe our empty plates from the table, we've both settled back into some semblance of ease.

Setting the plates in the kitchen sink, I say, "Thank you again, Jax. This was delicious." I swipe the sponge over my empty dish before pausing. "You know, it's kind of annoying that your name is so short. It's hard to give you a cute nickname."

"My nickname for you has nothing to do with your name. I guess I'm more creative than you." He shrugs, moving in next to me to dry a dish.

I press my lips together. "Honestly, you probably are because I've got nothing." I empty the leftover meal into a Tupperware before putting the pan in the sink.

"Let me clean that."

"No way. You cooked. I clean."

"I wanted to make tonight special for you. Let me do both."

"That's sweet, but no." I snatch the pan back. "Maybe your nickname should be Hog since you like to hog all the chores."

"That's a horrible nickname."

"Grinch could always make a comeback."

"No, absolutely not." He hip-checks me before crossing the kitchen to put the dry pan away.

"I can make it cuter and call you Grinchie."

"That's even worse!"

"Come on. I need something special to call you." An idea flashes in my head. "Maybe I need to lengthen your name instead of trying to shorten it. I'll call you Jaxon."

He bursts into laughter. "I don't know how to tell you that's an awful idea."

"You just did." I playfully shove his shoulder.

"Maybe you need to give this a little more time. Don't rush it and pick a name you'll regret."

"Okay, fine, Grinchie."

"I'm ignoring you." He holds his finger up in a matter-of-fact way before setting down the dish towel he used to dry the pan. He closes the two-foot gap between us, kissing me slowly. "How about we find something to do while you think a little more about that nickname?"

"Like what?"

"Well, we can't exactly go out in public, so do you want to play a game or something?"

"I have a game I used to play in college that could be fun!"

"Can just two people play it?"

"Of course."

I dash down the hallway, opening the tiny closet at the end and rummaging around. I quickly return to the living room with a box of cards, setting it down on the table and patting the spot on the couch next to me.

"The game you used to play in college is Uno?" Jax doesn't fight his laughter.

"Kind of. It's a more adult version of Uno. Sit, I'll explain it."

When he does, I immediately snuggle into his side. He smells so good, and his warmth is enough to spark a fire.

"Okay, so we'll play Uno like normal, but we have to do certain actions for certain cards. In college, any time someone played a skip or reverse card, the receiver had to drink. We can change that rule though." I press my finger to my lips as I think. "How about any time you play a skip or reverse card on someone, you get to ask them a question?"

"How do you play a reverse card on someone?"

"It's just whoever was supposed to go next but doesn't get to go because the card was played. Since there are only two of us, the person who doesn't play the card will tell a truth. Next rule: any time a change color card comes up, the player gets to choose a person to dare to do something. Again, in our case, any time I play one, I will give *you* a dare, and any time you do, you'll give *me* a dare."

His brows knit. "You really played this in college?"

"All the time. We did the stupidest thi—I mean, it's fun."

"I'm about to get into trouble, aren't I?"

"I'd never get you into trouble. I'm a perfect angel, remember?"

Chapter Twenty-Seven

Jax

"Okay, you definitely rigged these cards!" I reach for Lauren's hand to get a peek. "There's no way you have that many skips. You must have all of them."

She pulls them close to her chest, swatting me away. "Quit complaining. You have all the reverse cards."

"But you've also had *two* color change cards already."

"I'm not the one who shuffled the deck. The only person you have to blame is yourself."

"You suck." I throw down the only skip card I had in my hand and ask her the question I've been building up to for a while now. "Why are you taking a chance on me?"

"What do you mean?"

I quickly lose my nerve. It seemed like a good question to ask. Lauren makes me feel like a good man when I'm with her, but every time I think about the way we're hiding our relationship, my brain tells me it's because I'm not enough. I need to hear her assurance again.

Setting my cards facedown on the coffee table in front

of me, I explain. "I know I'm not known as a relationship guy, but here you are diving into one with me without asking any questions. I want to know what made you believe in me."

"I see the good in you, even if you don't see it yourself." That right there is enough to send warmth to my chest.

"You've done so many things to make me feel loved and supported, and I trust in your actions more than your lack of experience with relationships. I've seen that desire in you to be a good man when you've offered me your jacket, sent me thoughtful good-mornings texts, or stepped in to help with the ranch. Nothing you've done has led me to believe you can't be in a committed relationship if that's what you want to do."

Unsure how else to respond, I pick up my cards, throwing one down since I just skipped her turn. "Uno."

Disappointment floods her face, but she quickly recovers as she hovers over me. "Hmmm, what color do you have in your hand there, Grinchie?"

Her voice drips with sweetness, and I know she's trying to beat me at this game, but it does things to me anyway.

Refocusing, I say, "I'll never tell."

She studies me, carefully changing the blue six to a red six.

I toss my head back as I draw another ten cards until I get something I can play. "I hope you're ready to be annihilated because I have some good ones now."

I have literally no ammo to back my claim up, so on my next turn, I settle for playing a green card that's the same number as the last one she played. At least that will make the color something I can play on again.

My plan gets blown to pieces when she puts down a color change card. "Red."

"You're kidding."

"Nope." I hate that the smug smile on her face is so cute. It makes it difficult to stay mad.

"Don't make me do another dare. Your dares are lame."

"Well, excuse me for being nice with my dares, unlike someone." She places her hands on her hips.

"At least I actually do the things I'm dared to do."

Pressing her lips in a firm line, she ignores my remark. "I dare you to tell me where your head is at with our physical relationship."

"That feels like a truth to me."

"It's my dare. I get to pick how I want to use it."

"Okay. What do you want to know?"

She bites her lip. "You're known in town for sleeping around. I get that things are just starting between us, but I want to establish expectations before we get too far down the road."

"That's fair." Again, I place my cards down and open my arms for her to crawl into. "I'm sorry we haven't talked about it. I didn't want you to feel pressured. You're special to me, and I want to do things differently with you. I'd like the next physical steps in our relationship to mean something. I've never been in love with the girls I've been with. I told you you're not just another girl to me, and I want to prove it."

I rub her arm. "Don't get me wrong, I can hardly keep my hands off you, but I want to make that moment special when it comes."

"I'd like that." She peels herself off me. "Now you're going to have to try to keep your hands to yourself for a little while longer because you've still got a stack of cards left."

"Maybe we can ditch the cards?"

"No way! You wouldn't have said that if you were still about to win."

"Maybe not."

"It's your turn."

We go back and forth with no special cards for a little while. I guess I'm feeling nice. When I can't keep it up any longer, I throw down a reverse card to flip the turn back to me and then change the color to yellow. "I'll be nice to you and let you pick one. Truth or dare, Freckles?"

"Truth."

"What are you going to check off your list next?"

She bites her lip. "I don't know. There's really not much left on there."

With no warning, she leaps up from the couch, grabbing my hand and dragging me to her bedroom. We walk right up to the list, and she reads through the items that are left. "The first three are all checked off. Good job me." She pats herself on the back with a smile. *Why is she so cute?*

"Go to a concert. I checked that off in Tulsa."

"You did. Unless you had something else in mind. Was there a specific concert you wanted to go to?"

"No, I just wanted to go to one. I've only been to one concert in my life, and I was five. I hardly remember it." She continues reading the items that still need to be done on her list. "Do something for just me. Regenerative agriculture conversion on the ranch, which is in the works. Ride Lucky for fun again..." She turns back to me. "I don't think I can check off the regenerative agriculture idea for a while. The transition is going to take some time, but it could be fun to ride Lucky. Will you go with me?"

"You know I will. Just name the time and place."

"What about right now?"

I chuckle. "Name another time and place."

She bites the inside of her cheek, pulling her phone out to scroll through her calendar. I didn't realize it'd be such a hassle to pick a day.

With her nose still in her phone, she says, "What about an early morning ride? I don't have much time during the day, and it'd be nice to watch the sunrise like I used to in high school."

"Okay, how about we do dance lessons on Thursday night, and I'll stay over at your place so we can do an early horseback ride on Friday?"

She scrolls up and down. "I think that should work."

We make our way back into her living room, playing a few more cards before I change the color again. "Blue. Will you do a dare, or should I just do a truth?"

"Truth. I'm not falling into your dare traps anymore." She crosses her arms.

"I ask you for a one-minute lap dance *one* time as a joke, and suddenly I've scared you off?"

"Yes! I don't know how to do that." She tilts her cards slightly, gesturing in my direction. "What's your question?"

"What are you holding back from me?"

She frowns. "What are you talking about?"

"Something has been off all night. I've been trying to let it slide, but you could hardly find time to ride Lucky, and every time I look into your eyes, I see that you're tired."

"It's just been a long week." She sighs. "I'm sorry. I'm having a good time. I promise."

"You don't need to apologize. You're always running around and conquering the world, but it seems to me like you never take time for yourself, unless I make you."

As I say it, one question echoes in my mind: *Am I not good enough to share your struggles with?* Maybe processing Charlie's words and hearing the story about my mom has led her to the realization that I don't protect the people I love. But this moment needs to be about Lauren, not me. I'll just have to show her I can be enough.

She plucks at the threads on the rug beneath us. "I guess I don't know how to slow down. Even if I wanted to, I don't have a choice right now. Resting means the things on my never-ending to-do list won't get done. I have people counting on me."

"Things will still get done. I don't think you're capable of leaving a project and not coming back to it to see it through. You might find that taking time to rest will allow you to do things better than you otherwise would've done."

She raises her eyebrows and presses her lips together in a look of doubt. She's still not sharing exactly what's going on under the surface, and it kills me because I can't fix it if I don't know what's wrong.

Narrowing her gaze on me, she says, "I see that 'I can fix it' look on your face. I'm fine. Don't worry about me."

But I don't believe her. I grab her, holding her close. "I'm not the same man I used to be. I'm not just going to stand by and watch you suffer."

Chapter Twenty-Eight

Lauren

THE TRUTH IS, I'M EXHAUSTED, AND I DON'T HAVE TIME to rest. I wake up before five most mornings and spend several hours doing research, making sure all of our records are up to date, and finalizing our cover cropping plan. By six or seven, I'm out in the fields with the cowboys, moving cattle, mending fences, or tending to a sick calf.

When I finally come home, I barely have the energy to cook before I fall asleep on the couch, and on the days I have free time, I fill all the little cracks with time spent with Jax, Callie and Olivia, or my parents. If I told Jax that, he'd probably feel guilty for taking my time, but I *want* to spend time with him. Unfortunately, indulging in time with the people I love also means I don't have any to spend alone. I haven't even picked up the books Jax bought me in Tulsa, and I feel terrible about it.

Nevertheless, I don't know that I *want* the free time. I can't get my brain to turn off long enough to enjoy it. I'd just sit there reading the same page over and over again, ruminating on the fact that I should be working on my plans to make sure we're ready to implement regenerative ag this spring.

Ultimately, it's much better for me to spend all my time busy. This way I'm either working on things I need to get done or spending time with people whose company is enough to temporarily distract me from the things that need to get done.

It's torture not letting Jax in, but it's for his own good. He's done so much to help me since we created that list. I can't stand the thought of unloading on him. It'd be like telling him that everything he's done for me is a waste because I'm still drowning. I care for him too much to let him think that when I'm the problem. I need to figure out how to balance my life on my own. I'm grateful for his support in everything I do, but I don't want our relationship to be about Jax fixing me.

"How long have you felt like this?" He breaks my thoughts, and I look up at him.

"Like what?"

"I see the exhaustion on your face. If you won't tell me the extent of it, at least tell me how long you've felt this way."

"I don't know. Several months. I don't want to talk about it."

His eyes look sad, almost desperate, when he asks, "Why?"

It's then I realize that not sharing what's going on might be hurting him too. I need to give him something. "I don't talk about my problems." I shrug. "It doesn't do anyone any good. I just need to put my head down and work."

"You need to talk to someone about how you're feeling.

It's not good to keep everything bottled up." He rubs my back.

"It's worse to express it all. When I tried talking with Austin about it, he'd only remind me that he was dealing with similar stresses and was managing okay."

"That was Austin. He's an asshole!" His voice has a sharp edge that draws my attention immediately, but when he turns toward me, his voice softens again. "He had no right to invalidate your feelings like that. If you say you're tired and overwhelmed, it's no one's place to tell you you're not."

I nod.

"I'm not him. I want to know how you're feeling."

I didn't realize how badly I needed to hear someone say that. The overwhelming sense of validation causes a tear to slither down my cheek. *No. No. No. No. No.*

I quickly swipe it away. "Gosh, I'm sorry. I'm ruining our date. I don't want you to worry about me, okay? That's why I didn't want to tell you."

Something that almost looks like relief fills his eyes. "So it's not that you don't trust me?"

"Of course not. You're wonderful."

A dopey smile settles on his lips. "I'm glad you feel comfortable enough to express emotion in front of me." He gently swipes another tear from my cheek. "I know you want to spend time together, but I'd be a terrible boyfriend if I let all of this go and didn't work with you to find a way to get you some quality self-care time, so wait right here and give me five minutes. I'm going to help you relax."

"No, it's o—" But he's already gone.

———

As promised, Jax returns after ten minutes, a giant grin on his face.

When he grabs my hand, drawing me toward my bedroom, I can't help but ask, "What're you up to, Grinchie?"

"Is that really what you landed on?"

"No, but I like the way it makes you scrunch up your nose." I tap his nose. "It's endearing."

"I guess I'll have to try to stop scrunching my nose," he says, involuntarily scrunching it again and making me laugh.

When we reach the doorway of my bathroom, he pauses, letting me take in the scene before me. The bathroom light is off, but a couple of my tea light candles line a full bubble bath. My book rests on the ledge of the tub along with my Bluetooth speaker. The room smells like my lavender essential oil too.

"I'm impressed." I turn to him. "You threw all of this together in ten minutes? How'd you know what to do with the essential oils?"

"I didn't, but Google had some tips."

"This is incredible. Thank you." I pull him toward me, giving him a tender kiss.

"Okay, you better stop that or I'm not going to want to leave you alone, which defeats the whole purpose of this." He pulls away from me. "This is your time. Don't think. Just let yourself be. None of your problems matter right now. We'll deal with them tomorrow, okay?"

I give him a soft nod. I don't know how he manages to do that, but his words are really comforting. I actually believe them, and I think I can put aside the chaos in my mind for a few moments to let myself relax.

I sink into the tub, opening my book to the first page. I

don't come out until the water is cold and I'm about forty pages into my book. Jax is fast asleep on my bed, his phone resting on his chest. I can tell he fought hard to stay awake for me. I don't know how I got so lucky, but I'm not going to waste this. I remember Olivia and Callie's advice, and it hits me that I can't expect our relationship to go anywhere if I don't open up to him, and gosh, do I want it to go somewhere because my feelings for Jax are awakening parts of me I didn't even know existed. With him, I'm somehow funnier and kinder and better. He makes my smile brighter and my laugh deeper. At the end of the day, I *know* Jax will support me no matter what because it turns out the right person will be there to lift me up instead of tear me down. I can't believe I almost settled for less.

———

"This cold front just came out of nowhere. We've had such a mild winter this year." Cooper, one of our newest cowboys, brushes his hands off.

"We should've prepared for this anyway," I say, lugging the heater to the corner of the barn. "We should always be prepared."

"This isn't on you." Rhett touches my shoulder. His eyes are earnest, but his touch is stiff. I don't think he's used to comforting anyone besides Olivia. "None of us thought to plan ahead for this. We still have time to get it sorted out before the freezing temperatures hit tomorrow evening. We'll be fine."

"But I'm the one in charge now. I have all sorts of lists organized. I did research on emergency prevention before I took over the ranch. I *knew* we were supposed to prepare for this." I sit down on a bale of hay, placing my head in my hands. "How did I let this slip my mind?"

"You've had a lot on your plate. It shouldn't all be on you. That's what I'm here for." Rhett draws back, standing taller. Since Austin left the ranch, he's taken over as head cowboy. As much as I'd love to have full control over the ranch, I quickly realized I can't do it all, especially not up to my standards. If I'm going to trust anyone, it would be Rhett. He loves what he does, and he's great at it.

"You're sure your dad can't help with this?" Waylon asks.

"I told you, he's busy." The words come out in a growl, which immediately floods me with guilt. Waylon doesn't deserve that. He's sweet and has a heart of gold. It's just that my dad doesn't need the stress of managing the ranch.

I stand, joining Waylon by the water tank. "We need to learn how to do things without him anyway."

I nearly choke on the words as they come out, but it's true. Someday, my dad won't be around. Ideally, it'll be that he's able to retire from the ranching business. He's been doing well, and the doctors are optimistic his lifestyle changes can help decrease his blood pressure and resolve the issues he was having, but they also warned us he has to stick with these changes or his condition will worsen. As much as I hate it, today only shows we always need to plan for the unexpected.

"The good news is this heater should last a couple years," Rhett says, giving me a kind smile. He must sense how tense I am right now. I'll feel better when I know this is taken care of and I can enjoy my dance lessons with Jax tonight.

Cooper and Waylon work on the heater while Rhett and I line insulation along all the pipes. We want to make sure the water line doesn't freeze. We only have two tanks for the whole herd, and if one goes, there's no good way to make sure the cattle are all taken care of.

Bang! The two men on the water tank shuffle around as a surge of water sprays out.

"Shit!" Waylon shouts, stepping back and throwing his hands up in the air.

"Don't just stand there! Turn the water off," Cooper hollers at him.

In an instant, Rhett and I are standing over the top of them taking in the scene.

"What the hell happened?" Rhett growls.

"We punctured the tank."

"I thought you said this would be easy to install."

"It's supposed to be," Cooper says sheepishly.

"Is the heater still okay to use?"

Cooper bites his cheek.

"No, this thing is toast," Waylon announces, looking grim.

"What about the water tank?"

"We can try to patch it, but no guarantees it'll be effective."

"Oh my god." I suck in a breath. *This isn't happening.* "There's no way we can get another heater on such short notice."

"We can drive out somewhere. I'll drive all night if I have to," Waylon offers.

"No one is going anywhere until we know where we can find a heater. There's no sense in sending you out on a wild goose chase." I swivel on my heel, already making a mental list of places that might be able to help. "I'll make some calls."

I step out of the barn, calling everyone I know to see if

they have a spare heater. No luck. I call all the local stores followed by the ones I know of within an eight-hour drive. Nothing.

Overwhelm swirls inside of me, and instead of calling stores farther out, I call the only person I know who can make this better.

Chapter Twenty-Nine

Jax

My heart soars when I lift my ringing phone to
see Lauren's name on my screen.

I slide the button to answer. "There's my girl! Are you
ready for tonight? I've been practicing in my room. I'm a pro
now."

"Shoot! I forgot all about our lessons."

The panic in her voice makes my stomach turn. "Are
you okay? What's going on?"

"We're getting prepped for the cold front that's
supposed to sweep in tomorrow night, but there was an
accident when we were installing one of the heaters. It's
useless now, and there's a hole in the water tank too. I don't
know how we'll be able to get it all sorted out in time. I've
called every place I can think of, and everyone is sold out."

"I'll be right there." I grab my keys from my pocket.

"What? No, you don't need to do anything." I picture
her tensing up and holding her hands out in protest. "I'm

sorry. I'm just overwhelmed, and you were the first person I thought to call."

"I'm honored. Now hang on, I'll be there in five. I just gotta ask someone to cover for me at the bar."

"You don't need to—"

"I'll be right there, Freckles." I hang up, heading out the back door to my truck as I make another call.

In just under five minutes, I'm pulling into the Copper Hill driveway with reinforcements.

Callie bounds up to Lauren, wrapping her in a hug. "What can we do to help? I'm pretty good with the winterization stuff. I helped with your barn back in high school because—" She stops in her tracks. "I just know the process. I'm happy to help finish whatever needs to be done while the heater situation gets figured out."

A hint of relief crosses Lauren's face. "That'd be great."

Without waiting for further instructions, Callie surges off toward the barn.

Olivia steps forward. "What can I do?"

"Can you help me make more calls?"

Olivia nods, pulling out her phone and stepping aside for some privacy, leaving just Lauren and me.

"See?" I smile. "No need to be overwhelmed. You have a whole swarm of people who love you and are here to support you." I glance around before wrapping her in my arms and pressing a kiss to her forehead.

"You didn't need to do this." Her voice is weak. "I would've figured it out."

"I know, but I didn't want you to think you have to do it all alone."

"Thank you."

I hear a loud cough, and glance up to find Olivia, phone

to her ear, eyes wide as Mr. Rhodes walks toward us. Lauren leaps from my arms, and I don't have time to linger on the way that stings. Her dad looks paler than normal, and he doesn't carry himself with the same pride I've come to know.

Lauren rushes toward him, grabbing on to his arm and asking, "What are you doing out here?"

Mr. Rhodes straightens. "I came to see what all this commotion is about. What are y'all doing here?"

"We came to help." Olivia beams as she joins us.

"With?"

"Nothing," Lauren rushes out at the same time Olivia says, "With the water heater situation. Callie's working on the insulation, and I'm on call duty."

Lauren looks like she's about to pass out from stress or embarrassment, but Mr. Rhodes doesn't even look fazed. "And what about you, Mr. Greer?"

"I'll go wherever I'm needed."

"With the weather coming in, we'll need to move the cattle closer to the barn." Mr. Rhodes crosses his arms. "Are you still handy on a horse or have you gone soft working as a bartender?"

"Hey, I've been helping out around here a lot. Besides, I'd never forget what you taught me, sir."

"Good man." He claps his hand on my shoulder with a grin.

I head toward the barn to grab a horse as Mr. Rhodes turns to Lauren. "It's awfully nice of Jax to help out so much, huh?"

There's amusement in his tone that makes me think he's suspicious. *Already?* Apparently we suck at keeping this a secret.

"Yeah, I think Charlie's been asking him to keep an eye on me," she explains.

"Oh, I'm sure. I know how he just *hates* being around you." Mr. Rhodes chuckles.

———

"Should we say a toast or something?" Olivia smiles, looking sentimental. "It's kind of cool to have a group of us together like this."

I can only imagine how much gatherings like this mean to her considering she had no support system in San Francisco when she left.

"Can we do the toast after dinner, Wildflower?" Rhett hunches forward in exhaustion. "I'm starving, and based on the faces of everyone else here, I'm going to say they are too."

Olivia looks from Lauren to Callie to me. We're all grimacing.

"How long do you think my toast is going to be? I could've been done by now if you hadn't complained."

She holds up her glass of water. "I just wanted to say cheers to good friends who support one another. Y'all have been there for me as I've gone through one of the toughest times in my life, and I'm happy we were able to be here this evening to help Lauren in her time of need."

"Cheers!" Everyone clinks their glasses before digging into the tacos Olivia cooked for us once she found a water heater that was only forty-five minutes away.

"I still can't believe I missed that store." Lauren picks at her food.

"Don't beat yourself up." I reach out to her, then pause, my gaze flickering to Rhett. I know Olivia and Callie are aware of our situation, but I'm not sure if he is. As much as I want our secret out in the open, I'd like it to be because Lauren *wants* people to know. I'd hate to make things weird for her considering she has to work with Rhett every day.

Lauren's eyes widen, and she scoots away from my touch. I guess that means Rhett does *not* know. She quickly changes the subject, turning to Olivia and remarking, "Dinner is incredible! Thank you."

Rhett takes a monstrous bite of his taco, making me think maybe he didn't see, but Lauren keeps glancing in his direction, clearly looking for any indication he knows what's going on. I wonder if it's because she doesn't want Rhett to know or if it's because she doesn't want *anyone* to know.

I try not to let that get to me. I like Rhett, but he's kind of impossible to read. I'm not sure how to feel about him, so maybe that's how Lauren feels too. I'd much prefer that over the idea that my efforts to prove myself are failing.

"I'm happy to help." Olivia's response reminds me of the outside world again.

"Don't think I didn't notice you did stuff around the house too. I saw you emptied the dishwasher and pulled my towels from the dryer." Lauren lowers her taco. "Did you throw in a load of laundry for me too?"

Olivia smiles sheepishly. "I wanted to help however I could. I know sometimes it's the buildup of the little things that gets to you."

"You're hired."

"We should do this more often. It feels like we're a little family." Callie smacks her hands down on the table. "Oh my gosh! It's just like *Friends*."

"I like it." Olivia bounces up and down in her chair. "Who would be who?"

"I'm probably Phoebe, not going to lie." Callie shrugs as she takes another bite of her taco.

"That seems about right. You are the wackiest one of the bunch."

"Lauren could be a good Monica." Olivia points her taco in Lauren's direction. "She's got those type A genes."

"Hey! It's not like I'm busting out a little vacuum to vacuum my big vacuum," Lauren argues.

"Actually, I've seen her do that," I stage-whisper to Olivia, who bursts out laughing.

Lauren glares at me. "If I'm Monica, I'd end up with whoever our Chandler is, Jax or Rhett." Lauren scrunches her nose.

"It's perfect! Jax can be Chandler," Callie announces, smiling with pride until she sees almost everyone at the table giving her a look. "I mean, yeah, we might have to scratch this whole *Friends* idea. It just got weird."

"What about *How I Met Your Mother*?" Lauren offers. "There are five of them. That fits our group better."

We go on like this for a while, and Olivia was right, it is cool to have a group of friends together, enjoying food and good conversation, even if we didn't sit down to eat until almost eleven in the evening. It's been a while since I've had something like this. Charlie left a few years ago, and I haven't had a good friend since then.

By the end of the night, I even feel like Rhett isn't quite as scary as he once seemed. He gives me a handshake and a smile as he leaves, whispering, "I like you a lot better when you're hitting on Lauren instead of my girl." His reference to last July when I kind of flirted with Olivia at the Long Neck takes me a while to pick up on.

I step back with wide eyes, trying to figure out how to deny his accusation.

"It's so obvious." He smirks. "And Olivia thinks she's better at keeping secrets than she is."

Finally, I admit, "I'm sorry. I never meant to step on toes."

He shakes his head. "It's okay. I get it now."

"Get what?"

"You were afraid to let yourself love her. I've been there before." He nudges me in the side with his elbow, leaning in. "It gets so much better when you're both all in."

"We are."

He gives me a knowing look. "Keeping your relationship a secret is not going all in."

———

I hardly slept last night after Rhett made his stupid little comment. It was impossible to ignore the image of Lauren leaping from my arms when her dad was coming and then the feeling of her moving from my grasp when she thought Rhett might be watching us.

But what does he know? He's not the one in the relationship. Only Lauren and I know what we mean to each other, and we both adore one another. *Right?*

When her alarm goes off and she stirs awake, she presses gentle kisses along my collarbone and neck until she reaches my lips, whispering, "Good morning. Are you ready?"

"Of course."

"Good, because this time *I* have a surprise for *you*." She pauses, frowning as she takes me in. "What's wrong? Are you not excited about my surprise?"

"Of course I am." I force a smile on my face, which isn't

too difficult to do when I'm in her presence. I press a kiss to her forehead to further reassure her.

"We gotta hurry if we're going to catch the sunrise." She's glowing as she bounds out of bed, and it continues to melt away any concern I had about Rhett's words. *He's not us. He doesn't know us.*

Chapter Thirty

Lauren

Once Lucky and Charlie's horse, Tex, are tacked up, we head out onto the trails, silence falling over us for most of the way up. I'm grateful for the quiet company. It allows me to enjoy this moment with someone I care for deeply while still getting to soak up the feeling of riding Lucky for a reason besides work for the first time in years.

When we're about five minutes from the end of the trail, I break the silence. "My dad and I used to come out here every Sunday before family breakfast."

"That sounds nice. Why'd you stop?"

I shrug. "Life got busy, and I forgot what was important to me."

"Were you always close with your dad?"

"Yeah." I turn my gaze out to the horizon, which is slowly coming to life with the rays of the golden sun. "We were buddies from the start. He used to nap in his recliner with me on his chest, and I'd follow him around every-where. There's a picture of me when I was three, marching around in a pair of his boots and his cowboy hat. I wanted to be just like him."

Jax and Tex trot up next to me. "How have I not seen that? I need to see that picture."

"No, you don't. It's embarrassing." Trying to redirect his attention, I add, "I love my mom, of course, and we've shared bonds over rom coms and her sunflower garden, but Dad and I always had a special connection. When I had a crush on a boy in the seventh grade and found out he was going out with someone else, Dad was the one I talked to about it. It's weird, but, somehow, we've always understood each other."

I fight back the emotions clenching at my chest. "We got even closer when Charlie left because we bonded over the ranch. He's taught me everything I know."

"Is he the one who taught you how to bluff in poker like no one's business?"

I shake my head. "No, he's the one who taught me bluffing can't be taught. It's a skill you're born with."

He joins me in my laughter as we reach the summit—"summit" being a bit of a stretch considering how flat Roots is, but we're still at a higher elevation than when we started. Instead of staying there to take in the view, Lucky and I lead the way off the trail we've been following.

Jax leans to the side, peering around me. "Where are we going?"

"I want to show you my spot."

"Your spot?"

I nod. "No one else knows about this."

I swear that makes him sit up a little taller as we trek through the trees on the backside of the hill. After a couple more minutes of winding through the oaks into seeming nothingness, I stop.

"Here we are."

It's been years since I've been up here, but everything is just like I remembered it. The tree trunk I turned into a makeshift bench is still here. The initials I carved in one of the oaks years ago when I claimed this spot as mine managed to weather years' worth of storms. Even my tin lunchbox, full of emergency essentials, is still stashed below one of the tree roots.

I slide off Lucky, ready to open the box and reminisce, but before I can start unpacking it, Jax slides off Tex and grabs me by the waist, guiding me toward the bench.

"What're you doing?"

He tugs me down to sit next to him, holding me close. "Tell me what you see, smell, feel, and hear. If we're going to come out here to watch the sun rise, I want you to take a moment to truly appreciate it. It's something my mom used to do with me after—" He clears his throat and drops his voice low. "After things with my dad turned sour. It helped ground me. I thought maybe you'd enjoy it too as someone who is constantly going, going, going."

I nod, inhaling a deep breath. "I see the sun's rays coming over the horizon. It makes it look almost like there's an end to the earth. I see a patch of mistflowers that looks like a purple ocean out by what will be paddock twelve, and I see the light filtering through the clouds. Nana always said that the golden clouds in a sunrise and sunset were made that way by all our loved ones looking down at us."

"I like that."

"Me too." I catch on his blue-eyed gaze, noting the navy rim that surrounds the notes of gold in them. His sandy-blond hair is slightly askew as it sticks out the edges of his cowboy hat because he rolled out of bed this morning, but it only makes him look more charming and approachable.

"Okay, enough of what you see." He drags me out of my trance. "Close your eyes. What do you hear, feel, and smell?"

I follow his orders and try to focus on my other senses. The first thing I notice is Jax clinging to me in a way that makes me feel safe. His cedar scented soap wraps around my nose like a hug while his soft breathing mixes with the sound of a restless Lucky and a determined woodpecker in the distance.

There's a tiny part of me that feels like I need to do this exercise on my own. I appreciate all the ways Jax has been there for me, but I also need to have some moments of growth without him, so I sit there quietly, basking in his warm and gentle touch and his intoxicating smell. I listen to his steady breathing and note how my own breathing slowly matches his.

After several minutes, I say, "Thank you. I needed that."

"I just want to make sure my girl gets some down time to enjoy the beauty of life."

My lips curve into a smile. "Can I show you something?"

"Of course."

I get up from the bench, pull the tin lunch box from its hiding spot, and open it up to reveal a stale granola bar, a box of tissues, a picture of me and Charlie I stashed up here after he moved to LA, and something else I had forgotten was up here, something I didn't have the heart to get rid of.

I gingerly pull the colorful bunch of beads out from the box and lift it for Jax to see. "Do you remember this?"

He slips off the bench, squinting as he walks toward me. He reaches his hand out to look at the bracelet closer.

"It's my lucky bracelet."

I nod. "You remember when you gave it to me?"

His piercing eyes meet mine, and I can see everything swirling inside them as he tries to make sense of all of this.

"Of course I remember." He twirls the beads in his hand. "You really kept it? All this time?"

I shrug, feeling extremely vulnerable. I didn't plan on showing him. I forgot it existed until this very moment. "I just didn't want to get rid of it." I release a shaky breath. "I mean, it brought you a lot of luck that season."

"Oh."

Never mind the fact that I had a minor crush on him when he came to town, but nothing ever happened between us, and then Austin came along, and Jax went from being my brother's cute friend to my brother's annoying friend. When I started dating Austin, I spent less time with him, and when we were together, it was almost like a switch had flipped. Jax ruthlessly picked on me.

"So, this is your special spot?" He spins around, taking it all in.

"Yeah, I used to come up here when I wanted some space to clear my head. It's hard to feel overwhelmed when I'm removed from everything like this. It felt like all my responsibilities faded away here because no one knew where I was. If no one could find me, no one could ask anything of me."

"Do you still feel that way?" He places his hands in his back pockets. "Like everyone is asking too much of you?"

I bite my lip, moving back to the trunk bench. "I think now *I'm* the one asking everything of myself, if that makes sense."

He nods, joining me. "Did the other night help? With the bath? Or last night when we all came to help?"

"A little." I squeeze his thigh and give him a smile. "I

don't think I'll change overnight, but I'm learning I don't have to tackle everything alone. It showed me there are ways to find help and get rest."

"If you ever want to talk about it more. I'm here for you."

My heart jumpstarts in my chest. I haven't always had this kind of steady support in my life. Charlie has been there for me more and more recently, but he's still so far away. I've always been close with my dad, but his recent health condition has shifted our dynamic. I'm afraid of telling him anything, afraid of burdening him. Knowing Jax is there for me makes me feel... everything, almost too much. My feelings for Jax are building so fast and so deep. It'd be terrifying if his presence weren't so calming.

Jax pulls me into his arms. "Thank you for sharing your spot with me. It means a lot."

I press on a closed-lip smile, afraid I'm going to blurt out exactly how I feel, but I can't. It's too soon. We just started this thing between us. *Am I really capable of feeling all of these things already?* My brain says no, but my heart isn't convinced. It wants to give Jax a piece of me after every-thing he's done to advocate for me and push me to be a version of myself I'm proud of.

"I haven't been here in a while," I finally say. "It felt selfish to come up here once Charlie left and the weight of the ranch fell on my shoulders, but more recently, someone has showed me that it's okay to take a moment for myself." I slide a soft smile his way. "Even then, I didn't feel the need to come up here."

His eyes narrow in confusion, and I inhale a sharp breath, bracing myself to get as close to the truth as possible.

"I haven't felt the need to come up here because every time I'm with you, you give me the same feeling this place

once did. You wash away the weight of all my responsibilities, and you bring me peace every time you wrap me in
your arms. So, thank you."

There's a hint of relief in his eyes that catches me off
guard before he embraces me tightly. "Freckles, I can't tell
you how much that means to me."

He pulls me in for a tender kiss, but when he draws
away, there are shadows in his eyes that make me think he's
holding something back. There's a brief moment when the
look reminds me of Austin. He used to give me that same
feeling—the fear that he's hiding something from me, the
helplessness that I can't get him to openly speak his mind
and share his feelings.

Fear washes over me, but I ground myself again with the
touch of his lips and the feeling of his fingers splayed out on
my waist. Jax isn't Austin. I know that. These feelings are
just in my head. *I hope.*

Chapter Thirty-One

Jax

"Hey, ladies. Can I get y'all something to drink?" I ask as Lauren, Callie, and Olivia approach the bar Thursday night for swing dance lessons.

"Nothing to drink, but we might need a dance partner again," Olivia says loudly.

I glance from her to Lauren for guidance. Lauren leans over the counter, whispering, "She's apparently awful at keeping secrets." Turning to Olivia, she adds, "I thought you'd be better at this. You were kind of closed off when you came to town."

"There's a difference between being reserved and keeping secrets. I was never all that good at hiding things when people asked me questions. Plus, now that I have such a good support system, I don't want to screw that up by keeping secrets." She grabs a cup, filling it with water from the jug on the bar. "I think I'm doing a great job! I'm helping you."

"Helping them get caught," Callie murmurs.

Olivia's mouth falls open, and she gives Callie a playful smack on the shoulder. "Am not!"

I lean in and drop my voice. "It's okay. Lauren is going to be the one giving us away tonight anyway."

Lauren arches a brow. "Why would I do that?"

"Because I'm irresistible. You won't be able to tame yourself around my magnetic charm." I smirk and toss a wink in her direction, which instantly makes her blush. "Told you."

She presses her hands to her cheeks. "Not true. If anything, you can't resist *my* charm."

She bats her eyelashes playfully before pulling her purse off her shoulder and grabbing a tube of lip gloss. I almost forget I'm supposed to be resisting her while I watch her pucker her full lips and apply the shiny coat.

"Point proven." Her mouth curves into a devilish smile.

"I'm sorry for what I said, Olivia. It looks like these fools are going to give themselves away." Callie rolls her eyes as she walks toward the crowd forming to sign up for dance lessons.

"Nuh uh!" Lauren shouts back at her, but Callie is easily ten feet away already and shrugging her shoulders without looking back.

Lauren glances at me like I'm going to do something about it, but I hope we do give ourselves away. I'm tired of this charade.

Betsy starts up her mic and calls everyone forward to the dance floor. I pretend to be completely uninterested, but I'm just listening for my cue. As everyone joins up with partners, Betsy tsks. "Looks like we are one person short. Would y'all be okay with rotating through partners today?"

"Just make Jax join us," Callie suggests. "He's done the lessons before. I'm sure he'd be a good partner."

I glance up in fake horror, sure that my reaction could win me an Oscar. Once Olivia supports Callie's claim, as well as a couple other older ladies who have a hungry glint in their eye, I come out onto the dance floor.

"You should dance with Lauren. You two worked well together last time," Olivia says, shoving me in her direction. I don't even have time to fake protest.

Once Lauren is in my arms, I lean down, whispering, "You ready for this?"

"I was born ready. I'm going to kick your butt."

I choke on a laugh. "I could be wrong, but I'm pretty sure we're supposed to be partners in this, not competing with one another."

"You're right. Sorry, I don't know how to act."

"You don't need to act." I slide my hands down to her waist. A lick of fire ignites inside of me. Touching her already drives me wild, but touching her when I know I shouldn't be erases my ability to think straight. Everything around us melts into the background, Betsy's instructions, the other couples awkwardly trying to act out the steps as she explains, the clanking of bottles as my crew sets up for the night—it's all gone.

"What're you doing?" Lauren asks nervously, but she isn't glancing around, wondering what other people are thinking. Her hazel eyes are laser focused on me.

"I told you I was going to make you want to kiss me."

She places a hand on my chest, pushing away. "I'm not falling for that. Besides, if anything, *you're* the one who wants to kiss *me*. I can see it in your eyes already."

"Of course I want to kiss you, but I respect your boundaries. I'm not going to cave." I gently rub my thumb on her hip. "But I can't help it if you're impervious to my charm."

Betsy stops her instructions, turning to Lauren and me.

"Is there something you two would like to share with the class, or are you two going to actually pay attention?"

Murmurs float through the group. I don't have to hear them to know what they're saying. Lauren and I suck at keeping our relationship a secret. The whole town was already talking about how I've been seen with her on more than one occasion, from the diner to our first dance lessons together. The excuse that I'm just looking out for Charlie's little sister is no longer working. I can't help the fact that I don't look at anyone else the way I look at her.

Lauren's face sets on fire, and she freezes.

"I'm sorry," I offer, swooping in. "We were just talking through the steps as you explain them."

Betsy nods primly and resumes her instruction. When she turns us loose to practice the sequence she demonstrated with her volunteer, I take advantage of the moment to pull Lauren closer than I should. I let our fingers linger together longer than they're meant to, and I gently rub my thumb on her waist whenever it's in my hand.

It's working. She melts into my touch, her eyes going soft. God, I just want her to kiss me, right here, right now, in front of everyone. I want her to claim me as hers, and not just because Ms. Sanchez won't stop looking at me like she wants to eat me for dessert.

After I spin Lauren around to complete the sequence, she leans into me, pressing us chest to chest as her lips brush against my ear. "I see what you're doing, and it's not going to work."

She presses a soft kiss to my neck before quickly pulling away from me as if nothing ever happened, but now all I can think about is grabbing her and slamming my lips onto hers. Forget the lesson. Forget taunting her. I just want her, now. The game isn't fun anymore.

"You don't need to finish this lesson, right?" I give her hand a little tug, tilting my head toward the dark hallway that leads to my office.

"Are you saying I won?" she asks, looking smug.

"I don't think anyone wins unless we blow this popsicle stand."

Betsy helps Ms. Sanchez and her partner to our left, so Lauren leans in closer to me. "No, I definitely won. I'm not the one who wants to skip out on the rest of the lesson right now."

"It's not about winning or losing."

"Because you lost." She laughs, a look of pure glee on her face.

Betsy calls out words of encouragement to Ms. Sanchez and her partner, moving to Lauren and me. "How's it going over here?"

Lauren straightens, putting her hands behind her back. "Great."

"Really? It doesn't look like there's much dancing happening."

"I'm trying to get Lauren to let me lead, but she's refusing. I think we'll get the hang of it soon," I say, taking Lauren's hand and starting the sequence again.

Betsy moves on with a satisfied smile, throwing over her shoulder, "I know it's hard to give up control, honey, but it's so much easier when you do."

Little does she realize how perfect her words are. Still holding tight to Lauren, I lead her two steps to the left.

She picks up our conversation as we reverse the steps. "We can't just leave. People will wonder where we are."

"Does it really matter?"

She frowns as I spin her around. Once I pull her back to me, she lowers her voice so I almost can't hear her. "The whole point of keeping this a secret is to not let everyone know about us."

"How long do we have to keep it a secret for?"

"I don't know."

I stop dancing. "Is it something I've done wrong?"

"Of course not. You've been amazing. I'm just not ready." She motions for us to start the sequence over again.

"What will it take to make you ready?"

"I don't know." She looks upset, causing a hint of fear to settle in my chest.

"I'm sorry. I'm not trying to pressure you. I just want to understand. I want people to know you're mine and vice versa. The secret-keeping hasn't been as exciting as I thought it would be."

"That's because you're not even trying to hide it." She draws back.

"What did I do? Please don't be upset with me."

Betrayal flashes in her eyes. I don't understand! *Why is it so terrible that I want people to know we're together?*

Instead of coming from a place of compassion, I can't restrain my fears anymore. "Are you really that embarrassed to be seen with me?"

Her eyes soften, and a look of confusion settles on her face. "What? No. It's just—can we finish the lesson?" She holds her hands up, ready to take mine. "We should talk about this later."

"No, we should talk about this now." I guide her down the hallway to the office where we can hash matters out in private.

She glances around in horror, making sure no one is watching. Everyone seems to be pretty busy except for Ms. Sanchez, who arches her brow in curiosity when her partner dips her. Good, let her see. I'm tired of her looking at me like I'm a slice of chocolate cake.

Once we're in the safety of my office, I let go of Lauren's hand, and she unleashes on me. "Jax, you can't just drag me off like that!"

"You have to tell me what's going on, or I won't be able to fix it."

Releasing a sigh, she crosses her arms. "You don't have to fix everything for me."

My chest aches at her remark. "This isn't about fixing things for you. I want to know what we're doing in this relationship. In case you've forgotten, there are two of us involved."

"No, you're trying to fix me like you always do."

"I couldn't if I wanted to." Anger surges in me. Things have been building up for too long. "You won't let go of control for five seconds. Everything has to be just right, according to your standards."

She leans against my desk, her shoulders sagging. "What a pair: a control freak and a fixer."

I join her, leaning against the desk. "I guess we both have some things we need to work on, huh?"

She nods, staring at the ground. "I guess so."

When she glances up at me, there's regret in her eyes. "It's not just that I'm a control freak. I hate to admit it, but my relationship with Austin left me with some scars. The other day, when we went horseback riding, it felt like you were hiding something from me. It was like being back with Austin again, feeling you pull away the same way he did. It felt awful."

Instantly, I pull her into my arms. "I'm sorry. I'm not hiding things from you. I've opened up with you more than I have with anyone else."

"I know that, but I haven't been able to shake the feeling."

"I was a little off the other morning." I rub her arm up and down. "I feel caught between being excited about where things are going and being scared."

"Why are *you* scared?"

I don't want to make this conversation more difficult by telling her what Rhett said the other day, but I don't want to hold back either. If she already feels like I'm keeping things from her, hiding this won't help us move forward, so I fill her in on the conversation, adding, "It stirred up some of my own insecurities about not being good enough for you. I understand why you want to hide this relationship, but it's still hard for me to separate reality from the messed-up thoughts in my head."

She looks up at me, cupping my cheek with nothing but affection in her eyes. "You're more than good enough, Jax. I still have so much I need to overcome. I'm terrified I'll ruin this beautiful relationship developing between us if I open it up to all the external obstacles we might face before I overcome my internal ones." She tilts her head. "Does that make sense?"

"It does." I snake an arm around her waist. "You take as long as you need. I'm grateful we get to work through it all together. We'll share our relationship with the world eventually, but for now, I'm content to be us in whatever way that looks."

"Are you sure?"

"I'm sure." I give her a squeeze. "I don't want to push you to do something before you're ready."

The three little words that have rang true for years sit on the tip of my tongue, but I catch myself. I've had more than enough time to develop these feelings for Lauren, but she hasn't always felt this way about me. She fell in love with another man and planned a life with him. I don't want to scare her off by saying something too soon that I won't be able to take back. So instead, I offer her the best comfort I can. "I'm not going anywhere."

She bites her lip. "So, since we're already here, I guess they won't notice if we're gone a couple extra minutes, right?" She stands on her tiptoes to meet my lips, and I take everything I can get from her.

Chapter Thirty-Two

Lauren

I haven't stopped talking Charlie's ear off since I picked him up at the airport. We didn't always get along this well. In high school, we'd occasionally have life talks over ice cream, but Charlie had a wild streak I wanted no part of. After he moved to LA, his need to do crazy things that made me uncomfortable dwindled, and our relationship strengthened. He started calling more to check in on me or tell me he's proud of me. It's been the strangest, yet most wonderful, shift in the world.

"We definitely need to play a million games of poker while you're home, and maybe we could build a fire like old times."

"Yeah, that'd be great," he says, staring out the window. He's been plastered to that thing the whole drive. "I'll be gone for a few days for a hunting trip with Jax though."

"You will?" I park my truck and follow him toward the big house with a confused look.

He nods casually as he swings open the door. As soon as

his front foot crosses the threshold, everyone leaps out, cheering, "Surprise!"

Mom, Dad, and Nana reach him first, but Carol, Aimee, Jax, some of his old football buddies, and all the cowboys who've been with us since Charlie was in high school or college wait their turn to get a piece of him. While no one has said it, we all know this might be the longest he's home for another few years.

Charlie gives Jax one of those weird bro hugs where they clasp one hand and slap each other's backs with the other, smirking as he says, "How are you doing, Grinchie?"

Jax swivels to me, a look of betrayal shrouding his face. "You told him?"

"How could I not? Charlie is just as much a Christmas lover as me."

"How dare you!" Jax narrows his eyes at me, but when he gets close enough for just me to hear him, he says, "You're playing with fire, Freckles."

Charlie steps off to say hi to Carol and Aimee, who he always referred to as his second parents.

I take the opportunity to give Jax the most confident look I can. "I can handle a little heat."

"And I like a challenge."

"We already know how that went for you the last time. I wouldn't bother trying to humiliate yourself again," I tease, quickly stepping back from him before anyone can notice how close we are.

While his jaw falls open, I take the opportunity to ask, "So, you and Charlie are going on a hunting trip while he's here, huh? How long will you be gone?"

"Did I not mention it to you?" He looks genuinely surprised.

"No." I lean my shoulder against the wall. "Sorry, I'm

not trying to be clingy or anything. I just thought you would've wanted to tell me about it since we came up with the idea together."

"You're right, and I want you to be a part of it." He grabs me by the wrist and drags me over to Charlie, who's talking with Clayton, one of his old football buddies.

"I think we should take Lauren on the hunting trip with us," Jax announces to Charlie. "I've seen how hard she's been working on the ranch, and I know you've been worried about her slowing down. This could be a good way to force her to rest."

Charlie tilts his head in consideration. "That's not a bad idea, but do you really want to do that, Lo?" He scrunches up his nose like he just ate a lemon.

"I don't know." I shrug. "I didn't know Jax was going to suggest it until right now. I guess it could be fun to hang out with you more." I also think it'd be fun to spend time with two of the most important men in my life, and I love that Jax wants to include me.

Charlie drapes his arm over my shoulders. "I want to spend some time with my baby sister too." He pulls away, looking me in the face. "But if you're going to come with us, you need to know you can't talk while we're out hunting. We need complete silence."

"That's fine with me. I'd prefer to hang out with you while you can't talk anyway."

"You're the worst!" He pulls me in for a nuggie.

"Seriously, Char? I thought you would've outgrown the nuggie phase by the time you were twenty-five. Grow up."

"Never!" He gives me another nuggie, and when I shriek, Jax tenses like he's torn between putting a stop to this and trying to show he's on Charlie's side.

"Okay, that's enough." Jax carefully places himself

between Charlie and me. "We need to set a date for this trip. Mom and Aunt Carol want to do our annual cookie bake-off before Christmas, so it might need to be after."

Charlie's face lights up. "You should've seen the masterpiece Jax and I made several Christmases ago. Remember that?" He nudges Jax in the side, and Jax snorts.

I don't think I've ever heard Jax snort before. I want to make fun of him for it so badly, but I can't remember if that's something we used to do around Charlie, so I settle for asking, "What'd you make?"

Jax's face lights up. "Charlie and I decided we wanted to create a whole scene, so we made a gingerbread cowboy and sugar cookie woman from the city. We created this whole backstory for how they fell in love and created mutant half gingerbread, half sugar cookie babies. It was awesome!"

"Don't forget about their Pizzelle dog. He was as big as the people! We carved out a normal cookie once it was made. And the size of his crap—" Charlie closes his thumb and forefinger to create a circle the size of a quarter.

When I furrow my brow and glance between the two boys, Jax offers, "We used Hershey's kisses from my mom's peanut butter blossom cookies." Realization crosses his face. "You should come, Lauren. We can invite Rhett, Olivia, and Callie too. I wouldn't mind some fresh competition this year."

"That sounds fun." My heart flutters. "I'd love the opportunity to whoop both your butts. Plus, if you're inviting those three, I can team up with Callie, and Rhett and Olivia can be on a team."

"That's not fair. You can't get a professional baker for your team when I'm stuck with Mr. Overbakes Everything here." Jax thrusts his thumb in Charlie's direction.

"Rhett is a really good baker too."

"Okay, then this definitely isn't fair. I want a new partner."

The joke seems to go right over Charlie's head. He looks zoned out.

"Earth to Charlie." Jax waves his hand in front of Charlie's face. "I roasted you twice, man. Try to keep up."

"Y'all want to invite Callie?" His face has gone white.

"Oh, that's right." I wince. "We don't need to get everyone together if it's going to be weird."

He shrugs. "I just haven't seen her since I moved, but I promise it won't be weird. It's been years. I'm mature enough to handle it."

"Since when?"

Charlie shoves me hard with a grin on his face. "Shut up!"

"I'm not going to apologize for calling you out. You've given me *two* nuggies in the forty-five minutes since you've been home."

"Give me more credit than that. I had the whole car ride from the airport to torture you, but I was civil."

"Oh gee. Thanks for your kindness." I roll my eyes, but there's a smile on my face.

"Back me up here, Jax." Charlie throws his hands up in the air.

"I'm not getting in the middle of this."

"Since when?" Charlie crosses his arms, looking betrayed.

"I don't know. I guess I've just matured, unlike someone," Jax teases, a smirk tugging at the corner of his lips.

"Sounds like he's taking my side," I say, glancing at Charlie with a smug look.

"I'm not sure what the hell has been happening while

I've been gone, but it stops now. You two are being weird, and I don't like it."

My stomach drops, but I try to force a laugh. "Guess you haven't been home in so long that you've forgotten what things are like."

"Ha. Ha," Charlie deadpans.

When I meet Jax's gaze, there's fear in his eyes. It hits me then that keeping our relationship a secret still might not protect us from external obstacles, and if Charlie is the one who breaks us apart, that might hurt worse than any other form of heartbreak I could imagine.

Chapter Thirty-Three

Jax

"Welcome to the ninth annual Christmas cookie bake-off!" Mom throws her arms out in grandeur, her eyes gleaming with joy.

I take a beat to soak in this moment. Ten years ago, our Christmases were spent trying to keep my dad at home and off his phone or computer long enough to enjoy a family holiday that wasn't tainted by gambling or booze. The gambling in and of itself wasn't so bad, but when he lost a bet, he'd start drinking, and when he drank, he'd start throwing punches.

I'm relieved to have the comfort of friends and family around me now. I have an amazing girlfriend, even if I can't share that with everyone yet. My best friend is back for the longest he's ever come home since he left, and everyone I care about is safe, happy, healthy, and in one place.

"I'd like to introduce our guest judges this evening: Bennett Rhodes, Lacey Rhodes, Nana Rhodes, and Carol Greer." Mom can hardly contain her excitement. Since there are new competitors this year, we decided it would be fun to have a full judges' panel. The Rhodes family seemed to make the most sense since Lauren and Charlie were already competing. Plus, Nana Rhodes has been begging to be a part of this for years.

"Bennett, do you care to share with the contestants what they will be judged on today?"

"I would love to, Aimee. Thank you." Mr. Rhodes stands from his place at our dining room table, now deemed the judges' booth. Sporting a bright smile, he has a little more life in his eyes than a week ago when Lauren was trying to keep him away from the water tank fiasco.

"Today, my fellow judges and I will be choosing a winner based on creativity, holiday festivity, presentation, and, of course, taste."

As soon as Mr. Rhodes takes his seat, his wife stands. I bet they rehearsed this at home. I'm sure it was hilarious to watch.

"You will have three hours to make your creations. During that time, the judges will leave the baking area so as not to be swayed by anything that goes into each individual process."

"Plus, three hours is a long damn time to just sit here and watch y'all," Nana Rhodes adds.

"What my mother-in-law said." Mrs. Rhodes gestures in Nana Rhodes's direction, a smile spreading across her face as she takes a seat.

Nana Rhodes stands up proudly. "While there are no rules for this bake-off, we do—" She pauses and glances at her fellow judges. "Do I really need to say 'request'? That sounds kind of lame. I'm not going to say that." She swats a hand. "Essentially, don't intentionally sabotage anyone and make sure to share the oven because y'all are limited on time."

Aunt Carol stands from her spot once Nana Rhodes has sat down. "If you need anything from the store, you can contact one of the judges, and we can pick it up. Good luck and happy baking, y'all!"

We quickly disperse into separate corners of the kitchen and dining room while each team plots their creation.

"Please tell me you came with some good ideas, Mr. Hollywood."

Charlie rolls his eyes. "Just because I came from LA doesn't mean I'm going to have brilliant ideas, but yes I came prepared."

"What do you got?"

"I'm thinking we do a spinoff of my Nana and Papa's love story. They met at Christmastime in a Christmas tree lot. It's easy to pull off, it's got some creativity and a plot line that will tug at the judges' heartstrings."

"I like it. What do you think, Rhett?" I glance up at the man who is quietly standing opposite me. While setting up, we determined four teams would be too many if we only had one oven to share, so Mom and Aunt Carol offered to take a step back this year, likely because they knew they didn't stand a chance. They've quite frankly never been a threat. Then Rhett joined Charlie and me, and Olivia joined Lauren and Callie.

"I like it." Rhett nods. "We're going to crush the girls if they go with Olivia's idea. She wanted to do some sort of Christmas version of Resilient Paws. I told her she needs to learn how to stop working when she's not at work." He shakes his head, but there's an affectionate smile on his face.

Despite Rhett being difficult to read, no one has ever doubted he loves Olivia. A lot. I point an accusatory finger at him and ask, "How do we know you aren't working for the other side?"

He shrugs. "I guess you can't know for certain, but I'm telling you now, as much as I love that woman, I still want to crush her."

I glance at Charlie, wordlessly asking, *should we trust him?*

Charlie beams and offers his hand for Rhett to shake. "I like this guy! You'll be a nice addition to the team this year."

We start mixing the dough for the sugar cookies, plain and chocolate because Rhett insisted the chocolate will be great for turning into Christmas trees.

He orders us around the kitchen, and we grab supplies for Rhett as he asks for them. As much as it hurts my ego to be his servant, I can put aside my feelings of inadequacy for a moment if it means beating the girls at this competition.

"Okay, I think this first batch can be cut and put into the oven. Just bake them for eight minutes. We can cook them for a maximum of twelve, but we need to check them early. I don't know how hot the oven runs," Rhett instructs.

"Pretty hot. Our stuff gets burnt every year."

"That's because you don't have a single baking bone in your body," I say to Charlie.

"That's not true! I bake delicious chocolate muffins. Ask Callie."

I glance over to the girls' group as Lauren tosses her head back in laughter, and I forget what I'm doing for a second. I love to see her so happy. She's the most gorgeous girl I've ever met, inside and out, and her laughter is so infectious—

"Jax? If I didn't know any better, I'd say you were staring at my sister."

I go pale and immediately try to hide it by turning my

focus down to the cookie dough as I stick one of the Christmas tree cutters into it and wiggle it around a little. "I was just going to ask you how being around Callie has been, but I got distracted because I thought I heard the girls say something about their idea."

"We're already committed. We can't change things now," Rhett mumbles as he mixes up the plain cookie dough.

Charlie doesn't look up from his chore of cutting dough. "It's been fine. She hasn't said a word to me besides hello, but I guess I should've expected that."

"I'm sorry, man."

"It's all good." Charlie tosses a hand. "It's not like I expected anything different from her."

"You just let me know if you change your mind. I'm happy to play wingman again, especially for you two."

"You'd do that?" His eyes are shining.

"Of course. I like Callie. We've stayed friends since you left."

"What?" The shine in his eyes is gone as they narrow.

"It's nothing more than a *very* platonic friendship. Don't worry. I think we trauma-bonded a little over you leaving." I meant it as a joke, but the look of horror on Charlie's face shows it didn't land well. I guess I should shut up now.

He finishes placing cookies on the first parchment paper–lined sheet, and swivels from the counter to put them in the oven.

I thrust an arm into his chest. "How about I put them in? Wouldn't want you forgetting to set a timer. We can't overbake these if we are going to beat the girls. They have Callie's baking skills and feminine charm on their side."

He squints at me like I spoke to him in a foreign language. "What the hell are you talking about?"

"In case you missed it, three-fourths of the judges' panel is made up of women. You know when your sister does something, and you're just like *what the hell?*" He immediately nods. "Well, the only one who's going to be thinking that with us is your dad. The rest of the panel will be wrapped around their finger because they'll just get it."

He purses his lips. "Shit."

"Yeah." I take the cookies and move toward the oven. Lauren is also heading that way, and when her gaze meets mine, she presses her lips together to blow me a kiss. I bite my lip, trying to hide my smile, and trip over my own damn feet. The cookies go flying off the tray and onto the floor.

"What are you doing?" Charlie shouts, his voice strained. He's never done well with competition.

Lauren slips her cookies into the oven and then crouches down to the floor to help me pick up my mess. "It's okay. I'll help him."

"No way." Charlie inserts himself between us. "He doesn't need help from the enemy."

"Chill out, Char. I'm not going to sabotage your cookies." Lauren plucks a few off the floor. "They already need to be thrown in the garbage."

"They might not be. The judges didn't see them on the floor. Throw 'em in there. The oven will kill any germs."

Rhett moves into the scene. "Those are not going into the oven. Throw them away. We have plenty of dough, and I can make a half batch in less than five minutes if we need to."

"Fine." Charlie crosses his arms, pouting like a five-year-old as he stomps back to our station.

Lauren dumps a handful of broken trees on the baking sheet where I've been collecting them.

"I see you're trying to get in my head," I note quietly.

"I don't know what you're talking about." She continues picking at the floor, gathering up every last crumb.

"I'm going to report you for sabotage. You can't distract me like that. You know I'm a complete fool for you."

She bites her lip as her cheeks flush. "You know I love to hear that, but I didn't do anything."

"Yes, you did. You did it on purpose."

"Even if I did, you can't report me to the judges. How would you explain it to them?"

She's got me there.

"You're the devil." I get up from my spot crouched on the floor.

"No, I'm a perfect angel, remember?"

Lauren bats her eyes, looking way too satisfied with herself. *I'll show her. She wants to play? Game on.*

I dump the cookies in the garbage before retreating to our spot at the counter. Charlie has almost filled another cookie sheet already.

"Please tell me you saw what they're making?" Charlie says when I join them.

"No, but the girls are playing dirty, and we need to retaliate."

Charlie's face glows with excitement. "I'm in."

The two of us glance in Rhett's direction, and he shrugs. "Oh, what the hell? I'm in too. Olivia won't let me live it down if they win."

Chapter Thirty-Four

Lauren

"What was that all about?" Olivia asks when I return to our station at the dining room table.

"She was totally flirting with him!" Callie blurts. When I pin her with a glare, she lowers her voice. "You need to get your head in the game, Lo. I will *not* allow fraternizing with the enemy. I want to dominate." Callie pounds her fist into her palm.

"Did you see what my flirting did? I'm getting in his head."

Callie scans me for a moment, then a smirk blooms on her face. It's a little scary. "Did you do that on purpose?"

I press my lips together, and Olivia immediately calls me out. "That wasn't her goal. I can see it on her face."

Whose side is she on? She knows what it's like to be in love! Well, not that I'm in love...

"I couldn't help it." I shrug. "He gave me this look, and I immediately wanted to show him he's on my mind too. I don't know, our chemistry is so natural that sometimes it's hard to hide. I didn't mean to make him dump the cookies, but it's a nice plus, right?"

"That's a nice story, but we don't have time for moon eyes and chemistry right now." Callie thrusts the bin of cookie cutters into my hand. "Get cutting."

I'm a little taken aback. Callie is normally one of the first to support a budding love story, but she's been on edge today.

As she takes another tray of cookies to the oven, Olivia leans into me with a smile. "It's nice to see you so happy."

"Thank you."

"Have you thought about when you're going to start telling people?"

"A little." I wiggle my cookie cutter around in the dough and carefully peel the cookie up. "I don't have an exact timeline yet. There are still some things I need to work on before I subject our relationship to everything outside of us."

"All those external things you're talking about still exist now, even while keeping your relationship a secret. What's really going on?"

"That's it." I shrug. "There are still parts of me that need work. I need to learn to trust more. I need to learn how to ask for help and find time to relax."

Olivia sets an elf-shaped cookie on the baking sheet, arching an eyebrow. "How is keeping your relationship a secret going to help with that?"

"It doesn't inherently help, but at least it buys me some time to work through these things before we're exposed to more challenges."

"What challenges are you anticipating?"

"I don't know." Heat rises to my cheeks. I grab the rolling pin to flatten another clump of dough. "People might say I got with Jax too soon after my breakup with Austin."

"And?"

"What do you mean 'and'?"

"There must be something else if you're this determined to hide your relationship."

Callie rejoins us, instantly butting into the conversation. "What are we talking about?"

"Why Lauren insists on hiding her relationship with Voldemort."

"I have a guess! I have a guess!" Callie throws her hand up in the air.

"Yes, Callie. What's your guess?" Olivia graciously nods in Callie's direction, like a teacher calling on a student.

"I think she's afraid to go all in because of what happened with Austin."

"What a great guess. That's my top one too."

"Y'all are the worst. You know that?" I try to distract myself by taking the frosting Callie has mixed up and splitting it into bowls so we can add food coloring to them.

Unfortunately, the distraction doesn't work well at all. Maybe they're right, but I don't know what to do about it. I don't want to admit I have doubts about Jax. I mean, they're not even doubts about *Jax*. They're just doubts about love and my ability to find it.

"If you want my advice, I say you need to go for it. Just rip the Band-Aid off. Hiding the relationship doesn't exactly send the right message to Jax about what this is between you two, and it doesn't protect you from getting hurt."

"I second that," Callie says as she plops a bit of cookie dough into her mouth. "The longer you hide it the more you're telling him you want the option to run. That's not fair to him. I know you like to be in control, but there's no such thing when it comes to love."

That's not what I'm trying to do, at least not intentionally, but I have felt a little safer for it. It keeps people from seeing the shame if this goes down in flames. As great as things are going, there's a part of me waiting for the other shoe to drop because, as history goes to show, relationships end.

I try so hard to control everything that happens in my life, whether it's the approach we take with the ranch, swing dancing, or matters of the heart. I know I need to loosen my grip if Jax and I stand a chance of making it, but I don't know how to do that.

I open my mouth to ask them, but Charlie approaches us. "Do y'all have an extra spatula over here?"

"I see what you're doing. Get out of here, you menace." I press my hand into his chest to push him away, while he blatantly takes in our setup.

"They're not doing the animal rescue, boys!" he hollers as I keep pushing him away.

"Traitor!" Olivia calls to Rhett.

"Come on, Wildflower. It's just business." He shrugs.

It's like the use of that nickname takes any anger out of her body because she melts into a puddle on the floor before my very eyes.

As I come back to the table, Callie mutters, "It looks like both of you are going to be useless to me."

"Hey, we're doing our best," I say as I return to my frosting station. "What happened to all the food coloring?" I lift the bowl of frosting. "And I swear you made more frosting than this."

"What are you talking about? It's all right... there." Callie drops her hand as she realizes I'm right. "Thieves!"

She stomps over to Charlie, throwing her finger into his chest. "You stole our frosting. Give it back. You're not supposed to be sabotaging."

"I'd talk to Lauren about that. She's the one who made my teammate dump cookies onto the floor."

"Jax is just clumsy. Give us our frosting back."

Charlie arches a brow, a smile slipping onto his lips as he steps closer to her. "I didn't take your frosting."

She drops her hand, stepping back with a slack jaw like she's just now realizing how close they're standing. It takes a couple of seconds for the color to return to her cheeks before she swivels to Jax. "What'd you do with it?"

He holds his hands up to plead his innocence. "I didn't do anything."

She narrows her eyes at him, but when he doesn't give in, she turns to Rhett, a scowl on her face.

Inserting myself between Callie and the boys with a raised hand, I say, "This is getting ridiculous. We're supposed to be having fun. Just give us our frosting back, boys. If you don't beat us fairly, we'll never accept your victory."

Everyone falls silent. Even Charlie looks swayed, which is no easy feat.

Callie meets my gaze, and when I slightly tilt my head in her direction, she takes that as her cue to steal their mixer from the counter. *Okay. I guess we're fully owning the sabotage attempts now.*

Olivia and I fall into a fit of laughter as we block the boys from capturing Callie. Olivia pulls Rhett in for a kiss, which he willingly accepts, and I hop onto Jax's back, which does nothing to stop the man.

"What are you doing, Freckles?" Jax glances over his shoulder.

"I'm trying to stop you."

"You suck at this."

"Help!" Callie shrieks as Charlie stands over her, trying to tear the mixer from her grasp.

"We're a little busy," I call back, my arms still wrapped around Jax's neck as my feet drag on the floor.

Olivia pulls away from Rhett and leaps to Callie's aid, taking the mixer from her grasp before Charlie realizes it. She carries it under her arm like a football.

"She's headed for the door! Don't let her leave." Rhett tears after her and Charlie finally lets go of Callie, realizing she no longer has the mixer.

I slip off Jax's back and dart around him as I make a dash toward Olivia to offer help. Rhett reaches her at almost the same time, so we barely manage the handoff. I head toward the kitchen, the place that seems the least occupied at the moment, but the acrid smell floating in the air stops me in my tracks.

"What's burning?"

Jax takes the opportunity to dive toward me, snatching the mixer from my grip as Charlie yells in panic. "The cookies!"

Charlie pulls blackened cookies from the oven as I leap onto Jax's back again and Callie and Olivia try to trip Rhett.

Then Aimee walks in the front door. "How are my bakers doing? I thought I'd check—" The smile on her face whooshes off. "What on earth is going on in here?"

Chapter Thirty-Five

Jax

MOM LOOKS APPALLED, WHICH ONLY MAKES ME BURST into laughter. Tears form in my eyes as everyone laughs along with me.

Mom slowly joins our amused laughter, but after a few moments, she says, "Seriously, can someone please tell me what I just walked into? I need to know if I need to call Sheriff Baker."

"Ha. Ha. Very funny, Mom. We were just making sure the friendly competition truly was a competition."

"This is not what the bake-off is supposed to be about." She places her hands on her hips. "We told y'all not to sabotage one another. Should I tell the judges we've called things off?"

"No!" Charlie and Callie blurt in unison. Charlie's face is filled with desperation, and Callie throws some side-eye in his direction.

"Okay then. I can't believe I'm about to say this when you're grown adults, but y'all need to behave!"

"Yeah, Jax." Charlie gives my shoulder a playful nudge.

"You're the one who wouldn't let Lauren help me pick cookies up off the floor."

Mom clears her throat, getting our attention again. "I *did* come in here for a reason. There are only thirty minutes left. Will y'all be done and ready for the judges by then?"

"We can make that work. Thank you, Aimee," Lauren says sweetly. I'll have to give her a hard time later for being extra polite to my mom. I like that she cares about her image around her. It makes me think maybe Lauren's thinking beyond this secretive stage of our relationship.

"Well, get back to baking! The cookies aren't going to make themselves." Mom swivels on her heel to head toward the front door, but pauses, crouching down to drag a bowl out from under the shoe rack. Scrunching her nose, she asks, "Is this frosting?"

"That's where that went!"

Mom hands Callie the bowl. "Please don't put this on the cookies. I think there's dirt in it."

Charlie nudges me, muttering, "Nice hiding spot."

Rhett turns to me with a disapproving look. "You hid the girls' frosting under a shoe rack? Are you serious?" When he spins back toward the counter, I swear I see the hint of a smile on his face. I'm beginning to think Rhett isn't as intimidating as I thought.

————

"I can't believe y'all won! Our idea with Nana and Papa Rhodes was way better than whatever the hell your elf idea was." Charlie nudges Lauren's side, a teasing smile on his face.

"Oh, come on! Ours was creative. You just took a story that already exists."

"But we brought that story to life. Our cookies tasted like time travel," I argue. "Good punch line, by the way, Rhett."

"He gets that from me." Olivia tosses her hair.

"I do." Rhett snakes an arm around Olivia, pulling her in for a kiss.

"Boo! Get a room." Callie blocks her face, but I can tell by the smile on it that her actions are done in good fun.

"Oh, grow up!" Rhett throws a piece of cookie at her. "I'm not surprised the girls won. Between Olivia's marketing savvy, Callie's rampant imagination, and Lauren's organizational skills, it all came together perfectly."

"What about my baking skills?" Callie asks, frowning.

"You're just as good as me. We cancel each other out."

"I still don't think they should've won," Charlie grumbles. "'Justice for the elves'? Come on!"

"Hey, it's not our fault elves have been unfairly represented for centuries." Callie crosses her arms. "It's about time someone spoke up for them to let everyone know they're not the tiny little creatures we've been led to believe they are."

"It doesn't matter how silly the idea is, Charlie. It's all about how you present it," Olivia says.

"That's marketing talk if I've ever heard it."

"I don't think we are all capable of agreeing on how this bake-off was settled, so let's just move on," I offer, trying to keep the peace.

"That's what a loser would say. The vote was unanimous." Lauren gleefully spins in my direction, moving in close and then quickly dragging her addicting aura away from me.

I'm dying to get her alone. Her big hazel eyes and curves in those leggings have been distracting me all day. Trying to pretend my sole focus was on Charlie has been difficult to say the least.

"All right, well, I better head out." Callie stands from her seat. "Thanks for handing us the competition on a silver platter, boys. Maybe next time you can actually put in a little effort and make it fun?" She smirks as she heads toward the door.

"Yeah, we better get going too." Olivia gets up. "Maverick and I will be helping with the Resilient Paws table tomorrow at the Christmas festival," she says, referring to the dog she and Rhett adopted from the rescue last year. "Plus, this is my first Christmas in Roots, so my mom wants to show me everything the festival has to offer. I just know it's going to be exhausting." Despite her words, Olivia wears an affectionate smile as she gives Lauren a quick hug.

Rhett nods at Charlie and me, which I'm beginning to think might be the closest we will ever get to a bro hug from him. Oddly enough, I'm starting to accept his reserved nature.

"Are you two going to the Christmas festival tomorrow?" I ask Lauren and Charlie.

"Of course." Lauren's tone is matter-of-fact. "I have to work at the Copper Hill booth."

"You're going to *work* at the Christmas festival? No one should have to work at the festival, especially not Little Miss Whoville."

"That's what I told her, but she keeps refusing." Charlie frowns.

"Come on, Freckles. You need a break." I catch myself

reaching out to grab Lauren's hand, but it's too late. Charlie is already giving me a look, his brow raised. I can't meet his gaze. After years of friendship, I know he can see right through me. It's a miracle he hasn't already figured out what's going on.

"Someone has to work the booth. This is how I'm going to spread the word about our shift to regenerative agriculture," Lauren insists. "Plus, people come from out of town for the festival. Think of all the new customers and connections. The ranch can't afford to pass up this opportunity."

"But, again, the girl whose favorite holiday is Christmas deserves to enjoy the *Christmas* festival."

"I'll still enjoy Christmas day with my family."

I glance in Charlie's direction for some help. She may be mine now, but I still haven't figured out exactly how to get through to her.

"Let me help then," Charlie offers. "We can rotate shifts so you can enjoy part of the festival too."

"No way. This is the first time in years you'll be around for it. People are going to want to see you, and you deserve the chance to enjoy it."

"I don't exactly mind being stuck at the booth for a bit. I'm sure Jax will pitch in to help too." Charlie nudges me in the side, and funnily enough, a wave of relief rolls over me at the gesture.

The fact that he thinks he needs to convince me to help Lauren is laughable, but I do my best to play the part he expects. "Uh, yeah. I guess I can do that."

Hurt flashes in Lauren's eyes. This is getting too complicated already. I feel like I can't win with anyone while I'm keeping us a secret.

I rise from my chair. "Do you two mind helping clean up before you head out?"

Charlie nods, going into his natural helper mode. He may be a bit of a troublemaker, but he's also the best guy I know.

"What do you need me to do?"

"Can you take the garbage out? Lauren, maybe you can clean the counters off, and I'll get the floor?"

They both nod, and as soon as the door closes behind Charlie, I grab Lauren by the waist, pushing her up against the fridge and pressing my lips to hers. As much as I hate to do it, I quickly break apart from her. The look of amusement paired with the way her breath catches makes me want to pull her back in for more, but instead, I blurt, "I want to help you at the booth tomorrow. I just can't be super enthusiastic about it in front of Charlie. The version of me he knows wouldn't be."

She nods, a grin taking over her dazed expression.

I kiss her again. "He's going to be back in probably two more seconds, but I need to see you later. Hiding us all day has been torture."

"Charlie is supposed to stay over tonight."

I throw my head back, groaning. "That co—"

"But I can sneak you in later if you want." The smirk on her lips is enough to stop my heart.

"Yes, I very much want that." I unabashedly pull her in for another kiss, but the sound of the front door opening startles me. Instead of keeping my cool, I accidentally shove Lauren away. Now a solid two-and-a-half feet across the kitchen, she narrows her brows as if to ask *what the hell was that?* Or, I guess in Lauren-speak it'd be *what the heck was that?*

Charlie dusts his hands off. "What else do you need me to do?"

"I think that's it."

"That's it? You just asked us to stay and clean up, and all you had me do was take out a measly garbage bag."

"Yeah, I guess the kitchen is in better shape than I thought."

"You've been acting kind of weird since I got back. Are you okay?"

Honestly, I've never been better. "I could say the same for you, California Boy."

He rolls his eyes, draping his arm over Lauren's shoulders. "Come on, Lo. Let's go. I'm ready to swap whatever voodoo stuff is going on over here for an ice cream chat."

He tosses one more look over his shoulder before they head out, and I can tell the poor guy is genuinely concerned. It simultaneously warms and breaks my heart.

I do my best to distract myself by putting the last of the dishes in the dishwasher and starting it, but a buzz in my back pocket catches my attention.

LAUREN

My place. 11 pm.

Chapter Thirty-Six

Lauren

As soon as we are inside my house, Charlie rifles through my freezer. "All right. What flavors do you have?"

I slide onto a barstool at the kitchen counter. "You were serious about the ice cream talk tonight? We just baked cookies."

He turns to face me, a carton already in hand. "And I don't know about you, but one measly little cookie isn't going to ruin my appetite." He grabs the other carton from the freezer. "Since when did you start turning down ice cream?"

Since I realized an ice cream talk could last for hours and delay me seeing your best friend. "Okay, fine."

"Do you want chocolate thunder or mint chip?"

I peer over the counter top. "I thought there was a cherry chunk in there too?"

"Yeah, but I know you're just being the best sister ever and stocking that one for me because you refuse to eat ice cream that doesn't have chocolate in it." He beams, and it instantly churns something inside of me. It's been so long since we've had this. I've missed my big brother.

Handing me a spoon and the pint of chocolate thunder with a knowing look, he settles onto the couch with the cherry chunk.

"So, tell me, little sis, how's life?" he asks as I plop down next to him. "And don't give me fake fluff. This is our first life talk in ages. You need to be honest with me. I know you've had your fair share of shit handed to you lately."

I choke out a laugh. "That's one way to put it."

"How are you doing since the whole Austin thing?"

"Surprisingly really well."

He pauses his spoon mid-scoop as if he doubts me, and I flood with guilt. I want to offer more, but I can't tell him about the ways Jax has been there to push me out of my comfort zone and show me what I deserve. Even if I were ready to tell him about us, Jax should be part of the discussion.

I also can't tell Charlie how overwhelmed I've felt stepping into a lead role on the ranch because I don't want to make him feel bad for leaving. I'm proud of him for recognizing he wanted to try something else, and until recently, I had no reason to think things weren't going well for him in California.

At the end of the day, none of this stuff matters because I'm doing well, considering the stress of the ranch, Dad's condition, and my breakup with Austin. I just need to get through this busy season of life, but I'm fine.

"Seriously, Char, I'm good." I lower my carton of ice cream to my lap, looking him in the eye. "Things were pretty difficult at first, but I've had a lot of people supporting me lately, and with some time and space, I've come to realize Austin didn't treat me the way I deserve. I couldn't even fathom spending the rest of my life with him now. It's been good for me to explore who I am again. I lost myself somewhere between fifteen and twenty-three."

He locks eyes with me, like he's searching my soul. "And you're doing okay with everything that's been going on with Dad?"

"That part has been tough, but you know him. He's never going to give up. We had a minor emergency on the ranch last week, and he refused to sit back and let us deal with it."

"Classic Dad. He always wants to be in control, kind of like someone else I know."

I ignore his remark. I know he's right, but I don't want to go there right now.

Drilling my spoon into the chocolate heaven before me, I ask, "Do you have any questions for me about Dad?"

"You've kept me pretty informed, and he and Mom filled me in the other night. I'm not worried about him. He's a strong man." Charlie sticks his chest out in pride, but I don't miss the slight falter of his voice. "So, you promise you're okay?"

"I promise."

"After the whole dog-stealing incident, I didn't expect to come home and see you so at peace, but something has seemed different. It almost—never mind. It sounds ridiculous."

"Almost what?"

"Your energy today at the bake-off almost reminded me of your pre-Austin days."

I turn my face down to search for a glob of brownie,

hoping to hide the way my cheeks are turning bright pink. "Well, there's all the evidence you need. I don't lie to you, Char. I told you I'm good."

Except I am a big fat liar, aren't I? He should know what's going on between his sister and his best friend, two of the most important people in his life.

I savor the rich and melty chocolate notes, but they don't hit the same tonight with this awful guilt churning in my gut. Desperate to take the attention off me and rid myself of the possibility of telling Charlie a real lie, I ask, "How are you doing?"

He shifts uncomfortably, but before he can respond, I add, "I know you're going to say you're great because that's what you've always done around me. Maybe I shouldn't be worried, but I'm a little concerned about your sudden decision to come home for longer. I thought it was because of Dad, but it feels like something else is going on."

He shoves a massive bite of cherry chunk into his mouth, and that's all the answer I need. Something *is* going on.

"Come on." I extend my leg, tapping him with my foot. "I'm your sister. Tell me what's going on."

"It's not a big deal." He shrugs. "Work has been shitty for a while. I don't like the people I work with or the lifestyle of the people I hang around. It's made me miss my family and even made me miss Roots a little. There's something about the slower pace of life here. I've missed being outside every day, riding horseback, and being in touch with nature."

In an instant, I'm across the couch and wrapping him up in a hug. "I've missed you so much."

"I've missed you too." He squeezes me tight.

When I pull back, he pounces on the sad look in my

eyes, going into overprotective brother mode. "What's wrong?"

"Nothing." I force a smile. "I've just really missed having you around. It was hard on all of us when you left, and it's nice to hear you don't hate all of this, all of us."

"I could never hate you." He pulls me in for another embrace. "I was just young and curious, maybe even a little stubborn when I left. It had nothing to do with you or Mom or Dad."

"I didn't realize how much I needed to hear that," I mumble against him.

"I'm sorry it took this long for me to say it."

"Have you thought about coming home?" Hope floats inside of me. Everything I've been dealing with lately would be easier with my big brother around again. *Gosh, I've missed him.*

"I can't come back." He turns his eyes down.

"Why not?"

"I left so abruptly. People were counting on me. It's one thing for me to come back and visit, but I definitely can't move back here just because I'm having some sort of quarter-life crisis, not after what I did."

"No one cares about how you left anymore. We just want you home again."

He shakes his head. "It's not in the cards for me. I'm sorry." Setting his carton on the table, he straightens up a bit. "I'm trying to be better though. I'm calling home more and making family a bigger priority. I don't want to hide everything I'm going through from the people I love anymore, and it feels good to talk to you now."

I gulp, his words striking a chord. *I don't want to hide everything I'm going through from the people I love anymore. It feels good to talk to you now.* Meanwhile, I won't admit that I need help with the ranch or that I'm dating my brother's best friend, but my whole life has been spent hiding to keep everyone else around me happy.

Maybe there's a way to have more balance, but I don't know how to get there yet, so I keep my mouth shut, instead wrapping my arms around Charlie's neck. "I'm proud of you. I've missed you so much, and I need you to know that if you ever stop being so stubborn and decide you want to come home, I'll be here to support you."

He gives me a soft smile. "Thank you." When he pulls away, he gently punches my shoulder as he adds, "I love you."

I can tell from the punch that I got too sappy for him. Maybe Charlie isn't quite where he wants to be yet, but he's definitely opening up more than when he left this town.

———

While brushing my teeth, I type out my to-do list for tomorrow on my phone. I should create some pamphlets with information about regenerative agriculture and what it will mean for our ranch and Roots. I also need to print out an updated pricing guide for our products and maybe I should try to stop by the general store on the way over to the festival to get some cute Christmas decorations for the booth. *Gosh, I'm going to need to get up earlier than I thought.*

A wave of exhaustion rolls over me, but I power through and keep adding to my list because what else am I going to do? The work needs to get done, and it's important to me, the ranch, and my family.

I put my toothbrush away and inhale a deep breath, closing my eyes as I do so. My ringtone brings my eyes open as I grab my phone off the bed next to me, checking the screen and expecting to find Jax's name. Instead, it's Olivia's contact photo.

I answer hesitantly, sitting on the corner of my bed. "Hello?"

"Hey! I'm sorry for calling so late. We're at the vet right now with the puppy you got along with so well at yoga."

"Oh no. Is she okay?"

"She will be. There was an incident." A dog barks in the background. "She's going to need some stitches, and we need to find her a foster home where she can recover, preferably one that doesn't have other dogs she'll want to play with, so my house is out of the question. I thought maybe you'd be open to taking her?"

I pick at a stray thread on my bedspread. I can't fathom taking on more responsibility right now, but how am I supposed to say no to my friend and this poor dog?

"Of course I'll help out. What do you need from me?"

"They're going to keep her in the hospital overnight, but maybe you could pick her up tomorrow after the festival? She'll have the stitches in for two weeks. Once they're out, we can take her back at the rescue, unless you want to keep her."

The hope in her voice only adds to my building overwhelm. I can't believe I'm adding take care of a puppy to my never-ending to-do list.

"Two weeks sounds manageable." I try to keep my voice even.

"Thank you so much! We'll provide you with food, a bed, and all that fun stuff. I'll see you tomorrow, okay?"

"Sounds great."

When I hang up, there's a light tapping on my window. Jax's smiling face is peering through the glass. He's already in a plain white T-shirt and gray sweatpants, his eyes light with joy and a hint of mischief.

I slide my window open as quietly as I can because Charlie is staying in the guest bedroom on the other side of my bedroom wall. "Hey, handsome."

"Now that nickname I could get used to." He smirks. "Can you help me? I'm getting too old for this sneaking around stuff."

"You're only twenty-five."

"I hear that's when things go downhill. You wouldn't understand. You're still so young."

"I'm barely a year younger than you." I giggle, offering him a hand.

"Oh, what I'd give to be twenty-three again." He gives an exaggerated groan as he pulls himself through my window.

"You're ridiculous."

"Talk to me when you're my age. Then you'll get it." Once he's through the window, he wraps me in his arms, pressing a kiss to the crown of my head before drawing back to look me in the eyes. "How's my girl doing?"

"Better now that you're here."

I settle into the warmth of his touch, releasing a breath. I'm so grateful for Jax and his gentle comfort. Being in his arms relieves the weight of everything that was plaguing me moments ago. It's as if I no longer have a single responsibility except to be cared for by him.

"I missed you."

"We were with each other all day." He squeezes me tight.

"That's not what I meant."

"I know. I missed you too."

In an instant, his lips are on mine. In our frenzy to show

each other how much we mean to each other, I bump against my dresser, a surprised squeak escaping me. Jax chuckles as he maneuvers me to safety, but then there's a knock on the door.

"Is everything okay in there?"

Chapter Thirty-Seven

Jax

"What's all that noise?" Charlie asks.

Lauren moves quickly, shoving me into her closet and closing the door. As I'm thrust into the darkness, I trip over her shoes, unfortunately adding to the noise.

On the other side of the door, I can still make out slightly muffled voices.

"What's up?" Lauren sounds guilty as hell as she swings her door open. I can already picture Charlie narrowing his brows at her in suspicion. *Come on, Freckles! This is not how I want him to find out.*

"I heard something. Thought I'd check on you."

"You still don't trust that I'm okay, huh?"

"No, that's not it. I just could've sworn I heard someone else." Charlie's voice grows louder like he's stepped into her room. "It sounded like you were hurt."

"Oh, I was just going through my to-do list for tomorrow. I like to say it all out loud. Then I stubbed my dang toe on my dresser."

There's prolonged silence. I can only assume Charlie is staring her down, trying to determine whether he should believe her.

"You said you don't lie to me."

"I'm not lying to you. The noise you heard was me bumping into my dresser. I'm fine."

"You've been acting a little weird since I got home. Is there something in the water here?"

Lauren laughs, all high-pitched and nervous. *How on earth did she think it'd be a good idea to keep our relationship a secret when she's clearly terrible at it?*

"Don't be ridiculous, Char." She moves across the room. "I'm really tired and have a lot to do tomorrow, what with the festival and all, so I'm going to hit the hay."

Charlie's husky sigh could be heard all the way across town. "I opened up to you tonight, but you're still hiding something from me. That hurts."

My heart breaks on Lauren's behalf.

Strained silence fills the room, and the walls of Lauren's closet do nothing to cut the tension.

"You're making more out of this than it is. I'm fine. I need to go to bed. Good night."

There's defeat in his voice as Charlie moves toward Lauren's door. "Night."

When Lauren opens her closet for me, there's pain in her eyes, and it hits me then that there's something else there too. I don't know how I missed it before. She looks *exhausted*.

Without saying a word, I pull her toward the bathroom, and for perhaps the first time ever, she doesn't resist. I set her on the edge of the tub and braid her hair like I've been practicing, taking my time. Then I rummage through her bathroom cabinet, pulling out her face wash and the rest of her skincare.

Despite wanting to take care of her more, I give her the space to do it herself, a morsel of control I can tell she needs in this moment. It isn't until she's rubbing the last of her moisturizer into her skin that she speaks. "I think the secret-keeping is the hardest with Charlie."

I settle onto the ledge of her bathtub. "The ball is in your court. If you want to march over there right now and tell him what's going on, I'll handle whatever consequences there might be."

"I appreciate that. I do." She drops her head. "I just feel safer keeping things a secret. It keeps everyone else's opinion out of our relationship, and I've realized it gives me some semblance of control." She tucks herself into my chest, whispering, "I *want* to be ready."

"It's okay. You don't need to be ready yet." I rub her back gently. "We'll figure it out."

"How can you be so calm about this?" She pulls back to look at my face. "He's your best friend. This can't be easy for you either."

"It's not, but I know it's not forever. We'll tell him eventually. Right now, I'm trying to focus on you. I can tell something else is eating at you besides what Charlie said."

She sags. "You can tell?"

"I notice every little thing about you, Freckles."

That brings a soft blush to her cheeks, which I press my lips to. "Tell me what's going on."

She drops her gaze, not making eye contact with me. "I'm tired. I have a lot to get sorted out for the festival tomorrow. I'm sorry, but we should probably go to bed."

I can't help but feel disappointed. "I know something is bugging you. I can see it. Why won't you let me in? Don't you see I want to be here for you? I want to care for you through the good and the bad, mess and all. You've done that for me."

"Not like this." She scrambles out of my lap. "I don't want to hide things from you, but there's a reason I keep my feelings to myself, Jax. Sharing them has never done me well."

"Why not?"

She holds out her hand, ticking each reason on her fingers. "I've had to hide my problems from Charlie because I'm proud of him for going after what he wanted, and I don't want him to feel guilty. I've hidden my feelings from Austin because he didn't give me the kindness and care I needed. I've pretended like my dad is fine because he's too stubborn to admit he has a problem that could slow him down."

Now we're starting to get somewhere. "You've been there to pick me up when I've had a bad day. You've seen past my family's messy history and my reputation and shown me there's someone out there who thinks I'm a good man. Just let me in, please. I want to be there for you. I promise telling me won't change the way I think about you. It won't burden me. It'll just mean I can be there for you in your time of need."

"Won't that turn me into a burden?"

"No, I *want* to help you." I stand up, taking her hands in mine. "Plus, it'll feel good to let someone in, to stop hiding things from the people you care about."

Something I said, or perhaps the desperation in my voice, resonates with her because she looks back up at me, wincing the slightest bit. "I'm overwhelmed. You were right. I've been trying to be everything for everyone, and I'm starting to think I'm not good enough to manage it all."

In an instant, I'm dragging her to out of her bathroom

and sitting us both down on the edge of her mattress. "Not good enough? Don't you dare say something so ridiculous."

"It's true. I'm not doing a good job with the ranch, as proven by the heater incident. It took the help of three more people who don't even work for the ranch to get that situation sorted out because I didn't plan ahead."

She turns her gaze from me. "Before you showed up, I made my to-do list for tomorrow, and it turns out it's a mile long. I *knew* I was going to have a booth for the festival and that I'd need to prepare, but I haven't had a second to breathe, let alone do all the things I should be doing to make sure it's a meaningful contribution to the ranch."

She chews on her lip, her body tensing. "As I was realizing how behind I am, Olivia called me and asked if I could look after a puppy who just got stitches and needs a safe place to recover. I couldn't say no." She turns back to me, her eyebrows raised like she's asking for my understanding.

I pat her leg in reassurance, and she barrels on in a hushed tone so as not to alert Charlie again. "The cherry on top of it all is that my brother wants to know what's going on in my life, but I'm lying to his face, telling him I'm fine. I didn't mean to lie. I thought it was true, but, really, I miss him, and I wish he still lived here. I wish he could help with the ranch, and sometimes I think he would've been better at running Copper Hill than me."

She throws her arms up in exasperation. "Plus, I'm secretly dating his best friend, which I know is going to crush him when he finds out because it's already too late to tell him without hurting him. I should've told him from the start, but I'm too chicken, and I know you want to tell the world about us, but I'm here clinging to the safety of secrecy, so I guess that makes me both a bad sister *and* a bad girlfriend."

The look of defeat on her face physically pains me to see. I don't know what it's like to be overwhelmed by so many responsibilities, but I am familiar with the pain of thinking no matter what you do, you're not going to be enough. I hate that she believes her best isn't good enough.

Bringing my hands to her face, I say, "I need you to listen to me, okay?"

She nods.

"It's okay to accept help. It doesn't make you weak. Being unable to juggle a million things at one time doesn't mean you're not good enough. It means you're human. No one could handle the amount of things you have on your plate all alone. The fact that you've made it this far actually proves you're superhuman."

I pull away with a gentle smile. "Do you prefer Super-woman or Wonder Woman? Maybe Black Widow? She's kind of badass, and I wouldn't mind seeing you in that tight leather suit."

She bumps me with her elbow, a laugh slipping from her lips. "Jax!"

"Oh, sorry. I guess I'm getting a little off track." Except I'm not. I needed to see her smile and hear her laugh again. I can't take seeing her doubt herself. She needs to know how incredible she is.

"Thank you," she whispers.

"I'm not even close to done, Freckles. You're surrounded by people who worship the very ground you walk on, myself included, so don't be afraid to ask them for help. It's not a sign of weakness." I pin her with a look. "It's hard to open up, but I promise it's worth it. Now tell me one thing I can do to help."

"Could you and Charlie set up the booth tomorrow? If

you get the table set up, that'll give me time to create and print everything I need."

"I was already planning on it."

She traces lazy circles on my chest. "Okay, then can you also convince Charlie to cover for another thirty minutes, so I can sneak around the festival with you?"

"I would love nothing more than to sneak around the Christmas festival with the Queen of Christmas herself."

"I'm looking forward to it, Grinchie."

Laughter slips from my lungs, and I press another kiss to her forehead. "Thank you for opening up to me. It's okay to want to keep a little bit of control and to guard your heart. It's smart of you to, but I'm going to prove to you I'm worthy of sharing control with."

Her smile turns me into a puddle. I'm so far gone for Lauren. There isn't a thing I wouldn't do to get just the smallest hint of a smile from her. I'd let her call me Grinchie for the rest of my life if it meant hearing that musical laughter pour out of her. I'd braid her hair every night and let her drunkenly do her skincare routine on me if it meant she'd look at me with that dopey, loving glow in her eyes that I've come to adore. Being loved by Lauren would be the greatest honor of my life, and I hope someday soon she'll let down her walls enough to get there. Until then, I'll keep fighting for her.

Chapter Thirty-Eight

Lauren

There's no feeling better than waking up in Jax's arms. His strong yet gentle touch melts me like an ice cream cone in the Texas heat. His husky morning voice mumbling "Good morning" sends chills down my spine, and the smile slipping onto his face brings a smile to my own.

Everything about this moment is perfect. For the briefest moment, I forget about the festival. I forget about everything that needs to be done and all the ways I felt inadequate last night because how could I feel less than when Jax is looking at me like that? It almost makes me want to say three little words that just feel too soon to say. *Is it even fair to tell him I love him when I'm not ready to tell the world about us, when we live in this little bubble that isn't quite real life?*

Worst of all, being wrapped in Jax's loving arms makes me forget that my brother is right next door, and when he knocks on my door, calling out, "Happy Festival Day!" I have no choice but to leap out of bed and block him from my room.

He frowns at my abrasive approach, lowering the plate of eggs and toast in his hands. "What are you doing?"

"I just figured we should eat at the table. I'm not going to eat in bed." I take the plate, slipping past him toward the kitchen. "Why'd you do this?"

The look of hurt in his eyes tells me I said the wrong thing. All of this secrecy is getting out of hand. Maybe it's time to forget my reservations and tell everyone about Jax and me, but it's far from the right time to tell Charlie when his best friend is lying in my bed. I'd like to think Charlie will be okay with all of this, but he might not like that part.

Slipping onto a barstool at the kitchen counter, I say, "Thank you for doing this. It was really thoughtful." I scoop a bite of eggs. "Sorry for being weird. I've gotten used to living alone."

"I wanted to apologize for being so nosey last night." He grabs a plate from the cabinet. "Plus, I knew you were anxious about running the booth today, and I feel responsible. I know it should've been me."

"You always do this." I set my fork down while he dishes up a plate for himself. "It's okay that you left. I get stressed about handling all the ranch stuff, but I only worry because I care. I like the work I do, and I know you like the work you do, so you shouldn't feel guilty."

"Right." He shoves a heaping pile of eggs into his mouth.

We finish our food in silence, and then I pull my laptop out, opening up the document with the prices for our milk, beef, and tallow.

"I have some things to take care of this morning. Can you and Jax set up the booth for me?"

"Of course. I might have to drag Jax kicking and screaming based on his reaction yesterday, but I'll definitely be there."

I bite my lip as I ignore the urge to tell him he's wrong. "Okay, great. Thanks. I'm going to get dressed real quick."

I wrap my arms around Charlie's neck, giving him a quick hug, and then bolt into my room, closing the door behind me.

Jax scowls at me as he emerges from his hiding spot in my closet. "That's twice in less than twelve hours that I've had to hide here."

"I'm sorry! I just don't want Charlie to find out like this. I like you alive."

His eyes go round. "Do you really think he'd be that upset?"

"Not about us dating, but he might not like seeing you in my bed."

"Fair enough."

I tug him onto the mattress next to me, crawling into his lap. "I promise I'll make it up to you." I press a kiss to his cheek. "But just a heads-up, Charlie is going to call you soon to ask for help with the booth."

As if on cue, Jax's phone blasts out, a picture of Charlie making a stupid face lighting up his screen. Jax's eyes go wide as he scrambles toward my window. "That's his custom ringtone. He set it in high school, and I never changed it."

He slides the button on his phone to answer as he shoves my window open in a frenzy. He pauses in the window, leaning forward to give me a quick kiss before bolting, but I don't miss him saying, "You thought you heard my ringtone in Lauren's house? What're you on, man?"

As soon as I'm dressed, I open my door to find Charlie pressed up against it, listening.

"What are you doing? You're being weird."

"*I'm* being weird? I don't think so." Charlie barges into my room. "Where is he?"

My heart stops. "Who?"

"Jax. I heard my ringtone when I called him." He swings my closet door open to find nothing but clothing. "It was coming from your room." Charlie surges to the far side of my bed, looking underneath it.

"What on earth are you talking about? Your ringtone?"

"I called Jax, and I heard the song I set on his phone whenever I call. Why would Jax be in your room?"

"That's a great question. Why would he be in my room?"

His shoulders sag. "I don't know. Things have felt off with you two lately."

Well, that makes me feel guilty as heck. I may not have directly lied to Charlie, but I may as well have. *A lie by omission is just as bad, isn't it?*

"I'm sorry I've made you feel that way." I place my hands on both his arms. "I want to talk about this more, but I need to get going. I'll come find you as soon as I'm done with my trip to the general store."

I pull my purse from the shelf in my closet. "Let's hang out just the two of us again tonight, okay?" I grab his hand, meeting his eyes. "You're important to me."

"I'd like that."

———

THE GIRLS

ME

Y'all I need help

CALLIE

We've got you babe! What do you need?

OLIVIA

Is everything ok?

Charlie is getting suspicious but I want to be with Jax during the Christmas tree lighting

Also I need some time to give him a gift I made

OLIVIA

Awww we'll come up with something

CALLIE

You two are so cute I want to barf

Gee thanks 

CALLIE

I'd love to help but you have to promise not to leave me alone with your brother... things were a little weird at the bake-off

I'm sorry Cal!!

CALLIE

It's not your fault. It's just hard to act like the past didn't happen

OLIVIA

I'll cover for you!

CALLIE

And I'll help her practice her serious face

OLIVIA

Hey!!

CALLIE

You know I love you Ol

CALLIE

Also we need a better name for our chat.
The Girls is so unoriginal

Is it scary to be in your brain? You just ping
pong around from one thing to the next

CALLIE

I'm ignoring that

OLIVIA

Ohhh what are the people called who
follow Voldemort?

What?

**CALLIE CHANGED THE CHAT NAME TO THE
DEATHEATERS**

OLIVIA

YES!!!

What's happening?

CALLIE

We're showing our support for you and Jax

CALLIE

AKA Voldemort

Idk why I'm friends with you two

OLIVIA

Because we are going to help you be with
your man today

Oh that's right... love youuuuuu 

CALLIE

That's what I thought...

"How are things going over here with my favorite sibling duo?" Olivia asks, leaning against the booth.

Charlie smirks, turning to me. "Have I told you she's my favorite of your friends?"

Olivia swats at Charlie in fake humility.

"We're doing great," I say. "We've already sold a couple half cows for the spring, and a whole lot of tallow. People have been going crazy for that stuff lately."

"That's amazing!"

"How are things going with Carol at the Resilient Paws table? Are the ornaments working out how you expected?"

"Rhett is watching the booth right now, and they've been working like a charm. People love ornaments with their pet's faces on them." Olivia pulls her phone from her pocket, showing me a photo of a little boy with a puppy in his lap. "I also think I've locked in an adoption for one of the puppy yoga dogs."

"That's great!"

"That's why I do what I do." She beams, pulling her elbows from the booth and standing tall. "Anyway, I came over because the tree lighting is in about ten minutes, and I thought the biggest Christmas lover known to man should take a break to see it."

"Agreed," Charlie butts in. "We should all watch it together. The booth can manage without us for a few minutes. The whole town will be at the lighting anyway."

I glance at Olivia with wide eyes. I have no arguments to make with Charlie's logic.

"Sure!" I guess she and Callie didn't prepare for Charlie to go off-script.

When I give her my best *what are you doing* look, she tilts her head down at me to indicate I should follow her lead. I don't trust Olivia to be good at this kind of thing, but I don't know what other choice I have.

"Let me just text Rhett so he can meet us," Olivia announces loudly.

Within seconds, my phone vibrates.

THE DEATHEATERS

OLIVIA

Callie, get Voldemort ready

OLIVIA

Lo, get lost in the crowd. I'll stick with Charlie. We'll tell him you found Callie and are watching with her

Maybe this is planned better than I thought. As we weave in and out of people to get closer to the giant tree in the square, I slowly drift back. Once I can no longer see the two of them winding through the crowd, an arm wraps around my waist.

I squeal as that arm tugs me from the crowd and behind a giant inflatable decoration.

"Shhhh!" Jax presses a finger to his lips. "We're trying to be incognito."

"Then don't scare me like that." I give his shoulder a shove. "I thought I was being kidnapped!"

"Come on, Freckles. We're in Roots. There aren't any kidnappers here. The sheriff said it himself. You were the most exciting thing to happen to him in a while."

I roll my eyes. "That's not *exactly* what he said."

"You know what I mean." He swats his hand then pulls me in for a kiss, taking advantage of the privacy provided by the giant inflatable Santa and his eight reindeer.

When he pulls away, I ramble on about how excited I am for the tree lighting. "We used to go as a whole family. I'm not the only one who likes Christmas." I laugh, but Jax doesn't even smile. He's zoned out, watching the crowd as Callie helps us recirculate into it.

"Jax, are you okay?"

When he turns to me, he looks like an alien dropped onto this planet. "What?"

"You seem distracted."

He plasters on a smile that mirrors one the Joker would wear. "I'm sorry. It's nothing."

I inspect him once more, alarm bells going off in the back of my mind, as the three of us settle into the back of the crowd. It certainly doesn't feel like nothing.

Chapter Thirty-Nine

Jax

WHY DOES MY PAST ALWAYS HAVE TO HAUNT ME? JUST
when I think I'm moving on, something reminds me of the
darkness I'm trying to leave behind. Today, it was a letter
from my dad. In over nine years, we haven't heard anything
from him, but now he's sending letters to Aunt Carol's
house. *What the hell?*

I do my best to keep my focus on Lauren. Today is
supposed to be all about her, but it's hard not to run the
words from the letter over and over again in my mind.

"Welcome to the eighty-seventh annual Roots
Christmas tree lighting!" the mayor announces, bringing me
back to the present. Thank y'all for coming. Whether you
celebrate Christmas or not, this ceremony is about sharing
in the magic of the season. Will y'all help me count down?"

I keep my gaze on Lauren, willing away any thoughts of
the letter. Her eyes blaze with excitement as music starts
and the mayor leads the countdown. "Five!"

"Four!" The rest of the town has joined in by now. "Three! Two! One!"

The tree lights up in an array of dazzling colors. Tinsel and custom-made ornaments, one for each year the festival has been celebrated, glimmer as the light bounces off them. The crowd bursts with excitement, hugging one another and laughing.

The lights give Lauren's blonde hair a reddish tint on one side and a green tint on the other. Her hazel eyes are sparkling in a way that tells me everything that went into making this small moment between us work was well worth it. She nudges me with her shoulder, a smile creeping onto her lips, which I can tell is her subtle way of telling me she's happy I'm here with her.

As the excitement slowly wears off, and the crowd disperses, Lauren turns to me abruptly. "We need to find a quiet place. I have a surprise for you."

My heart skips. I don't think I can take another surprise today.

Callie squeezes between the two of us. "So, I guess my part is over?"

"Thank you, Cal." Lauren wraps Callie in a hug. "Don't worry. Jax owes me a shift at the booth still, so I'll come find you in a bit."

"I'm holding you to that." Callie points her finger at us and raises her brows.

Lauren giggles and leads the way as we weave through the crowd, keeping an eye on each other while trying not to make it obvious we're sneaking off.

When Lauren takes a sharp right turn between two of the buildings, I glance around and follow her. It isn't until we're safely behind them and winding down a path in the tall grass behind that I ask, "Do you know where we're going?"

"Olivia did a little research. She said this trail should take us behind some trees and completely out of the way from everyone."

The path we are on is hardly one at all. It's a clearing in the knee-high grass that's maybe a foot wide.

"Are you sure this is the kind of surprise I'll enjoy?" I do my best to keep my voice light. "I'm kind of fond of my life, so I don't think I'd like to be murdered."

She laughs. God, I needed to hear her laugh. I swear it's already dragging me out of my weird mood.

She crinkles her nose. "You *think* you don't want to be murdered?"

"I don't know. Maybe I'd find a little Romeo and Juliet situation romantic in the moment," I say, hoping to get Lauren to laugh again.

It works, making my heart pulse quicker in my chest, and for a moment, I'm able to focus solely on Lauren's glowing face. The sight of her makes three little words pop into my head. It's getting so damn hard to hide my love for Lauren because everything she does is a constant reminder of how I feel for her. It's one thing to hide it from the rest of the world, but hiding it from her much longer might actually be the thing that kills me.

Lauren sits on a boulder just off the path, patting the spot next to her. "Romeo and Juliet committed suicide. It wasn't murder."

I frown as I join her on the rock. "I'm sorry I'm not the Romance King."

"You might be. You have your shining moments." She nudges my leg with a smile.

It's hard to see the good in myself right now. The letter I

ripped open this morning was a not-so-gentle reminder of the ways I've been a failure before, but I'm not about to ruin our day by talking about my wounds.

I rest my hand on her thigh. "How are you feeling today? Any better now that all the set up for the booth is taken care of?"

"Sort of." She shrugs. "I still have a lot to do that goes beyond this festival."

"Is there something we can do in the short term?"

"I guess another cowboy would help." She swats away a blade of tall grass that brushes her knee. "I've been stretched thin trying to do both the management and the cowboying. I know you've been helping in your free time, but we need another person, or maybe even two, who can dedicate full-time hours to the ranch."

"I'll help you write an ad tonight."

She shakes her head. "I can't. I told Charlie I'd hang out with him later. I'm feeling guilty."

Me too. "I bet Charlie would be willing to help you with the ad. He loves you, and he'd do anything for you."

She plucks a blade of grass and crinkles it in her hands. "I can't ask him to do that."

"Why not?"

"He left this town to get away from the ranch. I don't want to force him back into that world while he's here. It's not fair."

I dig the toe of my boot into the dirt. "Have you ever considered it wasn't fair of him to leave without talking with you first? He didn't even pause to consider how you might have felt about taking over the ranch. He didn't care if you would accept the responsibility or not. He just decided it was time to leave."

A bird chirping in a tree overhead fills the silence that

washes over us. My words and harsh tone surprise even me. The events of this morning are definitely adding to my reaction, but I suppose I never processed how upset I was with Charlie for leaving. No one saw it coming. He always said he'd move back after college, but he didn't. It stung to know he didn't trust me enough, or care enough about me, to talk through the pros and cons or give me a heads-up. It was further proof that even the people closest to me don't think I'm enough.

"It wasn't like that," Lauren whispers.

"Maybe not, but it still wasn't fair."

She nods quietly. After assessing me for a beat, she adds, "What's gotten into you today?"

"Nothing. I'm sorry. I guess I have some unprocessed trauma." I chuckle, trying to keep things light.

She presses her lips together. "That's the second time today your Joker smile has come out. You're freaking me out."

I drop my head in my hands. I wanted to be better at hiding this. Lauren deserves a perfect day, and I'm screwing it up. I need to think of something quick.

"It's the hunting trip," I blurt, moving my hands to look at her.

She draws her head back like that's the last thing she expected me to say. Her eyebrows are still narrowed like she doesn't believe me, so I keep explaining. "I know we talked about this being a chance for me to find joy for myself. It's been so long since I've allowed myself to take a moment like that. I'm a little nervous I won't be able to enjoy it properly, but I'm also excited to spend time with two of my favorite people and focus on letting myself be happy."

Silence falls over us, and I wait for her to respond, to see if my words were enough to throw her off track. She doesn't need to take on the worry I have about the letter. She'd turn it into another thing she needs to make right and balanced, but this isn't Lauren's problem. It's hardly even mine. I just need a couple days to get over this, and everything will be okay.

Chapter Forty

Lauren

HE'S HIDING SOMETHING. I CAN SEE THE PAIN glinting in his eyes. No amount of Joker smiles or silly jokes will cover that up, but I can see from the look on his face he isn't going to tell me what's running through his mind right now. It stings.

I know Jax is a good man, but watching him sit here and pretend like nothing is wrong reminds me of the times Austin lied to me to be with other women. It stirs up all the feelings of inadequacy I've been working to fight off over the last month. He clearly doesn't think I'm strong enough to handle whatever he's got going on, and it scares the living crap out of me.

My surprise for Jax is still in my pocket. I was so excited to give it to him. I poured my heart and soul into making the beaded keychain. Similar to the charm bracelet he gave me sophomore year, it was supposed to be a symbol of strength to help him overcome his self-doubts, a reminder that I care for him, and a way of thanking him for showing me I deserve to be treated with respect and kindness, both from those around me, and myself. He's given me the gift of unconditional love, and I wanted to return the favor, but now it feels stupid.

Jax stares at me expectantly, and I realize I haven't answered him. "Okay," I say, my voice coming out hoarse.

He watches me, waiting for me to say more, but I don't. What else am I supposed to say?

"We should head back. Charlie will be wondering where I am."

"Wait, I thought you had a surprise for me?"

I laugh a laugh that does nothing to hide my level of discomfort right now. "This *is* the surprise. I just wanted to give us some alone time to talk."

He looks disappointed, but I can't give him the keychain right now. I can't make myself be vulnerable after he clearly lied to my face. I don't know what happens next for us, but I know I need to get out of here right now.

GRINCHIE

How's the puppy doing?

ME

She only had to get up once last night. Charlie gave her love this morning while I took care of some things. I think it's safe to say she's living her best life

And FYI we're calling her Bella

So you're keeping her?

NO! I just couldn't stand the thought of calling her something lame and impersonal like puppy

Uh huh…

———

GRINCHIE

Merry Christmas Freckles!

How has your day been so far?

ME

Merry Christmas!

It's been good! Mom made biscuits this morning and we're going to spend most of the day in pjs playing games. Wbu?

It's good but I miss you…

I miss you too

T-minus 22 hrs till I get to see you again. It can't come soon enough 🤍

———

Charlie has been in a particularly nasty mood this morning, and I can't seem to figure out why. We had a lovely Christmas Eve and Christmas Day as a family. I *did* cream him in poker, but we played for chocolates, so he can't be that upset with me.

Tossing a duffle into the bed of his truck, Charlie grumbles, "Jax is supposed to be here any minute. Where's your bag?"

"I already put it in the bed of your truck." I point to my navy-blue duffel pressed into the back corner of the truck bed. "What's with you this morning? I thought you'd be excited about going on a hunting trip with your best friend and your favorite sister. Not to mention your new favorite dog." I scoop Bella up and bat my eyes angelically at Charlie.

"You're my only sister."

"Ouch."

He sighs. "Sorry, I got a call from work this morning. They want me to come back early."

"How early?" I set Bella down. She's tied up to an extra-long leash so she can be out here with us.

"By the twenty-ninth."

"What? No. They can't do that! You're supposed to come with us to the New Year's Eve party at the Long Neck. Plus, I thought your office was closed through New Year's Day."

"The office *is* closed, but it doesn't stop all those maniacs from working." He surges into the house, and I follow him, helping him grab the pile of stuff he's gathered by the door.

"I thought you had a bunch of time off saved up?"

"I do, mostly because I never get to take it." He leads the way back to the truck and shoves Bella's dog bed into the back seat. "We're making a huge acquisition in the new year, and they need me around. Unfortunately, I'm good at what I do."

"What does that mean for the rest of your time here? Do we have to cut the hunting trip short?"

"It means I'll try not to be so bitter, but I need a day to wallow." He gives me a wincing smile as he climbs into his truck bed, shifting a few things around to make more room.

"As for our trip, we'll stay two nights and come back early the next morning. This way I can spend one more evening with Mom and Dad before I have to go."

My stomach sinks at the words. "I don't want you to go."

A tortured look flashes across his face, but he quickly replaces it with a smile. I hate seeing him put on a mask. That must be how Jax has felt, watching me insist I'm okay when he knew there was more going on underneath the surface. It sucks.

Charlie steps down and pulls me into a quick hug, mumbling something about how he'll be back as soon as he can, but we both know that means nothing. This trip was an anomaly. I can't expect Charlie to be home this long any time soon. Heck, I can't expect Charlie to be *home* any time soon.

Jax's truck rumbles into the driveway, and Charlie releases me, hustling inside the house and muttering something about one more thing to grab. I let him go, knowing he needs the distraction.

When Jax slams his door closed, he smiles at me like he just won the lottery. "Hey, Freckles." He wraps me up in a hug before I can hesitate. "Two days without you is too long. Never let me do it again."

I bite my lip, looking up at him in curiosity. Two days ago, I was convinced he was hiding something from me because he didn't think I was enough, but every text he's sent me and the way he's wrapping me up in his arms now is making me wonder how I could question the way Jax feels for me. He obviously cares immensely. I must've let my mind get the best of me yet again.

Jax pulls away, opening his tailgate. "Did you get the job posting up online?"

"I did, and Rhett agreed to keep an eye on any

applications that come through." I pull Jax's duffel down. "He won't hire anyone without my approval, but he'll let me know if someone comes along who would be worth interviewing."

"That's great!" He grabs his bow. "Are you ready to be away from the ranch for a few nights?"

"As ready as I can be. My little therapy dog helps too." I drop Jax's bag next to mine and gesture to Bella. "It's only been a few days, but she's already forced me to be back at reasonable mealtimes, and I got the okay from the vet to take her on a very slow, very short walk. I think she enjoyed it." I turn back to the chocolate furball at my side. "It was fun. Wasn't it, Bella?"

She nuzzles into my hand, blinking up at me with bright green eyes.

Jax shoves a couple things aside to make room for his bow before carefully noting, "It seems like she might be a good addition, maybe something that could become permanent?"

"We'll see." I grimace, trying not to get my hopes up that this could work. A few days over the holidays is hardly a good trial run with a dog. "Oh, by the way, our trip is only going to be two nights."

"Why?"

"Long story. Charlie will probably fill you in, but needless to say, he's not in a good mood." I lean against the truck. "You'll see soon, but he needs our support right now."

As if on cue, Charlie barrels out of the house, his hands full. "Thanks for the help, guys."

"See?" I whisper to Jax. "Char, you said you were going to get extra batteries. I didn't realize that was code for everything you could possibly carry from the tool shed."

"You can never be too prepared for a hunting trip. Right, Jax?"

"Right." Jax quickly moves to help Charlie load his items into the truck.

The second Charlie's arms are empty, he brushes his hands clean and announces, "The deer aren't going to hunt themselves. Let's go."

"This should be fun," Jax mutters.

I giggle as I help Bella into the back seat and then slide into the truck before Jax.

Once everyone is buckled, I turn to Charlie. "What are we going to do when we get there?"

"Unpack, obviously." Charlie pulls out of the driveway onto Roots Road. "Then I guess we can walk around the property a bit to look at tracks and see if we can get a sense of what their habits are. It's a bit late in the season. We're already past the second rut, but that means the whitetails are usually building more predictable routines. We don't have as much time as I'd like, but we can try to take advantage of getting there early to see what we find. We'll head out with our bows before dusk."

I blink a few times. "What's a rut?"

"It's the deer's breeding season and the best time to hunt for bucks because they're more active and less cautious. They're more focused on finding a lady than paying attention to their surroundings."

I nod my head in understanding. "So are human males always in a rut?"

Charlie glares at me, and I have to bite my lip to keep from laughing. "What am I going to do while you two hunt?"

"You're coming with us," Jax says, matter of fact. "That's why you're here."

"But I don't know anything. Won't I get in the way?"

"We'll teach you."

"I'm going to get killed with a bow and arrow this week, aren't I?" I straighten. "That's probably been your plan all along! Drag me out into the middle of the woods, where no one will find me, and make it look like I got in the way."

"That wasn't the plan before, but that's kind of brilliant. Way better than our original plan, right?" Jax glances at Charlie.

"You can't tell her that. Now she won't want to go out with us. We're going to need to come up with another way to eliminate her."

Even though I don't appreciate the fact that the two of them are talking about murdering me, the sight of Charlie's smile brings a wave of relief over me.

"Shit. You're right." Jax crosses his arms. "Back to Plan A, I guess."

"Or that's still your plan and you're trying to throw me off the scent!" I say, figuring I might as well play along.

That brings genuine laughter from the boys. "I promise we won't let anything happen to you, Lo." Charlie nudges me. "It'll be cool to show you the ropes. You're not bad with a bow and arrow. You could be a great hunter."

"I'm good with leaving that for you to handle. Besides, someone needs to look after Bella, and I have books to read."

"What's the point of coming out to the deer stand with us if you're just going to read?"

"You wouldn't get it. There's something about being in proximity to someone you care about while reading."

"What about someone you're just growing to tolerate?" Charlie nods his head in Jax's direction as he merges onto the highway.

Jax and I exchange a knowing glance. I try to think of

one of the insults Callie has given me for times like these, but I come up blank, so I wing it. "I think I more than tolerate you now, Char."

Charlie's smile is wiped clean off, as Jax covers his mouth, shouting, "Burn!"

"Lauren's the one who got burned because by suggesting *I'm* the one she tolerates, she's suggesting *you're* the one she cares for."

The truck goes silent. I don't know how to defend myself from that truth, and there's something searching in Charlie's eyes as he glances my way that suggests maybe he already knows exactly what's going on.

Chapter Forty-One

Jax

I brush my hands together in satisfaction as we step back into the Rhodes's family cabin. It's a couple hours outside of Roots and used exclusively for hunting trips. "I'd say day one was a success."

"You didn't get anything," Lauren deadpans.

"Maybe we would've if you hadn't brought the dog or squealed about how 'cute the baby deer' was," Charlie grumbles.

"Hey, we were quiet when the bucks came around. It's not my fault you have a crappy shot."

I choke on my sip of water, and Charlie nails me with a seething gaze.

"Sorry, man."

"I'm going to bed." He heads for the bedroom down the hallway where he dropped off his duffle earlier.

"But it's still early. You haven't even had dinner." Lauren leans against one of the dining room chairs, concern creasing her forehead. "Stay."

"I'm not hungry. I'm just tired." He gives her a quick hug and mutters, "Give me tonight. I've got a lot on my mind. I'll be fine tomorrow, okay?"

She nods hesitantly. When his bedroom door closes, she turns to me, her lower lip sticking out a little.

"He's going to be okay," I tell her, sweeping her up in my arms.

"I hope so. I'm worried about him. I think he's been putting on a face, and I'm concerned he's been doing it for longer than I realized."

"Sounds like a Rhodes family trait, but just like the other members of his family, he's strong-willed. He'll sort through it."

"Yeah," she says, but I can tell the urge to swoop in and smooth things over still has her in a chokehold.

"I brought pasta," I say, hoping to distract her. "I can treat you to some alfredo. We gotta carb load for day two of hunting. It'll be a marathon."

That puts a hesitant smile on her face, but I want more. I want her to be happy and carefree. I want to watch her tilt her head back as she releases some much-needed laughter. I want to listen to her ramble on in excitement about something Bella did or watch her dance with abandon in the kitchen.

So instead of pulling out the pasta, I pause and say, "On second thought, are you up for a drive into town?"

"What for?" She scoops Bella into her arms, like the dog is her shield.

"It's a surprise."

"You know how I feel about those. Plus, there's nothing in town besides a convenience store and a post office."

I grab my keys. "It'll be good for you to give up a little

control." I open the door. "Besides, I know they'll have exactly what we need."

———

"Okay, so my girl is comfy in her sweats, her belly is full of her favorite pasta, there's a dog in her lap, and she has ice cream waiting for her in the freezer." I put the last clean dish in the cabinet. "What else do you need?"

"Just you." She grabs my hand and drags me toward her. When we're chest to chest, she presses her lips gently to mine. "Thank you."

"It was nothing. I like seeing you happy."

"It's not nothing. Not everyone has the privilege of being in a relationship with someone who notices mood changes and takes the time to cook. I appreciate everything you do for me, and I savor every second we get to spend together. You make the everyday stuff feel extraordinary. Thank you for that."

"Thank you for being the kind of person who makes me want to do those things." I press a kiss to the crown of her head. "There was a long time when I thought something was wrong with me for not being able to fall in love with someone else. I thought maybe my past haunted me too much or that I clung to you because you were safe and unattainable. As it turns out, you're not all that safe, considering you're Charlie's little sister, but I want you, and I want to make every moment with you special."

This is the moment I should tell her I love her. I think she might be ready now, but, still, I can't bring myself to do it.

"Thank you, Grinchie." She curls into my touch, a smile growing on her face. "So, can we have ice cream now?"

"Yes, we can."

I pull the containers from the freezer and set them on the counter while she grabs bowls and spoons.

Once we've settled on the couch and given Bella a bone, Lauren turns to me. "Day one in the books. How are you feeling?"

"You're just jumping right in, huh?"

"That's how this works. The rule is if you eat ice cream with me, you need to be prepared to have a life talk. You signed the contract when you dug your spoon into the carton."

A chuckle escapes me. "Okay."

She spoons a bite of her chocolate fudge brownie ice cream, not taking her expectant eyes off me.

"It feels good to be out here with two of my favorite people in the world," I say, leaning back against the arm of the couch. "I'm slowly starting to recognize what I want in life and allowing myself to want it without judgment."

"What kinds of things do you want?"

"Well, for starters, I want to stop working at the bar." I don't wait for her reaction because I know I might lose my nerve. "I want to cowboy instead."

"You do?" Shadows darken her eyes.

"Yeah, I loved it back in the day with Charlie, but I thought it was because I was out there goofing around with my best friend. As it turns out, I enjoyed all the talks I went to at the conference, and helping you over the last couple months has shown me I love the simplicity of it: being out in nature, doing manual labor, having a purpose. I love doing the things it takes to run a ranch."

Lauren's shoulders rise to her ears, so I grab our bowls and set them aside. "What's wrong?"

"You're sure that's what you want to do?"

"Yeah. Why?"

She crosses her arms. "When did you realize?"

"I don't know exactly. I guess I've been thinking about it since the conference, but I didn't accept I could make the change for myself until recently."

The tension in her shoulders remains.

"What's going on, Freckles? Talk to me." I wrap her in my arms. "Your demons are my demons to fight too. We're a team."

Fears fills her eyes, but she goes soft in my arms.

"Did I do something wrong?" I hold her tighter.

"No, I'm really happy you found something you're excited about doing."

"Why'd you react like that when I said I wanted to work on the ranch full-time?"

She presses her lips together. "I know this is stupid, but a part of me has wondered if Austin only went out with me, and proposed to me, because he wanted the ranch. He buried himself in Copper Hill the second we were able to take any sense of control, and he loved it more than he loved me."

She grabs hold of her elbows, curling into herself. "Hearing you say you want to cowboy made me scared I had fallen into that trap again with you. Maybe you only like me because of the lifestyle you think you could have with me, or maybe you care for me now, but you'll come to love the ranch more. And possibly the worst scenario would be that maybe you never cared for me at all."

My heart splits in two. It's always been clear Austin's betrayal had an impact on the way Lauren saw herself and others, but it hadn't occurred to me she might still be fighting those demons in her head each day she's held me, kissed me, and told me she cared for me.

I want to fix it for her, but I realize the only way I can truly help is to keep doing what I've been doing. I need to keep loving and caring for her. Then, hopefully, one day she will understand Austin is an asshole who never deserved her.

"I'm sorry he put you through that." I kiss her temple. "I hate that he makes you question the way people see you, especially the way *I* see you. All I can say is that your position to inherit the ranch has nothing to do with why I'm with you. I'll work at another ranch as a plain old cowboy and be happy. I don't need to run Copper Hill with you to find the fulfillment I'm seeking."

I give her a squeeze. "And I'm going to keep telling you every day how amazing you are, how far gone I am for you, and how proud I am of you for continuing to be so brave. I'm only in this for you, the imperfect pieces just as much as the pieces of you that make me question if you're real because they're so perfect."

She bites back a smile that makes me think I'm doing something right, so I keep going. "I want to be around you all the time, and I want you to be happy above all else, okay?"

She nods silently before looking up at me with a hesitant smile. "I guess that's okay."

Leaning forward to grab her bowl, she remarks, "My ice cream is going to be a puddle now."

"We can get you a fresh bowl."

She shakes her head. "I'll eat it even as a melty puddle."

"Of course you will." I laugh, grabbing my own bowl. It's only halfway melted.

Silence washes over us. Lauren takes tiny bites of her dessert, letting it melt in her mouth. She looks so happy. I don't want to disrupt this moment, or the peace I see in

Lauren's eyes, but she released a weight from her shoulders, and now I need to take one off mine. I need to talk about this with someone, and I want that someone to be Lauren.

I take another bite of my ice cream, savoring the creaminess mixed with the Oreo flavor. "There's something else I want to talk with you about."

She crawls back across the couch, wrapping an arm around me in a way that mimics what I did for her a few minutes ago. "What's going on?"

I twist my spoon in the melted liquid at the bottom of my bowl, not looking up. "My dad sent a letter to Aunt Carol's house the other day. He's out of jail."

Chapter Forty-Two

Lauren

My jaw drops. I can only imagine how that letter must've made Jax feel. Putting all my focus on him, I squeeze him tight. "When did you find out?"

"I found the letter right before the festival."

This explains everything! That's why he was acting weird.

"Why didn't you tell me right away?" I have to rein in my frustration, knowing this isn't the time. Jax needs my support more than anything.

He rakes his hand through his hair. "I needed time to process everything. Plus, I didn't want to ruin the festival by telling you about the letter and making you worry."

I open my mouth and then close it, processing. I have so many questions.

Sensing the tension, Bella gets up from her spot on the floor, scampering over to us. I grab her before she has the chance to hop up on the couch and break her stitches. She immediately wiggles between us, setting a paw on my leg and her head in Jax's lap. It's like she knows precisely what we need.

I scratch Bella's back in the spot she likes. "I thought you said the drug charges would lock him up for a while."

"They did. He was there for over nine years, but he's out on parole now." Jax sinks his fingers into the soft fur behind Bella's ears. She must be in heaven.

"What'd the letter say?"

"He claims he's in Gambler's Anonymous, and that he wants to make amends."

I assess him carefully. "You don't believe him."

"How can I?" He shoves his empty bowl on the coffee table, throwing his arms up in the air. "He's never been someone I can rely on. He always said he'd do better when he sobered up, but that didn't stop the cycle."

"So what are we going to do?"

"We?"

"Yes, I want to be here for you."

He gives me a half-hearted smile before returning his attention to Bella. "We aren't going to do anything. He's on parole in Oklahoma, so he can't come to Texas." By the tone in his voice, he's trying to convince himself more than anyone.

"What'd your mom say?" I rub my hand gently on his knee "How does she feel about it?"

"She doesn't know."

"What do you mean?"

"I didn't tell her about the letter. She's been through enough because of that asshole. She doesn't need to be stressed out more."

My stomach sinks. I've seen Jax do a lot of growing over the last couple months, but this doesn't feel like a step forward for him.

"Are you sure that's what she'd want?"

"That's what she *deserves*."

This doesn't feel right. I don't think Aimee would want to be kept in the dark like this. "Jax—"

"It's the right thing to do." He tenses up. "My mom doesn't need to worry about this."

I lean toward him, keeping my voice soft. "And you're not at all curious about what your dad would have to say? You don't want to hear his apology?"

"Hell no!" His face turns red. "He only wants to do it to make himself feel better. I don't care. I don't want to hear it. I hope his guilt rots him."

I draw back, not sure what to say. I want to be supportive, but it's a lot harder to do when I disagree with him.

Regret flashes on his face at his harsh words. "I'm sorry. It's a sensitive topic. I'm trying to do right by my mom this time around. I won't repeat what I did to her before."

"Jax, you did nothing wrong. You don't need to fix anything."

"You weren't there." He shakes his head. "I need to do this for her."

Swallowing down any argument I have, I rub his back gently. "Then I'll do my best to support you. If you ever change your mind and decide you want to tell your mom about the letter, I'll support you in that too."

"Thank you."

Silence washes over us for a little while. Bella takes it as her sign to nuzzle her head under Jax's palm to get more pets. He grants her wish, and I watch him soften before my eyes. I wasn't kidding earlier when I called her a therapy dog.

Bella crawls all the way into Jax's lap as he says, "That's enough difficult conversations for one night, don't you think? Finish your ice cream and we can just sit on the couch together while you read."

"That sounds lovely, but I want you to do something you enjoy too. We came here this weekend so you could do something for you."

He nuzzles into me. "I've already told you being with you makes me happy."

"Grinchie." I do my best to sound stern.

"Fine. How about I play some music in the background, maybe a little John Michael Montgomery?"

I roll my eyes at his predictability, but a smile crosses my face.

———

Jax, Bella, and I lie on the couch like nesting dolls. Jax's back is pressed against the armrest with me propped between his outstretched legs as I read. Bella's happily curled up between my knees, breathing deeply.

I revel in the feeling of Jax's arms wrapped tightly around me as he leans his head back against a pillow. His eyes are closed, but I can tell he's still awake because he's been softly humming along to the music.

Normally any kind of noise while I'm reading would be a distraction, but I'm not bothered. It might also help that the character in my book is about to walk in on his best friend making out with his sister, and I'm very emotionally invested in what happens next.

As the song on the speaker reaches the chorus, Jax picks up his soft humming, pulling me in tighter to him, which I didn't think was possible.

"This is nice," he whispers, his lips brushing against my ear.

"You could turn the music up louder, you know."

"I don't want to disturb your reading. Besides, it's late. We can't risk waking Charlie and sending him into papa bear mode."

An easy laugh slips from my lips. "You're being ridiculous. We both know he sleeps like the dead."

"Yeah, but he seemed off today. It's not worth the risk."

I scooch a dozing Bella to the side as I sit up to face Jax. "Do you think he'll be okay with us being together when he finds out?"

"I don't know for sure." He bites his lip. "I hope so. If he isn't, we'll get him there." He kisses my cheek, setting loose a swarm of butterflies in my stomach.

A new song drifts from the speaker, and Jax's attention shifts from me to the music in the air. "I love this song. It makes me think of you."

I wrap my arms around his neck, moving in to kiss him. He accepts it, but he quickly draws away from me, slipping off the couch. "You have to listen."

"You just pulled away from me while I was trying to kiss you!" I drop my mouth open in disbelief.

"Because I'm constantly trying to figure out how to tell you what you mean to me, and all the words that tumble out of my mouth feel utterly worthless every single time. Maybe this song will do a better job than I can."

He pulls his phone off the table, sitting in the recliner across the room as he starts the song over. "The song is called 'I Love the Way You Love Me.' Will you listen this time?"

"I can do that."

He joins me on the couch again, draping his arm around me. I try not to let his touch distract me, focusing hard on the lyrics as John Michael Montgomery sings about how he loves every little thing about his girl, how she's managed to get him to start living his life for the little moments, like dancing in the rain, and how he ultimately loves how easily she loves every part of him.

The final soft note of the guitar plays, and one thought runs through my mind: *Jax loves me.* He may not have said it, but the song did. It fills me with a nervous energy, and the only way I know how to deflect it is with humor, so I turn to him and ask, "Was it the line about the two-hour baths that made you think of me? I'm sorry I stayed in so long that night, but you drew a *really* nice bath."

His lips quirk. "Is that all you got from the song?"

"No, I hung on every word." I cling to his arm. "It's beautiful, Jax. I want to listen again."

"I'll listen to it a hundred times if that's what makes you happy."

I'm quickly realizing Jax would go to the ends of the earth for me. With him by my side, I know I'm stronger than everything that's plagued me over the last several months.

Jax starts the song over then gets up from the recliner, holding out a hand. "Will you dance with me? No fancy swing dancing. I just want to hold you and sway to the music."

I take his hand in answer. With his hand on my waist and the other lacing our fingers together, I say, "I hope you know *I'd* do anything to make you happy. In fact, I want to tell Charlie about us tomorrow."

"Are you sure?" He looks hesitant, but there's a spark of hope in his eyes.

"I don't want you to feel like my dirty little secret. Besides, my best friends know about you and me. It's only fair your best friend gets to know about us too."

"This is different." He glances in the direction of Charlie's bedroom. "My best friend is also your brother."

"That's even *more* reason to tell him. Plus, I feel bad hiding it from him."

He grimaces. "Me too."

A combination of excitement and fear swirls in Jax's eyes as he processes what I just said. Finally, he mutters, "I might need to go home and grab my old cup just to be safe."

The laughter that escapes me is more like a cackle, and when Jax spins me around unexpectedly, it only grows louder. Bella wakes from her spot dozing on the couch, wagging her tail and letting out a bark of excitement.

"You think that's funny? You try getting kicked in the balls." Jax crosses his arms.

"Charlie won't kick you in the balls for dating his sister," I say, still giggling as I scoop a barking Bella into my arms and nestle her between our chests.

Despite the chaos in the room right now, Jax doesn't try to quiet me. He watches me, his eyes soft as he radiates his own happiness that's beautiful to see.

"I hope you realize how much I care for you, Freckles. I'm going to risk my balls for you tomorrow."

"You'll be fine. Charlie won't touch you." *I hope.*

Chapter Forty-Three

Jax

Before we left for our trip, Charlie and I agreed to let Lauren sleep in while we're here. She needs the rest more than she needs to be included in our almost inevitable failure this morning.

On my way to the kitchen, I grab Bella from her kennel and let her outside to do her business. Then I creep back to the coffee pot with her in my arms as I try my best to avoid all the squeaky spots in the floorboards. Even though it's been a few years since I've been up to the cabin, Charlie and I came here enough in high school and into college that I've practically memorized them.

Charlie joins me while the coffee brews. He's already dressed, which makes me wonder if he even slept at all, but he smiles brightly as he greets Bella and me. Maybe the time alone was exactly what he needed to get his head on straight.

The coffee maker stops, and Charlie isn't shy about taking the first cup. He's always been a coffee fiend.

"This is probably the first time we've been alone together since I got into town, huh?" he notes, blowing on the steaming mug.

"Yeah, I guess so."

"We'll have a lot to catch up on."

He's still smiling, but there's something in his tone that sends me into high alert. Ignoring it, I pull Bella closer to my chest. "Yeah, I want to hear all about your life in Hollywood, and everywhere else for that matter. Have you still been traveling a lot for work lately?"

He rolls his eyes. "You and I both know I don't live in Hollywood, and my life isn't that glamorous. I'm more interested in what I've been missing out on at home."

"Eh, you know Roots. Not much happens around here."

He sets down his mug, reaching for a thermos in the cabinets to take the rest of his coffee for the road.

"Want one?" He holds out a blue thermos with some cheesy saying about hunting on it.

"I'm good. I haven't been drinking much of the stuff lately. I'm already going to be jittery."

What I fail to mention is that I haven't been drinking coffee because Lauren doesn't drink it. She bought me coffee grounds and a coffee maker for her house, but I don't need the extra zing of energy in the morning anymore when I'm with her.

It's as if Charlie can tell I'm holding that information back because he eyes me closely, looking as if he wants to say something.

Pressing his lips together, he heads toward the door. "Are you ready to go?"

"Yup. Should we leave a note for Lauren to let her know when we left?"

"She'll be fine." His words have a bite to them, so I don't argue.

I put Bella in her kennel, muttering an apology before I head to the garage to grab my bow and the rest of our gear.

The deer stand isn't too far from the cabin, and the cold snap that swept through this part of Texas is long gone, so we opt to walk. It's a little more discreet than taking the four wheelers.

As soon as we've set everything up in the stand, Charlie turns to me, a creepy smile on his face. "You have to fill me in on what happened with that girl you were seeing. You know, the one who wanted to keep things a secret?"

The hair on the back of my neck prickles as I note his grip tightening on his bow.

"There's not much to tell."

"Well, are you still seeing her?"

I nod.

"Do you love her?"

I grab the bill of my hat, tilting it down a bit. "You know me."

"I thought I did." He crosses his arms.

"What's going on?"

He swivels toward me, anger in his eyes. "You tell me, Jaxon."

I scoff. "Dude, you know that's not my full name."

"Well, calling you Jax didn't pack enough punch."

"Did you slip something in your coffee this morning without me noticing?"

He frowns, pinning me with a stony-eyed gaze that makes my stomach drop. *He knows.*

"What are you doing with my little sister?"

"Nothing!" I blurt instinctively.

Clearly that was the wrong answer because his facial

expression darkens. "You call that nothing? I heard you two last night. I can tell you right now that's not nothing to her." He pokes me in the chest. "If you think I'm going to stand by and be okay with you messing around with her just because you're my best friend, then you and I don't know each other as well as I thought we did."

"That's not what I meant." I hold out my arms defensively. "I—we—I don't know. I wanted to tell you, but our relationship is a little complicated. She's been through a lot, so she was scared to tell people about us and have the chance for it to be ruined, but it's always meant something to me."

"So, you're not just screwing around with her?" He drops his hand.

"No. I love her. So much. I want to tell her, but I'm terrified she doesn't feel the same way."

"What do you mean?" His brows knit together. "I heard everything you two said to each other last night. She's clearly in love with you."

"You heard us?"

"You forget the cabin was built in the twenties. It has incredibly thin walls and next to no insulation."

I glance out into the field in front of us, processing everything. Finally, I turn back to him in disbelief. "You're the worst."

He chuckles. "If you didn't want to be heard, then you shouldn't have come here."

We sit in silence for a while, me watching the grass blow in the wind, and him keeping his gaze on me in a way that makes my skin crawl.

I know he can tell I'm ignoring him, but that doesn't stop him from asking, "So where do you two go from here?"

"I don't know." I shrug. "I don't want to screw things up."

"That'll only happen if you don't tell her how you feel."

"But she's been through so much. She's still learning to trust herself again and to trust someone else with her heart. I don't want to scare her off."

"Dude, she probably didn't think she was going to date again for a long time after Austin, but here you two are." He lifts his hand to gesture in my direction. "I know she still needs to work on not overloading herself, but she's clearly very happy. I think that happiness has a lot to do with you, so don't mess this up by waiting forever to tell her how you feel. She deserves to know she's loved after everything she's been through, don't you think?"

"Of course."

"My sister loves you, and you love her. Let it be that simple."

A deer creeps onto the field, but neither of us moves. The topic at hand is more important than the deer, and Charlie's words hit hard. I've been holding back with Lauren for all the wrong reasons. She deserves to know I love her. I've already waited nine years to tell her.

Charlie cuts off my train of thought. "Can I ask you something?"

"Would it matter if I said no?"

"Probably not." His lips quirk. "Why couldn't you two tell me? I know you've been keeping your relationship a secret from everyone, but why didn't you trust me with it?"

Guilt wraps its prickly tendrils around my heart. I reach out and clap my hand on his back. "It's my fault. I thought you'd be upset with me. I was too scared to face the possibility of you not approving, but we were finally getting ready to tell you. You just beat us to it."

"I'm sorry if I've been a crappy friend over the years." He winces.

"No, it's not that—"

He shakes his head. "I need you to know that as long as you treat my sister right, I'm going to be your number one fan. I'll even be your wingman if you want. It'll be just like old times."

"That's not necessary."

"Oh, come on. It'll be so much better than before because I'm helping you tell my sister you love her instead of helping you get some."

"You might still be helping me get some." I wiggle my eyebrows.

"Oh god!" He throws his head back. When he brings it back up to meet my gaze, he fake gags. "That's my sister you're talking about. I know I've been cool about things, but I'll change my mind in a heartbeat if this is how it's going to be."

"I'm just messing with you. Lauren is special." I pull my hat off, raking my hands through my hair. "I promise I'm not messing around with her. I've been in love with your sister for years, and I know she's been through the wringer. I wouldn't do anything to hurt her. I just want her to be happy and to see herself the way I see her."

Charlie softens. "If all that's true, I couldn't be happier for you two. My best friend and my sister. It doesn't get much better, right?"

I nod, nervous laughter slipping from my lips. "Yeah, I guess it doesn't."

"Let me know if you change your mind and want my help telling her you love her. I *do* know her pretty well after all, and I consider myself a bit of a Cupid."

"Cupid? When was the last time you even went on a date?"

"Why do you have to burst my bubble?" He throws his hands up in the air. "Besides, everyone knows Cupid doesn't date. He helps other people."

"Okay," I draw out.

His face turns serious again. "Also, it's my duty to let you know that if you ever hurt my little sister, I will kill you." He shifts his bow in a manner that is the opposite of subtle. "I'm not too bad with this thing, so you better be careful."

"Yeah, that's why we haven't shot anything yet, because you're so great with a bow."

Charlie's prideful smile falls from his face, and he shoves my shoulder, hard. "Shut up."

I snicker. My best friend knows about me and Lauren, and he's okay with it—*more than* okay with it. We're back to teasing each other like we always did. Everything feels right.

The buck is unfortunately long gone, so we sit in silence, watching the open field for a while longer before Charlie turns to me, rubbing his hands conspiratorially. "So, I know about you and Lauren, but she doesn't know I know. We could have some fun with this."

Chapter Forty-Four

Lauren

When Charlie and Jax come through the front door of the cabin, I'm ready to pounce on them for leaving me behind, but their arms are slung around one another and they're wearing bright smiles, which makes me hesitate.

"You two seem in a good mood. Did you get a buck?"

"Yeah, we did." Charlie stands straighter.

"That's great."

"Pretty sure it was because we left you behind, so thanks." He winks.

"You're such a jerk."

"You needed sleep, Lo. We're just looking out for you." Charlie pulls up a chair next to me. "Speaking of looking out for you, you're doing so great after your breakup with Austin, I thought maybe you'd be open to being set up with someone. I heard Rhett has a cousin who's supposed to come to town soon. He sounds like a catch: handsome, smart, kind. I guess he doesn't know much about ranching, but you're a pretty good teacher."

My mouth falls open, and I'm at a loss for words. I look from him to Jax, hoping he'll help me out, but he just shrugs.

Turning back to Charlie, I say, "I-I don't know about that." When I look at Jax again, he's biting his lip, his cheeks turning pink as he fights back laughter.

"What's going on?" I stand up from my chair, dragging Bella from my lap into my arms.

"I'm trying to set you up with Rhett's cousin. Why is this confusing?" Amusement fills Charlie's eyes.

Jax's back is turned to me, but it's impossible not to hear him wheezing in the corner.

"Why is Jax laughing hysterically?"

"I think he finds the idea of you dating Rhett's cousin funny."

I set Bella down and move across the kitchen, grabbing Jax's shoulder and spinning him toward me. Tears shimmer in his crystal blue eyes.

"Tell me what's going on."

"He knows," he manages between gasps for breath.

I tilt my head, silently asking if he's saying what I think he's saying. Jax nods.

"How did you find out?" I swivel in Charlie's direction.

He fills me in, causing heat to rise in my cheeks. I don't know what to say now that everything is out in the open, but I know I want to get Jax and Charlie back for what they did to me. "I need a moment alone with Jax," I say. "You don't mind, since you know about us now, right?"

"I guess," Charlie grumbles.

"I just need a few minutes. It's important."

Jax moves in my direction, cradling me instantly with his brows knit together. Guilt is already bleeding out of me, but I only feel so bad after what he just pulled.

"What's wrong?"

"We should go to the other room." I shoot Charlie a weary glance that does exactly what I want it to.

He strides to my side too. "You can't have that look on your face and then ask me to not be involved in whatever you've got going on. I'm your brother. I'm here for you too. In fact, I've been around longer."

"This doesn't concern you." I quickly look down to my feet, trying to hide the flash of a smile that blooms on my face in anticipation of what's to come.

"If it has to do with my little sister's well-being, then it has to do with me."

"Fine." I sigh heavily, turning to Jax. "I'm pregnant."

Jax's face goes white until realization hits him. We haven't yet done what's required for me to be pregnant, but I bet Charlie doesn't know that.

As expected, my brother swivels from me to Jax, pressing his finger into his chest. "What did you do to my little sister? I thought you said you were taking things slow. You said you cared about her."

"We are, and I do." Jax shoves Charlie back. "Freckles, tell him the truth."

"I *am* telling the truth." I bat my eyes innocently, but I must not do a good job because the tension releases from Charlie's shoulders.

"Why would you do that to me?"

"I did it to both of you to teach you a lesson." I cross my arms. "Don't mess with me, or I'll mess with you back."

"Okay, now that we've got our shots in, I think it's time for everyone to be civil, don't y'all?" Jax says, trying to keep the peace.

"I will if he will." I drop my arms.

"I will."

"Good because I've been dying to share this news with you two." I flounce into the chair I was sitting in earlier. "Rhett called this afternoon. One of the cowboy applications came through and looks promising. Although it sounds like we might be getting two new cowboys?" I glance at Jax for an answer.

"Are you sure you want me?"

I nod.

"Then, yes. You'll be getting two new cowboys." He pulls me from my chair, sitting down in it and dragging me into his lap as he presses kisses to my cheek and neck.

"All right! That's enough." Charlie shoots forward. "I may have been cool with you two being together, but I do *not* want a front row seat to your physical displays of love, okay? It makes me sick." He feigns a gag.

I grab a blueberry from the bowl I was snacking on earlier and toss it at him. "Grow up! This is what couples do."

He plucks the blueberry from the ground before Bella can get to it. "My best friend and my baby sister don't. In my mind, you two are merely special friends who hug. Please don't ruin the image for me."

Jax and I burst into laughter. I can't believe how good it feels to have this out in the open, and I *really* can't believe Charlie has been this cool about all of it, despite us hiding our relationship from him for a while.

Charlie's phone rings, interrupting our laughter. He picks it up, shrugging. "It's Mom. I'll be right back."

When he steps out onto the front porch, Jax takes advantage of our privacy. "What do you think of all this?"

"I'm really glad you and Charlie talked. And it sounds like you didn't need your cup, so that's a plus," I tease.

"Thank goodness. There were moments when I was worried."

"Was he hard on you?"

"He wasn't any harder on me than he should've been." He scoops a handful of blueberries from the bowl on the table. "I feel relieved. I hated hiding it from him."

"Me too."

"I think this calls for celebration." Jax shoves the last couple of blueberries into his mouth and gently brings me to standing. "Should I get the ice cream?"

He crosses the kitchen, not waiting for my response before he pulls the tubs from the freezer.

"Jax! It's too early." I giggle.

"Oh, come on, Freckles." His cheeks are rosy with joy. They're a stark contrast to Charlie's pale face when he walks back into the cabin.

My stomach plummets. "What's wrong, Char?"

"It's Dad." He stares at the ground, the shock apparent from the dead look in his eyes.

Fear curls around my body. "What happened?"

"He had a heart attack."

Chapter Forty-Five

Lauren

Charlie leads the way down the hall to Dad's hospital room, but I trail behind as my head spins with images of what I'm about to walk into. I imagine the pain he must've been in and all the scenarios that could've caused this. It's not lost on me that I was taking over the ranch to prevent something like this from happening to Dad, and as soon as I took a little time off, he ended up in the hospital.

Jax's gentle touch pulls me from the what-ifs, back into the brightly lit hallway. "Are you okay?"

I shake my head. "Not really. I don't want to see him. I don't want this to be real. It's like my worst fear just came true."

He stops walking, pulling me into a hug. "I promise it's all going to be okay."

"You can't make that promise. You're not a doctor."

"No, but I won't let you not be okay. Besides, you've grown so much over the last few months. I don't think there's anything that could break you."

His comfort brings a little peace to my heart. He's right. Between overcoming my breakup with Austin, holding the ranch together, and having Jax by my side, I don't think there's anything I can't handle.

I kiss him on the cheek. "Even if I can handle it, I don't want to lose my dad."

"We're talking about the man who has woken up at four a.m. every day for almost forty years. He's not going anywhere." His words pull a choked laugh from me as Jax places his hand on my lower back. "Come on. We'll go see him and prove to you he's going to be fine."

He laces his fingers in mine and doesn't let me release them, even when we join Mom, Nana, and Charlie in the hospital room.

Dad is hooked up to all kinds of IVs and drips, an oxygen mask strapped to his face. One of the machines by his bedside beeps steadily as the red lines spike and plummet in a manner that must mean something to the nurse who's watching it closely while the doctor speaks with Mom and Nana.

I try to listen, but the meaningless acronyms and complicated terms go in one ear and out the other. All I want to know is if Dad is going to be okay.

The doctor glances in our direction as the three of us newcomers stand awkwardly in the doorway, absorbing the sight in front of us.

"I'm sorry. If you're not family, you're going to have to leave." The doctor waves a dismissive hand. "There are too many people here."

Jax pulls me toward him, kissing the crown of my head as he whispers, "It's going to be okay. I promise."

When he unlaces our fingers and leaves the room, my

heart cracks. I believe I can handle this on my own, but I've also learned over the last few months that sometimes it's much better to wade through rough waters with someone you love by your side, and gosh, do I love Jax.

I watch Dad, lying in bed as only a shell of the man I know. Charlie instantly pulls me to his side, but he's not nearly as steady as Jax. The pain whirling in his body is evident, and I can sense his fear and heartache. This hug is for him just as much as it is for me.

I wrap an arm around him, playing my usual part of holding everyone together, even though I'm unraveling too.

When the doctor stops talking, she announces, "We're doing the best we can with Mr. Rhodes. We have a few more tests to run on him and then he needs to rest. Y'all can come back and visit him one at a time in a couple hours."

Mom and Nana walk toward us, but my strength falters, and I can't bring myself to leave as I watch Dad's lungs fill and deflate with the oxygen from the mask covering half his face. The awful beeping from the machine echoes in my ears, and I want nothing more than to be out of this room, but my feet are firmly rooted to the floor.

"Come on, Lo." Charlie tugs at my hand. "We'll come back."

"We can grab some lunch or something," Mom suggests, trying to sound chipper.

Nana nods. "There's a good sandwich shop nearby."

As all of this happens around me, I can't bring myself to leave my spot until Jax steps in the doorway. "Freckles, it's time to go. We'll come back soon, okay?"

His voice is soothing, his touch gentle. I relish his grounding presence the second he pulls me into his chest. In the safety of his arms, I realize I don't need to keep it together right now. After years of putting on a face and pushing myself until I'm buried, I let the tears flow and slowly allow myself to fall apart.

———

My sandwich still sits on the table in front of me, hardly eaten. With the results of Dad's tests still lingering, it's impossible to think about food.

"I can't keep waiting here." My chair screeches as I stand. Several other people in the crowded waiting room look up at me, but I don't care. "I'm going crazy."

Jax tilts his head to the side. "Let's go for a walk."

I take his outstretched hand and follow him down the hallway in the opposite direction of Dad's room. Mom and Nana's gazes lock on our connected fingers, but they don't say anything, and I don't have the energy to address it right now.

When we've walked in silence for several minutes, Jax finally asks, "How are you doing with all of this?"

My instincts are to put on a brave face and shield him from what I'm really feeling, but I recognize that's not the girl I want to be anymore. It felt good to cry in his arms earlier, and right now, the thing that would help me the most would be to tell Jax about all my fears and have him hold my hand through them.

I release a deep breath and squeeze his hand, admitting, "I'm not doing great, but I'd like to think I'm doing better than the old Lauren."

That brings a smile to his face. "How would the old Lauren be handling this?"

"She'd be blaming herself for resting while her dad was having a heart attack."

"Is there any piece of you that's still listening?"

"A small one." I glance down at the linoleum flooring, wondering why they chose beige. It's such a joyless color in a place that could use a spark of positivity. "The rational, more mature part of me knows my dad loves his work. He wasn't stepping back, and this could've happened any time, but the other part feels guilt at not being there to look out for him."

Jax stops walking, grabbing my other hand in his and looking me in the eyes. "Don't let old Lauren win, okay? This was not your fault. Everyone knows your dad has a hard time taking breaks because he's passionate about the work he does on the ranch. He's kind of like someone else I know." He squeezes my hands. "That fight in him is what's going to get him through this, and that same fight in you is what's going to get *you* through this. Maybe you should talk with your dad when he's ready. I think that might help clear the air."

"I think it would too." We continue wandering down the halls. We aren't talking, but nurses buzz past us, and announcements come over the intercom, filling what would otherwise be silence as I internally play out my conversation with Dad. Slowly, my thoughts drift to pride in myself for handling things the way I have today. I let myself break down. I've allowed Jax to be there for me instead of pushing him away. I might actually be changing for the better.

The thought brings me so much peace, and I can't help but wonder if Jax would feel the same way if he told his mom about the letter from his dad or the guilt he holds from years ago. Maybe he could find peace.

"You know, guilt can make us do some crazy things," I say. "I'm pretty sure if this had happened a month ago, I would've tried to push you away as a way of punishing myself for not focusing on my dad more." The weight of the truth hangs over us for a beat before I add, "Maybe it's time for you to talk to your mom and let go of your guilt."

Chapter Forty-Six

Jax

I DON'T EVEN TRY TO HIDE MY DISPLEASURE AT THE thought. It's wonderful that Lauren is growing, but I don't know that a conversation with my mom would help. It might just make things worse.

I scratch the back of my head. "Do I have to?"

"I'm not saying it has to be today, but I think the conversation would take a weight off your chest, just like me talking with my dad." She squeezes my hand in reassurance, looking so certain this is the right thing to do. *Maybe it is.*

We walk past a woman standing outside a room with tears in her eyes. A man wraps his arms around her in an effort to soothe her, but it doesn't stop her wailing. Lauren pauses her walking to watch, eyes wide. I quickly grab her, shuffling her down the hallway. I'm searching for a way to distract her from the scene when she says my name, her voice cracking.

"What if I don't get to talk with him? What if he doesn't pull through?"

"Don't you dare say something like that." I frown, drawing her into my side as we pass a receptionist desk decorated with a mini Christmas tree and a few lame pieces of tinsel. "You're going to have a lot more wonderful memories with your dad. He isn't going anywhere."

She looks up at me with an ache in her eyes that makes me feel helpless. I wish I could erase the last six hours for her, but I can't, so I settle for the next best thing. Casting my hand in an arch and putting on my brightest smile, I say, "I can see it now. We'll take over your family's Sunday breakfasts and invite my mom and Aunt Carol too. We'll have a couple little ones making a mess at our end of the table, and you'll be frantically trying to clean it up while your dad and I tease you about how silly it is to clean up their mess before the meal is over."

Tears shimmer in her eyes for the second time today. *No. No. No.*

I swipe a tear off her cheek. "Sorry, I was trying to cheer you up."

"You are." She laughs in embarrassment. "I just can't believe how badly I want that."

"You're going to have it, Freckles."

"I hope so."

I take both her hands, squeezing them tight. "Your dad is a fighter, remember? He's going to be back and kicking real soon. You'll see."

"Yeah." She glances down at the floor then back up at me. "Thank you for being here for me. You managed to put a smile on my face and pull laughter from my lungs when I didn't think either was possible today. You're always uplifting me, and your presence makes me feel so at peace."

"I'll always be here for you, Freckles."

She nods, a smile blooming on her face. "I know."

———

On the ride home from the hospital, I turn Lauren's words over and over again in my mind. *Maybe it's time to talk with your mom about your guilt.*

A day ago, I probably wouldn't have even considered it, but today has shown me how quickly people can be taken from us—what growth and healing can look like. I want that for Mom and me. I know the conversation will be difficult, but it will be good for both of us to sort through our pain from years ago and move on. I don't want to hang on to this hurt anymore. Nine years has been long enough.

The thought of moving on makes me feel lighter. A warmth fills my chest, but it's almost immediately replaced with dread when I pull into my driveway and my headlights flash over a shadowy figure on my front porch. *What the hell?*

I don't even bother parking my truck in the garage both because there's a truck blocking my way, and because I can't stand the thought of waiting to figure out who is showing up at my house unannounced late at night.

I shift into park in an instant, turn off the engine, and slam my door behind me. Adrenaline courses through my veins, and my heart pulses in my ears.

As I get closer, a pair of striking blue eyes meet my gaze. I know those eyes. They used to fuel my nightmares. I can still feel the bruises his fists left when the gambling losses got to be too much for him and the ache in my heart every time he let our family down. One glimpse into those eyes launches me back to my childhood, to the past I'd just resolved to let go of.

Chapter Forty-Seven

Jax

"Dad? What are you doing here?"

He bolts up from his spot on my porch chair, and I flinch. Growing up, I learned to prepare for the worst when he made sudden movements. Maybe I haven't changed as much as I'd hoped. *Come on. Be strong. Be brave. You're not a fifteen-year-old boy anymore. You can fight back.*

"Hey, bud." His blue eyes shine with something that almost looks like remorse, and his forehead creases with concern.

As I take him in, my shoulders relax a little bit. He's sober. That means I'm safe. But still, when he crosses the porch toward me, I take a step back.

"You're out of prison," I say awkwardly.

"Yeah, I am. They released me a little early on good behavior."

"But why are you here?" I stand at the top of the stairs, my mind swirling. "You're on parole, right? You shouldn't be able to leave Oklahoma."

"I got approval from my parole officer. I'm only here for the day, but she knows I need to do this to complete my program."

"Do what?" Dread spreads through me like a winter frost.

"I need to apologize."

I should be happy. All I ever wanted growing up was my dad to recognize the pain he'd caused our family. I wanted him to take responsibility for his actions and to be better, but now, it feels too late.

"I don't want your apology," I grit, clenching my fists at my side.

"Please, I need to apologize for all the terrible things I've done." Dad inches forward, sending me on high alert. "I had a lot of time to think about my actions and how they impacted you and your mom. I want to make it right. I checked myself into Gambler's Anonymous as soon as I got out of prison. I'm getting help for my addiction. I haven't gambled or had a drop of alcohol since I was arrested, and now that I've been out for a couple months, I need to make amends. That's how I make things as right as they can be, and that's how we all move on."

"I've already moved on. This apology is only for *you*, just like everything else in your life."

Rage flickers like a flame inside of me, and I'm surprised by the intensity of the burn, but why did he have to come back now? I was ready to move on, to move forward with the woman I love, and now he wants to tear my life apart again. He doesn't have the right to do that!

"I've lived without you for nine years." My fury builds. "I don't need you in my life. If you were really sorry, you would've stayed away because *that's* what is best for everyone. We're better off without you and your lies, manipulation, and abuse."

He flinches at the last word, but I don't stop.

"You want to apologize for all the things you've done, but you don't actually want to talk about them, do you? You recognize what a monster you are. I don't want anything to do with you, and neither does Mom. You're wasting your time by being here." I step down a stair, holding my arm out to show him the way off my porch. "You should go."

"No, I can't." Dad takes a few desperate steps forward. "I need to make this right."

"There's no fixing what you've done, and I don't feel like playing into your hand anymore. Growing up, all I did was bend to your will while you selfishly gave in to all the temptations that tore our family apart. I was too scared to stand up to you then, but I'm not anymore. You say you've changed and want what's best for us, but clearly you haven't because if you had learned from your mistakes, you'd understand the best thing you could do for our family is keep your distance."

The flame inside me is blazing now, but it's no longer just rage. The predominant emotion fueling my fire is pride. I always wanted to stand up to my dad, to let him know how badly he hurt our family. I used to long for the strength to say no to him and to push back, and here I am doing that. I *have* grown. I *am* good enough for the woman I love, and I'm ready to talk to my mom.

"You're right." He hangs his head. "It's awful of me to show up after all this time, but I need to correct my mistakes. I need to let you know you didn't deserve being abandoned and hurt like that."

"I don't want to hear any of that now." I shake my head. "Please leave."

Dad's face falls, and a shadow of guilt looms over me, but I quickly push it aside. He doesn't deserve my guilt after everything he's done. Coming back to fix things after all this time doesn't make it better.

Turning back to me, he asks, "Is your mom staying with your Aunt Carol? I'd like to see them, try to see if they'd be willing to hear me out while I'm here."

My protective instincts flare, and I step toward him. "You're not going near either of them." Mom might be strong enough to handle him now, but I'm sure she wouldn't welcome the surprise of him showing up on her porch.

"Come on." Dad's eyebrows pinch. "She deserves the chance to hear me out."

"She doesn't need you. I'm not going to let you hurt her now."

Something on his face shifts. "Jax, you know what happened back then wasn't your fault, right? It wasn't your job to protect your mom from me and my mess. We're your parents. *We're* the ones who were supposed to protect *you*. *We're* the ones who failed you."

Hearing those words releases a whole swarm of emotions I'm not ready to deal with. I want to bask in the comfort my dad is trying to offer. After all, I've wanted to hear those very words all my life, and to hear them filled with genuine remorse makes me feel things, but at the same time, hearing them come from the man who tore our family apart makes me think they can't be true. I guess I *am* a monster. I *did* fail Mom.

"I'll tell you what. I'll give y'all some space, and I can come back soon." Dad shuffles off the porch. "That'll give you some time to process and prepare, but I really think having this conversation will be healing for everyone. I'm not asking you to forgive me, just to hear me out. Do you think you can do that?"

Can I? I'm not even sure. As much as Lauren has given me a confidence I never had before, there are things I need to work on, and until I do, I don't think I'll be ready to hear my dad out. But I want to get to a point where I can be. I *want* to heal. I *want* to grow. I long for the peace I saw flash in Lauren's eyes when she told me she wasn't being dragged down by the old version of herself anymore. I just don't know how to get there.

"I'm not ready." I hate how shaky my voice is. This man has destroyed me even more than I realized. Healing isn't going to be easy.

Dad nods his head, and his gentle nature surprises me. Maybe he is changing, but it's difficult to believe it after all the times he's let me down.

Handing me a piece of paper, he says, "Here's my phone number. When you're ready, go ahead and give me a call." He turns on his heel and walks toward his truck, his head down.

As I watch him go, the hope and reason inside me evaporate, paranoia filling their place. *What if he's going to Mom and Aunt Carol's place right now? What if he doesn't respect my request and blindsides them?* I can't even imagine how upsetting that would be for Mom. She still thinks he's in jail.

And what if he lied about being in Gambler's Anonymous? What if what he really needs is money, like he always did? He could show up drunk and ready to throw fists!

I pull my phone out to call Lauren. She's the only person I know who could talk me out of this spiral. She will be my voice of reason and guide me down the right path, but as I hover my thumb over the call button, it hits me she's still at the hospital with her dad. She doesn't need to deal with my crisis right now. She needs rest, and if I tell her what's going on, she'll be ready to tackle this with me, just like she was when she found out about the letter.

I've already failed at protecting one woman I love from my dad. I need to be strong and figure out how to handle this on my own. I can tell Lauren everything once it's resolved.

Instead of doing what I know is rational, I hop in my truck and drive to Mom and Aunt Carol's, parking in the driveway to keep watch. The only sleep I get is interrupted by a nightmare I haven't had in several years.

Chapter Forty-Eight

Lauren

Jax's smile as he walks through the automatic doors of the hospital immediately lights up the room. While there are a few wreaths and string lights hung throughout the halls and waiting rooms, I've determined this city hospital could learn a lesson or two from Roots. It's sterile and lacks charm. After spending close to a full day here, I need a little ray of sunshine.

"Hi, gorgeous." Jax opens up his arms, and I easily slide into them.

"Gross." Charlie mutters, but I can see on his face that he's glad to know we're both happy and that I've found someone who treats me right.

Jax glares in Charlie's direction. "Aren't you supposed to go home soon?"

"I'll be leaving tomorrow."

"Good," Jax says, but I can feel the weight hanging over all of us at the thought. He glances down at me. "How's my girl doing?"

"I'm tired, but I'm much better now that you're here. How's *my* girl doing?"

"Bella's doing great." He releases me. "Although Mom says she's getting a little restless, like she wants to play."

"Poor thing. Tell her thank you again for me."

He nods, and it's then that I notice the shadows playing in his eyes. He looks both tired and wired.

"Are you okay?" I narrow my eyes on him. "Did you get any sleep last night? You don't look so good."

"Gee, thanks." He frowns.

"You know what I meant. I'm looking out for you."

"I know, and I appreciate it, but you don't need to worry about me. You've got a lot going on right now."

He places a kiss to my forehead and plasters on a smile that makes him look like the Joker, just like the other day at the festival.

I pull back from him, my stomach churning. "Everything about that just made me more suspicious. What's going on?"

"I missed you. It turns out I don't sleep very well without you by my side."

"That's my cue to leave," Charlie grumbles. "I thought I was okay with this, but the image of y'all sharing a bed is too much."

"Charlie, wait." I reach out to grab his wrist. When he turns back to me expectantly, I grab Jax's face and pull him toward me, planting a big kiss on his lips.

"Yup, I'm out of here. I'm going to check out the cafeteria food."

Jax arches a brow. "You'd rather eat hospital food than watch us kiss?"

"Yes, you're that gross." Charlie marches off.

I giggle, turning to Jax. Thankfully he's laughing too.

Maybe I was reading into things too much before. Maybe everything is fine.

"What have you been up to since I left? Did you get any sleep?"

"No, but I got a lot of work done." I give him a tired smile.

"You need sleep."

"You and I both know that's not happening yet."

He pulls me to sit down in an empty chair. "Have you heard anything from the doctors?"

"They said they got him in for treatment early enough to minimize the damage to his heart. They're going to hold him through tomorrow night, but then he can come home the next morning. He's going to have to take some medication to lower his blood pressure while he works on some lifestyle changes to reduce his stress, but he should be okay."

"That's great news! You should be relieved, right?"

I nod, worrying my lower lip. "I am, but I'm still *cautiously* optimistic."

He chuckles. "That sounds like my girl. Tell me what work you got done."

"I called Rhett this morning, and we've scheduled an interview with the cowboy I told you about. Dad's excited because it's the same morning he comes home. I might have to physically restrain him to keep him from showing up. He doesn't need to jump right into things as soon as he's out of the hospital."

"You know your dad."

"Yup, he's as stubborn as they come." I roll my eyes. "I'm trying not to get my hopes up, but I'm really excited about the cowboy we're interviewing. Did I tell you he has experience working on a regenerative ranch?"

I can't contain my excitement long enough to wait for

his response. "Oh, and speaking of regenerative ranches, we're going to start adjusting the fences for the pastures this week and plant some of the cover crops next week. That way we can slowly get the cattle used to the changes instead of all at once."

A family walks through the front doors, bringing in a sweep of cold air and sending a shiver through me. Without missing a beat, Jax takes off his sweatshirt and hands it to me.

I give him a soft smile in gratitude as I shrug it on. "I'm a little nervous the cattle won't forage the way they're supposed to. I read that it can take some time, but I believe it's the right move for Copper Hill. I just can't get distracted by the fact that if any of this goes wrong, it'll fall on me."

"Take a deep breath." He sets a comforting hand on my knee.

I do as he says. "Things finally feel like they're falling into place on the ranching front, but there's still that tiny bit of fear in the back of my mind."

"It's going to be great, Freckles. With the amount of thought and effort you've put into this, there's no way you could fail."

"Thank you." I place my hand over his and swipe my thumb across the back of it gently. "I did some research right before you got here. There are all kinds of grants offered for farms and ranches that get into regenerative ag. Securing one would really help us stay afloat until we settle into our processes and start seeing the benefits of the cost savings. I might need some help finding all the requirements for the applications though. Could you help me this week?"

"Of course."

I shift in my chair. It didn't take long for me to learn

these hospital chairs are extremely uncomfortable. "So, what have you been up to today?"

He freezes, looking almost guilty, and my guard goes up. I've seen the exact same look on Jax's face when he refused to tell me about the letter from his dad. I *know* Jax is a good man, but it doesn't stop the alarm bells from sounding in my head.

"What's going on?"

"Nothing."

"Grinchie, that's the second time your Joker smile has come out in less than ten minutes. Am I going to need to change your nickname?"

"Well, we *are* past Christmas, so it'd only make sense to give me a new one."

I cross my arms. "You're deflecting."

The smile on his face fades. "I'm dealing with something, but I'm not ready to talk about it yet."

"Okay," I say hesitantly, unsure how to feel.

He rubs my arm up and down. "When I'm ready to talk it through, you'll be the first one to know. In the meantime, you just focus on your dad, okay?"

I nod, feeling a bit better. I don't have any reason not to trust him. When he got the letter from his dad, he told me about it when he was ready. He's been thoughtful and honest during every step of our relationship thus far, and even though he hasn't told me he loves me, the song he played for me two nights ago and the look in his eyes whenever his gaze settles on mine tells me he does. We're going to be okay.

Chapter Forty-Nine

Jax

Lauren's dad is being released tomorrow morning, and she still hasn't slept a night in her own bed since he was hospitalized. She's been to the ranch, making sure everything is set for planting next week, taking Bella on gentle walks, and ensuring Rhett has the support he needs, but she has refused to sleep in her own bed until I dragged her out of the hospital tonight.

"You're going to be thanking me when you wake up feeling bright-eyed and bushy tailed for the first time in several days," I tell her as she walks into her bathroom.

She's been acting annoyed that I took her home, but she didn't put up a big fight, so I know she recognizes she needs rest. I'm proud of her.

"Yeah. Yeah. Yeah." She rolls her eyes, but there's a smile crossing her lips as she turns away from me.

While she pulls bottles from her cabinet, I ground myself in the sound of them clanking together, in the motion of her hands as she gently swipes the products across her face with care, and in the fresh scent of lavender and tea tree oils that emanate from the bathroom. It only works for a few seconds before my mind is drifting back to my dad's presence in my life again.

I've had two whole days to process his arrival and figure out what to do, but I've made no progress. I thought I'd be in a place to tell Lauren what's going on without burdening her, but I'm not confident I'll ever be able to forgive him for what he's done, and I don't want to intentionally put myself back where I was when I was fifteen. I've found peace now. I don't want to disrupt that. Plus, there's a part of me that doesn't trust him when he says he came back to make amends. That doesn't sound like the man I know, and I don't want to think about what it would mean if he were lying.

But I do anyway. He could show up unannounced. He might go to Mom, demanding money. *And what if he found out about Lauren?* I wouldn't put it past him to think her family's ownership of thousands of acres would mean they have money he could gamble away.

No. No. No. My mind spins out of control quickly.

"Do you want me to do your skincare?" Lauren asks.

Her voice makes me jump from my place on the edge of her mattress. She narrows her eyes as she stands in the bathroom doorway, her hands full of glass bottles. I focus on her, trying to pull my mind from the dark place it just went. Her blonde hair is pulled into a tiny braid that just barely passes the line of her T-shirt on the back of her neck, and her skin is shining from her moisturizer. Even with her eyes narrowed on me, I don't miss the way they swirl with a beautiful mix of blue, gold, and green.

It finally hits me she's waiting for my response, so I shift on the bed, telling her, "No, that's okay. I'm kind of tired."

"Me too." She plops on the bed next to me.

"You're still worried about your dad, huh?"

She grimaces. "What gave it away?"

"Well for starters, I had to practically sack-of-potatoes you out of the hospital today." I smirk.

She shoves my shoulder, dropping her mouth open. "You did *not*. I went willingly." When she laughs, it breathes a little bit of life into me.

"Sure you did," I tease.

"You're the worst." She crosses her arms.

"I am not. You like me, remember?"

"I do, but I can't remember why."

I pull her toward me, pressing my lips to hers. "Does that help you remember?"

"Maybe a little." She bites her lip. "Can I please do your skincare? I think it'll help me wind down more before bed."

"Fine." I get up and shuffle toward the bathroom. "Just for you."

"Don't look so happy," she calls after me, her voice dripping in sarcasm. "I'll have you know, my routine is the best in all of Texas—heck, in all of the country. You've told me that before."

"And you won't let me forget it."

Again, that chime of laughter brings the smallest flutter of joy back into my blackening heart.

———

The slam of the front door sends me upright. I immediately know what it means. He lost again. He's been drinking.

I lie in bed, holding my breath, hoping Dad will go

straight to bed and sleep it off. But seconds after the door across the hall creaks open, I hear murmuring. It grows louder and louder until it's full-blown shouting.

I storm out of my room and into my parents' bedroom. He's not going to lay a hand on her. I'm stronger now. Except when I reach the doorway, I catch a glimpse of my reflection in the mirror over the dresser. I'm not six-foot-four-Jax. I'm scrawny-freshman-Jax. I'm too-weak-to-stand-up-to-his-father-Jax. I'm good-for-nothing-but-standing-frozen-Jax.

Just like that, all the old fear floods back into me. I have no grasp on my own strength, only my weaknesses.

"You were never enough to protect her," Dad snarls. "And you're about to fail again."

He lifts his fist up, ready to strike, and it's then that I realize it's not just Mom cowering below him. Lauren is there too. And Aunt Carol. All of their faces are painted with fear as he— I wake up, gasping for air as I scuttle off the bed. My side of the mattress is drenched in sweat, and my skin is sticky. My vision blurs with tears as I try to separate my dream from reality. Breathing feels like the hardest thing in the world to do.

He's going to come back. He hasn't changed. He's going to hurt her again. I should've put a stop to this. I shouldn't have let him leave like that. I know I can't take chances with Dad. I shouldn't be sitting around waiting for something to happen. Except that's exactly what I've been doing, just like I sat by complacently when I was younger.

I move toward the door, and it feels like I'm floating. I still don't feel in control of my own body.

Hands grab hold of me, and a faraway voice cries out. "Jax! Jax! What are you doing?"

I swirl around, ready to throw my fists into Dad's face,

but a shriek of fear sharpens my senses. My gaze settles on a wide pair of hazel eyes, my favorite eyes in the whole world.

I drop my fist and let out a sigh of relief, dragging Lauren into my chest. My heart squeezes tight knowing she's here with me.

"I'm so sorry," I mutter.

"What's wrong? What happened?" Her voice is soft as she pulls me into her arms, lightly scratching my back.

We sit there for a while, and her gentle comfort almost brings my walls crashing down. I come so close to telling her what's been eating at me for the past few days, but when I look into her eyes, I see something in them that looks an awful lot like pain. It's like it breaks her heart to see me come undone like this, and seeing that look reminds me I'm supposed to put light in her eyes, not snuff it out by telling her just how far I've unraveled.

This isn't the time. I need to prove I've grown from the man I was at fifteen. The better version of me would protect not just my mom, but Lauren too. She's already going through a hard time. I can't add to that.

"I had a bad dream." I kiss her cheek, doing my best to plaster on my least Joker-like smile, but my hands are still shaking. "It was nothing."

"You were yelling and crying."

"It was just one of those dreams where I couldn't run. You know, the ones where it feels like you're trying to move through molasses? It was nothing. I'm okay now."

She gives me a look that makes it abundantly clear she doesn't believe me. Pulling me back into her arms, she whispers, "You know you can tell me anything right? I'm here for you. Your challenges are my challenges and vice versa. We're in this together now."

She meets my gaze, fear in her eyes. "I know you said

you needed space to process things, but you're having night-mares. I can't help you through this if you don't tell me what's going on."

I wipe my hands over my face. "I can't tell you."

"Why not?" She scoots closer to me, drawing slow circles on my back.

"You've got enough on your plate."

She draws her head back, confusion filling her eyes. "You've told me over and over again that it's good to let people help you. You've encouraged me to open up to you, even when I didn't want to, and I don't regret it for a second." Her sweet eyes latch on to mine. "Let me in, Jax."

I get up from the mattress, knowing I'll cave if I let her keep touching me and looking at me like that. "This is different."

"How is this different?" She follows me to where I'm leaning against the bedroom wall, resuming those hypno-tizing circles on my back.

I shrug out from under her, grabbing her hands and meeting her gaze, hoping she'll see the desperation in my eyes and understand. "I have to protect you."

She slips her hands from mine, shaking her head. "Don't give me that excuse. I hid my feelings from everyone I loved because I thought I was protecting them, but *you* showed me the right people will want to help. The rules don't change for you."

"They do in this case. I need to deal with this alone." My voice cracks as I add, "Please."

She stiffens, eyeing me. "Okay."

As she extricates herself from my arms, it's a sign of her emotional withdrawal just as much as her physical with-drawal. When the light in her eyes dims, I want to correct myself and tell her the truth, but it doesn't feel right. The dream proved I have to stop sitting around. I need to take action, and this time I don't just have my mom to protect. I have Aunt Carol and Lauren too. I'm the luckiest man in the world to be in a spot where I have so many people I love, but it also means I'm not going to risk putting them in danger. I'm doing what's best. Lauren will understand eventually.

Chapter Fifty

Lauren

"Tell me about your experience with regenerative agriculture." I try my best to pay attention to the words coming from the cowboy in front of me, but I can't focus. Images of Jax thrashing in bed last night swirl in my mind. I *know* something is torturing him, and I hate that he's hiding it from me. Then there's my dad who handed me a list of questions he made for my interview with the cowboy this morning. Nana Rhodes is looking after Dad to make sure he doesn't show up here unannounced, but we shouldn't have to do that. He just had a heart attack. He should know he needs rest!

Rhett asks another question. *Focus. You're almost done.*

"I put in five years at my last ranch, but I was ready for a change. My little sister lives out here. She has a two-year-old. I've had my years of bouncing around from place to place, but I'm ready to settle down somewhere, and I'd like to be around family. Plus, I'm tired of watching her kid grow up through pictures. I want to be around."

I cross my legs in my seat. "What would you say is your approach to problem solving? Are you more of a handle it on your own kind of person, or are you willing to ask for help?"

Rhett looks at me with narrowed brows. That question wasn't on the list he and I made. It may have been inspired by recent events, but it's still a fair thing to ask. After a beat, Rhett turns back to Zach, interested in what he has to say.

Zach launches into an explanation of how the situation would dictate his approach. I wish I could say I captured everything, but I think I got the gist. He seems like a great guy.

When he finishes, I ask, "And can you tell us about your experience with regenerative agriculture?"

He draws back, looking from me to Rhett with confusion. The room fills with silence for a full five seconds before I realize I've already asked this.

"I'm just kidding." I press on a smile. "I think that's all we need, right?" I look to Rhett for assurance, and he nods. "Thank you for coming in, Zach. We'll be in touch."

I hold my hand out to shake his, noting his firm and calloused grip. He has the handshake of a good cowboy. My dad taught me at a young age what to look for. He even told me I should shake a man's hand before I let him take me out on a date. He said it would weed out the ones that aren't worth my time. If I had listened, I wouldn't have spent eight years of my life dating Austin.

After Zach leaves the barn, Rhett stares me down. "Are you okay?"

"Yeah, I'm fine. I just missed lunch today. I guess I have a little brain fog." I do my best to give him a reassuring smile, but I'm certain I'm failing. *Dang you, Jax!*

"Olivia doesn't have any plans tonight. She's a great

listener and problem solver. She's also good at giving you a kick in the pants if that's what you need." He chuckles, and I can see in his eyes how much he adores that woman.

"Thanks. I'll keep that in mind."

"You should text her now." He scratches the back of his head. "Otherwise, she'll ask me how the interview was, and it'll be hard not to mention the fact that you asked the same question twice on *multiple* occasions. You and I both know she'll pester me for answers I don't have. Then she'll check up on you because she's already worried about how you're handling things with your dad. She'll end up coming over regardless. I'm learning it's a Parker trait." He smiles. "Save us all the trouble and just go to her now."

Genuine laughter slips from my lungs for the first time today. "I can do that." I pick up my phone, making sure he sees me press call on Olivia's contact before he finally leaves me alone.

———

Callie barrels out of her truck, her hands full with a catering box I'm sure contains some of her cupcakes. She gives me a squeeze so tight I have to gasp for breath when she finally lets go.

"I brought reinforcements," Olivia says, laughing as she steps out of the passenger seat, carrying a couple pints of ice cream, all of them chocolate.

"Y'all are the best." I give them a smile, but it doesn't reach my eyes. I should be happy my dad is home now, but instead, the events of last night are weighing on me. I thought Jax and I were on the other side of major obstacles, but, apparently, he doesn't trust me enough to tell me whatever he's going through now.

Olivia stacks the pints on top of one another, moving them to one hand and using her free arm to loop through mine. "I know that look. You're overthinking, and it's going to take you to a dark place." She leads us to the front door. "Don't go there. Let's go inside and talk through what happened over some chocolatey goodness, okay? A little bit of sugar goes a long way."

Callie grabs my other arm. When we're inside, she doesn't even ask me what I want. She just pulls a cupcake from the catering box and sets it on a plate with a fork. "I made ice cream sundae cupcakes, and I thought you'd be the best taste tester since you love ice cream so much. Batch one was a disaster, but batch two could be a real winner, so that's what I brought. You'll have to let me know though. My taste buds might just be tainted by how terrible my first attempt was."

Olivia sticks the cartons of ice cream in the freezer. "We can pull these out when we're ready, but I figured no one wants to drink a puddle of cream."

"That doesn't sound too bad." Callie sits up straighter, her eyes going round. "Maybe *that's* what my cupcakes are missing! I need to soak them in melted ice cream."

"Then they'd be soggy." Olivia scrunches her nose as Bella trots up to her to get some love.

"It'd be just like a poke cake. You know, when they poke holes in the cake and pour a liquid over it to make it moist?"

"Oh, you did *not* just say that word." Olivia groans.

"What word? Moist?"

Olivia clamps her hands over her ears. "La la la la la!"

Callie bursts into laughter, and I join in.

When we finally settle down, Bella curls up at my feet, giving me her best puppy-dog eyes as she eyes my plate. "You can't have this. Sorry, girl."

Callie takes a bite off her cupcake, groaning and rolling her eyes back. With her mouth still full, she mutters, "Batch two is definitely a winner."

I scoop up my own bite, making sure to get the perfect frosting to cupcake ratio. She was right. The chocolate cupcake somehow has a melty, fudgy texture, like it was infused with chocolate syrup, and the vanilla bean frosting melts in your mouth unlike any frosting I've ever had before. I pluck the cherry from my plate to complete the bite, and it's marvelous.

"How's your dad doing?" Olivia scooches closer to me on the couch.

"He's okay. He came home this morning, but he's already being a pain. He refuses to acknowledge what happened to him, and he wanted to sit in our interview with Zach this afternoon." I lean my head back against the couch. "He's so frustrating. I just want him to slow down."

"Hmmm another Rhodes family member who doesn't know how to take a break? That sounds familiar," Callie teases.

"Yeah, well, at least I'm *learning* how to do it. He still needs some work."

"Have you tried explaining to him that you just want him to take care of himself because you love him and want him to be around for the long haul?"

I drag both my legs up onto the couch, crossing them over one another. "No."

"Maybe you need to give it a try." Callie points her fork at me. "I can only imagine the thing that will finally get through to him is the love he has for his daughter."

"I hope so. If I'm being honest, I've been afraid to talk with him. I'm still trying to fight off the belief that taking a break to go on a hunting trip resulted in his heart attack." I take a tiny nibble of my cupcake. "Logically, I know it's in his nature to grind and never rest, but I'm afraid if I talk with him about it all, I'll realize it actually *was* my fault. Or even worse, *he* might realize it. That would kill me."

Olivia meets my gaze. "Do you know the reason I kept everyone at a distance when I first came to Roots?"

"It was to protect them, right? You thought your anxiety would be too much on the people you loved?"

"Sort of. There's a little more to it than that." She lowers her fork. "When I had my first panic attack in college, my mom ditched an important work meeting to help me through it. Her company missed out on a huge funding opportunity, so they fired her."

I wince. Olivia probably spun that to be her fault.

Seeing my reaction, she nods. "Yeah, it wasn't great. And I held on to the guilt for so long, but when I finally talked to my mom about it, she didn't blame me at all. She was thankful it happened because it helped her realize what's important to her. She created a beautiful life for herself after that incident, and she wouldn't have steered her life in a new direction if she hadn't gone through that hard thing."

Olivia sets her empty cupcake dish on the coffee table. Taking note of someone who no longer has her hands full, Bella rushes up to Olivia who happily scoops her into her lap, scratching behind her ears.

"I wouldn't have been able to let go of my guilt and let myself be happy if not for that conversation. Maybe that's what you need to do with your dad. Talk to him about what you're feeling. I'm sure he's going to tell you he would never once blame you, and if you're lucky, it might even be a trigger for him to make some positive change in his life."

She stops petting Bella for a brief second to pat my

knee. "I'm sure he'll also tell you he not only trusts in your ability to run the ranch, even when you're gone, but that his heart attack wasn't your fault."

I bite my lip as tears form in my eyes. Setting my cupcake aside, I sweep Olivia up into my arms, squeezing maybe a little too tight, but I can't help it. It means a lot to me that she's willing to share her story with me, and it only makes me realize I need to stop putting off this conversation with my dad. "Thank you."

"Of course." She rubs my back affectionately before pulling away. "Now what else is on your mind? Rhett said you were pretty distracted today. I know the thing with your dad has been weighing on you, but it usually takes more than that to throw you off your game."

"That's because it wasn't what was throwing me off today." I grab my cupcake off the table, taking a bite as I debate how much to tell my friends. I don't want to invade Jax's privacy by sharing about his nightmares. "Jax is going through something, but he refuses to tell me what it is."

"Jax isn't Austin," Olivia says, always the voice of reason.

"I know that. My heart and mind both know that."

Callie licks frosting off her fork. "You need to remember this man cares deeply for you. There's no denying it. Whatever's going on has nothing to do with you."

"I want to believe that, but everything changed so quickly. We went from seemingly being all in and ready to share our relationship with the world to him keeping secrets from me. After everything I've been through, it makes me feel—"

"Like it was all an illusion, and you should've known you couldn't have it?" Olivia says, her voice soft.

Gosh, did everyone around me know this was headed south except for me?

I pick at my cupcake on my plate. I've separated the frosting from the cake and have been slowly nibbling at the bottom, but the more this discussion progresses, the less I want to eat anything, which sucks because this cupcake is delicious.

Olivia reaches her hand out, stopping me from turning my cupcake into a bigger mess. "I didn't mean that's true. I'm saying it's easy to feel that way. That's how I felt when I started looking at jobs around here. It was my first attempt at going after what I wanted, and I was flat out told I was wrong for wanting it. That little rejection from one person sent me spiraling. I thought it was a sign I wasn't good enough, that I was stupid for ever thinking everything could work out, but, with some help from the people I loved, I realized I couldn't let one little incident knock me down and stop me from chasing after what I want."

A spark of hope ignites in my chest.

"I know you've been through some hard things." Olivia rubs my arm as Bella leaves her lap and curls up in mine. "Between what happened with Austin and now your dad's health complications, I know it's easy to believe you'll never catch a break. You start to question if you even deserve good things, if you're worthy of the love you want in life, but all those thoughts are just thoughts. They come from the shadows inside of you, and they don't deserve to be brought into the light. Instead of believing them, this is the part where you fight to show the universe you're stronger than you used to be. This is the part where you recognize your worth and make sure you get what you want."

"How'd you get so good at giving pep talks?"

"Because I know what it feels like to be rejected and to

question if you're deserving, but I also know what it's like to come out on the other side. Don't let Jax push you away. I tried to push Rhett away when I thought I couldn't make everything work. If he had stepped aside and let me, I probably wouldn't be in Roots anymore." She gives a guilty smile. "Maybe Jax just needs to know he has someone in his court who will fight for him."

"You're right. I need to talk with him." I nibble at my cupcake. "How do I do that?"

"Just be honest with him. Jax adores you, and all good relationships are built on a foundation of trust and honesty." Callie pats my knee.

Chapter Fifty-One

Lauren

I should be spending Sunday morning breakfast enjoying the beautiful meal Mom prepared and basking in the fact that Dad is home safe and I have a new cowboy to help out on the ranch, but instead, I pick at my food as I run my conversation with Dad through my mind a million different times.

He stands from the table as the meal winds down. "Before everyone goes their separate ways, I want to say how happy I am that we can all be here together for breakfast on this lovely Sunday morning. We're really looking forward to having you work on the ranch, Zach."

Dad holds up his nearly empty glass of water with a cheesy grin, and I share a knowing glance with Mom. We were talking this morning about how he's been extra sentimental since he came home yesterday.

Everyone raises their glasses to follow suit, and then we quickly disperse.

"I'm sad Jax couldn't join us this morning," Nana says as the two of us head into the kitchen with empty dishes. "Your second hire should've been here."

I don't look her in the eye as I pass her a dish to clean. She knows something is going on, and I really don't feel like talking about it now.

I texted him to try to find a time to talk, and he blew me off, giving some lame excuse about needing to help Carol with new puppies that came to the rescue this morning. The worst part is, I know Jax was lying about helping because Olivia confirmed there are no new dogs at the rescue right now. My stomach flip flops again at the thought.

"Yeah, too bad." I finish drying a dish and put it in the cabinet. "What'd you think of Zach?"

Nana pauses her scrubbing to narrow her eyes at me but answers my question anyway. "He seems nice. I'm glad he was able to join us so I could meet him."

"Me too. I know it helped Dad feel a little more involved in the ranch. He has such a hard time letting go."

Nana pauses with the dish she's cleaning, glancing up at me. "That bothers you, doesn't it?"

"What does?"

"Your dad's inability to take a break."

"Doesn't it bother you?" I take the next clean plate to dry. "Papa literally worked himself to death, and Dad is following in his footsteps."

"Of course it bothers me, but I learned a long time ago that the Rhodes men don't like being told what to do, especially not by their wife or mother."

"So, what do we do?"

Nana spins around, heading toward the dining room. "Bennett, your daughter wants to talk."

"Nana!" I drop my jaw, feeling more than betrayed.

"You're our best hope, dear. I'm sorry." She presses a quick peck on my cheek. "Speak from the heart and don't overthink it."

"But—"

"I watched you struggle at the hospital. It's clear something is weighing on you, and I know a conversation with your dad will fix it. He may have had a heart attack, but he's still here. Talk to him like you used to. You'll be glad you did."

She's right. *Be brave. This is how I grow.*

Dad glances up at me with a smile on his face as I come back into the dining room, pulling up a chair next to him. I can still see reminders of his heart attack from the way his smile doesn't quite reach his eyes, and the exhaustion etched into his face.

"What's going on with my favorite girl?"

I glance at Mom, who is still at the table with Zach.

"Zach, have you gotten situated in the bunkhouse yet?" Mom rises from her seat. "I can help you."

I give her an appreciative nod as Zach takes the hint, thanking us for breakfast and following Mom toward the front door.

I sit, taking my time settling in. I'm not sure how to start this conversation.

"What's bothering you?" Dad lays his hand on mine.

I take in a sharp breath, building up the courage to say what I need to say and quickly realizing I'm never going to be more prepared for this discussion.

"I need you to know I love you."

Dad smiles, swiping his thumb over my hand. "I love you too."

"You've been my best friend since day one. It was terrifying getting the phone call that you were in the hospital, and it was completely unbearable to just sit there, waiting, while they ran their tests."

I take in a deep breath. Here it goes. "I've been in this weird place lately because there's a part of me that blames myself for taking time off for the hunting trip and making you feel like you needed to step in and take over."

I trace a dark spot on the table, unable to meet his gaze. "I'm also mad at you because you've refused to rest even though the doctors tell you it will help you live a longer, healthier life, and yet I understand what it's like to love this ranch, and the work that comes with it, with your whole soul. So I find myself in a tough spot." I glance up at him, meeting his hazel gaze. "I want to blame myself, but I don't. I want to be angry with you, but it's only coming from a place of love and fear because I want you to be here for as long as you possibly can. You still have so much to teach me. You still need to walk me down the aisle someday and teach my kids bad habits that annoy me."

I sniffle as tears form in my eyes. I think I broke the dam when Dad went to the hospital, and I might not be able to put it back up. "I need you here with me." My voice cracks." I'm so sorry if I'm the reason you almost weren't. I'm trying really hard to keep the ranch afloat and to make it better, but—"

"I'm sorry, Biscuit." His words shock me, but when he drags me into his arms, I soak up his gentle caress paired with his use of my childhood nickname, which melts me every dang time.

"You're sorry?"

"I'm sorry I put you through that and that I haven't set a good example. You deserve time to take breaks and enjoy life. I promise I'm going to work on stepping back. It's just so difficult to let go of this ranch. The thing that brings me life is the same thing that almost ended me, and it's heartbreaking."

His eyes shine with tears, and seeing my idol break down in front of me is like a knife to the heart.

He quickly plasters on a smile, some of the light returning to his eyes when he says, "I guess it's time to find something new to love, like supporting you from the sidelines. Some grandchildren soon might not hurt either." He smiles, placing his hand over mine. "I heard about you and Jax. It's about damn time that boy made a move on you."

"What?"

"He's been looking at you like he loves you since he came to town all those years ago."

"I—" I don't know what to say. I don't even know where Jax and I stand right now. The last twenty-four hours of our relationship haven't been good ones. I know Olivia said I need to fight for him, but how do I know it's worth it? Heartbreak sucks, and all of my instincts are screaming at me to get out while I can.

Dad gives a sheepish smile. "I don't mean to embarrass you. You had to have known this was going to get back to me though. Your Nana can't keep her mouth shut."

"No, she can't." I laugh, swiping at the tears in my eyes.

"He's a good man. It's good for you to have someone else in your life to look out for you because I've clearly done a crappy job. I should've noticed the way my diagnosis was putting pressure on my girl. You've been through so much over the last few months, and I'm used to you handling it with such grace and strength that sometimes I forget I need to check in on you." He pauses, taking my hand and looking me in the eyes. "You're doing an amazing job, Biscuit. You're running this ranch better than I did in the thirty years I had control of it. Your regenerative ag shift is *genius*. I have no doubt you're going to take Copper Hill to new heights."

My heart clenches, and new tears form in my eyes. I had no idea how badly I needed to hear those words from him.

"Thank you." My lip quivers as I drag him into a hug. "You know, you don't need to give up every part of the ranch. You could horseback ride for the joy of it again. I recently started doing it for fun, and I highly recommend it."

He flashes me a genuine smile that warms my heart. "That sounds amazing. Will you go with me?"

"If you're there, I'm there. You already know that." I squeeze him firmly but not too tight.

"Come on. I know I had a heart attack, but you can give me a real hug." Dad pulls me tighter to him.

When we pull apart, he looks me in the eyes, concern lining his face. "Does Charlie know about you and Jax?"

"Yeah, I guess we royally sucked at keeping the secret. He figured it out before we could tell him."

"How did he handle it?"

"Surprisingly well."

"We should have Jax over for dinner soon. You know I love the kid, but I still need to have my 'Dad Talk' with him." He sits up straighter, puffing his chest out. "I didn't have it with Austin, and it's one of my biggest regrets."

"We can probably arrange that, but I have some things I need to sort out with him first."

"What happened?" His prideful smile turns into a frown.

"I don't know. He's been acting weird."

"That probably makes you want to run for the hills."

I shrug. "Kind of."

"I can tell you love him." There's a bittersweet look on Dad's face. "I didn't see that love in your eyes when you looked at Austin, but I've seen it between you and Jax, and darlin', that's the kind of love you fight for."

Chapter Fifty-Two

Jax

I zip up my duffel, slinging it over my shoulder. I didn't need to be at the Long Neck or Copper Hill today to work. The same committee responsible for decorating the bar for the New Year's Eve party tonight will also be bartending, so this is my chance to go to Oklahoma and set things straight with my dad.

The mixture of adrenaline and determination coursing through my veins nearly mutes the sound of my phone ringing in my back pocket when I walk out the front door, but the added vibration is enough to bring my attention to it.

"Mom? What's up?"

"Jax Greer. What have you done?"

"Well, hello to you too." I scoff. "I'd love to stick around for my inevitable ass-whooping, but I'm in the middle of something. I'll call you later, okay?"

"This can't wait."

The anger in her voice stops me in my tracks. "What's going on?"

"I was dusting your old room like I do every couple of weeks, and I found a letter. From your father."

The ground falls out from underneath me. This wasn't supposed to happen. She must be so freaked out. She thought she was safe and now she knows my dad is free in the world again.

"I'll be right there."

————

Mom is waiting on the porch when I drive up. Pulling her into a hug, I say, "I'm so sorry. You weren't supposed to find out like this. You're safe though. I promise. I'm not going to let anything happen to you. He won't hurt you ever again."

She pushes me away, her brows slanting.

"What on earth are you talking about? The letter says he wants to make amends. Why did you hide it from me?" Her voice is rising an octave per sentence until she's practically supersonic.

"I picked up your mail the other day, and when I saw the handwriting on the letter, I recognized it immediately. I knew him coming back into our lives would probably upset you, so I kept it to myself." I shrug. "I guess I thought there was no sense in telling you when I knew he'd be on parole and wouldn't be able to just show up in Roots. I failed to consider the fact that he could get permission to come here and make amends with his family."

"Wait, he was *here*?" She sounds really angry now, and I can't help but feel surprised. I thought she'd be grateful I stepped up this time around.

"He completely blindsided me and showed up on my

porch the night I got back from the hunting trip. He insisted he wanted to make amends, but I asked him to leave and to stay away from you. It was time I protected you the way I should've all those years ago."

"That wasn't your job to do." She shakes her head. "You should've told me he was here. I would've liked to hear what he had to say."

"Have you lost your mind?" I throw my arms up in the air. "Dad tore our family apart. He drove us into all kinds of debt. He's the reason we had bruises when we came to stay with Aunt Carol. He's why you and I both have to constantly convince ourselves we aren't terrible people."

I'm pacing the length of the porch now. "He tortured us, mentally and physically. I wasn't going to let him come back into our lives and pretend he's sorry. It's too late for that. If he cared, he wouldn't have gone back to gamble after the first time you begged him not to. He wouldn't have continued drinking, knowing the monster it turned him into. He would've taken care of us the way he was supposed to, but he didn't do any of those things, did he?"

I stop pacing, grabbing the rail with white knuckles. "I just wanted to protect you from that monster. Our lives have been so much better without him. You don't need him coming back around to make things complicated."

Mom steps closer, and the fire in her eyes terrifies me. I've never seen her like this. "Did you think I was going to welcome him back with open arms after everything he did? Do you really think I'm so weak that I couldn't protect us back then? That I can't stand up for myself now?" She looks hurt, and she doesn't wait for me to answer before blurting, "Of course I wouldn't let him come crawling back! I recognize the things he did to our family. I'm sorry I didn't get us out of that situation sooner. I was blinded by love, and I thought he could change. I'm much stronger now, and it stings that you didn't think I was."

"I know you're strong." I drape an arm over her shoulders. "I didn't think you'd take him back, but I didn't see his presence doing any good. Whatever apology he has is worthless to us now."

"Speak for yourself. I wouldn't mind hearing him swallow his pride to say he was wrong for everything he did."

"But how can you even believe him after everything he's done to us?"

She shrugs, staring out at the gray clouds accumulating in the sky. "Maybe he'll be full of crap, but at least I'd get to hear the words I've most wanted to hear come out of his mouth."

Silence falls over us for a moment as we both watch the wind shake the trees. Finally, she says, "You shouldn't have had to handle this on your own."

"I need to make up for the times I didn't handle him before. I need to keep everyone safe. I didn't do that for you before, but I'm trying now."

"And keeping secrets from me is the way to do that?"

"I was protecting you. You didn't need to know he was back."

"I know you're a grown man now, but you're still my son. It'll never be your responsibility to protect me or make decisions for me. If your dad hadn't hidden his gambling before it got too late, maybe I could've helped him. It sounds like he's getting help now, but just imagine if he had asked for help and gotten it fifteen years ago. Think about how different our lives could've been. You shouldn't keep secrets, even if you think you're protecting someone."

"I'm sorry." I toe one of the splintered floorboards. "I

guess you were right. The Carter men are scum. *I'm* scum. Even when I try to be better, I just ruin everything."

"Scum? What would make you say that?"

"You've said it yourself. Plenty of times. 'The Carter men are scum.' I come from a line of lying, cheating, assholes, and I've done a terrible job of breaking the mold."

She pulls me into a hug. "The Carter men don't include you."

"What do you mean? I know my legal name is Greer now, but it doesn't change where I came from."

"You were raised by two Greer women. You're a Greer through and through." She says it with pride. "You're not scum. You messed up, but now you do what Greers do, and you make things right."

"How do I do that?"

"Did he give you a way to get in contact with him? I'd like to hear him apologize, and I'd love it if you would be by my side through it."

"He did, but I don't—"

"Don't do it for him. Do it for yourself. Having him pop up in your life again has been causing you a lot of pain, hasn't it?"

I nod. "I've been having nightmares again, and this time they're worse. Everyone I love is there now, not just you, and I still can't do anything to protect y'all."

"Don't you want to move past that?"

"I do, but how do I know hearing his apology will help?" I adjust my grip on the railing as thunder claps in the distance. "I don't think I'd even believe him."

"You won't know until you try."

I toss my head back. "Why do you have to be right?"

"It's a perk of being a mom." She smirks. "Have you told Lauren about all of this?"

I whip my head toward her. "What?"

"You two are an item, aren't you?"

"How did you know?"

She tosses a hand. "I could see the way you looked at her on Thanksgiving, and I swear you could've cut the tension with a knife at the bake-off. I'm happy for you."

"Thank you." I nudge her with my shoulder, and she forces me into a hug. It's a relief to have this secret out in the open.

I draw back. "She knows about the letter, but I didn't tell her about dad showing up. She's had a lot going on with her own dad, and I didn't want to burden her until I figured this out on my own."

"Jax, did you push that poor girl away?"

"It was for her own good. I was going to tell her eventually."

She swats me. "That was not for her own good. That was for *you* and *your* selfish reasons. You're trying to be the hero, but all you're doing is hurting the people you love."

I wince as an image of Lauren's face flashes through my mind. She looked so defeated when I told her my dream was nothing for her to worry about.

"What else was I supposed to do? I *love* her, Mom. I just want what's best for her."

"If you love her, then you need to be honest with her. You don't push her away with the lame excuse that it's the noble thing to do. That only breaks both your hearts, which doesn't do you any good."

I cover my face in my hands. "I screwed up. I screwed up so badly." I glance at Mom. "What do I do?"

"You have to move past your fear of not being good enough. Pushing her away is just as bad as not showing up for her in the way she needs."

"But Lauren deserves the world, and I've never even been in a real relationship before. I did you such a disservice growing up by not standing up for you and—"

"No, you didn't. Remember, we just established it wasn't your job?" She gives me a pointed look. "If you hadn't let me sort through that situation on my own, I never would've realized I deserved better. You allowed me to spread my wings and find safety. You gave me confidence in my decision to leave so I wouldn't always wonder 'what if.' By standing back, you gave me the greatest gift of all, the chance to grow on my own."

It's as if those words are exactly what I needed to hear all my life. The knife in my chest is magically removed after years of constantly digging in and twisting. The scars I've carried heal.

"I hope you're not just saying that."

"No, I wouldn't do that to you. I meant every word."

I bite my lip, trying to contain the immense emotions swirling inside of me. "I love you, Mom."

"I love you too, honey." She wraps me in a hug.

I return my hands to the railing, which has become my crutch in this conversation. "I'm still scared. I thought I was doing the right thing for you by hiding that letter, and it turns out I was screwing up."

"We all make mistakes. It's what you do after that counts. I can't guarantee things will work out between you and Lauren. There aren't many guarantees in life, but you'll definitely get things wrong if you never try."

"I don't even know where to begin." I bite my lip. "She's been hurt before. She's already doubted herself after being left by Austin, and I probably made all of that worse."

I was so consumed in getting everything right this time.

I thought I was being smart, that I was protecting her. I was trying so hard not to hurt her, but I did anyway.

"I guess you better get ready to do some groveling." Mom smirks. "You need to show her you've learned from your mistakes. Show her you love her and believe she's more than worthy of standing in the rain with. Heck, forget *standing* in the rain. Lauren is wonderful. Show her she's more than enough to *dance* in the rain with."

As if on cue, a clap of thunder roars overhead, and raindrops slowly pepper my warm skin.

"What if I screwed up too much? What if she realizes she's too good for me?"

"You're the one in control of your actions. Be the man Lauren deserves. I know you're capable." Mom rubs my shoulder with a smile.

The gentle pitter patter of the rain turns into a downpour as fear and hope dance together inside of me. I know what I need to do.

I shoot toward my truck, but Mom's arm stops me. "Where are you going?"

"To show Lauren I'm willing to dance in the rain with her."

Chapter Fifty-Three

Lauren

Sandra Bullock's character, fresh out of the shower, is fighting off a little white dog as she tries to get a towel when the on-and-off drizzle we've had throughout the day turns torrential.

"Did y'all know it was supposed to storm today?"

The girls shake their heads as I turn up the volume a couple of notches.

Callie leans into me on my left-hand side, whispering, "Are you doing okay?"

I nod. I still have a lot I need to figure out with Jax, but my conversation with my dad today was encouraging. In a lot of ways it was exactly what I needed. A movie day followed by researching and applying for grants with Mom should clear my to-do list enough for me to come up with some way to prove to Jax I'll always be there for him. I'd like to make up with him before ringing in the New Year tonight.

Callie continues to eye me carefully as she draws back.

"Watch the movie." I point to the screen. "She's about to run into a naked Ryan Reynolds. You can't tell me you're not all over that."

She gives me a smirk, looking a little reassured that I can at least make a joke right now. I've still been a little off today, distracted by my constant attempts to figure out exactly what I need to do for Jax to get through to him.

Just as Callie settles back in, her phone lights up, bringing a deluge of light into the dark room.

I glance in her direction, simply because the light catches my eye, but I could've sworn I saw Jax's name on her screen before she quickly flips it over. I'm going crazy. Maybe I need to stop overthinking this and just show up on his doorstep tonight.

A guilty smile creeps onto Callie's face. "Sorry, no texting in the theater. I'll turn it off."

I turn back toward the TV, smoothing a hand over Bella's back as she curls into my side, lightly snoring, but out of the corner of my eye, I see Callie turn her brightness down to look at her screen.

"Is everything okay?"

"I'm about to see Ryan Reynolds's sweet bottom. I couldn't be better."

"Oh my god!" Olivia grimaces. "Please never say that again."

"Come on. Ryan isn't your type? He's brunette like Rhett." Callie wiggles her eyebrows.

"He's a good-looking man, but I still don't want to hear about *anyone's* 'sweet bottom.'" She shudders.

"Then close your ears because I'm about to rant about it." Callie leaps up as Sandra Bullock's character barges straight into Ryan Reynolds's character, unleashing chaos.

Once the actors stop shouting at one another, Callie

pops up from the couch. "I need to pee real quick. I'll be right back."

She heads toward the front bathroom around the corner, and I don't miss the fact that she snagged her phone off the couch too.

I pause the movie and glance in Olivia's direction. "What do you think that's all about?"

"Don't look at me. I love the woman, but I don't always understand her."

A sharp knock cuts through the sound of the rain, and I groan as Bella's head shoots up. I have to grab her to keep her from lunging off the couch and ripping her stitches. She still has about a week until she can get them out.

As I walk toward the door, I wonder who could possibly be showing up on my porch right now. All the cowboys should be out in the fields.

I slip off the couch, and pad toward the door, swinging it open to find a damp Jax, wincing. "Hey, Freckles."

"Jax."

A flood of conflicting thoughts whirl in my mind at the sight of him. I want to fly into his arms and assure him that I'm here for him, just like I've been planning to all along, but there's also a part of me that wants to run far away and protect my heart from that golden smile that's flashing on his face.

He wrings his hands together. "We need to talk."

I glance back at Olivia, and she gives me a nod, taking Bella from my arms. I know that's her way of telling me *you have to try*.

"Yeah, we do." I join him on the covered porch, closing the door behind me and crossing my arms. The rain patters insistently on the roof overhead.

"I screwed up. I've been keeping things from you, and

it's not fair. I'm really sorry." There's pain in his eyes as his brows pinch together. "I thought I was doing the right thing, but all I was doing was hurting us both."

"I hate that you pushed me away, and I'm not the same girl I used to be." I have to raise my voice a little to be heard over the pounding of the rain all around us. "I'm not going to wallow and think that it has to do with me not being enough. I'm going to recognize my worth. I'm going to recognize *our* worth and fight for us. You don't get to push me away when things get too hard." I drop my shoulders, realizing they've been creeping toward my ears as my frustration builds. "You don't get to do all these wonderful things that make me think we're moving forward and then pull back. You need to open up to me. I want to help. I—"

He grabs both my hands, pressing them between our chests. The action makes me melt back into him. Between the anger and hope mixing in my chest and the fact that I'm so close to Jax that I can smell the familiar scent of oak on him, my heart is pounding.

I wrangle my feelings back in, going rigid. I want to give us a chance, but he doesn't get to come back and think I'm going to immediately forgive him. I want to fight for us, but I need reassurance this won't happen again. I'm not going to be in a relationship that cycles back and forth between hot and cold. Not again. I deserve better.

"I'm sorry for being so stupid. My fear of not being enough got in the way, and I suppose my ego did too. It told me I needed to fix this problem on my own to protect everyone. I'm not perfect, and I know I never will be, but I'm going to fight like hell to be good enough for you because you deserve it."

Thunder booms, shaking the ground. The storm is rolling in closer.

"You're my favorite person in the whole world, and there's no one I'd rather go through life's ups and downs with than you. It's always been you, Freckles. Please just give me a chance to prove it to you."

It's always been you. A swarm of butterflies unleashes in my stomach, but I bite my lip, trying to remain steady. "You really hurt me when you pushed me away. You acted like you didn't believe I was enough to stand by you when life gets hard."

"I'm sorry. You were never the problem." I open my mouth to speak, but he presses on. "I've spent so much of my life hiding: how I feel for you, what happened with my dad, and the fears plaguing my mind, but I'm done hiding." The rain picks up, pouring over the edge of the roof in dredges, but Jax's focus doesn't waiver from me. "Freckles, I love you with every fiber of my being. I have for years. I've wanted to tell you for so long, but I always got in my own way, just like I did over the last few days, but that's over."

He releases a puff of air, building more confidence. "I've been in love with you since I was fifteen. Your kindness, your laugh, your sense of humor, your wisdom, your passion, your drive, they all immediately drew me in, and as much as I've tried, I haven't been able to keep myself from falling head over heels for you. When you were with Austin, I *tried* to push you away and bury my feelings, but it was pointless. My heart was made to love yours."

My mind swirls. This is all so much to take in. Not only does Jax love me, but he apparently has for years. *How did I not know?* My heart aches for all the time we could've had together instead of suffering through the pain we've both endured over the last several years, but then again, I don't think we were ready for one another any sooner. We've both grown a lot just in the last couple months, and we're still continuing to grow. Maybe we collided at just the right time.

"You've loved me for that long?" I swallow, trying to tamp down the butterflies in my stomach.

He nods, squeezing my hands. "And I'm going to do everything in my power to be worthy of you because I need you in my life more than I need air."

The sky lights up with a flicker of light, and only a few seconds later, thunder shakes the ground. My eyes widen in shock, and Jax holds me tighter. "I already missed my chance with you once because I didn't tell you how I felt. No more secrets, okay?" His blue eyes swirl with hope and desperation. "Anything you want to know, I'll tell you."

"Really?"

He nods earnestly.

Unable to hold myself back any longer, I lunge into his arms, grabbing two fistfuls of his T-shirt as I crash my lips into his.

I pull away for only a second to say the words I've been dying to say for so long. "I love you."

"I love you too. So damn much. I love you. I love you. I love you." He grins goofily. "I've been wanting to say it for so long, and now that I have, I'm afraid I won't be able to stop. I love you."

A giggle slips free, but I quickly turn serious again. "It's exciting, but it's also slightly terrifying. I've loved someone before, but he broke my heart, and now—"

"I'm not going to mess this up again. I see what a gift you are. I'm not going to take you for granted and risk losing you."

Another flash of lightning brightens the whole sky as I tug Jax to the wicker chairs on my front porch. "Can you tell me what's been going on with you over the past few days?"

"My dad came to Roots."

"What?" My jaw drops, and I reach out for his hand. I know how tumultuous his relationship was with his dad, and I know the terrible things that man did to Jax and his mom. "Are you okay? How did he get here? I thought you said he was on parole?"

Jax fills me in on everything from his dad showing up on his porch to his mom finding the letter.

"What does your mom think about all of this?"

He picks at the flaky wood on the arm of the chair. "She wants to hear him out."

"How do *you* feel about it now that you've had some time to process it?"

An ominous cloud of thunder rumbles, but it sounds a little further away than the last one. "I don't feel like I owe him anything after what he's done to our family, but I want to move on from the pain."

"You deserve that."

He pauses picking at the wood to look up at me. "I don't want to do it without you by my side though. I know it's going to be hard to sit there and let him talk, but I think I can do it if you're with me." He glances out at the sky as lightning flickers in the distance. "All of this has helped me realize I can't carry the weight of everything on my shoulders alone. I need to find someone I can dance in the rain with. Will you be that person?"

He stands, taking my hand and pulling me from the cover of my porch, down the steps and into the mud. Callie's truck starts up, and her headlights flash on. She gives me a thumbs-up from the driver's seat before turning her radio on at full blast. John Michael Montgomery's "I Love the Way You Love Me" streams out of the truck.

"I love you, Freckles, more and more with each passing second. I messed up, and I want to make it right. When you're at your weakest, and you only have ten percent to give, I'm supposed to help carry the other ninety percent for a little bit, but I'm also supposed to let you do the same for me. Relationships are about give and take." He slips a hand to my waist. "They're about learning to dance in the rain, and I need you to know, with you, I'll freaking frolic in the rain any day."

He squints at me as rain drips down his face, but he's still wearing a smile. "Will you dance in the rain with me? Both literally and metaphorically?"

I laugh at the cheesy metaphor, nodding eagerly. "I love you, Jax. I love you so much. I'm always going to be there for you, even when our minds play tricks on us. It's you and me from now on, okay? We're going to be honest with one another and support one another no matter what."

He spins me around then pulls me close, pressing his lips to mine. Rain drips down our faces. It seeps through my clothes and chills me to the bone, but with Jax's strong arms holding me steady, I let it all go. Let the rain soak me. Let people think what they want about our relationship. Let my mind play tricks on me because I know in my heart that Jax and I together are stronger than anything we might face.

Chapter Fifty-Four

Jax

MY NERVES TUMBLE AROUND MY STOMACH AS WE PULL into the parking lot of Dad's new place in Oklahoma. Mom and Aunt Carol shuffle out of their seats seemingly as soon as I stop the truck, but I'm still sitting in the driver's seat, twisting the beaded keychain Lauren gave me before we left in my fingers. Each bead on it represents a part of our journey, whether it's a whiskey glass for the night she tried to kiss me or dancers for our first swing lesson. Lauren said it was supposed to bring me luck and remind me that I'm loved.

I don't think I need it when I have her by my side, but I slip it into my pocket anyway, releasing a sigh. *I can do this.*

Lauren gingerly slips her hand into mine, quieting all the noise in my head and easing my stomach. "I'm by your side the whole way." She kisses my cheek. "Thank you for letting me be here for you."

I squeeze her hand. "Thank you for not giving up on me."

She gifts me one of her beautiful smiles before nodding toward the truck door behind me as if to say *let's do this*.

Aunt Carol knocks on my window. "Is everything okay?"

I open my door. "I can't say I'm ready for this, but then again, I don't think I'll ever be."

Mom loops her arm through mine on the opposite side of Lauren, and we all walk toward the external stairwell together.

Mom does the honor of knocking, and Dad opens the door seconds later. He must've been waiting on the edge of his seat for us to show up. His desperation to make amends is evident from the pleading look in his eyes. I can't reconcile the man standing in front of me with the man I knew growing up.

He wasn't always an addict. I have fond memories of him when I was younger, like when I was six and he took me to an OSU football game. It was our first trip just the two of us, and I remember it vividly because that's when I learned how to throw a football.

Dad's downward spiral started around the time I was in fifth grade, rendering those fond memories worthless. Mom and I lived in the hell he created for about five years before we got out.

Lauren gently squeezes my hand in hers as Dad guides us all to his tiny living room. There isn't enough seating on his lounger and two-person sofa, but he placed a dining room chair next to the couch to account for Aunt Carol. I'll admit, I admire the thought he put into this. It makes me think maybe he has changed a little.

Noticing there aren't enough chairs, Dad looks between Lauren and me with a nervous smile. "Who's this?"

On instinct, I throw my arm in front of Lauren to cover

her from the danger of this man, but she tugs on my arm, indicating for me to drop it.

"I'm Lauren, his girlfriend." She holds out a hand. "I've heard a lot about you."

When he takes her hand, I note a bead of sweat on his brow. "Probably not many good things."

"Nope." She crosses her arms.

"I promise I'm not trying to cause any harm." Dad twists his hands in front of him as he turns to me, silently asking if I'm willing to hear him out now.

I thrust my hand in his direction to indicate the floor is his. "Go ahead." *Let's get this over with.*

Dad's shoulders drop in relief as we all take a seat. When he exhales, hope fills his eyes. "I know I can't fix everything I've done in the past, but I am trying to get better, and I want you to know it's because I recognize all the harm I caused you two, the people I love most in the world."

I tense up, fighting my instincts to argue with him. *If we are the ones he loves most in the world, then why were we the ones he hurt?*

He must see the question in my eyes because he explains, "I've learned we often hurt the ones we love the most because we take them for granted and believe they'll love us through all of our mess. You two provided me a safe and loving home, and I took advantage of that. I convinced myself that no matter how bad things got, you wouldn't leave. But eventually you did, and it felt like my life was over. I buried myself further in my gambling, trying to fill a void that could never be filled."

He sighs, glancing down at the floor and then back up, looking into my eyes. I quickly shift my gaze away, feeling like it's too much, but he continues. "I'm sorry I took you two for granted, and I'm sorry I took my anger and feelings of inadequacy out on y'all instead of acknowledging I had a problem. I should've worked to be better."

At those words, Mom squeezes my hand so tight that my knuckles have turned white, but I don't say anything to her because I know my hand in hers is what's keeping her together. This man used to be the love of her life.

"Is that it?" I ask, unable to completely harness the anger still swirling inside of me.

"No. I need to thank you for leaving me. It pushed me to my rock bottom, and I fear if I didn't hit it, I never would've gotten better. I'm thankful you two found safety and people who love and care for you." He looks from Aunt Carol, who's sitting in a chair with her arms crossed and eyes narrowed, to Lauren, who's sitting rod-straight on the arm of the couch instead of the chair Dad got her so she can hold my hand. She looks like she's ready to pounce at any moment.

"I'm sorry I wasn't one of those people." Dad chews on his lip. "It should've been me. I don't expect anything from y'all. I know my mistakes are unforgivable, but maybe you'll allow me to come see you sometime, to prove to you that I'm dedicated to being better?" He scoots to the edge of his chair, raising his eyebrows.

I glance at Mom as fear inflates in my chest. Her lips are pressed together, and she's in a daze, like she's mentally somewhere else, likely trying to make sense of how her life ended up this way because I know that's what I've been doing.

Lauren brings her other hand to me, wrapping herself around my arm, and it reminds me that I'm safe, that I have people who love me. Everything that happened with Dad is in the past, and I am in control now. I get to dictate whether we allow him to come back, and if I choose to let him back in, I know I will have the most incredible women by my side.

I squeeze Mom's hand in a gesture of solidarity, and she gives me the smallest of nods before I turn back to Dad. "Yeah, maybe we can get to that point someday."

Aunt Carol's mouth drops, and she gets up from her chair to protest, but Mom reaches out to her, motioning in a way that says *it's okay*. She sits back down, but even when her mouth is closed, it's evident she's clenching her jaw. Aunt Carol never liked Dad.

Dad sits up straighter while he presses his lips over his teeth to hide a hopeful smile.

Not liking the hope on his face, I quickly add, "I don't forgive you for what you've done, but I'm man enough to acknowledge what it took for you to admit you were wrong and to ask for help. Thank you for doing that."

"I'm glad you're getting the help you need, Rick." Mom pats his knee, giving him a strained smile. Determination is etched on her face, a sign of her bravery to push through the discomfort because she knows we both need the closure.

Dad nods and reaches a hand out. I stare at it, almost waiting for him to use it for violence, but Lauren gives me a subtle nudge. I take his hand, meeting his gaze as I add, "If you ever step a toe out of line, I will not be forgiving in the future. I have too much at stake now. I'm not going to give all this up for you."

"I completely understand." Dad nods like a bobble head. "You've built a beautiful life for yourself, surrounded by strong women. Don't mess it up like I did."

"I won't," I snap just as the women around me chime in with, "He won't." It brings a warmth to my chest and releases an immense weight from my shoulders. *I'm not my dad.* I protect my family. I make mistakes, but it doesn't take a stint in jail to get me to own up to them and try to be better.

"Would you like to stay for dinner?" I think Dad knows the answer to the question before he even asks it because there's no spark in his eyes.

"No, we need to head back."

"I'll see y'all again though, right?" Dad's eyes are wide.

Mom nods. "Just give us some time."

"Of course." He lingers, watching us as if he wants to give hugs but recognizes that may be crossing a line.

Mom gives him a head nod, indicating his apology is as far as she will let him go, and with that, we head out the door, closing that chapter of our lives with it.

———

When we drop Mom and Aunt Carol off at their house, the rain, which has been incessant for most of the day, has stopped. The ground is a muddy mess, but the air smells clean. It feels symbolic. I've wiped my guilt away, and I'm ready to step into life as a better man who keeps himself accountable without letting fear take over.

It isn't until we pull into my driveway that Lauren speaks. "I'm proud of you."

"Thank you. I couldn't have done this without you."

She tilts her head to give me a knowing look. "You could've."

"I don't want to though. You're my person. I want you with me all the time."

"And I want to be with you all the time." She glances out the window at the muddy mess that is my yard before looking back at me. "Where do we go from here?"

I turn the engine off, leaning back against my seat. "I think we finally get to let ourselves be happy."

"I like the sound of that."

"Me too." I take her hand in mine over the center console. "I'm going to tell Tony I'm done with the Long Neck tonight. I'm ready to stop punishing myself and to be happy. I want to work on Copper Hill if you'll still have me."

"You already know the answer to that."

"Then it's settled." I plant a kiss on her lips. "So, I guess we need to tell the rest of the town about us, huh? How do you want to start?"

"What do you think about being my date tonight for the New Year's Eve party at the Long Neck?"

"I think nothing would make me happier."

Chapter Fifty-Five

Lauren

THE DEATHEATERS

CALLIE

Olivia, Rhett, and I are here. Where are you Lo?

ME

I just pulled in. Jax should already be in there somewhere. He had to talk with his boss

CALLIE

Hurry! You've already missed the first hour!

It's been a long day

CALLIE

Well the good news is I bribed the DJ so he's going to play some Shania for us. It should be coming up any song now

You did NOT

OLIVIA

She did! She flirted her butt off for that

CALLIE

I think you mean I flirted my sweet bottom
off for it

OLIVIA

Ew NO!

LOL

Jax is waiting for me when I step out of my truck. He rushes up, opening me door. "Are you sure you're ready for this?"

My stomach is doing a series of twirls, but it's nothing compared to the way my heart flutters at the thought of no longer needing to hide our relationship.

"I'm ready. Are you?"

"I'm *so* ready. I've been waiting for this moment for years." The lopsided grin that appears on his face makes me melt.

He laces his fingers in mine before pressing the doors of the Long Neck open. The bouncer eyes our clasped hands but doesn't say anything as he gives us the nod to go in.

The dance floor is covered from wall to wall with gold and white decorations: balloons, tassels, and streamers. Lights are strung overhead and fill empty champagne bottles on the center of the picnic tables. There's even a new golden disco ball overhead.

"Wow, did y'all buy out the Dollar Store for this function?"

Jax adjusts his ball cap. "It's a lot, huh? Decorations weren't my responsibility. I've never been good at that kind of thing, but I've been trying to decrease my involvement in the bar anyway." He leads the way toward our friends. "I think Tony knew all along. He wasn't even the least bit surprised when I told him I was putting in my two weeks."

"But he was okay with it?"

"He was more than okay with it." He presses a kiss to my cheek, and I try to ignore the murmurs that immediately ensue in response to the action. "I even offered to help out any time he needs an extra person for the next few months."

"Good. I don't want him to think I'm stealing you."

"He'll be fine. Besides, I kind of want him to think you're stealing me." He wraps an arm around me, pulling me close and planting a kiss behind my ear just as Callie and Olivia come up to us.

"Ew, PDA!" Callie announces, pointing at us.

"Oh stop." I lower her arm.

"We have a table over there. Rhett is holding down the fort. Come join us."

We make it two whole steps from where we were when a new song comes on. Callie grabs Olivia and I by the hand, dragging us out onto the dance floor. "This is my request. We have to dance!"

I glance back at Jax as we are whisked away. He's laughing. "I'll help Rhett hold down the fort. You three have fun."

The smile on his face, paired with his assurance that he wants me to have a good time, makes me feel so loved, like everything is right in this world. We are finally free to just be.

Once we're out on the dance floor, I register the song. It's "Whose Bed Have Your Boots Been Under."

Callie and I share a look and burst into laughter before matching the footwork of the crowd.

"What are you two laughing at? Is it my dancing?" Olivia doesn't look up as she tries to follow along to our movements without bumping into us. "I've been practicing, but I still suck."

"No, it's not your dancing. Callie blasted this song for Austin when we tried to take his dog."

Olivia frowns. "I still can't believe you two got into trouble without me *again*."

"You're not exactly the trouble-making type," Callie offers as her feet shuffle to the beat.

"Neither is Lauren, but she's been included in the trouble twice now."

"To be fair, both times were because of my terrible love life." I step my right foot forward and back. "Be thankful you've had Rhett to keep you out of that mess."

"I guess," she grumbles.

"I'll tell you what, next time we're going to do something stupid, we'll stop to make sure you're not out of town and call you if you aren't with us." Callie smiles.

"Are you mocking me?" Olivia stops, placing her hands on her hips. The motion causes Mrs. Liens to bump into her.

Callie tugs Olivia to get her back in the right position. "No, I swear we'll include you next time."

"Okay." Olivia smiles as she accidentally grapevines in the wrong direction. She throws her head back groaning. "One of these days I'm going to nail a line dance."

As we scuff our boots and turn to a new wall, I glance over at the table where Jax and Rhett are watching us carefully. Rhett has a look in his eye that makes it abundantly clear he is so in love with Olivia, even if she falters the steps.

"Well, whether you do or you don't, you have a whole lot of people who love you."

She stops trying to dance, glancing from me and Callie over to Rhett with a soft smile. "I know. So do you."

I nod.

The song ends, and we clear the dance floor, but when the opening line of the next song comes over the speaker, I instantly recognize it as John Michael Montgomery.

Reaching out to Jax, I ask, "Are you ready to make our debut?"

"Hell yeah."

I laugh as he leads me out onto the dance floor while John Michael Montgomery sings about how his lover's belief in him is the reason he continues to get up and try to do things he believes are out of reach.

Jax's hand finds my waist once we're out on the dance floor, setting loose chatter around us. It makes me laugh. "People in this town can be so nosey."

"I'm just glad they finally know you're off the market. I've been terrified someone would come and sweep you out from under me."

"You have *not!*" I laugh, giving his chest a gentle push.

"I have." He twirls me around in a circle and then returns to swaying with me from side to side.

"You must know by now I'm completely gone for you. I'm not going anywhere."

He smiles. "Yeah, I do. But just because I know you're gone for me doesn't mean I'm going to stop trying to impress you each and every day or stop fighting to be worthy of your love."

Without hesitation, I wrap my arms around his neck, pressing my lips to his. Words don't feel like enough to express the way I care for Jax. I need him to feel how much I love him, and I want everyone else in this town to see it too. Jax isn't going to be my secret anymore. I don't care what anyone else thinks of us.

Being this close to him, sharing this moment of intimacy, the rest of the world quiets. There's no more music, no more people whispering about us, just the two of us happily in love. It's incredible.

"I guess everyone knows now," Jax whispers, his forehead pressed against mine.

"I *knew* it!" Austin stumbles across the dance floor. "He was always pining after you and trying to steal you out from under me. It makes sense you'd end up with trash like him. You have no sense of self-worth."

Jax swivels on his heel toward a very drunk Austin. "You don't get to talk to her like that."

"I can talk to her however the hell I want. Stay out of this, Greer." Austin turns toward me, but it's clear he's keeping an eye on Jax. He may be a drunken jerk, but he's not stupid. "Where was I? Oh, yes, your lack of taste, your lack of self-worth, and your overall inability to do anything on your own." He throws his head around as he says the words. "You couldn't even handle your job at Copper Hill without feeling overwhelmed. I bet the ranch is falling apart without me."

Jax lunges at Austin, but I grab on to his arm. "Don't."

"He doesn't get to treat you like this. Apparently, he needs to be taught *another* lesson." He turns from me back to Austin. "Don't you dare talk to her like that." He shoves him back. "Hell, don't talk to her at all."

I tug Jax back again, pressing my palms to his cheeks. "I love that you want to stand up for me, but I need to fight this battle on my own. I'm ready to stand up to him and let that pain go, just like you did with your dad. Will you allow me to do that?"

Jax laces his fingers in mine. "Yes, but I'm going to be right by your side while you do it."

"Thank you," I whisper. As I turn back to Austin, I

notice all the nosey Roots residents who have fallen silent around us, congregating to watch the show. "Let's talk outside."

Austin stares at me, his eyes glistening. He sways a little before finally saying, "There's nothing to talk about. You never deserved me. I was always too good for you."

I feel Jax's body go rigid as he physically restrains himself from knocking Austin out cold. His restraint only lasts a few seconds because after a beat, he grabs Austin by the collar of his T-shirt and drags him outside.

"She said she wants to talk," Jax grits out.

I hate to admit it, but it's really satisfying to watch Austin get dragged out like that, especially after he tried to tell me he's too good for me. *Tell me, Austin, are you still feeling too good?*

The second the crisp winter air hits me, I begin rambling, desperate to get this over with before I overthink it or lose my nerve. "You don't get a say in who I'm in a relationship with, Austin. You're the one who cheated. You don't get to care about what happens after you chose to ruin our relationship."

I take a few steps closer to him as my anger builds. "I spent years of my life thinking I wasn't enough. You trained me to believe my feelings were invalid, that I was weak because I couldn't carry the weight of the world on my shoulders." I take another step forward, poking him in the chest. "You conditioned me to think it was selfish to want things for myself and that I shouldn't even bother asking for them. I'll admit, I was weak back then, but it was only because I put up with your crap."

Austin draws back as if I've hit him. I'm sure it's weird to see me stand up for myself after I failed to do it time and time again in our relationship. It feels a little foreign to me too, but the pride in my chest as I tell Austin off after all this time is addictive.

I step forward again, covering the distance he just put between us. "I've always cowered when you put me down, but I'm not that girl anymore. You cheating on me was the best thing that ever happened to me. It helped me learn how I *don't* want to be treated."

He drops his gaze from me, not meeting my eyes, but it doesn't matter. I'm on a roll. "Now I know how to go after what I want and how to ask for help without being apologetic. Me standing in front of you right now, telling you off with Jax by my side, is in big part because of you. So, thank you for finally setting me free because I've never been happier."

It finally hits me how close I am to Austin, so I take several steps back. Austin looks like a scorned child as he stands there, watching me.

I hold a finger up in the air. "Oh, and one more thing. You don't get to talk to me like this anymore. You don't get to call me or text me or show up out of the blue. You don't have any claim over me, and you never did. So *please* leave me alone."

I swivel on my heel to head back inside, leaving a gaping Austin behind.

Jax follows, lacing his fingers with mine again. He leans into my ear, whispering, "That's my girl."

When I glance over my shoulder, Austin is already gone, and Jax says, "Do you realize you just checked the last item off your list?"

"What are you talking about?"

"You just did something for yourself and no one else. Telling off Austin was for you, not for me, and definitely not for him. You did it the way you wanted to because *you* needed it."

The pride on his face slowly morphs into humor, and he snickers.

"Why are you laughing?"

"I'm picturing Austin's face when you told him off." He doubles over as he keeps laughing, gasping for air before adding, "And leave it to you to then ask him to *please* leave you alone."

I join him in his laughter. "Hey, I've grown a lot over the last few months, but I haven't forgotten who I am."

"I love that about you."

"I love *everything* about you." I wrap my arms around his neck. "Thank you for sticking by me through it all."

"I'd rather stand in the rain with you than enjoy the sunshine with anyone else, Freckles."

Epilogue

Nine Months Later

Lauren

"Lauren, get off your phone. Let's go," Callie shouts from my front door.

"Just a second. I need to finish writing this down," I call over my shoulder as I type out another note on my phone about tweaks we're going to make next year to help the regenerative agriculture transition go even smoother. Things have gone extremely well this year. Costs have been lower, the cows have been thriving, and I have high hopes for our yields, but I know there's still room for improvement.

Olivia sits on the porch steps with me, finishing up an Instagram reel she wanted to make for the rescue. As her fingers move furiously, her engagement ring glitters in the orange sun.

Callie barges down the steps, tugging my phone from my hands. "Get off your phone. If we don't leave now, we're going to miss the sunset."

"Olivia's on her phone too." I thrust my hand in her direction. "Bug her."

"I had to finish this reel while the idea was fresh, or it wouldn't look as good when I make it later." Olivia sets her phone down and holds up her hands. "I'm done now."

"Well, I need to finish writing down these changes before I forget them." I turn back to my phone, rereading what I've typed. "Crap. I don't remember. It was something to do with paddock nine."

Callie scoops her hands under my armpits and drags me off the step I'm sitting on. "Remember when I said it would be cool to go on a sunset horseback ride? It won't exactly be a *sunset* ride if the sun has already set, will it?"

"I don't get why you want to do this anyway. It feels like all three of us are going on a date."

"Maybe I wanted a little romance in my life for once." Callie fake sniffles.

"You're being ridiculous." I gently shove her as laughter breaks free from my chest.

"No, that outfit is ridiculous." Callie gives me the elevator look, a frown painting her lips. "Go change. You can't wear that."

"What are you talking about? This is what I always wear to ride."

"Not if you're going on a date with me." Callie surges past me, down the hall, and into my bedroom, heading straight for my closet. "We agreed we were going to finally get some cute pictures of the three of us. Let me help you pick something out."

She pulls several tops off the hanger, laying them out on my bed along with a different pair of jeans. "These ones make your butt look good."

"But they're not as comfortable when I'm riding."

She holds up a white top. "But they will look cute with this top, which looks *so* good on you when you have a tan."

"What are you up to?" I look from her to Olivia, who is standing in the doorway with a suspicious smile on her face. "Olivia, tell me what you two are doing."

"Nothing." Her voice is two octaves too high, and her cheeks are flushed.

Ignoring her, Callie says, "I already told you. I want to take pictures at sunset. We have no pictures with the three of us. Come on. It'll be cute."

"Can't we do them another time, so I don't have to wear these jeans?"

She thrusts the white top and jeans into my arms. "Please just put them on. We don't have time to argue about this. The sun is setting by the second."

Sighing, I get changed and meet the two of them at the front door. Olivia is looking at me all misty-eyed.

"Why are you looking at me like you want to remember what I look like before I die? It's creeping me out."

Callie shoots a scary look at Olivia before she leads us out the door to the barn.

"What's Jax doing tonight? Is he still working? It's getting late." Callie slides the door open and hands me the gear to tack up Maggie, the horse I learned how to ride on and the only horse Olivia trusts to get on.

"He came in from the fields, and we had dinner together before you got here. I think he's hanging out with Rhett tonight, isn't he?" I turn to Olivia.

"Oh, yeah, they are. It's great they're getting along."

"I knew they would if we forced them together enough." I grin.

"Rhett just takes time to come out of his shell, but he seems to really like Jax."

I finish tacking up Lucky and help Callie with my mom's horse so we can leave.

Callie takes the lead, heading out on the main trail behind the barn.

"So, since this is a date, do we have to ask each other awkward get-to-know-you questions?" I tease.

"Oh, come on! We're well past a first date. This is like our one hundredth date," Callie quips.

"What do you do on a one hundredth date then?"

"I don't know. Y'all tell me. I'm the single one here."

Not for long, I think. But I know better than to say that out loud. Callie just might bite my head off for a remark like that.

"I don't think Rhett and I have made it to a one hundredth date," Olivia says. "In a little over a year of being together, that would require us to go out almost every three and a half days. Do you think you and Jax have been on one hundred dates, Lo?"

"Practically? No. In my heart? It feels like we've been on a million. I know it's silly, but it feels like we know each other on a soul-deep level."

"Barf," Callie mutters, but she's smiling so wide.

We make a turn onto the trail that leads up to my spot. I didn't think anyone else knew this trail was here besides Jax.

"Do you know where you're going?"

"I'm just exploring," Callie says over her shoulder. "I promise I won't get us lost."

Silence descends over us as we crest up the hill, taking in the sunset painting the horizon brilliant oranges and reds. It looks like the sky goes on forever. I get so wrapped up in the painted cotton candy clouds to our right that I don't even notice what's happening in front of me until we stop, right where my spot is.

Instead of my usual fallen tree bench, there's an actual bench in its spot, and Jax is waiting on it. I look to Callie and Olivia, and neither of them are any good at hiding their overflowing joy right now. My stomach does a million cartwheels as it hits me what is about to happen.

"Don't leave him hanging. We'll watch Lucky," Callie says, her words barely above a whisper, like she's afraid of ruining the moment.

I slip off Lucky and meet Jax at the bench. He immediately takes both my hands in his, his smile lighting up his face. "Hi, Freckles."

"Hi." My heart pounds like a million horses in my chest, and my stomach flutters as if a swarm of butterflies was released inside it.

When Jax gets down on one knee and says my name, all of those nerves melt away. It's just us, finally getting our happy ending. We earned this. After fighting so hard to both be better, we grew and learned to accept ourselves. We learned our past doesn't define us, and we allowed love in. It's all been so worth it.

Jax's voice shakes as he looks up at me. "From the moment you walked into my life, I knew you and I were meant to be. We connected on a level I couldn't even comprehend at the time, but I still knew that whenever I was with you, I felt on top of the world. I felt like a better version of myself, one who was strong, brave, and capable. These past eleven months have been some of the most challenging yet most beautiful months of my life. You have pushed me to be open and to face my demons. You showed me I'm worthy of love, even when I'm a complete mess." He chuckles. "And you helped me learn the storms will come, but I don't need to fear them. I just need to find someone who will dance in the rain with me. I've found that person in you, and I don't want to let you go. I know ten months together isn't that long, but I've waited long enough to spend the rest of my life with you. I'm all in."

He takes my hand. "I can't guarantee I won't make mistakes along the way, but I can promise you I'm going to do my best every day to continue to show up for you, to help you never carry too much weight on your own, to show you how beautiful you are inside and out, and to make you feel loved. I love you so damn much."

He flicks open the velvet box in his hand to reveal a ring with a gold band and an elegant white diamond in the center. "Will you please spend the rest of your life with me? Will you please have babies with me and take care of this ranch with me and keep creaming me at Uno, even when we're old and gray?"

My laughter is ragged as tears stream down my cheeks, and I nod. "Yes. Yes, I will. I want you by my side through it all."

He slides the ring on my finger, stands up, and presses his hands to my cheeks as his lips meet mine. We both do a beautiful dance of taking and giving, trying to show each other how much this commitment means to us.

Rhett and Charlie come out from behind a tree, and Mom, Dad, Carol, and Aimee come from behind us. I don't know how I missed all of them, or the fact that six horses were missing from the barn earlier, but I don't care because I'm surrounded by all the people I love for one of the most special moments of my life.

It's crazy how a year ago, it felt like my life was over. My fiancé left me. I was drowning in work and desperately trying to find a way to keep the ranch afloat on my own, but it turns out uprooting my whole life was exactly what I needed to grow and find my place in the world. Because now I have all these wonderful people surrounding me. I've learned how to love myself and fight for what I'm worth, and I've somehow managed to fall in love again.

Bonus Epilogue

Six Years Later

Jax

"Ouch!" My three-year-old tugs away from me while I try to braid her blonde hair. She scrunches her nose at me, and it's crazy how much she looks just like her mother.

"You're the one who asked for French braids." I shrug. "I'm still learning how to do them. I could've done a flawless normal braid."

She crosses her arms, looking displeased as she climbs off the stool she's sitting on. "I want Mommy to do it."

Lauren walks into the bathroom, a smile on her face while our eighteen-month-old clings on to her leg. "You want Mommy to do what?"

"Braid my hair, please," Addie says.

"Will you take Bennett?" Lauren hands me our little boy. He's got my blue eyes and Lauren's soft blonde hair sprouting from his head.

I take the brand-new toy he hands me and tell him what

a perfect gentleman he is for sharing while Lauren undoes all my hard work. "Hey, I spent twenty minutes on that!"

She looks down at Addie. "Did he?"

"No, he took years!" Addie insists, throwing her hands up in exclamation.

"I need more practice."

"You'll get it, but maybe not five minutes before everyone is supposed to come over. There are going to be pictures today. We need our little girl to look like a princess, right?" Lauren asks Addie as she finishes the left braid already. *Show off.*

The doorbell rings, and I get up from the ledge of the tub, taking Bennett with me. "I'll get it."

I dash down the hallway, chasing Bennett toward the door. His laughter is a welcome distraction from my nerves over who may or may not be at the door right now.

I swing it open and find Mrs. Rhodes. Nana Rhodes is trailing behind, trying to push Mr. Rhodes away from her, insisting she can carry her "own damn presents."

"Merry Christmas!" Mrs. Rhodes smiles as she hands me a casserole dish and shrugs off her coat. "Has your house been as chaotic as ours was this morning?"

"Oh, yes. Between our two little rascals being excited about their toys and trying to get everything ready for brunch, we've had our share of chaos."

"She knows we weren't expecting her to still host when she's seven months pregnant, right?"

"Yes, but she loves it, and she asked for help when she needed it," I say over my shoulder as I put the casserole down on the kitchen counter.

Addie, with two perfect French braids, darts down the hallway, plowing into her grandma's legs and wrapping her arms around them. "Nana!"

"Hi, sweetie."

"Did you bring presents?"

"Addie!" Lauren scolds in disbelief as she joins us at the front door.

"I brought you loads of presents," Mrs. Rhodes says as Mr. Rhodes and his mother walk into the door, both of their hands full.

"Yay!" Addie spins around, showing off her new dress.

Before I can close the door, another car pulls into the driveway. Mom and Aunt Carol step out, excited smiles on their faces as Mom calls out, "Merry Christmas! We're going to need some help with all these presents for the kids."

"Presents!" Addie screeches as she dashes out the front door to help carry the gifts in.

Bennett watches from the doorway with shy curiosity, which he definitely gets from his mother.

"Thank goodness you're not as crazy as your sister," I say to him, ruffling his hair.

"If he's anything like his father, he'll grow into his wildness," Mom says as she kisses my cheek.

"Great." I frown at Bennett, and he bursts into laughter. I turn to Lauren. "Did I make a face?"

"No, Grinchie. Your face is just always that funny." She laughs at her own joke then places a consoling kiss on my cheek, followed by one on the top of Bennett's head.

"Have you heard from Rick?" Lauren asks Mom as she takes some gifts from her hands.

"Not yet, but he was excited for this. He'll be here."

I've been trying not to let myself get worked up over the possibility of Dad showing up for his first Christmas with our family. He hasn't given me any reason to doubt him in the six years since he showed up at my doorstep to apologize. He's been sober. He hasn't gambled or gotten into trouble with the law. He even has a new wife, who is lovely, but there's still a part of me that recognizes how much is at stake now if I let him in again.

Lauren must be a mind reader because she wraps her arms around me, whispering, "He's going to be here, and it's going to be great. Don't let his mistakes make you doubt his victories over the past several years. Remember how great it is to let all that go?"

I nod. She's right. Moving on felt amazing. It has allowed me to start building a relationship back with my dad, one more like what we used to have when he took me to OSU football games, but it's hard not to let the doubt creep in every once in a while.

More people flood into our home while Lauren and her mom set the table for brunch. Charlie pulls me into a bro hug while his two-year-old shoves himself in front of me, trying to grab my attention. "Uncle Jax, look what I got today!"

He holds up a toy firetruck, his green eyes aglow.

It's his toothy grin and childlike innocence that ground me again, ridding me of the doubts I've had. Even if my dad doesn't show up today, I'm still incredibly blessed. Never in a million years would I have expected to have such a beautiful life with an amazing wife and the sweetest children, surrounded by loads of family who love us.

"Wow, look at that!" I crouch to his level. "Where's your mama and sister?"

"Mama's at the café finishing up the dessert with Isa."

"Is she making something good?"

He crosses his arms. "Mama *always* makes good desserts."

"Of course."

As the table fills with delicious food, Lauren attempts to wrap her arms around me, which is made difficult by her growing belly.

"This one is going to be a boy. I just know it." I rub her belly gently.

We learned the sex of the baby for our first two kids, but with the third, we decided we wanted to wait. It's been torturous not knowing and a constant point of playful banter between the two of us.

"I still think it's going to be a girl. Bella has been following me around again just like she did when we had Addie." Lauren gestures to the chocolate mutt at her feet.

"Bella hasn't stopped following you around since before we got her. That dog fell in love with you at puppy yoga. You have all the pictures and videos in the world to prove it."

She laughs. "Maybe, but I still have a feeling it's a girl."

The ring of the doorbell interrupts us, and I zip toward the door. It has to be Dad. Everyone else is here. My heart is pounding in my chest, and as soon as I open the door, seeing him with his arms full of presents and a smile on his face, I feel it grow three sizes more. My dad is celebrating Christmas with us again. He's sober, and he came through on his word. It's amazing how many things have fallen into place for us.

"I'm so sorry I'm late. I know you told me not to bring presents, and I really tried to, but I couldn't show up empty handed. It was a scramble to wrap these up last minute." He leans in toward me, whispering, "I found a homemade bird-house kit that Addie will love. We can build it together and look at the birds whenever I come to visit. And you know I had to get Bennett a *very soft*"—he emphasizes the word knowing that Lauren will freak out if she overhears—"football. He's not too young to get him started on his rise to stardom."

"He might not want to play football." Lauren holds out a hand. "Maybe he'll be into something safer, like no sports at all."

I chuckle, kissing her on the forehead before turning back to Dad. "They're going to love them. Thank you. I'm happy you're here."

"Me too."

I help Dad and his wife set their gifts under the tree and then we join everyone at the table, saying a quick prayer before digging into the delicious food in front of us.

"Hey, Bennett, has your mama showed you how we used to make Santa pancakes?" Mr. Rhodes asks his grandson.

Bennett shakes his head, and Mr. Rhodes quickly takes it as his sign to show the kid how to tear the pancakes apart, decorating them with fruit and syrup.

"Dad, we're trying to teach him good table manners, not how to pull apart his food at the table," Lauren chides.

"Come on! He loves it. Bennett has plenty of manners. Right, kiddo?"

"Right!"

"I want Santa pancakes too," Addie insists.

"Papa." Mom addresses Mr. Rhodes by the nickname we've been using to keep him separate from our son. I love that we decided to name our little boy after Mr. Rhodes. He's a wonderful man who has played a role in raising both Lauren and me, but it got confusing real quick to have two Bennetts running around Copper Hill. "Please tell me you're participating in the bake-off later. I want your creativity on my team."

"No way, I want Dad!" Charlie insists.

The table erupts into chaos as everyone argues over who gets to be on a team with whom, and amidst the raised voices and laughter, Lauren and I meet each other's gaze. I can already tell she's thinking the exact same thing as me. We made it.

We have everything we had ever dreamed of: the big family breakfasts, her dad here to teach our children bad habits, and a family we love who wants to carry on holiday traditions with one another. We have it all.

Author's Note

Each book I've written thus far has challenged me in new ways, but I think it's safe to say *Uprooting* has challenged me the most.

The success of *Putting Down Roots* thrilled and terrified me. I was convinced I couldn't write something as deeply relatable and well-rounded again. I told myself the characters in book 2 wouldn't get the love they rightfully deserved because their struggles weren't as relatable as panic attacks or because Rhett and Olivia had already stolen everyone's hearts. On top of that, Lauren and Jax were supposed to be the characters for book 3, but I got about halfway through writing what I *thought* was book 2, and I suddenly realized Lauren and Jax needed to be next. Needless to say, things did not go as planned.

I finally decided to write this brother's best friend story I had in my head, and I was feeling good. I thought I knew what the book would be: a love story with an emphasis on Lauren's journey of finding herself after being in a bad relationship. As the novel unfolded, Lauren's struggles became about so much more than her ex. It turns out she's a people-pleaser, a girl who wants to keep her friends and family whole and happy, which is beautiful but exhausting.

I always try to pull aspects from my own life into my books because I want to create characters with struggles people will relate to. I want my books to not only be an escape but an affirmation that you, the reader, aren't alone in your struggles. Unfortunately for me, that made writing *Uprooting* harder because I was still learning the lessons Lauren needed to learn as I was writing the book.

I imposed accelerated deadlines on myself that I struggled to reach because of everything I was balancing in my own life. I put in late nights and disregarded self-care in exchange for working on my book or spending time with loved ones, and I put on a face because my boss at my day job quit, leaving me to take over a controller role when I didn't even have a whole year of experience in my prior role. So, I guess you could say I learned my lesson, but I didn't do it the easy way.

Despite the challenges this book put me through, or perhaps because of those challenges, I will always have a deep love for this story. I proved to myself I can get through tough deadlines and that I can write more than one good book that will mean something to someone. And as I faced all these struggles, I found new love with these characters. Lauren, Jax, and the rest of the Roots characters have become my friends. They've brought me so much joy during some of the hardest parts of my life, and being apart for them makes me ache.

Now, I get to share them with you, hoping they will become your friends too, that they'll bring you light when you're in the dark, laughter when you're in tears, and hope when you think all is lost. Whenever you need them, these sweet, goofy, loving characters will be here waiting for you, just like they were for me.

I'll see you back in Roots soon!

With love,
Jenna

Acknowledgments

To the love of my life, thank you for sticking by my side through this book. I'm forever grateful for your endless support, whether it was stopping your work to listen to me spew words about a million different scenarios for my ending, getting excited over my characters with me, or making logistical suggestions to make sure Lauren didn't see her proposal coming. Thank you for helping me celebrate all my victories, from book signings to finally finishing my developmental edits. You were by my side cheering me on through every step of the journey, and there are no words to convey how much that means to me. I love you infinitely!

Kimberly, I am so thankful we have been able to continue working together. Thank you for answering my questions when I got stuck, being kind and supportive, and pushing me to make this a better story. The editing process is easily one of my least favorite parts, but you make it manageable and sometimes even enjoyable.

Melissa, thank you for creating the most beautiful cover for this book. You are such a delight to work with, and you absolutely surpassed my expectations with this cover. I am so in love with it! I can't wait to complete the series with you.

Britt, you are a rockstar! Thank you for taking such care with the copyedits for Uprooting. I appreciate how thorough you were and how you left so many little notes about parts in the book you loved.

Mom, thank you for reading both versions of my ending for me in a ridiculously quick turn around time and for being supportive whenever I told you I needed to get some editing done. I love you so much and am so grateful I was blessed with you as my mom and best friend.

Jeffrey, thank you for being the kind of brother that I know has my back at the end of the day. My relationship with you has been a big inspiration for Charlie and Lauren's relationship. I hope you know I will always be there for you. I love you.

Dad, you are the reason I wanted to create a story where the female main character had a special bond with her father. I will always look up to you for showing me the power of empathy and kindness as well as the importance of family and always showing up for your loved ones. I love you more than you know.

Thank you, the reader, for picking up this book and treating it with the care it deserves. This story took a lot to create, but I'm so proud of the final product. I hope it touched your soul like it did mine and that it brought you laughter, joy, and a sense of belonging.

About the Author

Jenna Rogers loves crafting heartfelt, closed-door contemporary romance stories. When she's not writing, you can find her curled up with a good book, baking something sweet, or pumping iron at the gym. Jenna calls the Pacific Northwest her home and enjoys all the beautiful sunrises and sunsets the region has to offer. Her debut novel, *Where the Sun Lights the Shadows*, marked the start of her professional writing journey, but Jenna started writing when she was seven years old. Even then, she was captivated by love, writing a story about cows falling in love and another with a romantic plot set along the Oregon Trail. You can find her on her website at www.jennarogersbooks.com, where you can buy signed copies of her book and sign up for her email list. She is also found on the following social media platforms:

instagram.com/jennarogersbooks

threads.com/@jennarogersbooks

tiktok.com/@jennarogersbooks

goodreads.com/jennarogers

Also by Jenna Rogers

Standalone Novels

Where the Sun Lights the Shadows

Roots Series

Putting Down Roots - Roots Series, Book #1

Uprooting - Roots Series, Book #2

Roots Series, Book #3 - Coming 2026